TIME TSUNAMI

Book One: The Time Counselor Chronicles

Danele J. Rotharmel

Published by Prism Book Group
ISBN-13:978-1523314294
ISBN-10:152331429X
First Edition, 2016
Published in the United States of America
Contact info: contact@prismbookgroup.com
http://www.prismbookgroup.com

THE TIME COUNSELOR CHRONICLES:

Time Tsunami
Time Trap (coming soon)

For my parents, Don and Joan Rotharmel, with all of my love.
This book would not have been possible without you.

Excerpt from Timewave Dynamics 805

What is a Time Tsunami? It is a phenomenon that is set in motion when a time counselor destabilizes a captured timewave causing it to split in half. When the two halves begin rushing toward the temporal shore, the fabric of time unravels. It is our responsibility to insure that a Time Tsunami never occurs.

Dr. William Ableman

ॐ

The Five Immutable Laws
1.   A case subject's past must be thoroughly researched.
2.   A case subject must undergo extensive interviews before being selected.
3.   A case subject's tipping point toward evil must be determined.
4.   A time counselor must never reveal his or her last name or personal history.
5.   A time counselor must never be blinded by conceit or supposition.

TEMCO Code of Conduct, 5th Edition

ONE

TEARS FLOODED GIL Montgomery's eyes as Daniel Winston was strapped down to a gleaming metal gurney. She blinked back the moisture. She knew Daniel wouldn't appreciate her pity. She also knew her tears were inappropriate. His crimes had been violent.

Gil shuddered as heavy buckles were tightened across Daniel's chest. She'd known that observing executions would be part of her job when she joined the TEMCO program at National Science University, but she hadn't considered the harsh realities of watching a life being extinguished.

As another shudder ripped through her body, a deep voice whispered, "Are you okay?"

Gil nodded and squared her shoulders. With a glance at her adviser, Dr. William Ableman, she said in an unconvincing voice, "I'm fine."

William's soft, warm eyes peered into hers. She knew he was discerning enough to recognize her words as a lie. Looking down at her hands, she desperately tried to regain her composure.

"It'll be over soon," he murmured.

"Seven minutes at the least or two hours at the most," she mumbled.

"I'm sorry you have to see this."

"It's part of a time counselor's job. I can handle it."

"I know, but I'm still sorry."

Gil glanced up at William. He was in his mid-thirties and was handsome even though the lower half of his face was hidden by a wiry beard. As his gaze captured hers, the compassion she saw caught her by the throat. She looked away swiftly and bit down on the inside of her cheek. She was going to lose it if she wasn't careful, and breaking down would *really* impress the TEMCO Review Board. If she wanted to earn her Time-Counselor License, she needed to get control of herself.

She watched as William reached toward her shoulder. Before he touched her, he stopped short and said, "The first execution's always hard to watch."

"Does it get any easier?"

"Honestly? Not really. Not ever. But at least you know what to expect after your first."

Digging her fingernails into her palms, she nodded and reminded herself that she was there to bring hope to a hopeless situation. She looked back through the glass at the man strapped to the execution gurney. His burn-ravaged face was twisted into lines of defiance. His body was held rigid and unrepentant. As she watched, his arms were swabbed with alcohol in preparation for cannula insertion. He had only a few minutes left to live—alcohol sterilization seemed like some kind of macabre, ghastly joke.

As if feeling her gaze, Daniel looked at her with his uninjured eye—his other eye was shriveled in its socket. She expected him to look away, but he didn't. As her tears threatened to fall, a flickering change came over his face. Suddenly, she could see past his defiance to the regret and fear he was trying to hide. As they stared at each other, Daniel's face softened and a tear slowly gathered in the corner of his eye.

Across the viewing room, a voice hissed, "That's right! Cry! I hope you feel yourself dying. I hope you feel more pain than my wife ever felt. I hope you go straight to—"

Gil stopped listening to the ranting words and continued staring at the inmate's face. Although he winced as two intravenous cannulas were introduced into his arms, he refused to look away from her. It was as if he were gathering strength from her and using it to help him through his final moments. Gil felt an overwhelming wave of sadness as slender plastic tubes were attached to his cannulas. She hated what she was seeing. She knew he was evil, but she also knew there was good in him. She'd seen that goodness during their interviews. She'd heard it in his voice when he sang softly in his prison cell. He wasn't a complete monster—the good in him was hidden to most people, but she knew it was there. It went deep, and it was worth fighting for. *He* was worth fighting for.

As attendants attached Daniel to a heart monitor, his layers of hate and anger seemed to be stripped away, leaving him with a vulnerable, emotionally naked appearance. As she watched, sorrow filled his face.

I'm so sorry, she mouthed silently to him.

One corner of his mouth twitched up as he shook his head and mouthed back just as silently, *Don't be.*

"Daniel Winston," the warden said solemnly, "do you wish to make a final statement?"

Daniel nodded, and at last, his single tear fell. For the first time since he'd captured it, he broke his gaze with Gil. She watched as he looked over at the angry man behind the glass. "I want you to know how sorry I am about your wife and unborn daughter," he said in a choked voice. "I didn't mean to shoot your wife, but it was my actions that put her in danger and it was my bullet that killed her. If I could change what happened to your family, I would. I hope my death will bring you the closure you deserve."

The man jumped forward and slammed his fist against the glass. "Save your fancy speeches! Just die! You hear me? Just die!"

Gil watched as Daniel swallowed hard and stared at the knot of furious people in the viewing room. "I'm so sorry," he murmured thickly. "I know I deserve this. I should've died in the fire. My life has brought nothing but pain. I know how evil I am, but I wasn't always this way. I used to be good, and kind, and..."

His voice trailed away as a hiss rose from the relatives of his victims. Biting his lip, he said to Gil, "Perhaps the thread of my existence can be changed. But if it can't...I'm glad it's finally over."

The warden signaled for the execution to begin. Reaching over, Gil grabbed her advisor's hand. William jerked and looked at her in a startled fashion. Gil's breath turned into strangled gasps as three drugs were injected sequentially into Daniel's cannulas. William awkwardly stepped closer and put an arm around her shoulders. Collapsing against him, Gil stared with blurry vision through the Plexiglas window.

Daniel watched as William tightened his arm around Gil. Seeing the golden girl held close to her adviser—and also seeing the rapid way the doctor was breathing—a smile came to Daniel's lips. Suddenly, his eyelids began to flutter. He knew that the first drug inserted into his cannula, a short-action barbiturate, was about to render him unconscious. It was the State's final act of mercy before the second drug would cause sustained paralysis of his diaphragm, and the third drug would stop his heart. He peered over at Gil's pretty face—he wanted it to be the last thing he saw. His body shivered and spasmed. Her blonde hair seemed to swirl into a cloudy storm of gold. She was inexpressibly lovely. He tried to focus on her eyes, but they seemed to explode into thousands of bits of bluish light.

As Daniel Winston's eyes slowly rolled up toward the back of his head, he murmured softly, "Here's to second chances."

Two

DRIVING THROUGH THE outskirts of Washington D.C., William looked over at Gil in concern. It had taken Daniel Winston forty-seven minutes to die, and each minute had taken its toll on her. By the time her first case subject had been pronounced dead, her face was chalk-white and she was barely speaking. During the car trip back from Virginia, she stared out her window with a single-minded absorption that he didn't like at all.

She was at a dangerous juncture in her training—witnessing an execution was the moment some senior cadets washed out of the program. He didn't blame them. The less brutal aspects of scientific research could be seen as preferable to the harsh realities of the struggle between life and death during the reorganization of time itself.

He couldn't see Gil's face—she had it averted—but he could see her clenched fists. He didn't want to lose her. He didn't want to get the call saying she'd dropped out of TEMCO.

He cleared his throat. "What are your plans tonight?"

Gil slowly turned toward him. "Why are you asking?"

6

"Because I'm concerned. You shouldn't be alone. You need someone to talk to."

"Are you offering?"

This time, he was the one who averted his eyes. Fixing his gaze on the bumper of the semi-truck ahead of him, he said, "Only if you need me. After all, I still have that violet I promised to give you."

"It's still alive?"

"Barely. I keep alternating ritual drownings and droughts—I don't know what my sister was thinking when she gave it to me. If you don't have any plans, we could swing by my place, pick up the violet, and then find a taco stand."

"Are you asking me out on a date?"

A slight blush crawled up William's neck. "Dating students is frowned upon by NSU."

"Frowned upon, but not forbidden."

"Regardless, making sure you're all right falls within my duties as your advisor."

"Vigilant about your job, are you?" she asked dryly.

"I try to be."

"Well, bully for you."

He blinked rapidly. "Gil—"

"NSU should be glad they have such a diligent professor on their staff."

"Gil—"

"It must be a drag to be constantly hassled with keeping your students on an even keel. I appreciate your willingness to put in some overtime on my behalf."

"That's not what I meant, and you know it."

"Do I?"

"Look, if you need to talk I'll be happy to spend time with you, but if you have other plans I'll drop you at your apartment. Just tell me what you want. Do you want to grab a taco?"

"As a student being helped by her professor?"

As he nodded, he heard her sigh. "Actually, I'm awfully tired," she said. "Besides, I have a three-hour final in the morning."

William blinked. "I'd forgotten about the exam."

"You can afford to," she sputtered. "All you have to do is sit in front of the class and watch your students struggling through your ponderous questions. I, on the other hand, have to take the silly thing."

"You're not planning an all-night cram session are you?"

"My brain feels numb. Studying wouldn't do me a lick of good. I'll pass or fail on what I know already." She stretched. "Tonight I'm gonna take a bubble bath, order pizza, and be a couch potato. After the day I've had, I don't want to concentrate on anything complicated."

"That sounds like a good plan." He hesitated. "Are you sure you're all right? Watching someone die, especially someone you've been interviewing, can be—"

"I'm fine."

"I know today must've bothered you. Should I be concerned?"

"Are you asking as my friend or as my advisor?"

"Does it make a difference?"

"Of course it does." She hunched a shoulder. "If you're asking as a representative of the review board, you're not getting a single word out of me."

"As your friend then—how are you doing?"

"If you want the absolute truth, I'm a little shaken but all right."

"You're sure?"

She nodded. "Seeing Daniel die was horrible, but that's why I joined TEMCO. We look at harsh realities and do something about them. I'm going to fight to give Daniel his second chance." She shifted in her seat and faced him. "I'm not going to wash out. I'll see this thing through, and you're gonna be astonished at what I accomplish."

Feeling a rush of relief at her words, he said softly, "I'm sure that I will be."

"Can we change the subject?" she asked, tucking a lock of hair behind her ear. "I need to stop thinking about Daniel's death for a while."

He looked at her pale face in concern. "What do you want to talk about?"

"I'm not sure," she replied. Her voice took on a slight teasing tone. "After all, you're a stodgy *old* academic who has more in common with a dusty dictionary than with me."

Stopping at a red light, he looked at her with a raised eyebrow. "You think I'm old?"

Her eyes twinkled. "I think you could give Methuselah a run for his money."

"Come on, I'm only a few years older than you."

"A few? Nine years is *practically* a decade."

"For your information, I'm only seven years older."

"You're thirty-four? I knew I'd get you to tell me your age eventually."

"Be careful," he said as the light turned green, "or I'll add another page of questions to your final tomorrow."

"You wouldn't dare."

"Stodgy *old* professors can do anything they like."

Gil's lopsided dimples danced. "True, but students can get even in inventive ways. Rumor has it your office got a decorative touch recently. You should start coming to the gym again—you're obviously getting too out of shape to pay attention to what's going on around you."

He grunted, refusing to rise to her bait.

"So will I see you at the pool in the morning?"

He hesitated.

"Honestly! It's like you've become allergic to chlorine. I don't understand why you've stopped coming."

He remained silent.

"For pity sake, the least you can do is tell me why. Answering a simple question won't trigger a Time Tsunami."

"We're here."

"Pardon?"

"We've arrived at your apartment," he replied.

"I can see that, but you haven't explained why—"

"I'm not going to."

"I can't believe *women* are considered the secretive sex."

Remaining silent, William pulled up at her front door. As she gathered her belongings, he shut off the engine and watched her. She had no idea how graceful she was or just how beautiful. Seeing her reach for the door handle, he said softly, "No, allow me."

"I can manage," she said. "Stay in the car, it's blowing a gale outside."

She opened her car door, and a rush of wind stirred through her hair. William breathed in the scent of her perfume and forced himself to hold his tongue.

As she started to rise, he reached for her arm. Stopping himself before his fingers touched her, he said quietly, "Call me if you can't sleep. Remember you couldn't do anything to save Death Row Daniel, but in a couple of days you'll get your chance to save little Danny."

10

She nodded. "Goodnight. See you in class—or at the pool if you change your mind."

William watched as she walked to her building. The wind was playing with her golden hair and tugging at her blouse. Once she was safely inside, he laid his forehead against the steering wheel. After a few moments, he raised his head and slowly drove away.

THREE

GIL WANDERED AROUND her apartment in aimless circles. The bubble bath hadn't relaxed her, and the pizza was sitting in her stomach like an undigested stone. There was *no way* she was going to be able to sleep. She kept hearing the angry clamor of the relatives in the viewing room. She kept picturing the poison creeping its silent way into Daniel's arm.

Making a disgusted sound, she looked over at the clock. It was almost 10:30—what were the odds that William was still awake? She reached for the phone and then hesitated. Only a brain-dead idiot would wake up her professor the night before her final exam. Besides, she'd already blown the opportunity to spend time with him. She should've taken him up on his offer, but the way he made his dinner invitation sound like a duty had been too irritating to ignore.

Flopping onto the couch, Gil flipped through the TV channels. After a few minutes, she groaned. Hundreds of options, and *nothing* was interesting. Tossing the remote on her coffee table, she stood and peered out the window. *Did Daniel feel himself dying?*

Before she could change her mind, she tugged on a sweater and went out the door. William's house was within easy walking distance. She'd stroll over and see if his lights were on. If they were, she'd ring the bell and ask for the violet. If not, she'd simply march on by and he'd never be the wiser. Either way, a breath of fresh air would do her good.

Walking quickly, she tried to out-distance her churning thoughts and erase the memory of Daniel's final moments. Her steps slowed when she reached William's house. She'd never been inside his home, and she wasn't sure how he'd react to finding her on his doorstep. Now that she was there, she could think of a thousand reasons why she *shouldn't* ring his doorbell and only one reason why she should—she wanted to see him.

His lights were on and there was a shadow moving behind his blinds. Before she could lose her nerve, she pressed the doorbell. As the sound of echoing chimes filled the air, she heard an alarming series of small crashes coming from within the house. She didn't know what was happening, but it was obvious that she'd caught him off guard.

As she waited for William to open the door, she pinned on her most becoming smile—a smile that was transformed into a look of bewildered impatience as she was kept waiting. She tentatively rang the bell again. There was still no response. Just as she turned to leave, the door swung open. Gil's jaw dropped. William's beard was covered in orange paste, and he looked horribly embarrassed.

"What *on earth* happened?" she gasped, trying her best not to giggle.

"A blender accident," he said ruefully. "I forgot to fasten the lid before I hit liquefy. I've managed to wash my face, but I'm afraid my beard's still messy."

"I'll say it is. That funny paste is setting up like concrete. Seeing the state you're in, I guess I'll forgive you for not opening the door sooner."

"Glad you understand," he said, leaning up against the doorframe. "It was childish, but I didn't want to let you in until I looked more presentable."

Gil tried to hold back a laugh, but couldn't manage it. "If this is presentable, you must've looked disastrous when I first rang the bell."

"You can say that again." William smiled. "Now, to what do I owe this pleasure?"

"I was taking a walk and thought I'd drop by and rescue the violet."

"Come on in. I'll get it for you."

Gil passed inside and looked at his living room with frank curiosity. It was well decorated, but it also had a lived-in feel that made her instantly at ease.

"Make yourself at home," he said. "The violet's in the bedroom where it can get the morning light. I'll go fetch it, and if you'll give me a minute, I'll see if I can scrape this gunk off my beard."

"I think that'd be a good idea." She laughed.

As he left the room, Gil wandered over to his entertainment center and looked at the photographs arranged on top. She could see faint dust lines where several frames had been removed. A giggle churned in her throat, fighting to get free. She'd bet her bottom dollar that his blender accident wasn't the only reason he took so long to answer the door. She was sure that all the embarrassing photographs of him as a gawky teenager had just been consigned to a drawer. She looked around the tidy room— she'd also bet that he'd performed a frantic pick-up job on his living room. If she opened the door to the coat closet, she'd probably find a slug of newspapers and dirty dishes bursting to get free. When she heard him entering the room, violet in one hand and towel in the other, she took one look at his face and knew she was right.

She pointed at the photographs. "Where'd the rest of them go?"

He cleared his throat and placed the violet on the coffee table. "If you think I'm letting you see the baby picture of me in the bathtub, you're not as smart as I thought."

Gil allowed her eyes to twinkle at him as he dried his beard with the towel. "Let me guess," she said. "Your mother thought every moment of your life needed to be photographically chronicled—even the embarrassing ones?"

"Especially the embarrassing ones." He tossed the towel onto the back of a chair. "How'd you know I moved the pictures?"

"For a genius, you aren't very bright." She ran her finger over the entertainment center. "You forgot to dust. I can see the outlines of the missing frames. You shouldn't try to fool me—you don't stand a chance of succeeding."

"I'll remember that."

Gil smiled and picked up a picture of a beautiful woman playing a violin. Cocking an eyebrow, she asked in a coy voice, "Your girlfriend?"

His lips twitched. "I don't have a girlfriend. That's my sister, Angelina."

"The concert violinist?" Gil peered at the picture. "She's a knockout. When was this taken?"

"Last Christmas—the night she played at Carnegie Hall for the first time." He pointed at another picture. "That's my brother, Alex."

"Is that the cabin he's been building?"

William nodded. "Over spring break, I flew to Colorado and helped him build his front porch. Angelina wanted to help, but she was stuck in L.A. giving a string of concerts. She sent Alex a unique housewarming gift, though."

"Oh? What?"

He chuckled. "The ugliest-looking cookie jar you've ever seen. Considering Creekdale's limited shops, Alex has me scouring D.C. flea markets in hopes of finding something equally ghastly for him to give her—but I think it's a lost cause. I don't know where Angelina found that cookie jar, but it's sure a humdinger."

Gil laughed and set Angelina's picture back on the entertainment center. "Where are the pictures of your parents?"

"They're down in the drawer. I don't know why, but I always manage to look awful in family pictures."

"Vain, are you?"

"Let's just say a touch self-conscious."

"All the time or just with me?"

He gave a sputter of laughter. "No comment."

As she studied a picture of him with his coworkers, he asked, "How about your family? We've talked about so many things, but I don't remember you mentioning them much. Any brothers or sisters?"

She shook her head. "I was an only child. It would've been nice to have some siblings. My parents traveled a lot."

"They didn't take you along?"

"Not after I turned ten. By that time, Mom and Dad thought I could fend for myself."

"Ten is awfully young. Did they leave you often?"

"More than I liked and for days at a time. My friends used to envy me my freedom, but freedom isn't much fun when it's storming outside and the lights go out."

"I can understand that."

She looked at him curiously. "Why? Did your parents ignore you too?"

"Not at all. I had lots of cover to run to when I was younger."

"That sounds nice. Your parents must be pretty wonderful."

"They are. They're flying to D.C. in a few weeks... Would you like to meet them?"

Her eyes flew to his face. "I'd like that."

"I'll make sure it happens." He cleared his throat. "How about your parents, any chance they'll be coming to D.C.?"

"They died my senior year of high school."

"I'm sorry. I didn't know."

He didn't ask, but she could see the question in his eyes. She sighed. "They were touring the Rocky Mountains, and the brakes on their rental car failed. They didn't stand a chance."

"I'm sorry," he repeated. "I'll bet you miss them."

"I suppose so, but really, by the time they died, they'd become strangers to me. I think I missed them more before their funeral than after it. At least when they were dead they had an excuse for ignoring me." Hearing the bitter note in her voice, she bit her lip and shook her head. "I'm sorry, that sounds awful, doesn't it?"

"No. Just truthful."

She shrugged a shoulder and picked up a picture of a black-and-white collie. "This must be a special dog to rate his own frame."

"He was. I was heartbroken when I left for college and had to leave him behind."

"Did you eventually find an apartment that accepted pets?"

"In a manner of speaking. I couldn't find a place that accepted dogs, but I found one that accepted other pets, and Iggy's been with me ever since."

17

"Iggy? Doc, if you ever get married, your wife had better name your children." As William chuckled, she asked, "So what type of animal is Iggy? A fish or a bird?"

"Neither." Giving her a wicked grin, he said, "Look down."

Gil turned her attention to the floor and jumped about two feet in the air. Backing up against the entertainment center, she stared in horror at the iguana waddling toward her. Sputtering a bit, she asked, "What in the world is that...*thing?*"

"Thing?" William grinned and picked the lizard up in his arms. "Careful, Iggy's sensitive. You'll hurt his feelings."

"It's not his feelings I'm worried about—it's his teeth." Gil took a cautious step forward. "Does he bite?"

"Not usually."

"That's comforting," she said dryly. "If I touch him, will I be minus a finger?"

"Doubtful. Iggy's good tempered—just move slowly until he gets used to you."

Wrinkling her nose, Gil extended a hesitant finger toward the lizard's back. She scratched him gently and then grinned as the iguana seemed to close his eyes in pleasure.

"Like him?" William asked.

"His skin feels *really* weird, but I think he could grow on me."

"Iggy's probably thinking the same thing about you." William chuckled. He set the lizard on the floor. "Now, why don't you tell me why you came over tonight?"

"I came to get the violet."

He shook his head and motioned for her to sit on the sofa. "We've been friends too long for me to be fooled by that excuse. Today upset you badly, didn't it?"

"Not enough to quit," she said quickly. "Just enough to have trouble turning things off."

"You're a compassionate person, it's no wonder you're having trouble winding down. What's the one thing about today that's bothering you most? If we talk about it, maybe we can make it seem less awful."

"That's doubtful."

"Give it a try."

"In that case, does dying by lethal injection hurt?"

"I don't know, but the pentobarbital they gave Daniel should've blocked most of the pain. I'm sure he was out cold before he started having trouble breathing."

Gil shuddered. "It was justice, but it definitely wasn't pretty."

"Death never is."

"I guess I thought he would peacefully drift to sleep. I didn't think I'd have to watch him struggling for air."

"His body was dying. Struggle was inevitable."

"I know." She looked down as Iggy walked across her shoe. "Did it bother you too?"

"More than you know."

She sighed and rubbed the lizard's head. "Do you think I'll be a good time counselor?"

"If I didn't, I never would've recruited you."

"I still don't know why you did."

"Let's just say I saw something special in you and leave it at that, shall we?"

She let his cryptic comment slide. "Do you really think I'll be able to help Daniel?"

"You're going to pass your field exam with flying colors." He stood to his feet. "But you're never going to pass my written exam unless you get some sleep. It's getting late."

She groaned. "You should hear what last year's seniors had to say about your final. *Death by Examination* and *Cruel and Unusual Punishment* were common themes."

"I never promised to be easy on any of you—just fair. I want you to be prepared for whatever you may encounter on your time surfs. You'll thank me later."

She grinned a little. "That's what all narcissistic dictators say. Napoleon, Nero, Stalin—"

"Watch it!" He grabbed his car keys. "Let me run you home."

She shook her head. "It's silly to drive—it's just a step to my apartment."

"You shouldn't be walking alone this time of night." He put the violet in her hands. "But I'm giving you fair warning—considering the state of my beard, I'm hiding behind you if we see anyone we know."

"Will you give me extra credit for providing you with cover?"

"Not a chance," he replied as they left his house, "but I may just spring for coffee on the day of your field exam."

"Extra credit sounds better, but coffee will work. Hey, as long as we're negotiating, what will you do if I pass my written exam tomorrow?"

"Die of shock."

Laughing, Gil gave his shoulder a quick nudge. As he led her to his car, she studied the cute way his hair stood in an untamable tuft at the crown of his head. He started talking about Iggy, but she wasn't paying attention.

Briefly closing her eyes, she concentrated on his voice. It was smooth as silk and deliciously husky. Just listening to it made her knees go weak. Gil silently groaned. This was a perfectly wretched time to realize she'd fallen in love!

FOUR

GIL LOOKED AT her test questions and nibbled her eraser. The questions were swimming in front of her eyes and trying to concentrate on them was murder. After all, who cared about oscillation rates of transverse timewaves with sinusoidal tendencies? What she cared about was the fact that William was looking scrumptious in a heather-gray suit. Her nose twitched appreciatively at the scent of his cologne. Even his beard looked better today. *And his eyes...*

Gil slowly studied his deep, brown eyes and melted a bit in her seat. Giving a gusty sigh, she put her pencil down and gazed at him. Suddenly, she saw William glowering at her. Gil sat up swiftly and peered at him in a startled fashion. His lips narrowed into a tight line as he tapped his watch. She got the point. Oscillation rates might not be as interesting as William's eyes, but she'd better pay attention to them if she didn't want to flunk.

Later, in the smothering quiet of Broglie Hall, William pulled Gil's test from the stack in front of him and reached for his red pen. He hoped she hadn't blown the exam. He could've wrung her neck when he caught her staring off into space instead of working on the test.

He groaned when he saw that her first three questions were incorrect because of silly mistakes. *Where had her mind been? She knew better than to confuse wavelength and amplitude! If the rest of her test was as screwed up as her first few answers, she'd never pass.*

Tossing his pen aside, William stood and paced around the empty classroom. After a few minutes, he took a deep breath and sat back down. When he saw that her answer for question four was correct, he began to relax. The minute hand of the black utility clock ticked away as he continued grading her paper. When he was finished, he gave a deep sigh. Eighty-six percent. She had passed.

Over in Hawking Hall, Gil entered the TEMCO lab with a tired groan. William's final for *Timewave Dynamics 805* had been worse than rumor reported. She really liked him, but his class wasn't exactly a cakewalk.

Behind her, a cheerful voice called out, "Hey, Gil, did you survive?"

Looking over her shoulder at Ryan Adams, she groaned expressively.

"That bad?"

"Worse."

Ryan chuckled. "Something for me to look forward to next year, huh?"

"Dread is more like it."

Marc Kerry, another cadet in Ryan's class, joined them and asked, "Was the *Dynamics 805* final a killer?"

"Well," Gil moaned, "I'm not dead, but I'm definitely maimed a little."

Marc cracked his knuckles. "I was hoping to take *Timewave Dynamics* with Dr. Ableman next fall, but registration's already full. I may have to take it from Dr. Moosly instead."

Gil winced. "You have my pity. Doc's classes are murder, but I've heard that Moosly's are duller than ditchwater. I've avoided them like the plague."

"I know, but what can I do? I want to get *Timewave Dynamics* finished before the spring push and my practicum field exam."

"I can understand that. Leaving that killer class until my last semester was pretty stupid." She paused. "You know, since I'm graduating, Doc's gonna need a new teacher's assistant. I'll bet if you were his TA, he'd let you into one of his full classes in the fall. There's always room for a folding chair in Broglie Hall if you look hard enough."

"That's good advice." Marc gave her a cheesy grin. "So do you think you aced his class?"

"Not a chance," Gil replied. "But hopefully, I pulled through with a B-."

Seeing Crystal Stuart, a blonde woman with big glasses, walking over and hovering on the edge of their group, Gil asked, "So what are you three doing in the lab?"

"Extra credit," Marc replied. "Director Matthews said we could help run the GAP Staging Platform when Zeke Masters comes home."

Crystal spoke up excitedly, "I can't wait to get my hands on the controls."

"Even so, I don't know why you're here," Ryan said with a smile. "We all know you're pulling a 4.0."

"I don't care about the extra credit," Crystal replied with sparkling eyes. "I want the experience. GAP fascinates me! Besides, I can't wait to see Zeke. He—"

"Hey, Gil, why are you here?" Marc asked. "I would've thought that after Doc's exam you'd be headed straight home for an aspirin and a nap."

"I plan on taking both as soon as possible, but first I need to help the lab techs with the final calibration of Danny's game cartridge. Director Matthews left me a message to come in today for another scan."

"I'll bet you're excited," Marc said, tossing his backpack on a chair. "The field exam is so *unreal*. I can't believe you're going to be leaping through a TV and traveling through time."

Crystal pushed at her owlish glasses. "Time surfers don't leap through televisions, Marc. The Staging Platform opens a small time portal right in front of a child's TV, so it appears as if the surfer is going through the screen, but no one could really jump through a television. I'm afraid you're falling for a common misconception."

Marc pursed his lips. "Oh?"

She nodded. "Personally, I think the television paradigm is limiting TEMCO. Lab techs could attach a time portal to a wall just as easily, and I don't see why the portals have to be so small. Although it takes a tremendous amount of energy to harness a timewave, I believe that with a few tweaks to GAP, a portal roughly the size of a doorway could be created. I have several ideas that I'd like to run past Director Matthews when he has a chance to listen."

"I'm sure you do," Marc said dryly. "I can't believe how *fortunate* I am to have an expert like you explaining things to me— please continue."

"Oh, I'm not an expert," she said earnestly. "But I don't mind clarifying things. Understanding portals can be tricky…"

Hearing Crystal's voice trail away, Gil winced. She knew that Cris was finally figuring out that Marc was making fun of her.

With a bright red face, Crystal mumbled, "But you already know about portals, don't you? I mean, we're taking the same classes. I mean…" She turned away sharply and tripped over a chair.

Marc rolled his eyes. "Pack up your breakables—Klutzy Crystal's on the loose."

Ryan glared at Marc and put his hand on Crystal's shoulder. "Don't mind him."

"I need to learn to keep my mouth shut," she mumbled. "No one wants to hear me ramble on."

"That's not true. I like hearing you talk." Ryan gave her a smile. "Are you going to the Bible study in Heisenberg Hall this week?"

Crystal shook her head so vigorously that her messy bun came undone.

"You haven't attended for the last two months. We all miss you."

"I've been really busy, Ryan, I've got…"

As Crystal and Ryan walked away and their conversation faded out of range, Gil turned on Marc. "Cris is a really nice girl. You should give her a chance."

Marc didn't reply. Instead, he looked over at the lab door. "Who are they?"

Gil glanced over at the group of people entering the lab. "My guess would be next year's freshman recruits. I'll bet they had their interviews today." She groaned a little. "What a *lousy* afternoon for me to finish up my practicum scans. With a freshman tour slowing things down, I'll never get a nap."

"Don't worry. I hear Director Matthew's voice in the hall. He'll get things running smoothly."

At that moment, a tall man with brown hair and hazel eyes entered the lab. Tossing his lab coat over a chair, he addressed the milling crowd of students. "Freshman recruits, please take a seat. A time retrieval is about to take place, and I'm sure you'll find it fascinating. Junior cadets, take your places at the GAP controls." Director Peter Matthews motioned for Gil to join the freshmen. "After Zeke arrives home, the techs will finish your practicum scans."

Gil nodded and grabbed a chair. Beside her, a woman with golden freckles sat down and said, "Isn't this the most thrilling thing you've ever seen? I can't wait to find out if I've been accepted into TEMCO."

"Me either," said a man on the other side of her.

Gil smiled. "I'm afraid you'll both have to wait a little while. I don't think the acceptance letters will be mailed for a few more weeks. By the way, I'm Gil."

"Phoebe Reynolds," the woman said with a dimpled grin.

"And I'm Drake Procerus," the man said, offering his hand.

"I'm pleased to meet you both. Welcome to TEMCO."

"Do you work here?" Drake asked as white-coated techs rushed around the room.

Gil shook her head. "I'm just a senior cadet, but if I pass my field exam I hope to become a professional time counselor."

"I can't believe it takes four years to get your master's degree through TEMCO."

"It's not just a master's degree," Gil replied. "It's also an internship and a chance to earn your Time-Counselor License. Once you earn that, you may be chosen to join TEMCO's staff."

"Is the program hard?"

Gil gave a snorting chuckle. "It's *murder,* but it's the most exciting thing I've ever done. I think I'll die if I don't earn my license."

"Is that a possibility?"

She nodded. "Every senior cadet is required to take a practicum field exam, but not every cadet earns their license. The standards are pretty high."

"It seems like a lot of work on a gamble," Drake mumbled.

"Not really," Gil said, pushing back her bangs. "Even without a license, once you earn your degree, you can pretty much choose your own job in the private sector. I've already had six job offers from firms around the country, and I haven't even graduated yet."

"Are they good jobs?"

"They are if you like earning a lot of money, but that's not my goal. Some students use TEMCO as a stepping stone to fabulous careers in other fields, but I *want* to work here. Becoming a professional time counselor is..." Gil's voice trailed as the Staging Platform began to shimmer with a faint blue glow.

"What's happening?" Phoebe whispered.

"Last week, Zeke Masters traveled nineteen years into the past on a counseling assignment. He's a professional time surfer, and he's about to come home."

Over the intercom Marc's voice intoned, "Contact in three, two, one..."

The cloudy light on the platform brightened and swirled. Behind the captured timewave, Gil could see a large-nosed man with thick glasses standing beside a fifteen-year-old boy.

"Zeke," Director Matthews said, "it's good to see you."

"You too. What's the status?"

The director turned to a bank of computers on the adjacent wall. "I think I'll let one of our third-year cadets tell us that."

Crystal's excited voice rang out, "You're at a one hundred percent probability factor. Your case subject's life is back on track."

"Hey, Cris"—Zeke laughed—"have you finally got your hands on the controls?"

Crystal nodded. "I sure have, and I'm never going to budge now that I'm here."

"You'd better watch out, Director." Zeke chuckled. "Someone's after your job."

"I'm not worried." Director Matthews smiled. "TEMCO has several positions available for someone with Miss Stuart's qualifications."

Zeke turned to the teenage boy on his left. "Well, Andy, it looks as if things are finally looking up. A one hundred percent probability factor means your future's out of danger."

"I'm so relieved," the teenager said in a voice choked with emotion. "I never would've gotten through this without you. When I think about what I was planning—"

"Don't think about it—it's over now. You have a bright future ahead of you." Zeke smiled through the time portal. "Cris, just for fun, why don't you tell Andy what he becomes when he grows up."

Crystal bent forward—her fingers flying across her keyboard. Suddenly, she motioned for the director to draw near. "GAP won't let me see what Andy becomes. It keeps telling me to observe *Condition Gold Protocol.* I've never even heard of *Condition Gold.*"

"What does that mean?" Andy asked anxiously. "I thought I was in the clear."

"You are," Zeke said firmly. "*Condition Gold* means you're going to become something so important that we don't want it revealed to the public. I should've realized your future would be classified. Trust me, *Condition Gold* is a *very* good thing."

Andy bit his lip. "I'm never gonna see you again, am I?"

"That's not necessarily true. Practice the racquet ball returns I taught you. If we come across each other in the future, I'll challenge you to a game."

"You've done so much for me," Andy choked out. "I can never thank you enough."

"You don't need to try," Zeke replied, putting a friendly hand on Andy's shoulder. He looked through the portal at the people in the lab. "Are you ready for my retrieval?"

Ryan nodded. "Staging Platform is set and prepared. You can come through any time."

Zeke smiled at Andy and stepped through the shimmering curtain of blue light. Several blinding flashes illuminated the platform as he entered the lab.

"Don't forget the things we talked about," Zeke said, looking back through the portal at the teenager. "Forgiveness is key. Bitterness will destroy you."

Andy nodded and waved. The swirling blue light began to disperse. Within seconds, the timewave had vanished, leaving the platform dark and quiet.

Crystal jumped out of her chair and ran toward Zeke. "I *really* missed you!"

"The feeling's mutual. How about grabbing a bite to eat? That is, if you can bear to rip yourself away from GAP controls."

As Crystal nodded, Marc and Ryan strolled toward them.

"Would you two like to join us?" Zeke asked cheerfully. "After living on nothing but TEMCO energy bars, I can't wait to get my teeth into a nice, juicy steak."

"That'd be terrific," Marc replied. "It'll be my treat."

Crystal fell back a step. "Zeke, I have an errand to run. You and the guys catch up. We'll meet later, okay?"

"Sure," Zeke said slowly, "if that's what you'd prefer."

As Zeke's group moved to the other side of the lab, Phoebe looked at Gil with glowing eyes. "Time retrieval's awesome!"

"It is pretty exciting."

"I'll bet you can't wait for your turn to time surf," Drake said as a tech invited the freshmen to begin touring the lab. "When will you get your chance?"

Giving a nervous giggle, Gil replied, "Tomorrow afternoon."

"Oh, you lucky thing," Phoebe gushed. "Who are you counseling?"

Gil smiled. "A ten-year-old boy named Danny."

FIVE

AT THE UNHOLY hour of 5:00 a.m., Gil drove to NSU's fitness center and parked her car. Yawning widely, she scanned the barren lot for William's car—it wasn't there. Puffing out her cheeks, she tried to decide if she wanted to go to the bother of swimming after all. Suddenly, her eyes began to sparkle. Just because William's car wasn't in the lot didn't necessarily mean he wasn't at the pool. Sometimes, he parked over at Hawking Hall and walked to the gym.

Grabbing her duffle bag, she went into the gym and saw Ryan, Marc, and Kyle Carson lifting weights. She waved at them and continued toward the women's locker room.

"Hi, Gil," Ryan said cheerfully. "Getting some exercise before your big afternoon?"

She nodded. "I have some nervous energy I need to expend. Are you the only ones here this morning?"

"Kailee and June are back on the ellipticals," Marc replied, "and Jake's in the sauna."

Kyle smirked. "If you're wondering about Dr. Ableman, we haven't seen him this morning. Were you expecting him?"

"Not especially," Gil replied in a frosty voice.

Kyle's smirk deepened. "What's up with you two?"

"I don't know what you mean."

"Oh, come on. I'll bet there's more than swimming going on during your early morning *exercise* sessions."

Gil's eyes shot sparks as she stepped toward him. "Just what do you mean by that snide comment?"

Kyle started to reply, but Ryan interrupted. "He didn't mean anything. We all know that you and Dr. Ableman are straight arrows."

"We are," Gil said stiffly. "The doc's my friend. That's all."

"Maybe so." Kyle grinned. "But you want to be more than his friend, don't you?"

"That's none of your business!"

Kyle opened his mouth to make another comment, but Ryan gave his shoulder a rough shove. "Will you shut up? Leave her alone."

"Don't get testy. I'm just having a little fun."

"Well, I'm not," Gil snapped, stalking toward the locker rooms.

"Hey, don't go away mad," Kyle called out as she stormed past. "I'm just giving you a hard time."

Ignoring him, Gil went into the locker room and slammed the door. After she had changed into her swimsuit and slipped into the empty pool, she looked over at the men's locker room and sighed. She was hoping that William would join her, but she had a feeling he wouldn't. If he'd heard a comment like Kyle's, it might explain why he was avoiding too much private time with her. She grimaced. It might explain part of it—but not all of it. Something else was holding him back. She hoped it wasn't anything major and that he worked it out soon. If she wasn't put on staff, she'd be leaving D.C. at the end of the month to accept a job in Seattle.

As Gil floated across the pool, her thoughts drifted to Daniel's execution. It had been horrible, but she'd get her chance to do something about it soon—in a few hours to be exact. Pushing the memory of the execution aside, she began making a mental to-do list. The first thing she needed to do was go home and clean out her fridge—boring but necessary. She sighed. What she was *dying* to do was talk to William—but she wouldn't. For the next few days, she should be focusing all of her attention on ten-year-old Danny Winston.

$S\!I\!X$

LATER THAT AFTERNOON as Gil waited in the TEMCO lab for her field exam to begin, twenty-four years in the past, Danny Winston was riding his bicycle down Paradise Avenue in Charlesberg, Colorado. The autumn air was streaming past his ears and ruffling his hair. As he pedaled toward his house, he watched golden leaves dancing toward the ground in the fading October light. He smiled softly.

Suddenly, an angry voice shattered the peace around him. "Danny, come here!"

Danny wobbled and almost lost control of his bike. Across the street, a flock of startled blackbirds flew out of a tree.

"Danny! Now!"

Danny's eyes widened in his pale face as he caught sight of his babysitter, Rick Olsen, standing impatiently on the curb. Avoiding eye contact, Danny pedaled as hard as he could toward his garage. Seeing Rick's knotted fists, he winced and scrambled off his bike so quickly that his feet became tangled in the spokes. Desperately, he tried to chain his bike to a metal ring in the sidewalk. As his uncooperative fingers fumbled with the lock, he peeked over at Rick. It was obvious that he was drunk. It was also obvious that he was furious. A cold fear settled into the pit of his stomach.

"What are you? Spastic?" Rick growled. "How hard is it to chain a bike? Are you trying to make me mad?"

Danny anxiously shook his head. His breathing became ragged as he accidently dropped the lock.

"Can't you do anything right?"

Danny didn't reply. When the lock finally slid into place, he stood up. Wiping his sweaty palms on his jeans, he tried to hide his fear, but he was trembling so much that his dread was obvious.

"You're such a wimp," Rick said in a voice that made Danny flinch. "Your mother should've drowned you at birth."

Hunching a shoulder, Danny climbed his front steps.

"Maybe I should dunk you in the bathtub until you quit kicking."

As Danny tried to slip past him, Rick laid a massive hand on his shoulder. Putting his face next to Danny's, he whispered, "Did you hear what I said?"

Shuddering, Danny looked up with eyes that held a mixture of shrinking terror and desperate courage. "You won't kill me. You'd go to jail."

"I'm too smart to get caught."

Rick pushed Danny into the house and slammed the door. Inside, the strong smell of beer and perspiration filled the air. Knowing what was coming next, Danny spun around and put his back to the wall. He felt a nauseous wave of overwhelming fear as Rick drew near.

"What are you looking at?" Rick snarled, giving him a stinging slap on the cheek.

Danny flinched and tried to get away, but Rick grabbed him by the collar and shook him.

"Let me go," Danny begged. "*Please.*"

"Please?" Twisting his hand in the front of Danny's shirt, Rick raised him off the ground. "Scrawny cowards make me sick."

Desperately, Danny began to twist and squirm, clawing at Rick's hands. Rick threw him against the opposite wall. As Danny fell in a crumpled heap, Rick kicked him in the ribs. Danny shuddered and drew his legs up to protect his stomach. Rick kicked him again and then reeled down the hall. From his vantage point on the floor, Danny watched as Rick lurched toward the couch and sat down. Holding his breath, he remained absolutely still as Rick flipped on a football game.

Willing the time to go faster, Gil tossed back her blonde hair and looked at the clock on the wall. Waiting for her field exam to begin was torture. Across the room, a glowing beam of blue light twisted on the GAP Staging Platform. Over the intercom, a tech began a countdown. In just twenty minutes, Danny would play the game and she would launch into the adventure of a lifetime.

Rising from her chair, she began pacing. She looked at the spiraling blue light and the white-coated techs hurrying around the room. There was so much to see. So much to anticipate. She felt adrenaline screaming its way through her veins. She couldn't wait to get into the field and give Daniel Winston his second chance.

When Danny was sure that Rick was engrossed in the football game, he rolled to his feet and stole into the kitchen. If he was lucky, he could grab something to eat and hide in his room until Rick left.

Being careful not to make a sound, he took a soda from the fridge and reached for some crackers.

"Danny!"

Danny dropped the soda can. It hit the floor with a sickening thud. "Yes?"

"You have a package on the table. You haven't been ordering junk from some website, have you?"

"No."

"Well, get your lousy stuff off the table."

Danny picked up the soda can and sighed. He wished his dad was alive—his dad would know how to handle Rick. He sighed again. If his dad were alive, there'd be no Rick.

Gil glanced at the clock and resumed pacing. Maybe coming so early hadn't been a smart idea after all. The countdown was getting closer, but her adrenaline rush was turning into a bad case of nerves. She looked around for William. He'd slipped out a few minutes ago and hadn't returned. He was the one thing keeping her calm, and with him gone, she could feel her anxiety kicking into overdrive.

Danny looked at the stack of mail with a puzzled frown. He was surprised Rick hadn't opened the package, but his surprise evaporated when he saw the empty beer bottles piled in the trashcan. Beer must've been more inviting than the mail today.

Danny gave the nondescript box a tiny shake. The package didn't have a return address, and he wondered if it was a mail bomb. If it was, he wished Rick would've opened it.

Balancing his package and snack, he slipped into the hall. He held his breath as he crept past the living room. Rick was slumped down on the couch, cursing as his team fumbled the ball. Danny tiptoed into his bedroom and locked the door.

Sighing, Danny went to his hideout—a corner partitioned off by thick black curtains. Slipping inside, he flicked on a lamp with a red bulb. An angry red glow filled the tiny space. Danny settled into a beanbag chair in front of a battered TV hooked up to a secondhand PlayFest gaming system. As he flipped open the tab, his soda began to fizz over. His mom didn't like him to curse, but he felt close to it. With Slim hassling him at school, and Rick hassling him at home, he was at his breaking point.

When the fountain subsided, he shook pop from his hands and put the cold can against his cheek. Raising his shirt, he looked at the bruise spreading across his ribs. He'd gotten off easy. Everyone said Rick was charming, but Rick sure didn't bother wasting that charm on him.

William sat in his office with hands clenched so tightly that his knuckles were turning white. Taking a shuddering breath, he focused his attention on the forms cluttering his desk. Grabbing a pen, he went to work. After only a minute, the pen dropped from his hand. He reached up and fingered the silver chain hidden beneath his shirt. Lines of tension formed beside his eyes. William jolted violently as someone knocked on the door.

"Are you finished with..." Director Matthew's voice trailed away as he entered the office. Shoving a jar of pencils to one side, he sat down on the edge of William's desk and studied his face.

"Give me a few minutes, Peter, and I'll have the forms ready for you."

"Are you all right?" the director asked quietly.

"I'm fine."

Giving him a measured glance, the director said firmly, "Then pull yourself together and get back out there. She needs you."

Putting down his soda, Danny picked up the package. He paused with the idea of a mail bomb still lurking in his mind. "Oh, well," he mumbled, "who cares anyway?"

Plunging his pocketknife into the packing tape, he raised the box flaps. When nothing happened, he swished his fingers through squeaky Styrofoam peanuts. As packing filler spilled onto the floor, his groping fingers found a hard object. He pulled it out and looked at it in amazement. It was a PlayFest game called *Extreme Exam*.

"What a weird name for a game," he murmured.

Gil breathed a sigh of relief as William entered the lab carrying two cups of coffee.

"Miss me?" he asked, handing her a cup.

"Starting to," she admitted, taking a sip. "Where've you been?"

"Tying up loose ends." His eyes widened as he stared at the bags at her feet. "For Pete's sake, couldn't you pack any lighter? When I left, you only had a duffle bag. Where'd the rest of the luggage come from?"

The dimples in Gil's cheeks danced. "It was over in the corner."

"You're only going to be gone four days. Surely you don't need *that* many clothes."

Gil pulled a shocked face, her anxiety beginning to dissipate. "Four days? I thought the exam was over in two. Maybe I should go home and get that extra sweater."

William laughed and shook his head. "Don't blame me when your case subject runs away and you're too weighed down with skirts and shoes to follow."

"If Danny tries to run, I'll toss my baggage into a bush and take off after him."

"If you're just looking for a convenient shrub to toss that mess into, there's a nice one below this window. If you'd like, I could give that big suitcase a toss."

"No, thanks." She chuckled. "I'll look for a handy bush after I travel through GAP."

William stroked his beard and mumbled something inaudible.

Gil smiled. Her nervous tension was broken. She was herself again.

Danny looked at the PlayFest game in wonder. Rummaging through the box, he spilled more packing peanuts on the floor. He kicked at them absently and continued digging. At the bottom of the box was a letter. Scanning it quickly, he came to the words: *Free Test Game.*

Smiling widely, he picked up the game and looked at the holographic laser drawing of a university on its cover. Suddenly, 3-D sprays of color shot out of the picture. Blinking in amazement, Danny touched the rays and watched as they went through his fingers. He closed his eyes as they danced over his forehead. He could feel his scalp tingling and could almost see the colors dancing inside his brain. He felt the rays stop their motion, and when he opened his eyes, they were gone.

At NSU, Gil watched as Dr. Moosly came bustling out from the swarm of techs merging Danny's neural scan into their computer calculations. As she looked at him, the bald man frowned and approached. "Miss Gillyflower Montgomery?"

"Please call me Gil." She smiled. "My parents had a sadistic sense of humor when they named me."

If possible, Dr. Moosly frowned even more. "I could not help but overhear your laughter, and I feel it is my duty to remind you of the importance of the field exam."

Gil blinked. "I *am* taking the exam seriously, I—"

"I sincerely hope so," he snapped. "There's significant danger of damaging the fragile psyche of the child you are counseling if you make a mistake. It may seem impossible to adversely affect the future of a death-row inmate, but I assure you that it can happen much easier than you realize. If you neglect to handle things properly, your case subject may start his path of violence earlier and the body count of his victims may rise."

"I promise I'll be careful, I—"

Dr. Moosly held up an impatient hand and glowered down at his clipboard. "I see here that you hope to be put on staff. If your test performance is substandard, you won't attain licensure. Not everyone who aspires to work for TEMCO gets that opportunity."

"I know. I'll do my best. I've studied hard and—"

"I'm sure you believe yourself to be ready, but so have other cadets who have failed."

At his words, Gil felt a knot tightening in her stomach. She glanced nervously at William for reassurance and ended up stifling a grin. He was staring at Dr. Moosly with an exasperated expression. She'd seen that look before and knew he was slowly and silently counting to ten.

Dr. Moosly continued, "Although GAP has been used for exam purposes for several years, there's still significant risk when dealing with time displacement. As one of your evaluators, I caution you to approach this technology, and the exam procedure, with proper respect. Do you understand?"

"Yes," she said quietly.

"I trust that you've read all the manuals covering the exam?"

Not wanting to lie, Gil shifted uncomfortably and tried to think of an answer that wouldn't land her in too much hot water. The five-inch manuals were collecting dust underneath her bed. They'd proven so dry that she'd consigned them to oblivion and gathered her information from friends who had been through GAP. The information they provided may not have been technical, but it *had* been interesting.

Not waiting for her reply, Dr. Moosly glared at William in distaste. "You're Miss Montgomery's advisor? I might have known."

William's eyes gave a brief twinkle. "It's good to see you too, Dr. Moosly."

Ignoring him, the bald man turned to Gil. "After reading the manuals, you know that time surfing isn't the picnic that someone like Dr. Ableman makes it out to be. If you feel unprepared to take the exam, I'll arrange for it to be postponed and for you to be given a different advisor. I'd hate for you to be at a disadvantage during such a critical juncture in your training."

Hearing the way that William's abilities were being maligned, Gil's face hardened. "Dr. Ableman has done an excellent job of preparing me."

Dr. Moosly raised a skeptical eyebrow. "That remains to be seen, doesn't it? I hope your faith hasn't been misplaced."

"It hasn't." Gil's tone was so rigid that it bordered on rude insolence.

As Dr. Moosly pursed his lips and glared down at his clipboard, Gil glanced at William. A smile was tugging the corner of his lips. She knew he appreciated her defense of him, but she also knew it hadn't been necessary.

As Director Matthews joined them and engaged William in conversation, Gil peeked at Dr. Moosly. Seeing the offended tilt of his chin, she knew she'd better try to mend a few fences. "You wrote one of the manuals, didn't you?" she asked in a suitably subservient voice.

"Yes, I did. My book is called *The Technical Design and Inner Mechanics of TIME GAP Displacement at the Atomic Level in Conjunction with Historical Theorems and the Application of Modern Theory.*"

"I thought so." Gil looked at the sour-faced evaluator and thought a little judicious flattery might not come in amiss. She hadn't read his book, but she assumed it contained quite a bit of information. Convincing herself that she wasn't exactly lying, she said with a smile, "Your book was my favorite of all the manuals... It was very in-depth."

"I'm glad you appreciated it. What did you think about the chapter on the subatomic development of cyberspace neurolinks and the present program design?"

In the distance, Danny heard the muted ring of the telephone and the low growl of Rick's voice. Dropping his new PlayFest game, he scrambled out of his hideout and sprinted to the door to make sure it was locked. The knob turned violently as Rick pounded on the door.

"Danny, open up!"

"Just a minute," Danny said desperately. "I'm...I'm changing clothes."

"Whatever for?"

"I...I..."

"Never mind," Rick said impatiently. "I just got a call. They need me at the plant." Suddenly, Rick slammed his fist against the door causing Danny to jump back several feet. "I don't like locks! Keep your bedroom open from now on, you hear?"

"Sure, Rick. I'm sorry."

With his heart pounding in his throat, Danny listened to Rick's heavy footsteps moving down the hall. He waited cautiously for the front door to slam before slipping into his hideout and collapsing on the beanbag. Passing a shaking hand over his forehead, he tried to calm his rapid breathing.

In order to keep her eyes from glazing over, Gil began to count the words in Dr. Moosly's sentences. When that pursuit paled, she diagramed his sentences in her head. Her automatic nod and mechanical *"Oh, really?"* were all the evaluator needed to keep him going.

"Excuse me," she said as William called her name. "I have to go, but thanks for talking with me."

As Dr. Moosly turned away, Gil went to William and demanded in a soft hiss, "What took you so long to rescue me?"

"I thought it served you right, you little hypocrite. You're the one who expressed interest in his book." As Gil gave a sputtering laugh, he said, "I toyed with the idea of letting Dr. Moosly explain the paradox of neurolink degradation and sinusoidal loops, but I took pity."

Gil's reply died on her lips as a group of techs brushed past her and took their places beside the Staging Platform. Seeing Dr. Moosly's bald head bobbing among them, she shifted uncomfortably.

"Stop worrying," William said firmly. "You'll do great with Danny. Don't let Dr. Moosly's Cassandra-like bleatings bother you. His verbosity could make a hangnail seem like a terminal disease. I'm surprised how fast you breezed through his manual."

"I didn't. The first chapter was all I could manage to read, so..." Seeing the change in William's expression, Gil's words stumbled to a halt.

"You didn't finish it? How could you cut corners?" William exclaimed. "On that admission, I could cancel your exam."

"You wouldn't," she gasped. "Would you?"

His jaw tightened. "If you didn't study the manuals, how'd you pass the orals?"

"Edible bribery. I cooked dinner for last year's graduates. By the time I served my raspberry cheesecake, I had tons of information."

Gil watched anxiously as William fingered his beard. After a moment, he said slowly, "What you did obviously worked. You passed the orals with flying colors."

"So you won't cancel my field exam?"

He shook his head. "Considering your scores, I'll let you continue. After all, manuals covering temporal physics aren't necessary for a successful time surf. A student needs a counselor's instinct—something you have. But if you hadn't aced the orals, we'd be having a serious talk with the director right now."

Danny took a sip of pop and ate a cracker. Taking a last look at the game's cover, he stuck the cartridge into his PlayFest console.

"We have contact," Director Matthew's voice boomed over the intercom. "I repeat. We have contact."

Gil turned and looked at the blue glow on the Staging Platform. Through the shimmering curtain, she could finally see Danny's face. She couldn't believe she was looking at the child version of Death Row Daniel. As she stared at him, she could see that his eyes held sadness, even now, as he was engrossed in the opening stages of the *Extreme Exam* game. She felt a tug on her heart as his eyes seemed to call to her.

SEVEN

"AWESOME," DANNY WHISPERED as the TV came to life with a glittering picture of a university. He watched with awe as tiny rays of color reached out from the screen to touch him. The beams of light danced around his hideout, spiraled back, and became sparkling fireworks. As the sound of *Pomp and Circumstance* filled the air, students began pouring out of the university wearing mortarboards and huge smiles.

Danny listened intently as a computerized voice began to speak. "Welcome to *Extreme Exam*. Before a prospective time surfer can graduate, he or she must complete a field exam, and *you've* been selected to help. During this exam, you'll work closely with one of our student cadets. If you agree to help with the testing procedure, press your B button."

Danny watched as a swirling river of Bs flooded the screen and became a whirlpool of psychedelic colors. When he pressed his B button, the whirlpool vanished and an avatar of a blonde-haired woman with twinkling eyes and lopsided dimples appeared.

"This is Gil," the game's voice said. "If you agree to help Gil take her *Extreme Exam*, press your Y button."

The screen turned neon yellow as twisting Ys danced. When Danny pressed the appropriate button, the dancing letters disappeared and the blonde avatar entered the university. She walked through pillared halls, up a set of marble stairs, and into a room marked TEMCO Lab. Suddenly, the screen exploded with whizzing rainbows of color. Drops of color burst from the television and sizzled when they hit the floor. Danny reached toward one drop. It effervesced when he touched it. Looking at it in amazement, he touched it again.

When the rainbows disappeared, a blinding blue light filled his room. He gasped in wonder as the PlayFest game took on the appearance of real life. As he watched, people hurried around the lab. A bald man with a big frown stomped across the room, consulting his clipboard. Danny could see his face clearly and feel the vibration of his footsteps. Suddenly, his attention was caught by a blonde lady resembling the game's avatar. She was slipping on a backpack, and beside her, a bearded man was struggling to pick up a suitcase. As the man dropped the suitcase with a thump, a pretty lady with red hair approached the blonde.

The game's voice intoned, "While Gil's getting last minute instructions from Dr. Nelson, let's double check to make sure you're still willing to participate. If you wish to continue, press your B button."

William looked down at Gil's enormous suitcase and groaned. "I think I just pulled a muscle in my back."

"If that's true," Gil laughed, "you *really* need to start swimming again—your lack of exercise is becoming painfully apparent."

"If you had to grade a mountain of term papers, you'd be skipping out on the gym too."

"So that's your big excuse? Grading papers?"

He started to reply, but was interrupted when Dr. Laura Nelson walked over and said, "Miss Montgomery, may I have a moment of your time? According to new regulations, Danny has completed the necessary steps to free TEMCO from liability, but before you go through the time portal we need to talk."

As Gil nodded, Dr. Nelson took out a computer pad and went down a checklist of last minute instructions. "I trust you've had your inoculations and Class Two injections?"

"I had them a week ago," Gil replied.

"That's fine. The inoculations are just a precaution—there were some nasty things floating around twenty-four years ago. The Class Twos you took should curb any partial paralysis initially accompanying your trip through GAP. If you do feel any paralysis, don't worry, the effect will fade after a few minutes." Dr. Nelson's eyes moved down the list. "Don't forget, since GAP's only calibrated to Danny's neural pathways, only he will be able to see you."

She handed Gil an electronic journal. "Please write daily entries concerning your contact with Danny. We'll use this notebook as part of the evaluation procedure, so make your entries exam quality. GAP will gauge your progress, and your progress with Danny will be the main criteria in determining if you earn your license."

Dr. Nelson tapped her computer pad with a polished nail. "When you cross over, remember to take *Extreme Exam* out of Danny's gaming console and put it someplace safe. The cartridge is your ticket home. You must know where it is at all times, and it's vital that you avoid leaving it in a running gaming system. After eight hours in a console, a cartridge could be damaged. If that happens, you'll be stranded in the past. The game's waterproof, but keep it dry to avoid mishaps."

"I'll be extra careful," Gil promised.

"Good," Dr. Nelson replied. "Every night at 10:00 p.m., put the cartridge in Danny's PlayFest console for a conference. After we confer, remember to take it out again." A smile tugged Dr. Nelson's lips. "Be aware that after you stop the game, the connection may take several minutes to fade if you neglect to turn off power to the gaming console. I've heard a surprising number of embarrassing things when students failed to completely sever the connection."

Dr. Nelson looked up at Gil. "The final thing to keep in mind is that Danny's an extremely troubled youth. If his feet can be set on the right path during this crucial window, he may be able to avoid his violent future. We don't expect miracles—just a few solid results. If anything in this boy's tragic future can be averted, it'll be a gain for society." She turned off her computer pad. "Now, if you're ready, we'll begin."

Taking a deep breath, Gil gave a nervous smile. "I'm as ready as I'll ever be."

Munching on a cracker, Danny watched as the blonde and the bearded man drew near. He could almost smell the woman's perfume and feel a breeze coming out of the TV. As the music blared, the bearded man smiled at the blonde. Danny could see the words "*good luck*" forming on his lips. Suddenly, the lab was a bevy of activity. The blonde looked nervously over her shoulder as technicians rushed around the room. As the bearded man spoke again, Danny lip-read the words, *Let me know if you need me.*

Danny watched the woman nod and step closer to the TV. Her image began to blur around the edges. The screen filled with whirling blue light as the game's voice announced in ringing tones, "*Extreme Exam* begins in five, four, three, two, one..."

Suddenly, blue light oozed out of the TV and encompassed Danny—spiraling around him and forming clouds above his head. There was a blinding flash and then a bedroll landed on his lap. Danny yelped and jumped to his feet. Pressing up against the wall, he stared down at the bedroll in disbelief. More blinding flashes took place and a large suitcase, a duffle bag, and a backpack landed on the floor. Danny's muscles froze. With his breath catching in his throat, he watched as a hand engulfed with light reached out from the TV. Danny stared in horrified disbelief as a woman with blonde hair slid through the screen.

"I'm through, Doc," she said cheerfully, turning back to the TV. "Everything's fine."

"Do you feel all right?"

"Terrific. No dizziness. No paralysis. It was just as easy as you said it'd be."

"Good! I knew you could do it. We'll talk to you tonight. Be careful."

The woman turned toward Danny. Seeing that she was focused on him, Danny let out a strangled scream and tried to run away. He tripped over the suitcase and landed on the beanbag. One of his flailing legs sent his soda can flying through the television. His scrabbling hands squashed the crackers flat. Packing peanuts squealed frantically as he tried to push his way through the curtains.

Moving her luggage aside, the woman put her hand on his shoulder. "Hey, it's all right. There's nothing to be afraid of."

"Get away!" he gasped, breaking through to his room.

He watched in fear as the woman put *Extreme Exam* into her backpack and slowly walked toward him. Seeing her approach, Danny ran to the door and fumbled with the lock.

"Hey, it's all right," the woman said in a soothing voice. "It's me. Gil. You agreed to help me pass my exam."

"I never agreed to nothing!"

"You pressed the right buttons."

"That was a game," he shouted, twisting the knob frantically. "I didn't agree to this!"

Seeing Gil reaching her hand toward his shoulder, Danny backed toward the window.

"I'm not going to hurt you," she said gently. "I'm here to help."

"Stay away," he yelled, opening the window.

Gil leaned against the wall. "Hey, I'm *just* a girl. What can I do to you?"

Danny slung his leg over the windowsill. "Lady, you just jumped out of a TV. Who knows what you can do!"

EIGHT

"THIS IS TOTALLY unacceptable," Dr. Moosly growled as he wiped soda from his face. "That pesky child threw that can on purpose!"

Ignoring him, William watched with amusement as Gil vaulted out the window in pursuit of Danny. As the GAP beam faded away, he whispered, "God speed, Gil, go get 'em."

At that moment, Kyle approached William, holding Danny's soda can in his hand. "May I keep this, Dr. Ableman? It's a limited edition that's worth quite a bit of money online."

William's eyes narrowed. "We do not surf through time to collect souvenirs. If you want to sell that soda can, sell it for charity. I'll expect the receipt for the sale and the receipt for your charity donation on my desk by the end of the day."

With his heart pounding, Danny sprinted across the yard. Kneeling beside his bicycle, he began yanking on the padlock. Looking over his shoulder, he saw Gil climbing out the window and landing in a clump of prickly evergreen bushes.

"Hey, where are you going?" she yelled. "Wait a second, will you?"

Seeing her pelting across the lawn, he jumped over his bicycle and raced down the sidewalk.

"I'm in good shape," Gil yelled. "I can run just as long as you can. Give me a break! I just wanna talk!"

Ignoring her, Danny sprinted to the house next door where his neighbor, Mr. Jacobson, was sitting on his porch drowsing in the late-afternoon sunshine. As Danny ran up to him, the old man rose from his chair and sputtered, "For goodness sake, what's the matter?"

"Help me, please!" Danny gasped. "Someone's after me."

"Is it that Rick fellow? Is he bothering you?"

"No, sir. It's..." His voice trailed off as he tried to explain something beyond explanation.

Stumbling up the porch steps, he landed in a heap beside the old man. Mr. Jacobson brandished a flyswatter and stepped protectively in front of him. Danny saw Gil's headlong pursuit come to a stop. He sighed and closed his eyes.

"Whoever was chasing you has given up," Mr. Jacobson said. "There's no one on the sidewalk."

"What...?" Danny looked up—straight into Gil's face.

"Please don't yell," she said, crouching on the top step. "Don't upset this nice old man. Just hear me out. Remember the game? The blue light? That light makes me visible to you—"

"Mr. Jacobson," Danny said in an agonized voice, "are you *sure* no one's around?"

The old man shoved his glasses further up on his nose and looked in every direction. Danny watched in amazement as he looked through Gil as if she weren't even there.

"I don't see anyone at all," Mr. Jacobson replied.

"Do you mind if I stay here for a while?" he asked, scooting closer to the old man.

"Don't mind a bit. Take your time and catch your breath."

Chewing his lip, Danny turned his shoulder on Gil and watched as Mr. Jacobson sat down. A cat jumped onto the old man's knee. Mr. Jacobson chuckled and scratched the cat behind the ears. "This here's Sheba. She thinks she's queen of all the land."

"I've seen her running through our backyard," Danny said absently, glancing cautiously at Gil out of the corner of his eye. "She's a pretty cat."

"That she is." As the cat began to purr, Mr. Jacobson said gently, "Danny, are you in some kinda trouble? Is there something I can do to help?"

Danny studied Gil who was wiping sweat off her neck with a messy looking tissue. "I'm not sure," he said. "Can I just sit here for a while?"

"Sure thing. But if you do decide to tell me what's wrong, I'll listen. I have a grandson on the Westfield Police Force and another grandson who's a black belt. If you decide you need help, I'll see that you get it."

As Danny nodded, Gil moved closer to him. When he cringed back, she said softly, "I'm sorry you're so frightened. You don't need to be."

Danny shifted his weight and pressed closer to Mr. Jacobson. The old man gave his shoulder a pat and began to hum.

"I'm not gonna hurt you," Gil said. "Just listen to me for a minute, okay? When you played *Extreme Exam*, it asked if you'd be willing to help me take my field exam. I know you thought it was just a game, but the blue light was from my university. It scanned your brain—"

Danny gave her a horrified glare.

"Don't worry," she said quickly. "The light didn't hurt you. It just let you see me. I'm no one to fear. I'm just a college kid. All I wanna do is pass my exam and graduate."

Danny glanced up at Mr. Jacobson. The old man seemed completely unaware of Gil's presence. Nervously clenching his hands, Danny gave Gil a slight nod.

With an encouraging smile, she said, "I know you're in a pinch right now. My job, the way I can pass my test and get out of your hair, is to give you a hand over the next few days."

Danny raised an eyebrow and looked skeptical.

"I may not look tough," she said indignantly, "but I promise I can help. Think of me as a secret warrior."

He looked at her with a speculative gleam in his eyes.

She laughed. "It's kinda sinking in now, isn't it? Having the invisible woman on your side could be pretty cool, huh?"

Gil shifted positions, and Danny saw Sheba whipping her head around. With a tail puffed like a bottlebrush, Sheba gave a feral hiss and ran through the cat door into the house.

Mr. Jacobson chuckled. "Silly cat, probably saw a bee. Sheba's been terrible afraid of bees ever since she ate one by accident when she was a kitten."

Gil said to Danny, "I can't be seen by anyone but you—and maybe that silly cat—but I'm chock-full of good ideas that I'm super anxious to put into practice. Will you let me help you?"

Danny stared at her for a long moment and then stood to his feet. "Mr. Jacobson, thanks a lot. I think I'll be going now."

Rising from his chair, the old man put arthritic hands on Danny's narrow shoulders. "Just remember I'm here and my grandsons are only a phone call away. I'll vouch for you if you want to talk to them."

"Thanks, sir. I might take you up on that."

NINE

GIL SWUNG IN beside Danny as he jumped off Mr. Jacobson's porch and went into the shadowy forest behind the subdivision. The fading afternoon sunshine was playing peek-a-boo with the ground as they weaved through a grove of wind-stirred aspens and came to a tiny brook. As Gil walked, she silently prayed for wisdom. She'd been warned that if first contact went awry, it was hard to salvage a time surf.

Danny sat down on a moss-covered log and drew his knees beneath his chin. "Okay, I'm listening. I'm willing to believe you're not here to hurt me. So talk."

"What do you wanna know?" she asked, putting her hands in her pockets.

"Who are you? First and last name."

"You just *had* to ask," she groaned. "Can't we start with a different question?"

Seeing his critical stare, she wrinkled up her nose and said in a voice full of dignity, "It's against TEMCO rules to reveal my last name, but my first name is Gillyflower Meadowlark Deleena Rosemarie."

Danny choked and laughed. "You gotta be kidding. *Gillyflower? Meadowlark?*"

"Hey, no cracks about my name. It's a sore spot."

As Danny grinned and peeked up from beneath unkempt bangs, Gil felt a tug on her heart. "What else?" she asked, squatting beside him.

"What college are you from?"

"National Science University in Washington D.C."

"Never heard of it."

"That's because it doesn't exist yet. In about fifteen years, the government's going to establish NSU and staff it with our country's finest minds."

Danny rolled his eyes and threw a stick in the water. "Stop pulling my leg."

"I'm not. Think a little. You've never seen anything like *Extreme Exam*, right? That's because the technology doesn't exist yet. It won't exist for another nineteen years."

"You're from nineteen years into the future? You gotta be kidding."

"Twenty-four years actually," she replied. As silence fell between them, she began doodling on the muddy bank with a stick. After a few moments, she gazed over at him. "I know what it sounds like, but I'm telling you the truth."

"So what's going on here?" he asked, studying the swirling eddies in the water. "Am I some future world leader, and you're here to keep me safe from killer robots?"

"I don't understand."

"Don't you watch movies in the future?"

"Of course we do, but old classics aren't really my thing."

Danny shuffled his feet in the leaves. "So why are you here to help me?"

"Because the GAP computer indicated that you could be time counseled and saved."

"Saved from what?" he asked, wiping his nose with his sleeve.

Gil looked down at her doodles. She had drawn a house that was broken in half and on fire. Scratching it out with the stick, she stood up. "I don't think we should discuss that right now. It isn't the right time, and there are other things that—"

"Look, lady, if you wanna hang out with me, you gotta be straight. Tell me what's gonna happen, or I'm walking away and you're flunking your precious test. Am I gonna be hit by a bus or something?"

"No. You're safe from buses."

Squatting down, Gil looked Danny straight in the eye. She looked for so long that he began to squirm. Swallowing hard, she plunged in, making a quick decision. "Don't freak out, okay? But in less than two days you'll kill Rick Olsen with a butcher knife in your kitchen." As Danny blinked, she hurried on, "You'll be sent to Juvenile Hall, and you'll become involved with a bad bunch of boys. A few years into your sentence, the prison will catch fire and you'll be badly burned."

She paused, but when Danny remained silent, she continued, "When you get out of prison, you'll have trouble finding work. Eventually, your old juvie hall buddies will talk you into robbing convenience stores. This will escalate into home invasions and bank robberies. You'll become meaner, and tougher, and more violent, until ultimately you'll kill a man and his wife during a robbery. You'll be found four weeks later, and during a standoff with police, you'll fatally shoot five police officers and one innocent bystander—a woman who was eight-months pregnant. You'll be sentenced to death by lethal injection." She shuddered. "You just died. Three days ago. I attended your execution in—"

Standing up abruptly, Danny stumbled toward the stream. Gil jumped to her feet and walked beside him. As he looked at the water, tears began flowing down his face. "Am I really gonna do all those b-bad things?"

"Yes," she said quietly—the catch in his voice breaking her heart.

"I don't wanna hurt nobody. Maybe you should just kill me."

"That's not why I'm here," she said soothingly. "I've seen you die once. I'm not gonna let it happen again. I'll help you make all the bad things go away."

"How?"

"By showing you other choices you can make. You're not an evil person—at least not yet—you're just in a bad situation that's too big for you to handle. We've looked at your case carefully, and you don't have to go down a corrupt path. You have a good heart and are highly intelligent."

He roughly brushed away his tears. "You gotta be joking. I'm flunking out."

"We have your IQ on file, and believe me, it's *very* high. Some extremely smart professors believe you can become a tremendous asset to society."

"Really?" he asked, scuffing his feet in the dirt.

"Do you think I'd travel twenty-four years into the past if I didn't think so? By the time I'm through with you, you're gonna become something wonderful in the future—something to be proud of."

"Are you sure?"

"Very sure. Last semester, my friend June counseled a boy who was gonna be responsible for a plane hijacking. After her work with him, he turned out to be the future governor of Maine."

"Are you joking?"

"Of course not. The GAP computer looks for people with good hearts and high intelligence who have basically had a bad break—a *tipping point* it's called. The computer calculates who can be transformed into assets for society providing the tables are turned in their favor. You're a pretty special kid. Only a few people out of millions are selected for time counseling. That's a good indication of how much faith we have in you."

Danny's smile wobbled and turned into a frown. "But isn't messing around with time dangerous? In *Star Trek* you aren't allowed to change the past because it alters the timeline. Even talking with me would be in violation of the *Temporal Prime Directive*."

"Kid, you watch *way* too much TV." Gil laughed. "What's wrong with stopping a killer from killing?"

"But is this even legal?"

"Sure it is. The *Temporal Counseling Program*—TEMCO for short—operates under full government approval. After GAP was invented, Congress voted to—"

"Wait a sec, what's GAP?"

"It's TEMCO's *Grappling-And-Positioning* computer. All around you are radio waves, cosmic waves, and electromagnetic waves. Timewaves are no different than those other invisible waves— they're sailing around you at this very moment. GAP harnesses timewaves and allows us to surf them."

"And you use GAP to help people?" he asked.

She nodded. "Since Congress voted to allow time surfing, the number of violent crimes has dropped significantly throughout our nation."

"I don't see how," he said gruffly, tossing a rock in the brook.

"Look at the ripples from the rock you just threw. If you take a violent person and transform him into peaceful person, that act ripples through time. One person's positive change echoes throughout the years, making things better."

"Do you ever fail?"

Gil hesitated. "Only rarely and never with someone as young and good-hearted as you. You *are* gonna be a success. I feel it in my bones, and my bones never lie."

"So what do we do first?" he asked, giving her a wobbly smile.

"First, we go to your house and throw away the kitchen butcher knife." Gil laughed and tousled his hair. "Then we get down to some *serious* business."

TEN

MR. JACOBSON SAT ON his porch and waited for Danny's return. He was of half a mind to call the police, but he wasn't sure he should. He sighed. He'd definitely be keeping an eye—two eyes—on what was going on next door. It was good to mind one's own business, but it was also good to keep an eye out for a youngster who needed help. He'd never liked the look of Rick. He couldn't understand why a nice lady like Danny's momma let him hang around her house.

Mr. Jacobson felt a rush of relief as Danny walked out from the forest. "Hi, there," he called, lifting a blue-veined hand in greeting.

He watched as Danny waved back and then the boy paused and cocked his head like he was listening to something. Mr. Jacobson tapped his fingers against his knees. Something strange was definitely going on.

Danny walked over to him. "Sir, I've thought about your offer. Can I talk with your grandson—the one who's a policeman?"

"Sure thing. Nathan's coming over for supper tomorrow at 5:30. If you like, you can join us. That work for you?"

"Yes, sir. Thank you."

"You gonna be okay until then? I can call Nathan and get him over here tonight."

"No, that's fine. I'll see you for supper tomorrow."

As Danny moved away, the old man rose from his chair. He was going to call his grandsons and get some advice.

Gil placed a hand on Danny's shoulder as they walked down the sidewalk. "That was perfect," she said. "By getting a policeman involved, we're getting the ball rolling in the right direction."

"What's next?" he asked as they walked toward his house.

"Next, we take a serious look at your homework."

Danny groaned and made a face. "I thought you were here to help me with Rick—not school."

"I'm here to help you with *everything*. Education's important."

"You sound just like my mom."

"I'm gonna sound even more like her in a minute. After we look at your homework, we're cleaning up your room. It looks like a tornado hit it."

Twenty-four years into the future, Ryan entered a classroom on the eighth floor of Curie Hall. It was time to take his *Quantum Mechanics 645* final, and he was hoping like mad that he was prepared. Although the final for *Quantum Mechanics* was reputed to be much easier than the one for *Timewave Dynamics*, Ryan knew that any test designed by Dr. Ableman was probably a killer.

Stepping into the crowded classroom, he spotted Crystal in her customary spot—front-row center—and smiled. She'd saved him a seat. Sitting down beside her, he tapped a finger on her desk to get her attention. "Where were you last night? I tried to call you, but you didn't answer."

Crystal blushed and looked uncomfortable. "Sorry about that."

Ryan groaned. "You lost your cell phone again, didn't you?"

"I didn't *lose* it. I just *misplaced* it. There's a world of difference."

"Not much. Where'd you misplace it this time?"

"I think on the lawn between Student Union and Hawking Hall. Either that or in the library. Or maybe in the Tech Lab. It's not in my car or under my sofa cushions—I checked. But it might be in the pocket of my dirty blue jeans, or maybe it's at Zeke's house."

"That sounds like the definition of lost."

"I wouldn't say so. *Webster* defines 'lost' as *unable to be found or no longer possessed*. I have every expectation of finding my phone, and even though it's not currently in my hand, I certainly still possess it—I just paid my phone bill."

Ryan raised his hands in surrender and laughed. "I never could triumph in a verbal battle with you—it's pointless to try now."

Crystal flashed him a smile. "So, why were you trying to call me?"

"I was hoping to pick your brain. Black Body Radiation and the Planck Constant were giving me fits."

"Do you want me to explain them?" she asked, opening her notebook.

"No need. I finally figured them out around 2:00 a.m."

Crystal winced. "You pulled an all-nighter? Are you okay?"

"Sure, I took a few catnaps between classes today." Stretching his arms over his head, he yawned and quirked an eyebrow. "I was so desperate for help last night that I went to the library to find you, but you weren't there."

Crystal's lips twitched. "Okay, I'll admit it—I wasn't studying at all. I was painting the town red."

"I'll bet you still get an A+." Reaching over, he tugged a curl bobbing beside her ear. "Sometimes it's a pain to be around a genius who doesn't have to study."

"I study," she protested. "I study a lot! I've been preparing all week for this final."

Ryan grinned and changed the subject. "So what part of the town did you paint?"

"Zeke took me to this cool Japanese restaurant, and I tried sushi for the first time."

"Did you like it?"

"That depends on whether I listen to my taste buds or brain."

"That comment needs explaining."

"It's simple. My taste buds kept telling me that sushi was absolutely yummy, but my brain kept rebelling at the thought of eating raw fish. Whenever my brain got the upper hand, my gag reflex kicked in. I spent the night licking my chops while trying not to barf. It was an interesting sensation, to say the least."

Ryan grinned. "I'll bet Zeke had a blast introducing you to Japanese cuisine."

Crystal's face fell. "He did at first, but then he had another migraine."

"It wasn't as bad as the one he had Easter Sunday, was it?"

"It was worse. We had to leave the restaurant early. I drove him home and then took a taxi to my apartment."

Ryan whistled in disbelief. "Zeke must've been half-dead to end the night like that."

"He was in so much pain he didn't even insist on giving me cab fare—not that I would've taken it. I wanted to help him to bed and sleep on his couch, but he wouldn't let me. He said it wouldn't look right."

"It wouldn't have."

Crystal glared. "Don't you start too! You guys and your silly sense of honor. Zeke's my friend, and he was in trouble. In times like that, propriety can take a hike."

Ryan shook his head but let it pass. "Has he seen a doctor?"

"Several of them, and they all say the same thing. He needs heavy-duty medication. They want him to carry an EpiPen and inject himself at the first sign of trouble."

"Sounds reasonable."

"Maybe, but he won't do it. His father had a history of substance abuse, and Zeke doesn't want to get dependent on any chemical—even a helpful one."

Ryan sighed. "So what's his plan?"

"He doesn't have one. The stiff-necked jerk's gonna suffer through the pain until his head explodes."

"I suppose that's his prerogative."

"Maybe for a while, but soon, he won't have a choice. His migraines are coming more frequently and are escalating in intensity. The EpiPen is going to become a necessity before long." She chewed her lip. "I just hope the medicine's enough."

Seeing her worried face, Ryan said softly, "You know something about his migraines, don't you?"

"I don't *know*—I *suspect*." Giving a gusty sigh, she opened her notebook to a paper-clipped section of neatly written dates. "I've been collecting data and I've figured out that every time Zeke comes home from a time surf, he ends up experiencing a migraine. I think it has something to do with cranial resistivity and cascading synaptic irritation due to magnetic field diffusion when sinusoidal timewaves are disseminated."

Trying to mentally untangle her last sentence—and utterly failing—Ryan asked simply, "How long have you been keeping track?"

"For over a year. I wanted to be sure I was right about the cause."

"You're sure now?"

She nodded. "At first, the migraines occurred a few days after Zeke came home from an assignment. Now, they're occurring within hours. If the pattern continues, he'll eventually experience incapacitating migraines immediately after stepping through a temporal portal at the start of an assignment."

"That'd end his career as a professional time counselor, wouldn't it?"

As Crystal nodded miserably, Ryan asked, "Have you told him?"

"I doubt he'd believe me, and even if he did, he'd refuse to do anything about it. Time counseling is his life."

"I wouldn't blame him for ignoring the facts. I'd hate to leave TEMCO."

"He doesn't have to leave, he just needs to stop going through temporal portals. He'd still be in the mix of things if he switched career paths and became a lab tech."

"Would that end his migraines?"

"Not completely," she replied, flipping to a page of mathematical equations. "But after crunching the numbers, I've concluded the risk of migraines would be negligible. He'd still be exposed to timewaves in the lab, but the exposure would be of an indirect nature. As long as he worked reasonable hours and avoided stress, hopefully, his migraines would be manageable with medication."

Ryan looked at her calculations and scratched his head. He couldn't begin to understand the complicated math, but he knew Crystal was smart enough to get it right. Not wanting to appear completely moronic, he studied the numbers for a while before he said slowly, "I see what you mean. Are you going to tell Zeke?"

She closed her notebook. "Like I said, he wouldn't listen if I did. When it comes to his work, he's as stubborn as they come."

"Then you need to talk to Director Matthews."

"Go behind Zeke's back?" Crystal looked horrified. "I couldn't do that!"

"If it's a matter of his health, you don't have a choice. The director will rope Zeke into lab work without hurting his pride."

"I don't know," she said, cramming her notebook into her backpack. "I need to think about it some more."

Seeing her worried frown, Ryan changed the subject. "You actually drove Zeke's eggbeater last night? I can't believe you got it to run."

"It only ran after a fashion," she said with a weak chuckle. "I killed it a thousand times. I kept popping the clutch and stalling at stoplights."

"Sounds like an interesting ride."

"It wasn't interesting, it was *awful*! The blasted thing wouldn't go into second. We crept home at a snail's pace."

"I'll bet you're glad your rust bucket's an automatic."

"That's an understatement. After graduation, I'm going to buy a new car, but I'm gonna make doggone sure it's an automatic too. And when I buy it, my new car's gonna be small enough to make parking a breeze. I'm sick of parallel parking huge boats."

"But, Cris, you parallel park so bea-u-tifully."

She rolled her eyes and laughed. "Don't give me problems. You're the one who asked me to park your car yesterday."

"I said park it, not squeeze it in so tightly I couldn't move it later."

"You're lucky I didn't abandon your car in the middle of the road. That tiny space was the only one available for miles. Next time you toss me your keys and ask for a favor, the answer's gonna be no."

"Have a heart."

"I have one, and it's definitely agreeing with me."

Before Ryan could respond, Marc slid into the desk next to him. Ryan saw Crystal's laughter dying on her lips. As she turned away and became occupied with studying her textbook, he sighed and said to Marc, "So, are you ready for the test?"

"I hope so," Marc replied with a pointed glance in Crystal's direction. "I'll be fine unless Miss Einstein breaks the bell curve again."

Ryan watched as Crystal hunched her shoulders and twisted a bit of hair around her finger. She was obviously upset. Just then, William came into the classroom, balancing a briefcase and a stack of exams.

"What's the matter with Dr. Ableman?" Crystal whispered. "He looks like he's under a ton of stress."

Ryan shrugged and whispered back, "He looks okay to me."

"But his hands are shaking," she said impatiently.

"Maybe he drank too much coffee."

"But he's wearing mismatched socks!"

Before Ryan could reply, William cleared his throat. "Today's final is timed. All papers will be collected in two hours. I'll hold a recapitulation session for *Quantum Mechanics* this Thursday at 11:00 a.m. in Hertz Hall. At that time, your graded finals will be returned."

Marc asked, "Is the review session required?"

William shook his head. "It's only recommended. However, I'd advise those desiring to work for TEMCO to be sure and attend."

William put down his briefcase. "A sign-up sheet has been posted in the main office for those wishing to assist in the summer shutdown of the lab. As juniors, this will be your first opportunity to actually participate. It's an experience you shouldn't miss."

While William handed out the finals, Ryan whispered to Crystal, "Doc sounds the same as usual. Are you still convinced something's wrong?"

She nodded. "Now more than ever. He just split two infinitives."

$\backsim$

When they walked through Danny's front door, Gil wrinkled her nose at the overwhelming smell of beer. "You don't drink, do you?"

Danny shook his head. "The booze belongs to Rick. Me and Mom never touch the stuff."

"Good. There wasn't anything in your file about alcoholism, and you never mentioned it during our interviews, but I—"

"Wait a sec! You talked with the grown-up me? What was I like? Was I tall? Rick says I'm scrawny. Do I get big?"

"I'll say you do. You're over six feet tall."

"Am I good looking?"

"The fire scarred your face, but it couldn't hide the fact that you're gonna be awfully cute when you grow up."

"Did you like the grown-up me? Was I nice?"

Gil bit her lip and hesitated. "You were on death row when I met you, but you were polite to me." Seeing his face fall, she said quickly, "I'm sure if your life had turned out differently you'd have been a *very* nice person—someone I'd like for a friend." As he smiled, she said, "Hey, did you know you can sing?"

He shook his head. "You sure about that?"

"Positive. I heard you singing in your cell one day. You have a magnificent voice. Who knows? Maybe you're gonna become a rock star when we get things straightened out." She went over to the kitchen counter and threw away some empty yogurt containers. "What time does your mom come home tonight?"

"Not until midnight. She's working the late shift at the hospital."

"Is she a nurse?"

"Nah, she's the receptionist at the emergency room. She always wanted to be a nurse, but she never got the schooling."

Gil began brushing breadcrumbs from the counter. "And Rick—when will he be back?"

"Not until tomorrow afternoon. He was called into work."

"Does he live here too?"

"He'd like to, but Mom won't let him. She says it ain't proper."

"*Isn't* proper," Gil corrected. "So, we don't have to worry about seeing him for a while?"

Danny nodded.

"Well, then, let's get the first order of business done. Where's the butcher knife?"

Danny went over to a drawer and pulled out a lethal-looking knife.

Seeing it, Gil shuddered. "Does your mom use it very often?"

"Nah, she works so much that she never cooks anymore."

Gil shoved the trashcan toward him with her foot. "In that case, I'll let you have the honor of throwing it away."

Danny tossed the knife in with the empty beer bottles and asked, "Does this mean I'm not gonna kill Rick?"

"I can't see how you can stab him without a knife, can you?"

Danny laughed, tied up the bag, and took it to the garbage can in front of the garage. When he came back inside, Gil did a little jig and said gleefully, "You realize we've just taken a great big step in reconstructing your future, don't you?"

As Danny smiled, Gil put a broom in his hand. "Let's do something nice for your mom. You sweep, and I'll do the dishes. Where do you keep the dish soap?"

"Under the sink."

"Okay, spill," she demanded as she turned on the faucet. "What's going on between you and Rick? Why's he here?"

Danny stopped sweeping and mumbled, "Mom was worried about me being alone when she works late, so Rick offered to keep an eye on me. I think he wants to be Mom's boyfriend and is trying to impress her."

Hearing the tone of Danny's voice, Gil set the dish soap on the counter and asked, "You don't like him very much, do you? Does your mom know?"

He shook his head. "Rick's Mr. Charming when she's around, and I don't wanna worry her. She has enough problems."

"Having someone around that you don't like is a problem too. You should tell her."

"I don't know. Maybe he'll be nice if I can figure out what I'm doing that's making him mad. It wasn't bad when he first came over. He just kinda ignored me."

"What about now?"

"Lately, he's been drinking and..." Danny shrugged.

Seeing the tension in the boy's face, Gil asked gently, "Is he hurting you?" When Danny wouldn't meet her eye, she said quietly, "I need to know. If he's hurting you, it isn't your fault."

Danny's grip tightened on the broom handle. "He hits me where the bruises don't show."

"*Oh, Danny!*"

"Last week he messed up and punched my face really hard. When Mom saw the bruise, he said he'd been teaching me how to catch a baseball. He said I was clumsy and missed."

"*That—!*" Biting off an expletive, Gil said softly, "I'm sorry you've been hurt."

"It's not your fault." Danny wiped his nose with the back of his hand. "Besides, Mom was so upset about the bruise that Rick's started slapping my face instead of punching it. Slapping doesn't hurt as bad. I can take it."

"You shouldn't have to! Abuse is wrong." Gil's furious eyes turned thoughtful. "If Rick is abusing you that may explain a few things. I'll bet in two days, Rick's gonna attack you in the kitchen and you'll feel the need to defend yourself. Does that sound right?"

"Maybe...I don't know. What did 'future-me' have to say about it?"

"He just said Rick had it coming." She chewed her lip. "I wish he'd given me more information. I'd like to know what triggered the stabbing."

Danny shuddered. "I can't imagine sticking a knife into someone."

"Well, it's not gonna happen. We know the date your D-day occurs, and—"

"D-day?"

"Disaster Day."

"Oh."

She gave him a reassuring smile. "Don't worry. The butcher knife's in the trash, and I'm gonna make sure Mr. Jacobson's grandson is in the house with you on D-day."

"That's why you want me to talk with him?"

She nodded. "If he can't be here, we'll get you out of the house when the stabbing's supposed to happen. We're gonna win this one,

I promise." Shutting off the water, she began attacking the dishes with soapsuds. "Does Rick ever hit your mom?"

"No. Like I said, he's Mr. Charming." Danny balled his hands into fists. "I'd never let him hurt her."

Gil swung around, leaving a trail of soapy water. "Hey, maybe that's the answer! Maybe he attacks your mom, and you try to defend her."

"What did the court records say?"

"They didn't say much…" Gil began washing a pot with unnecessary force.

Danny tugged at her sweater. "What aren't you telling me about Mom? Remember our agreement? You said you'd to be straight with me."

"Okay," she said slowly. "But *remember*, it isn't gonna happen. We're gonna change it."

Danny nodded.

"The night you were arrested, Charlesberg police reports say your mom hung herself."

"I don't think so," Danny said quietly.

"It would've been a hard time for her. Suicide is—"

"You don't understand! Mom's uncle killed himself. She says suicide is selfish. *She hates it.* She wouldn't do it. Maybe Rick killed her, and when I saw her body, I stabbed him."

"Maybe, but I think her body would've been found when you were arrested."

"Could those people in the TV find out?"

"When I make contact tonight, I'll ask them. But remember, it doesn't matter in the long run. I'm here now, and since you think your mom may be involved in the fight with Rick, I'll make sure to keep her safe."

"Promise?"

Gil gave him a quick, soapy hug. "Promise. Don't forget, we're gonna get the Jacobson clan on our side. Between us all, we'll keep her alive." Turning back to the dishes, she smiled over her shoulder. "Continue sweeping, young man, and spill again. What's up with your school work?"

Danny rolled his eyes. "I'm just dumb. I just can't read good and my spelling stinks."

"When you take a test, do you get all the way through?"

"Nah, I only get halfway. The questions don't make no sense."

"*Any* sense."

Grinning, Gil wiped her hands on a dishtowel and took a book out of her backpack. When she opened it, a homemade card landed at Danny's feet. On the front was a caricature of Gil flying to the rescue in a superman suit.

"What's this?" he asked, picking it up.

"A good luck card from my classmates. My friend, Ryan, drew the picture."

"He's pretty good."

"If you like his drawings, you should see his wood carvings. Go ahead and read the card. I can tell you're dying to."

Danny opened it up and whistled. Every square inch was covered with well-wishes and scraps of advice. As he looked at the messages, he squinted down at a string of math formulas. Seeing his puzzled look, Gil laughed. "That's a note from Crystal."

"What does it mean?"

"Truthfully, I don't really know. Half the time I can't understand what she's saying. I think the formulas are her attempt to quantify the odds of a successful surf in terms of linear-time increments."

"Huh?"

"My thoughts exactly." She chuckled. "Cris is a strange girl, but she has a heart of gold. I'd bet my last dollar that circulating the card was her idea."

"You have nice friends."

"They're a good bunch." She took the card and tucked it inside her backpack. Pushing aside various debris, she laid a book on the table and motioned for Danny to draw near. "I want you to read this passage to me."

He looked at the text and sighed. "I'm really bad at reading."

"That's okay. It's just you and me, and I have a hunch about what's going on."

Sitting down, he began to struggle through the sentences. After a few minutes, Gil stopped him and put a pencil and sheet of paper in front of him. As she gave him an impromptu spelling test, the more he spelled, the bigger her smile became.

Danny brushed a bead of sweat from his forehead and chewed his lip. "I told you I was stupid. You must be pretty disappointed."

"Oh, Danny," Gil said cheerfully, "you're *not* stupid. You're dyslexic."

"Dis-what's-it? What's that?"

"Dyslexia's where your brain interprets material a bit differently than other people. Some doctors believe it's a mark of brilliance."

"It doesn't feel brilliant," he grumbled. "Why am I so stupid at spelling, and reading, and stuff?"

"You're *not* stupid. Einstein and Edison were both dyslexic. Your brain just needs a little retraining. Tomorrow, we'll see about getting you some help. We're gonna lick this as well." As Danny started to smile, Gil said gleefully, "We're on the road, my fine young friend. Not only that, we're traveling down it at a fast rate of speed!"

$\mathcal{E}$LEVEN

IN CURIE HALL, Crystal looked at the clock and sighed. She'd finished her test in less than forty-five minutes, and she'd spent the last ten minutes double-checking her answers. More than anything, she wanted to turn in her exam and get food, but she needed to wait until another student was finished. Her rule of thumb was that if one wanted to win friends, it didn't pay to look like a showoff.

She pushed at her glasses nervously. Regardless of her best efforts, she was still having trouble fitting in. Being careful about test etiquette wasn't going to be enough—she needed to monitor her speech. She'd been making an effort to use contractions when talking with her peers, but colloquial speech patterns wouldn't help in the long run if the majority of her conversation revolved around mathematical theory. It had jolted her when Ryan said it was a pain to be around a genius. She knew he was joking, but the joke wasn't funny to her. As a Harvard undergraduate, she'd been alienated by students who thought she was an academic know-it-all.

After Crystal checked her answers for a fourth time, she looked over at William. He was sitting motionless at the table in front of the classroom. His arms were extended stiffly on the tabletop, and his hands were clenched into fists. She was certain his thoughts weren't pleasant. The tension around him was so thick she could cut it with a knife.

∾

When the house was clean, Gil showed Danny how to use a cookbook. Since he'd neglected to bring home his homework, she gave him a lecture about academic responsibility as they made stew. Later, when it was time for bed, she picked up her sleeping bag and asked, "Where can I spread this so I don't get stepped on?"

Danny scratched his head. "Even when it's late, Mom comes in after work to say goodnight. Would she trip over you even if she can't see you?"

"I'm not sure," Gil replied. "I know I can move things, but I don't know if my body mass can be tripped over."

"The people in charge should've told you that," Danny protested. "It's kinda important to know if people walk *through* you or *into* you."

"Well, my professors did try to prepare me. There were some gigantic manuals I was supposed to study, but—"

"You mean after lecturing me about homework, you didn't do yours?"

"It's not the same." Seeing his justifiable skepticism, Gil laughed and admitted, "Okay, I guess it's *exactly* the same. I really goofed, didn't I? So what do you suggest? We can't let your mom trip over me."

"You're asking me what I think?"

"Given your IQ, I know you can problem solve. So out with it, what should I do?"

"Just how big is my IQ?" he asked with a visible gleam in his eye.

"Big enough to give you a big head if I told you. But remember, having a gigantic IQ isn't worth anything unless you—"

"—apply myself, I know. I heard your lecture the first time. It's pretty funny that you scolded me about doing homework and now you're in the hot seat."

Gil tossed her pillow at him.

Laughing, he tossed it back. "Let's keep you outta traffic tonight by putting your sleeping bag beneath the window."

"That's a good plan. What else?"

"Tomorrow, let's do a test run and put you in the path of someone to see if they hit you or walk through you—but not Mom, I don't want her freaking out. Could I be the guinea pig?"

"I'm afraid not, we need someone else. Who do you suggest?"

"Maybe this is evil of me, but there's a guy in my class who's a real pain. He's always pushing me around. Do you think we could use him? I wouldn't be sorry if he freaked."

"That's an excellent idea."

"Cool." Danny smirked. "So when do you contact the 'mother ship?'"

She looked at her watch. "In thirty minutes. Why? Do you wanna stay up and watch?"

"Can I?"

"It's not normal procedure, but I can't see what it'd hurt. If I were you, I wouldn't want to miss an opportunity to talk to people from the future...although come to think of it, they're in this time too. They're just kids and teenagers." She began to laugh.

"What's so funny?"

"I was thinking about Dr. Moosly," she admitted. "I suppose it's awful of me, but I was wondering if he walked like a penguin when he was a kid or if that was a characteristic he acquired as he got older."

"Was he the bald guy with the clipboard?"

She nodded. "He wrote one of those huge manuals I couldn't get through. He talks through his nose, and when he speaks, his eyebrows wiggle and his nostrils flare. Keep your eyes open and see if you notice it."

"I can't wait until we make contact."

"Me either. But in the meantime, we might as well get into our PJs. Do you want the bathroom first or last?"

"I'll run over and change in Mom's. You can use mine."

"Sounds good," Gil replied, struggling to pick up her suitcase. Dropping it back to the floor with a solid thunk, she started dragging it over to the bathroom.

Five minutes later, his ablutions complete, Danny sat on his bed, waiting for Gil to get out of his bathroom. Fifteen minutes after that, he began to scowl. Glancing at the clock, he jumped up and pounded on the bathroom door. "We gotta make contact in five minutes! What are you doing in there? I've been waiting *forever*. Hurry up! I don't wanna miss this!"

Gil opened the door, and he fell back with a gasp. She was dressed head-to-toe in fuzzy pink pajamas. Her face was smeared with green goo, and her hair was up in blue curlers.

"Good gravy!" Danny sputtered.

"I know. I'm in the suds. I always underestimate the time at the most inconvenient moments. This facial still has several minutes until it's supposed to come off. How soon until we gotta make contact?"

"Four minutes."

"*Nuts!* I don't even have time to wash it off now. How bad do I look?"

At a loss for words, Danny shook his head. "What are those things on your head?"

"These? They're curlers. Doesn't your mom use curlers to curl her hair?"

"She gets a permanent when we can afford it. Why don't you?"

"Don't like the smell. There are some hot rollers I'm *dying* to try. You spray on conditioner first, and —"

"Are you for real?" he interrupted with a sputter. "Hair care? My eyes are glazing over. I'm a guy for Pete's sake!"

"Sorry, Danny," she laughed, "but you asked. Never ask unless you wanna know."

"Look, we're outta time. We gotta set up *Extreme Exam*. It's only a couple of minutes until contact."

Glancing at the clock, she nodded. "You're right. Where's my backpack?"

Danny looked at her blankly. "I don't know. I don't see it anywhere."

"Me either!" Gil moaned. "I can't believe this! I was supposed to make sure I didn't misplace the game! Look, Danny! Hurry!"

Danny scurried around the room. As he threw the covers off his bed, Gil picked up her sleeping bag and tossed it to one side.

"It's not here!" she exclaimed. "What'd I do with it? How could I be so careless?"

"Mom says when you lose something, sit down and think where you had it last."

Together, they plopped down on the bed. As Gil tapped a pink, furry-clad foot, Danny said, "Don't worry, we'll find it."

"In thirty seconds?" She groaned.

"She's late." Dr. Moosly grumbled, crossing his arms over his chest and glaring at the shimmering GAP beam.

"It's only ten minutes past," William replied. "Give her time. She'll come through."

∽

Danny sprinted back to his bedroom with a grin on his face. "Find it yet?"

"No!" Gil wailed as she went through the clothes hamper. "This is hopeless!"

"You think so? Huh? Look what I found!" Danny crowed, pulling her missing pack from behind his back.

"*You gem!* I told you that you had a high IQ. Where'd you find it?"

"On a chair pushed beneath the kitchen table. You put it there when we scrubbed the floor, so it wouldn't get wet."

As Gil ran over to him, Danny laughed at the sight of her PJs. He hadn't noticed before, but the feet had built-in bunny slippers. With her green face and blue curlers, she *really* looked weird. Actually, even weirder than before. In the frantic effort of the search, the green goo on her face had started to crack and peal. She looked *seriously* diseased.

"Got it!" Gil said jubilantly as she rummaged through the backpack. "Let's get the game in the PlayFest console."

"Don't you wanna wash your face first?"

"No time! I'm already...goodness...twenty minutes late. What are they gonna think?"

"I don't know, but I think you need to wash your face," Danny said in a quivering voice.

"Let's just get going. Dr. Moosly's gonna have a field day about my tardiness."

TWELVE

"TRANSMISSION COMING THROUGH," intoned Director Matthews. "Contact in five, four, three, two, one…"

The opaque beam dancing on the Staging Platform gradually became transparent. As the ghostly image behind the beam solidified, the review board could see Danny and next to him…

"What on earth?" Dr. Nelson whispered softly.

William's laugh was loud and bellowing.

Trying to ignore her appearance, Gil pasted a smile on her face and addressed the review board in a deliberately cheerful voice. "Hello, there! What's up?"

"I might ask you the same thing," snapped Dr. Moosly. "Do you realize how long we've been waiting?"

Beside her, Danny grinned and whispered in her ear, "I see what you mean about the nose and the eyebrows—"

"Shh!" she said, trying hard not to laugh.

"Gil," William said with twitching lips, "may I ask what's on your face?"

"Oh, this?" She smiled, and as she did, a green strip became dislodged and began to waggle beneath her chin. "It's a rejuvenating facial. Guaranteed to make your complexion as sparkling as dew on a rose petal."

"Ah. Quite so. Marvelous. I can tell it's working already."

Gil's smile widened. Another strip rolled down her cheek and dangled. Danny reached over and pulled it off.

"Gross," he yelped, shaking his hand. "Get it off me! It won't let go!"

"It won't hurt you," Gil said, handing him a tissue.

"I don't wanna take the chance," Danny replied. Wiping his gooey fingers, he looked through the portal at the doctors. "So, how's the future treating you?"

"Quite well," Dr. Nelson replied. "And how are you adjusting? Over the shock are you?"

"Yes, ma'am."

"Is Miss Gillyflower treating you well?"

Gil winced as Danny snickered at the mention of her proper name.

"*Gillyflower Meadowlark* is treating me fine," he said with a cherubic smile.

"Watch it, smarty-pants," she whispered out of the corner of her mouth. "It's Gil to—"

"Miss Gillyflower," Dr. Moosly blustered. "I fear you are ignoring the gravity of the situation. This is a serious proceeding. Now, do you have anything to report other than completion of first contact?"

Before Gil could reply, Danny spoke up, "Yes, sir, we think Rick murdered my mom. I know she's not gonna die 'cause we're gonna change the future, but I wanna know if that's why I stabbed Rick. Can you find out?"

"Miss Gillyflower," Dr. Moosly growled, "you told the boy about his future? Revealing disturbing information during the first twenty-four hours of a counseling assignment is strictly prohibited. The manuals are *explicit!* The shock could irreparably damage a youth's fragile psyche, coming, as it were, after the traumatic upheaval of time-travel entry by a stranger."

"Does he always talk like that?" whispered Danny.

"Yes," Gil whispered back, "usually worse. Shh!" She turned to address the board. "Danny likes things straight—no evasion. I thought it best to inform him."

Dr. Moosly glared. "It was irresponsible and—"

"Obviously, it didn't do any harm," William interrupted. "Danny seems fine. Aren't you, Danny?"

"Fit as a fiddle!" he chirped. "Hey, how high is my IQ? Gil won't tell me."

"High enough that you should know I'm not going to answer that question either."

Dr. Nelson chimed in, "Danny, we'll do some digging into your mother's death. If there are grounds for suspecting homicide, we'll let you know."

"Thanks, that'll be a relief."

Dr. Moosly stood to his feet. His face was rigid with disapproval. "This is intolerable! Miss Gillyflower, it is highly irregular to let a child enter into a practicum conference." His nostrils flared. "Highly improper is what I would call it. You need to review TEMCO protocol and—"

"Hey, lay off her," yelled Danny. "She's my friend, and I asked to be included. I know what's going on, and it concerns me more than it does you. I don't wanna end up sticking a knife into someone. I wanna be a pro...a pro..."

"Productive," whispered Gil.

"I wanna be a *productive* member of society, and I'm gonna be. You just watch! And Gil's gonna be the best what-you-ma-call-it yet. She's already figured out I can't spell because I'm dys...dyspeptic."

"Dyslexic," Gil corrected.

"Whatever! And she's got a plan on how to keep me and Rick from tangling. You just leave her alone! She's doing fine. We both are!"

"Danny," Dr. Nelson said soothingly, "as far as I'm concerned, even though it's unusual, you have just as much right to be included in our conferences as we do. After all, it's your future we're discussing. You're welcome to join us unless Gil feels it would be counterproductive. How does that sound?"

"Fine, ma'am."

Dr. Nelson nodded. "Gil, unless there's anything else you wish to report, we'll let you go until tomorrow night. Danny needs his sleep, and unless I miss the mark, you need to wash your face. I left a facial on too long once, and when I peeled it off, it took part of my skin with it."

"I think she should keep it on," William said with a laugh. "She looks quite fetching tonight. Rather like a moldy Easter bunny."

Rolling her eyes, Gil picked up a wad of paper and threw it through the temporal portal.

"Bull's-eye!" Danny squealed as it hit William squarely on the chest.

"Until tomorrow, my dear doctors," Gil said sweetly. With dramatic flair, she pulled *Extreme Exam* out of the gaming console and shut off the machine, severing the GAP connection.

Smiling, William tossed Gil's wad of paper in the air and caught it. "She's doing great."

"I quite agree," replied Dr. Nelson. "She's quite irreverent, but exactly the type of candidate who'll get through to Danny. Did you see how he defended her?"

"I sure did. They've already formed a close bond."

Dr. Nelson tapped her lips with a polished nail. "I believe Danny may be right about his mother's death. When we tested Daniel Winston on death row, he scored very high in protective instincts. His first homicide has always puzzled me, but it would make sense if his mother was murdered." She turned in her chair. "Peter, what do you think?"

"It sounds like a reasonable hypothesis," the director replied. "I'll see if I can discover a connection between Rick Olsen and Mrs. Winston's suicide. I think we're off to a good start."

"I disagree," spat Dr. Moosly. "Miss Montgomery is lacking in decorum. How can she properly guide an unruly youngster like Danny? That impudent child needs to be restrained, not encouraged. She isn't the proper match for the boy."

William shook his head and smiled. "I think you're wrong. Gil and Danny are the perfect combination."

THIRTEEN

AROUND MIDNIGHT, SUE Winston kicked off her shoes and tossed her coat on the couch. Giving a weary sigh, she quietly opened Danny's bedroom door. The soft glow of the hall nightlight streamed past her as she slipped into the room. Wisps of honey-colored hair escaped the braid looped over her shoulder as she bent down and kissed her son's cheek. "Sleep well, little man," she whispered.

Danny sat up. "I'm awake, Mom. Did you like the stew?"

"I just got home and haven't had any yet," she replied, sitting down on the edge of his bed. "But it smells heavenly. Did Rick make it?"

"Nope, I did. I cleaned the house too."

"That was thoughtful of you," she said, running a hand down his cheek. "I was going to clean it tonight, but now I can just go to bed. Thank you, love." As Danny smiled, she said, "Now, what are you doing up? Can't you sleep?"

"I'm too excited. I met a new friend today."

"That's wonderful. What's his name?"

Danny grinned. "*Her* name's Gil."

"Oh," Sue said with a chuckle. "*I see.* You'll have to tell me all about her tomorrow, but now it's time for sleep. Morning's coming soon."

"Was work okay?"

"A little hectic, but fine." She wrapped a bit of frayed blanket around her finger. "Where's Rick?"

"He got called into work."

"That's happening quite a bit lately."

"Yah, but I don't care. I can take care of myself. I don't need him hanging around."

"Yes, you do." Sue began combing Danny's hair with her fingers. "What would you do if a fire started?"

"Call 911. I'm not a baby. I know what to do."

"Regardless, it worries me when you're home alone. I want you safe."

Sue watched as Danny chewed his lip. "Mom," he said slowly, "if I found someone else to watch me, could we get rid of Rick?"

Hearing the tense note in her son's voice, Sue froze. "Honey, has Rick done something wrong?" When Danny refused to meet her eyes, she felt her heart tighten. "Danny, talk to me. Tell me what's going on."

After a small pause, Danny whispered, "Rick pushes me around. I...I don't like him."

Keeping a soothing hand on her son's back, Sue said in a tight voice, "That bruise on your cheek. You didn't get hit with a baseball, did you?"

He shook his head.

"He's hitting you? Oh, Danny, why didn't you tell me?"

"I thought I could handle it." His voice cracked. "It w-wasn't bad at first, but it's getting worse all the time."

"I'm *so* sorry! I can't believe I trusted him."

"That's okay," Danny said, giving her a fierce hug. "You didn't know. He was always nice when you were looking."

Sue held her son close. "He's never coming near you again. I'll make sure he doesn't come tomorrow, and when I see him on Wednesday, I'll tell him he can't watch you anymore."

"He's dangerous, Mom. You'll be careful, won't you?"

"Of course I will." She squeezed his hand. "I'm working the afternoon shift tomorrow. After school, ride the bus to the diner."

"Can I study in the library instead? Mr. Jacobson invited me to supper."

She nodded. "After work, I'll come next door and get you."

"Hey, Mom, Mr. Jacobson's always home. I bet he'd be willing to watch me."

"I'll talk to him, but even if he can't help, I'll find someone who can. The most important thing is to keep you safe and happy."

As Danny sighed and snuggled against her, Sue kissed the heart-shaped freckle on his jaw. "I love your little freckle," she teased him with a long-standing mom-and-son joke.

"Aw, Mom," he protested right on cue. "I think it looks silly."

"I think it looks cute."

"A guy isn't supposed to look cute! He's supposed to look strong and handsome."

"You'll grow up to be both. But in the meantime, remember freckles are where the angels kissed you, and the angels must've loved you bunches to shape your freckle like a heart." As Danny pulled a face, she laughed. "And when you're all grown-up and see your freckle in the mirror, remember it's where your mama always kissed you and that she loved you *very much*."

Danny sighed and smiled.

"Okay, young man, lie back down. It's time to go to sleep or you won't be able to wake up in the morning."

"I love you, Mom."

"The feeling's mutual," she whispered, pulling the covers snugly around his chin.

As the door closed behind his mother, Danny gazed up at the dark ceiling and sighed.

"Your mom's pretty terrific, isn't she?" Gil said softly.

"She sure is," he replied. "I wish I could make things easier for her."

"Her job at the hospital's tough?"

"Yah, but her job at the diner's tougher."

"She works two jobs?"

"She has to." Danny flipped over on his side and peered through the darkness at Gil. "When Daddy got sick, there were tons of bills. Someday, when I get big, I'm gonna give her enough money that she can quit working and relax."

"That sounds nice."

He nodded. "She's all alone except for me. She needs to get married again, but not to anyone like Rick. To someone good."

Later that night, Gil got up and stretched. The moonlight acted like stabbing silver beams and it was keeping her awake. Afraid that her tossing and turning would disturb Danny, she tiptoed past his bed and out the door. As she crept down the hall toward the kitchen, she heard the sound of muffled weeping. Frowning in concern, she peeked through the crack in Sue's bedroom door.

Danny's mother was curled up on her bed with an arm flung over her face.

Gil watched as Sue's whole body shook as she suppressed her sobs. "Oh, God, how could You let Rick hurt Danny?" Sue wept softly. "Have I drifted so far away that we don't matter to You anymore? Can't You see what we're facing? Are You even there?"

Leaving the doorway, Gil stole to the living room and sat on the couch—Sue's soft cries still echoing in her ears. Smoothing a wrinkle from the arm of her pink PJs, Gil breathed a prayer of her own. "God, please show me how to help this family."

In Washington D.C., William sat on his couch and tried to concentrate on a late-night movie. When the movie's heroine screamed and he had no idea why, he finally gave up in disgust. He looked down at Iggy. The lizard seemed to be contemplating him with a beady-eyed stare.

"What are you looking at?" William asked gruffly.

As Iggy blinked and butted his hand, William sighed. "I had to let her go, Iggs. I didn't want to—I had to." He peered over at the clock and groaned. "I wish practicum conferences were held morning and night. I won't be able to talk to her for another eighteen hours. A lot can happen in eighteen hours—"

Sitting up swiftly, William grabbed the television remote. *Surely something was on...*

FOURTEEN

THE NEXT DAY, GIL awoke with Danny tugging on her arm. "It's morning," he said. "You'd better get a wiggle on if you want to come to school. If last night's anything to go by, it'll take you *hours* to get ready."

She yawned and blinked. "Are you through with the bathroom?"

Danny nodded. "Mom's making blueberry pancakes for breakfast. Wait until you taste 'em. They're super-delicious... Hey, how are you gonna eat? I watched a movie about an invisible man, and when he ate, everyone could see his food digest. It was really gross."

Gil laughed and shoved his shoulder. "You *definitely* watch too much TV."

"Maybe so, but how are you gonna eat without freaking Mom out?"

"Easy. I have a whole stash of energy bars that came with me through GAP. Like me, the bars can't be seen. Why'd you think my suitcase was so heavy?"

"Clothes?"

Gill tossed her pillow at him. "I'll give you that, but my suitcase also has a huge supply of food in it. But even if I'd eat your food, your mom wouldn't see it digest. It's inside my body, so it'd be invisible."

"So why'd you bring the energy bars?"

"Because mysteriously moving forks tend to attract attention." She finished rolling up her sleeping bag and kicked it into a corner. "Go get your breakfast. I'll eat an energy bar while I get dressed. How soon until we have to go?"

"About an hour."

"*Only sixty itty-bitty minutes?*" Gil groaned, pushing him to the door. "You gotta be joking."

William dove into NSU's swimming pool and began a vigorous set of laps. As he cupped the water and pushed it away, he mentally tried to push away his worries. He swam until he was breathless, and when he couldn't swim another stroke, he flipped onto his back and floated.

Listening to the quiet lapping of the water around his ears, he tried to capture a feeling of peace, but peace didn't come. He looked over at the women's locker room door. It was hard for him to realize that Gil wasn't going to be coming out of it. In his mind, he could clearly picture her skipping over to the pool in her little red swimsuit. He could see her testing the water with a cautious toe and then sliding in with a gasp and a giggle.

Uttering a choked sound in his throat, he spun around and began another set of laps.

Licking syrup from his fingers, Danny tapped on his bedroom door. When he stepped inside and saw that Gil was ready, he blinked. He thought she'd be strolling around in a bathrobe. "How come it took you forever to change into your PJs and only a few minutes to dress this morning?" he asked.

"Motivation," she said, tying back her hair. "Hey, Danny, do you own a Bible?"

"Sure, Mom and Dad gave me one for my seventh birthday." As Danny handed her his Bible, he watched as Gil turned to Psalm 139.

"Ask your mom to read this passage to you, okay?" she said.

"Sure thing," Danny replied.

He went to the kitchen where Sue was wiping off the table and tackled her in a bear hug. "Hey, Mom, can you read me a Psalm?"

"Why sure," Sue replied, tucking a strand of hair behind her ear and tossing the dishcloth into the sink. "Which one?"

"The one by the bookmark, please."

They sat down at the table, and Sue opened to the marker and read, *"O Lord, You have examined my heart and know everything about me...I can never be lost to Your Spirit! I can never get away from my God...How precious it is, Lord, to realize that You are thinking about me constantly. I can't even count how many times a day Your thoughts turn towards me. And when I waken in the morning, You are still thinking of me."*

After she finished reading, Sue brushed moisture from her eyes and cleared her throat. "Would you like to pray together?"

Danny nodded. He felt a warm glow in his heart as his mother took his hand and prayed, "Lord, thank You that we're never lost or alone. Thank You for showing us through Your Word that You care about all our problems and worries. Forgive us when we doubt Your love, and help us feel Your presence today. Amen."

"Thanks, Mom," Danny whispered. "I enjoyed that."

"So did I," Sue replied. "Let's make it a habit."

As Sue closed the Bible, Gil whispered in Danny's ear, "Ask your mom for a note. I want you to be tested for dyslexia."

Nodding, he said, "Hey, Mom, a friend of mine saw my spelling and said I might be dyslexic. If you give me a note, the school counselor can have me tested and get me help with reading and stuff."

"Are you falling behind?"

"A little, that's why I wanna see the counselor."

Sue picked up a pad of paper. "I'm proud of you for tackling this problem head on. What else have you been up to lately?"

"Oh, nothing much," he replied. "Except I've learned I got a high IQ and can sing."

Sue smiled. "I knew about your high IQ. You used to escape your crib by climbing down a coat rack. It scared me to death, but your daddy just laughed. He called you his little genius."

"Really? He did?"

She nodded. "The singing's news to me, though. I'm anxious to hear you." She pointed at the clock. "But not right now. You need to brush your teeth before they grow over with purple fuzz. Grape juice mixed with syrup doesn't seem normal to me."

"Ah, Mom, it's yummy!"

"Yummy or not" —Sue laughed—"you need to scoot."

FIFTEEN

FIFTEEN MINUTES LATER, Gil and Danny began walking up Paradise Avenue on their way to Fairfield Middle School. Gil sniffed the tangy breeze and watched the autumn leaves dancing down from the trees.

As they got closer to school, she dropped the maple leaf she was twirling and said, "You need to point out which boy we want to use as our crash dummy."

"There won't be any question," Danny grumbled. "He hassles me every day. His name's Pete, but he's so tall everyone calls him Slim. Except me. I call him the goon."

"So where will we find this goonish fella?" Gil asked.

"Up ahead. He's the kid in the green cap."

"Stay here and pretend to tie your shoe," Gil said. "I'm going in."

Gil sprinted forward and planted herself in the middle of the sidewalk. When Slim turned around and saw Danny, he laughed and rushed toward him—hitting Gil in the process.

As Slim landed on his backside, Gil shouted gleefully, "Let's make tracks, Danny! We just found out what we needed to know. *Whoopee!*"

As Danny crossed the street, several boys surrounded Slim and asked what happened.

"I don't know," Slim said, scrambling to his feet. "I just don't know."

Gil let out a war whoop as she and Danny turned the corner. "That was awesome!" she cried. "Look at me! I'm the invisible bionic woman! I'm a force to be reckoned with. I'm a—"

"—futuristic weapon!"

"You bet I am!" she exclaimed. "If Rick comes after you, I can karate chop him to bits and he'll never see me coming."

"But, Gil, when Slim ran into you, you fell back. That means you can be hurt. I don't want you tangling with Rick."

"That's sweet, but don't worry about me. I'm a certified white belt in karate."

"A white belt? Never heard of it."

"Oh, really? It's an impressive belt—something to be feared." Giving Danny a cheeky grin, she said in a British accent, "Tallyho! To the counselor's office, old chap."

"Right-O," Danny replied in his own British accent. "You know, I'm actually looking forward to going to school."

Gil grinned and started to whistle.

Walking down the second floor hallway of Hawking Hall, Marc paused outside William's office and nervously cracked his knuckles. William usually kept his door open, but this morning it was firmly closed. Marc hesitated at the unfamiliar sight and tried to decide what to do. He didn't want to disturb William, but neither did he want the TA position to slip through his fingers because he was too spooked to ask about it.

As Marc tried to make up his mind, Director Matthews came up behind him and asked, "Problems, Mr. Kerry?"

Marc jumped and shook his head. "I was wondering if Dr. Ableman was available."

The director's lips twitched. "You'll never find out by standing in the hall."

As Director Matthews opened the door to the main office and disappeared inside, Marc grimaced. He liked the director, but he always ended up looking like a fool around him. Turning back to William's door, Marc took a deep breath and knocked.

"Come in," William called.

He stepped inside. "Hi, Dr. Ableman. Can you talk?" Marc saw William sighing and looking down at the mountain of exams he was grading. "If this is a bad time...?"

"Not at all," William said. "What can I do for you?"

Marc sat down and cleared his throat. "I was talking to Gil, and she suggested I apply for the TA position she's leaving vacant."

Marc fidgeted in his chair as he saw William's eyes beginning to twinkle.

"Has something more than a desire for my company prompted this offer?" William asked.

"Well," Marc nervously replied, "I was hoping you'd allow me into one of your closed classes next semester. Registration's already full, and I'd rather take *Timewave Dynamics* from you than Dr. Moosly."

"I think that could be arranged." William spun a pen between his fingers. "But you don't need to sacrifice your free time. I'll let you into the class without attaching strings."

"Being your TA wouldn't be a sacrifice. I'd like a chance to work with you. Is the job still available?"

"In a manner of speaking. I offered the position to Crystal, but she told me yesterday she was turning it down."

Marc blinked. "Why'd she do that?"

"It's possible she heard you were interested in the position and decided to step aside."

"I'm sure that's not it. Cris and I hardly know each other." He hesitated. "Would you consider me for the job?"

"Wade Kingston applied as well. He hopes to join our teaching staff when he graduates."

Marc sighed and nodded. "Wade's a good choice."

William smiled. "I said Wade applied—not that I'd hired him. The TA position is yours."

"Thank you!" Marc exclaimed. "I promise I'll do a good job."

"I know you will. If I didn't think you would, I'd give the position to Wade."

Marc stood and shook William's hand. "By the way," he asked, "how's Gil doing?"

William looked down at his pile of test papers. "Just fine. First contact went well."

"If anyone can nail the practicum exam, she can."

William nodded, and as he did, Marc noticed that William's hands were shaking.

"Now if there isn't anything else," William said, putting his hands in his pockets, "I need to grade these exams. You'd better be prepared—next semester, I'll have you do it for me."

"It'll be a pleasure."

William gave a grunting laugh. "No need to curry favor. You've already got the job."

$\mathcal{S}$IXTEEN

GIL AND DANNY EMERGED from the counselor's office and stretched. With fantastic luck—which Gil called *cosmic God-timing*—the lady who oversaw dyslexia testing was at school that day. Danny had been tested and an academic plan was created to get him the attention he needed.

"Where to now?" Gil asked, ruffling Danny's hair.

"History." Danny looked at his hall pass and moaned. "I wish I didn't have to go to class. My brain feels like mush."

"I can believe it. We were in the counselor's office so long that my backside's numb. How's anyone supposed to sit in those plastic chairs? I feel like a pretzel."

"I guess you just get used to it. I nearly died when you tipped your chair against the wall. I was sure you were gonna get caught."

"I know. I goofed. I forgot I was the invisible woman. But seriously, those chairs are killers. I'm gonna need to go on disability. How far away is your history class?"

"It's through the cafeteria and past the gym. Why?"

"I'm hoping to walk out some of the kinks."

As she began to lurch forward like a three-legged mule, Danny giggled. "Oh, Gil, you're a real crack-up."

"And you, my young genius, are an impressive fellow. I'm proud of all the work you did this morning. In fact—" Stopping short, Gil pointed to a poster on the wall. "Hey, look at that. They're holding auditions for *The Sound of Music* after school. That's better than perfect! You'd make a wonderful Frederich or Kurt."

"A who or a who?"

"The Von Trapp boys in *The Sound of Music*. If you get a part, the rehearsals will give you a place to go after school. Have you ever been in a play?"

"I was a talking tooth in first grade, does that count?"

"You bet," she said enthusiastically. "You're already a pro! I'll talk you through your audition, and even if you don't get a part, it'll be good experience. Sound like a plan?"

"If you say so. After all, who am I to argue with a super-bionic chick from the future?"

As Marc left the air-conditioned comfort of Hawking Hall and made his way into the bright sunshine, Ryan Adams swung in beside him and asked, "So, how'd it go?"

"Fantastic! You're looking at Doc's new TA." Marc grinned. "He's already threatening to bury me under a mountain of paperwork."

"I don't know whether to congratulate you or commiserate with you."

"Both." Marc chuckled. "Gil's always complaining that Dr. Ableman's a hard taskmaster. I guess I'm gonna find out for myself."

"It'll be worth it, though. Getting to work with the doc's a chance of a lifetime."

"It sure is." Marc's forehead puckered. "Hey, Ryan, what do you know about Crystal?"

"In what respect?" Ryan asked slowly.

"Doc offered her the TA position, but she turned it down. He seemed to think she might've refused the job to help me out. I don't know her well...do you think it's possible?"

"Why are you asking me? Why don't you ask her?"

In Colorado, the morning was passing swiftly. By the time Danny went to math, Gil was dying to find a safe place to sit. Sighing a little, she heaved herself up and sat cross-legged on a low bookshelf.

Mrs. West, the math teacher, was having students do problems at the blackboard, and when it was Danny's turn, Gil noticed that although he did the problem swiftly, he transposed two of the numbers, making his work incorrect. She shook her head. *No wonder the poor kid is having trouble.*

As the teacher called the next batch of students up to the board, Gil heard an ominous cracking sound. She sprang off the shelf just as it collapsed. As students jumped from their desks and chaos reigned, Gil slithered to one side, clutching the wall until she reached the front of the classroom. When she looked over at Danny, he was shaking his head and grinning from ear-to-ear.

After class, Mrs. West called Danny aside and asked him to do several math problems while she observed his work. Gil was pleased to see that the boy did them correctly. Later, Mrs. West gave Danny a list of makeup work and extra credit problems. She also gave him the first academic compliment he'd received all year. As he left the room, Gil watched his face glow with excitement.

"Did you hear what she said?" he exclaimed. "She said I had an excellent grasp of mathematics!"

Gil grinned. "I heard."

"She said I was *advanced* for my age."

"That's what I've been telling you."

"*I really am smart*, ain't I?"

"Of course you are," Gil said with a smile. "But you'd be even smarter if you'd direct me to the cafeteria. I'm so hungry I could gnaw off a couple of my fingers."

With a spring in his step, Marc strolled over to the hamburger stand in Student Union. As he glanced around the atrium, he noticed Crystal sitting at a table by herself. She was surrounded by a teetering pile of textbooks, and as she ate, she kept her eyes glued to a thick book on quantum physics. Marc stared at the book with raised eyebrows. He knew the heavy tome wasn't required reading. That meant her taste in recreational reading was *interesting* to say the least.

As he watched, Crystal pushed at her glasses and attempted to take a sip of soda. The straw scraped up the side of her nose. Still keeping her eyes glued to the book, Crystal began seeking the straw with her lips. Marc chuckled. She looked like a frustrated goldfish. Eventually, her mouth found the straw and she took a long drink. With her eyes still on the book, she began groping blindly for her fork. Marc shook his head. Crystal was definitely...unique.

A puzzled frown wrinkled his brow as he watched her. Dr. Ableman seemed sure Crystal had stepped aside because of him. If that was true, it was an extremely nice thing for her to do. His frown increased. Maybe he was wrong in writing her off.

"Sir, may I take your order?"

Marc stared blankly at the cashier. After a moment, he said, "I need to talk to someone first."

As the cashier murmured a vague reply, Marc walked over and sat beside Crystal. She was so engrossed in her book that she didn't notice. As she brought a forkful of salad up to her lips and kept it hanging while she read, he felt a bubble of laughter expanding in his chest. He gently cleared his throat. She still didn't look up. Obviously, whatever she was reading had her full attention. Marc's brow puckered. He knew he was handsome—he'd have to be an idiot not to know it—and he wasn't used to working for female attention.

"Crystal," he said softly, putting his hand on her arm, "may I talk with—"

Crystal jumped wildly, knocking over her glass. A cold stream of diet cola flooded the table and cascaded in an icy wave onto Marc's lap. As he leapt to his feet, he saw Crystal making a desperate grab for a stack of napkins. Her fumbling hands sent her salad plate spinning. Marc sprang back as the salad with its oily dressing bounced off his hip and landed upside down on his shoe.

Crystal gasped and stumbled to her feet. As she pushed the napkins toward him, her arm knocked over the ketchup bottle. It hit the floor with a bounce, squirting ketchup on his leg.

"I-I'm s-so sorry," she stammered.

Marc looked down at his messy clothes and made a valiant attempt at a grin. "No problem. I needed to do laundry anyway."

"Oh," Crystal replied awkwardly. "G-good." With a bright red face, she began rescuing her textbooks from the pool of soda and drying them with a handful of napkins. "Did you want to talk with me about something?"

Marc nodded and tried to wipe the ketchup from his pants. "I spoke to Dr. Ableman. He gave me the TA position."

Crystal began mopping up the table. "That's nice, but what's that got to do with me?"

He peered over at her. "Did you turn the job down to help me out?"

She blinked at him and turned her head. Her long, blonde hair fell over her cheek and hid her face. "Why would I do something like that?"

"I don't know. That's why I asked...I just wondered—"

"Well, stop wondering," Crystal said fiercely. "If you think I make decisions about my life based on *you* then you're more conceited than I thought."

Marc fell back a step.

Crystal turned away and threw a handful of soggy napkins onto her tray. "Was there anything else you wanted to ask?"

Marc shook his head.

"In that case, I have a lot of reading to do."

Marc stared in open-mouthed disbelief as she sat down again and opened her book. He wasn't used to being ignored, but it was obvious she deemed their conversation closed. He stared at her bent head, and after a long moment, he turned and walked away.

As he stalked past the hamburger stand, he glanced back at Crystal. Her face was covered with her hands, and she was shaking. He didn't know if she was laughing or groaning. What's more, he didn't care.

After Danny got a lunch tray, Gil went with him to the schoolyard and they sat beneath a tree. "So, what do you think?" she asked as she unwrapped a TEMCO energy bar.

"I think it's gonna to be a lot of work to catch up," he groaned.

"You're right about that, but at least you have great teachers to help. A good teacher makes all the difference. I should know, Dr. Ableman's terrific."

"You really like him, huh?"

"You bet. He's the one who convinced me to become a time counselor."

As she took a bite of her energy bar and made a face, Danny asked, "So, what does that stuff taste like?"

"Kinda like rubbery cardboard with a hint of almond."

"That good, huh?"

"Hey, what do you expect? A big punch of nutrition *and* good flavor?"

"It might be nice."

Gil laughed and wrinkled her nose. "You've got that right. This bar's simply *ghastly*."

Danny smirked. "As ghastly as your first name?"

"Stop giving me problems," she sputtered with a chuckle. "At least I could shorten Gillyflower down to Gil. Some names are so atrocious they can't be used at all. Dr. Ableman goes by his middle name. I'll bet his first name's something horrible like Humperdinck."

Marc stalked toward Hawking Hall with his wet pants clinging to his legs. As he passed the library, he saw Kyle walking toward him. He groaned. The last thing he wanted was to answer questions.

As he picked up his pace, Kyle called, "Hey, Marc, what's the rush?"

Marc stopped and shrugged a shoulder. "I had a little accident."

"I'll say you did." Kyle laughed. "What the dickens happened to your clothes?"

"Two words: Klutzy Crystal."

"I told you she was a menace. There needs to be a warning label printed across her forehead: *Approach with care*."

"Forget that," Marc grumbled. "I'd rather not approach her at all."

SEVENTEEN

AFTER SCHOOL, GIL rushed Danny to the auditorium where auditions for *The Sound of Music* were in full swing. At her instruction, Danny signed up to audition last, so he could become familiar with the music. When it was his turn to sing, Gil watched as his face turned pasty white. Seeing that he was about to freeze, she gave his shoulder a reassuring squeeze and his back a firm shove.

Danny stumbled toward the piano, and the teacher said briskly, "I'll play two measures and then you may begin."

Danny nodded vaguely, but it was obvious to Gil that he had no idea what the teacher was talking about. Regardless, he began at just the right point. When Danny started to sing, a hush came over the auditorium. Bored students who'd been chatting idly fell silent. Even Gil blinked in astonishment at the rich voice that came from Danny's slender body.

The music teacher, who'd been listening to a string of students butchering *Edelweiss*, smiled widely and said to the assembly, "It's obvious that we've found our Captain Von Trapp. Fay Hennly will have the part of Fraulein Maria. All other parts will be announced Friday."

While the teacher continued to speak, Danny slipped to Gil's side and whispered, "Did I do good?"

"I'll say you did." Gil laughed.

As students began shuffling out of the auditorium, the teacher handed Danny a script and said, "I'm going to enjoy working with such talent. It's obvious that you have a rare and wonderful gift."

Danny goggled at Gil as the teacher moved past him. "Did you hear that?"

Gil grinned. "Which part? Rare and wonderful?"

"Yah, and talented."

Gil watched as Danny smiled with growing confidence. After a moment he said, "Hey, how 'bout we go to the library and whip out my homework before we go to Mr. Jacobson's?"

"You're actually volunteering to do homework?"

"You bet," he replied. "Maybe I can even tackle a few make-up assignments."

"With your brains and talent, I wouldn't put it past you."

Danny tucked his hand inside hers. "I *am* brainy and talented, ain't I?"

Feeling a soft tug on her heart, Gil nodded and said gently, "You're something *very* special, Daniel Winston—never forget it."

Feeling his bruised ego reviving under Kyle's irreverent banter, Marc sat on a bench in front of Hawking Hall and put his hands on his knees. In the hot sunshine, his pants had finally dried. Running a hand down one leg, he began to scratch at the crusty ketchup clotting on the material.

"It's your turn," Kyle said. "But I'll bet you can't come up with a better Klutzy Crystal joke than the one I just told."

"I could beat you without even trying," Marc replied.

"Prove it."

"How many Klutzy Crystals does it take to change a light bulb?"

"I don't know. How many?"

"Two. One to drop the bulb, and one to explain that according to Schroeder's theory her klutziness doesn't matter. The bulb's simultaneously broken and unbroken because when quantum superposition ends, reality collapses into one possibility or the other.

"That doesn't make any sense."

"Neither does she."

As Kyle laughed, Marc looked up and saw Crystal standing on the sidewalk staring at him. She'd obviously heard his lame joke. A guilty blush stained his cheeks.

Narrowing her eyes, Crystal said dryly, "I believe the theory you're discussing is Schrödinger's theory. Schroeder is the piano-playing character created by Charles Schulz."

"Oh, really?"

She gave him a disdainful nod. "And unless you're *trying* to display an astonishing amount of ignorance, you need to revise your punch line. The bulb wouldn't exist in both states due to the termination of quantum superposition. You're just making an idiot of yourself telling it that way."

Gritting his teeth, Marc watched as Crystal flipped her hair over her shoulder and walked away. Turning to Kyle, he said deliberately, "It's your turn—and make it a zinger."

In a corner of the school library, Danny looked over at Gil and grinned. "I can't believe how much homework we got through. You were right. When my dyspepsia—"

"Dyslexia—"

"—is helped, I'm awfully sharp."

"You bet you are."

As he closed his science book, Gil pointed at the clock and said, "Hey, we'd better scoot. We only have ten minutes to get to Mr. Jacobson's."

"Where'd the time go?" Danny asked.

"Don't ask me," Gil replied with a laugh. "I'm a temporal dynamics student, but that question still confuses me."

As they walked down the empty hallway, Danny paused in front of a poster advertising the school musical. Grimacing a bit, he said, "I hope I didn't disappoint you by not landing the role of Frederich or Kurt."

"Why on earth would I be disappointed?" Gil asked.

"I'm only a sea captain. I probably only got two lines."

"Danny, Captain Von Trapp's the leading male role. Only Maria has more lines."

"Are you serious?"

"Sure I am. Captain Von Trapp is Frederich and Kurt's father. He falls in love with Maria and they—"

"Wait a minute," Danny sputtered. "I fall in love with Maria?" His face took on a look of horror. "Are they gonna make me *kiss* her?"

"I doubt it—this is a middle school production—but you'll probably hug her."

"No way," he said flatly, crossing his arms in front of his chest. "I'm quitting the play."

"For heaven's sake, why?"

"Fay Hennly is Maria. I don't want to snuggle up with her."

"Are you girl-shy?"

He shook his head. "Hugging any other girl wouldn't be a problem, but Fay is awful! She cornered me in the cafeteria once and tried to kiss me."

"I told you that you were good looking," Gil said with a smirk.

"Look, I'm not gonna hug Fay. She gives me the creeps."

"Just think of her as Maria."

"I can't."

"Sure you can. Acting's only make-believe. We'll run through your lines together until you're comfortable with your role."

Danny's eyes began to twinkle. *"You'll* be my Maria? I like the sound of that. I'd like to have you for my girlfriend."

Gil gave a sputter of merry laughter. "Well, look who's suddenly become a raving Romeo. I'm awfully flattered. If I were twenty years younger, I'd jump at your offer."

"You're not that old."

Gil reached over and playfully shoved his shoulder. "Compared to you, I'm practically one of the geriatric brigade."

As their shoes squeaked rhythmically on the newly waxed floor, Danny gave her a crooked grin. "Maybe I like older women. Did you ever think of that?"

"Maybe you're full of beans. For two cents—"

Before Gil finished her sentence, they turned a corner and Danny ran headlong into a boy leaning up against the lockers. Recognizing Slim, Danny's face turned white and his newfound confidence oozed out the bottom of his sneakers. Beside him, he heard Gil's laughing voice changing into a low rumble that reminded him of an angry bumblebee.

"Been waiting for you, Danny-boy," Slim sneered. "What took you so long?"

"Look, I don't want any trouble."

"I don't care what you want. Somehow you tripped me this morning, didn't you?"

Danny swallowed and remained silent.

"I thought so." Slim shoved Danny up against the lockers. "You're gonna regret messing with me."

Suddenly, Slim's feet went out from under him. Danny glanced over at Gil who had just tackled Slim's legs. Danny's lips quirked up into a grin as he mouthed silently, *White-belt maneuver?*

Gil nodded grimly and flexed her biceps.

"Now, you're in for it," Slim snarled, rolling to his feet. "No one pushes me around!"

As Danny flinched and raised his hands to protect his face, Gil grabbed Slim's jacket and swung him to the floor. Seeing Slim blinking up at him in amazement, Danny grinned. "I think you'd better leave me alone."

"Not a chance! When I figure out how you're messing with me, you're dead." Glaring wildly, Slim sprang to his feet. Danny watched as Gil tripped him. "You're dead meat!" Slim shouted from the floor. "You hear me?"

Scrambling on all fours, Slim dove at Danny. Gil planted her foot on his back and held him down. "How are you doing this?" Slim scowled.

"It doesn't matter," Danny replied. "Stay down. You can't win this fight."

Slim struggled to his feet and was immediately sent back to the floor. Banging his fist against a locker, he shouted, "What's going on?"

"Do you need it spelled out? You're through bullying me. Deal with it."

Slim got up swinging, but Gil pushed him down. He gave a half-hearted lunge at Danny, but when Gil held him down with her foot, the fight drained out of him. Seeing the change, Danny put out a hand to help him up. When Slim hesitated, he said, "No tricks, I promise. Let's end this thing. I'd rather be your friend than your enemy."

"Why would I be friends with you?" Slim asked in a stony voice. "You're weird."

"You're even weirder, but I don't care. I'd bet we'd get along."

Silence fell. Keeping his hand extended, Danny quirked an eyebrow and wiggled his fingers.

"You're definitely a weirdo," Slim replied with a slow smile, "but maybe you're all right." Taking Danny's hand, he scrambled to his feet. "Thanks."

Danny gave an answering smile. "Don't mention it."

"How'd you move so fast?" Slim asked. "You're faster than Jackie Chan."

"You like martial art movies?"

"They're the greatest," Slim replied. "My pop used to watch 'em with me."

"Maybe sometime you can come over to my house, and we can watch one."

Slim blinked. "You're inviting me over?"

"Sure." Danny shrugged. "After all, stranger things have happened."

As the boys got ready to part at the door, Slim shuffled his feet and mumbled, "Hey, Dan. I'm sorry."

"No worries. No harm."

Giving Danny a grin, Slim ran down the sidewalk.

"I'm so proud of you," Gil said, speaking for the first time. "I was afraid I was gonna have to toss him inside a locker to get him to stop. How'd you know what to do?"

Danny shrugged. "I just did the opposite of what Rick would do. When Slim was on the floor, he reminded me of myself after Rick gives me a sucker punch. Maybe it was another *cosmic God-thing?*"

"Maybe it was. Who knows, maybe you'll be a good influence on him."

"I'll just be happy if I'm not hassled by him every day."

"So, do you think you'll enjoy being friends with a goon?"

"I don't think the goon exists anymore. Hopefully, all that's left is a guy named Slim."

EIGHTEEN

DANNY HAD TO run all the way to Mr. Jacobson's, but he managed to get there right on time. As he rang the doorbell, Gil whipped a comb out of her pocket and brushed his hair.

"Hey, I'm a kid," Danny protested, batting her hands away. "I'm supposed to look messy."

Laughing, Gil gave his bangs one more swipe. As she pocketed the comb, she said fervently, "I'm glad no one can see me. I'll bet my hair's flying in all directions."

"You've got that right." He snickered, giving her a mischievous glance.

"Is it that bad?" Gil dug a mirror out of her backpack, gasped, and frantically began to comb her hair.

"I thought no one could see you?"

"*You* classify as someone, and *I* classify as someone. I've seen myself now, and I can't stay in this *awful* condition."

He chortled and rang the bell again.

"Danny, good to see you," Mr. Jacobson said, opening the door.

"You too, sir. Thanks for inviting me."

"Come in. Let me introduce you to my grandkids."

Mr. Jacobson ushered Danny into the kitchen where two men in their mid-thirties were lounging against a counter. Next to them, an exotic-looking woman was stirring a pot of spaghetti sauce. Grabbing the nearest man by the shoulder, Mr. Jacobson said, "This here's my grandson, Nathan. He's the Westfield policeman I was telling you about."

As Nathan smiled and shook Danny's hand, Danny looked at him with an approving eye. Nathan was 6'2", and his T-shirt did little to hide his muscles—he'd easily be a match for Rick.

"Pleased to meet you," Nathan said. "My grandfather said you wanted to talk to me?" As Danny gave a nervous nod, Nathan said gently, "No problem. I'll be glad to lend you an ear—even two of them."

At his words, Danny smiled and felt a rush of relief. Before he could reply, Mr. Jacobson bustled him over to the lovely woman. "This here's Zara, Nathan's wife. They met when she came over from Jamaica to go to college. She's the bee's knees and the best cook in three counties. Our family sure won a prize when she came into it."

"Oh, go on," Zara said in a voice that held a delightful Jamaican accent. Taking a spoon, she scooped up some sauce and handed it to Danny. "Try some. Tell mi ef it needs anything."

Danny popped the spoon in his mouth. "Mmm, that's good! All it needs is noodles."

Zara chuckled and hugged his shoulders. "Wise mon, yuh be right 'bout de noodles."

As Danny put the spoon in the sink, Mr. Jacobson drew him over to the other man. "This is my grandson, Samuel. He's a black belt. He lives down the block and pastors the church across from your school."

Samuel shook Danny's hand and said with a smile, "Call me Sam, Samuel's too formal between friends."

As Danny nodded, he studied the big, strong man—he never would've guessed Sam was a preacher. The only preacher he'd ever known was Reverend Felder, a wispy old man who tottered as he walked. He'd always been secretly afraid that a brisk wind would blow Felder away. Sam didn't look like Felder at all. He looked like he could stand in the face of a hurricane. *Mr. Jacobson sure grows his grandsons big*, Danny thought as he gave Sam's muscles an admiring glance.

Sam's blue eyes began to twinkle. "Do I pass inspection?"

Realizing he'd been caught staring, but also that it was okay, Danny grinned. "You sure do. How 'bout me?"

"Truthfully, I like the look of you. You have an honest face. I'm glad we're gonna get to know one another."

"Me too," Danny said—a bit more fervently than he intended. Hearing the note of desperation in his voice, he bit his lip and lowered his gaze.

Sam clasped his shoulder. Danny looked up and studied his face. Sam's eyes were so sympathetic that he suddenly wanted to tell the preacher all of his troubles, but there was no time. Even as he opened his mouth, Zara bustled the men out of the kitchen, telling them to set the table while she put the garlic bread in the oven.

As the men went to work, Mr. Jacobson took a stack of plates from the china hutch and said, "Now, Danny, can you talk to Nathan while Sam and I are in the room, or do you need some privacy?"

Danny looked over at Gil, and seeing her silent prompting, he replied, "I don't mind talking in front of you."

Nathan motioned for the boy to sit beside him. "In that case, tell me what's wrong."

As Danny fidgeted and struggled to find the right words, Sam said gently, "Just take it slow and tell us how we can help."

"Is it that Rick fellow?" Mr. Jacobson asked, plunking down plates in an agitated fashion. "I never liked the look of him. Why does your momma let him hang around?"

"He watches me after school," Danny replied in a hollow voice.

Placing his hands on the table and leaning forward, Mr. Jacobson asked, "Is he bothering you?"

Danny nodded, and his words began to tumble out in a rush. "He hits me. He's really mean. Mom didn't know until this morning 'cause I didn't tell her. She works at Stubby's Diner and she's gonna tell Rick tomorrow that he can't come over anymore. I'm afraid he's gonna get mad and hurt us."

As Sam sat down beside him, Danny continued, gulping a little over his words, "Dad died, so it's just us at home. Could one of you be at our house tomorrow when school lets out?" His eyes pleaded with Sam and Nathan. "I don't know how to explain, but it's important. I'm learning how to cook. I'll make supper. We have a TV. You could watch a football game...please...I mean, if you can?"

Danny's stumbling words came to a halt. Silence filled the room. He watched as Sam and Nathan looked at each other and then seemed to come to a decision. "If you feel so strongly about it," Sam said, "we'll make sure it happens."

"What time do you want us?" Nathan asked.

Danny let out a deep sigh. He felt so relieved that tears filled his eyes. "I get home at 3:15. Rick usually comes at 3:30."

Sam nodded. "One of us—or both of us—will be waiting on Grandpop's porch. When we see you, we'll walk you home and stay with you. Okay?"

"That's better than okay. Thanks so much!"

"You see?" Mr. Jacobson said. "I told you my boys could help. Now, how are you and your momma gonna replace Rick?"

Danny licked his lips. "Today, I got a part in the school musical. Between rehearsals and studying at the library, I can stay at school until 6:00. The problem will be when Mom works late at the hospital. Sometimes she doesn't get home until after midnight."

"I thought you said your mom worked as a waitress at Stubby's?" Sam said.

"She works both places. When Daddy was sick, his treatments cost lots of money."

"It's been pretty rough, hasn't it?" Sam said with a face full of sympathy. "You know, my church hosts an after-school program. If you want to come when your mom works, I'll walk you home afterwards and stay with you until she arrives. Does that sound good?"

"It sure does," Danny replied, wiping his nose with his sleeve.

"When can we talk with your mother? She may've made other arrangements."

"She's gonna get me around 7:30."

"That's perfect," Mr. Jacobson said, slapping his knee. "We'll get everything squared away tonight." Pursing his lips, he said, "You know, Danny, there's someone else who can help you besides us. John 3:16 says God loves you so much He sent His Son to die for your sins. If He loves you that much, don't you think He loves you enough to help with Rick?"

As Danny slowly nodded, Sam asked gently, "What do you know about God?"

"Well, when I was little, we used to go to church. When Daddy got too sick to go, he'd lay on the couch and read me Bible stories about Jesus."

"Have you asked Jesus to forgive your sins and come into your heart?"

Danny shook his head. "Daddy died before he told me how, and Mom was too sad."

"Do you want me to explain it?" Sam asked.

Danny nodded. "I wanted to ask Mom, but I wasn't sure how."

"Salvation's pretty simple. We've all sinned, but Jesus came to earth to die for our sins. Because He paid sin's price, we can go to heaven if we ask for forgiveness. We get off the hook like death-row felons going free because Jesus was executed in our place."

"But what happens if people don't ask God to forgive them?"

"They have to pay sin's price themselves. Acts 4:12 and John 14:6 say believing in Jesus is the only way to get to heaven. If there'd been another way for sin to be forgiven, you can bet God would've chosen *that way* rather than letting Jesus die such a painful death." Sam paused. "Danny, would you like to ask God to forgive your sins?"

"Do you think He would?"

"Of course I do. Romans 6:23 says salvation's God's free gift."

"But what should I say?"

"Romans 10:9-10 tells us to believe in our hearts that Jesus is Lord and confess with our mouths that God raised Him from the dead. When we do that and confess our sins, 1 John 1:9 says God will forgive us."

"But what if I don't ask right?"

"God sees your heart, and He listens to it even more than your words."

Nodding, Danny bowed his head. He prayed silently for a moment and then said, "I think God did it! I feel better!"

Sam gave him a hug. "I know He did! And He's gonna help us with Rick too."

123

Over Sam's shoulder, Danny saw Gil beaming in the corner. Feeling the knot in his stomach loosening for the first time in months, he sighed and smiled.

"Do yuh men-folks 'ave de table set?" Zara called from the kitchen. "De noodles are done, and de garlic bread is browned to perfection."

Quickly tossing forks by the plates, Nathan replied, "All finished, honey. Everything smells wonderful."

"Go on, mister-flattery mon." Zara laughed merrily, bringing in the food.

As they sat down, Mr. Jacobson motioned for Sam to say grace. Looking around the table, Danny felt a warm glow in his chest. These were *good* people. Gil was right to have him ask for their help.

⌐IINETEEN

BY THE TIME supper was finished, Danny felt completely at home with the Jacobson clan. He fit right in, drying dishes while Nathan washed.

"Grandpop, why don't you have a seat," Sam said, taking the salad bowl from his grandfather's hand. "I'll finish clearing the table."

"I believe I will. Thank you, Sam."

As Nathan handed him another dish to dry, Danny watched as Mr. Jacobson went to the stool where Gil was perched. Danny could tell she wasn't paying attention. She was bent over staring at the cat. Sheba's fur was bristled, and it was obvious the cat could sense Gil's presence. It was also obvious that Gil didn't realize Mr. Jacobson was about to sit on her.

"Gil!" Danny shouted.

Looking up quickly, Gil slid to the floor as Mr. Jacobson sat down.

"Gil?" Nathan said in a puzzled voice. "What do you mean?"

Danny grinned as inspiration hit him. "I meant to say *guilty*. I guess a frog got in my throat. I'm *guilty* of overeating—that pasta was yummy."

Nathan smiled at his wife. "It sure was. When you get married, look for a kind-hearted woman with a worn-out cookbook."

As Zara swatted Nathan's rear with a tea towel, the doorbell rang.

"I bet that's Mom," Danny said in an excited voice as he finished drying a plate.

Mr. Jacobson rose from the stool. "I'll bet you're right."

"Don't get up, Grandpop," Sam said. "Danny and I will let her in."

Outside room 468 in Heisenberg Hall, Crystal took a deep breath and peeked through the window in the door. The classroom was packed. The Bible study had tripled in size since she'd last attended. She was pleased more people were coming, but she knew she was going to miss the coziness of a small-group setting. If she'd been attending regularly, she wouldn't have paid attention to the increase in size, but a few months ago, Marc had started coming and she couldn't bear to be there.

Leaning her forehead against the door, she watched as Zeke led worship. The music surrounded her in a peaceful cloud. She'd been avoiding Bible study for too long. She wasn't going to be a coward anymore.

Smoothing her hair, Crystal turned the knob and stepped inside. Suddenly, she caught sight of Marc. His eyes were closed, and his hands were raised in worship. She blinked rapidly and lost control of her breathing. As she stared at Marc, she noticed Ryan looking directly at her. Her face went white as he motioned to the empty seat next to Marc. With Ryan's invitation to join them, she couldn't follow through with her plan to sit in the back and sneak out early.

Nervousness washed over her in a sickening wave. She despised herself for her weakness, but she knew she couldn't stay. If spending five minutes in Marc's company was uncomfortable, the thought of sitting next to him for over an hour was torture. She wouldn't be able to control her breathing, and Marc would be sure to guess...

Shaking her head at Ryan, Crystal turned sharply and went out the door. Some things in life were best left alone—this was one of them.

Sam went to the front door with Danny and watched as the boy gave a happy little skip.

"I can't wait for you to meet Mom," Danny said. "You're gonna love her."

"I'm sure I will," Sam replied, smiling at the boy's enthusiasm and opening the door.

When Sam saw the woman on the doorstep, he blinked. Sue was standing in the moonlight with her lips curved into a gentle smile, and she was wearing a blue blouse that accentuated the beauty of her eyes. Her honey-colored hair was flowing in soft waves around her shoulders and the porch light was making it sparkle like pure gold. Sam swallowed. Danny's mother was extremely pretty. She certainly wasn't the matronly, browbeaten woman he'd been imagining. As he tried to think of something charming, or witty—or at least *coherent*—to say, Danny took his mother's arm and drew her into the room.

"Guess what, Mom?" the boy exclaimed. "I asked Jesus to come into my heart!"

"Why, Danny, that's wonderful," Sue replied, hugging her son. "Asking Jesus to be your Savior is the most important decision you'll ever make." Holding Danny close, she murmured, "I'm sorry I didn't make God a bigger part of our lives after your daddy's funeral. I was sad, but that's no excuse. I've asked God to forgive me. Will you forgive me too?"

"Oh, Mom, you know I will," Danny replied, giving her a strangling hug.

"Making God part of our lives is going to be a priority from now on. Jesus is the best friend you'll ever have. I'm glad you asked Him into your heart."

"Sam told me how to do it. He's the best!"

Sam felt himself blush as Sue turned to him. "Thanks for telling Danny about Jesus," she said. "His father was doing it before he died, but..." She bit her lip. "Thanks for stepping in and filling the gap."

"My pleasure, ma'am," Sam replied softly.

"Please, call me Sue."

As Sam nodded, he saw a tiny hint of pink coloring Sue's cheeks. She was looking at him as if she knew him. "Have we met before?" he asked.

"Not officially," she replied. "But I've seen you around town. Every morning, you walk past the diner where I work."

"Next time I'm by Stubby's, I'll have to stop in and say hello."

"Do that," she said. "I'll buy you a cup of coffee."

"I'll look forward to it." He grinned. "In the meantime, come meet the rest of the family. They've all taken to Danny. He's a great boy."

"Thank you." She smiled. "I think so too."

As they entered the kitchen, Mr. Jacobson rose. "Sue, it's good to see you. I see you've met Sam. This here's Nathan and Zara. They live a few miles east of here in Westfield."

"It's nice to meet you both," Sue said. She smiled at Zara. "If I remember right, you brought us a delicious chocolate cake when we moved here. I intended to write a thank you note, but with unpacking and starting work, I'm ashamed to say it didn't get done."

"Dohn worry 'bout it. I'm glad yuh liked it. Chocolate cake's like butter pon a cat's paw fah making a bodi feel at home."

"It was scrumptious. I'd like the recipe if you'd be willing to share it."

Zara's eyes sparkled. "I'll be happy to gi' it to yuh."

Mr. Jacobson beamed and said to Sue, "Zara's recipes are really special. She's the best cook around."

"I can believe it," Sue replied. "I've never tasted a better cake."

"We all think Nathan caught himself a peach of a girl," Mr. Jacobson said proudly.

Sam groaned inwardly when he saw his brother glancing his way. Knowing what was coming, he tried to interrupt Nathan, but couldn't do it in time.

"Sam still hasn't managed *anything* in that department," Nathan told Sue with an impish grin. "I keep trying to find him a girl, but he says he's too busy. Not that I buy it. He's such a slowpoke that he never gets outta the starting gate. Some enterprising lady needs to set a fire under him to get him moving."

Sam felt himself blush as Nathan laughed and gave Sue a cheeky wink. "You know, attention from a pretty lady like you is *just* what my brother needs."

Sam's blush intensified as he glanced over at Sue. "Please ignore him. Nathan's more addicted to matchmaking than any

129

granny I've ever met. Unfortunately, he's about as subtle as a jackhammer."

As Sue gave him a reassuring smile, Sam's eyes widened a fraction of an inch.

Zara motioned for Sue to sit down at the table. "Here, sugar, 'ave a piece of pecan pie. I set it aside fah yuh. Danny says it's one of your favorites."

"It sure is. Thank you."

As Sam went to the fridge to pour Sue a glass of milk, Mr. Jacobson put his hands on his knees and cleared his throat. "Now, honey, I don't want you to think we're presumptuous, but Danny says you're in a spot of trouble. We'd like to help."

Sue choked on her pie. "I don't want to impose—"

"Don't worry about that. We're a direct family, and we pride ourselves on doing what needs done. Rick's a smooth-talker, but no good. I've seen his type before—friendly on the outside, but pure poison underneath. We want to help keep you and the boy safe."

"Don't let Grandpop's directness trouble you," Sam said soothingly as he handed her the glass. "Just know we're willing to help. Do you think it'll be difficult to get rid of Rick?"

"It's a possibility, but the thing I need most is help with Danny. After school, could he check-in with one of you until I get my schedule changed?"

"Of course," Sam replied.

"It won't be for long—a month at the most. I work two jobs, and my hours are unpredictable. That's why I let Rick watch Danny." Sue bit her lip. "I didn't realize Danny was being hurt. I never should've gotten so busy that I missed the signs."

"Listen," Sam said softly. "It isn't your fault Rick wasn't what he seemed."

"Maybe not, but I should've figured it out sooner. I know that by working so much I'm neglecting Danny, but at the moment I don't have a choice. It's been a struggle since my husband died."

"He didn't have life insurance?"

She shook her head. "We didn't think we needed it. Bill was so young. We didn't expect him to get s-sick."

As her voice broke, Sam's eyes filled with compassion. "I'm sorry."

"So am I," Sue said softly. "Bill was a wonderful man." Straightening her shoulders, she took a drink of milk and cleared her throat. "I had a good job back home, but it didn't pay enough to cover Bill's medical bills and funeral expenses. For the last several years, I've been trying to dig myself out of debt. When Tri County Medical Center held a job fair and wanted to hire me, I jumped at the chance."

"Tri County prides itself on its salaries and benefits, doesn't it?"

"It does, but when I moved here to start work, I was told there'd been a mix-up and the full-time position I'd been promised wouldn't be available until November. While I waited, the hospital gave me an on-call position, but I had to get a job at Stubby's to keep things floating. That's when Rick volunteered to help with Danny."

"He's your boyfriend?"

She shook her head. "He asked me out once, but when I refused, he didn't make a fuss. He never gave any indication he was violent. I'm usually a good judge of character. I don't know how he managed to fool me so completely."

Zara squeezed Sue's hand. "Dohn worry, honey, yuh dohn haffi explain. A smooth-talking mon cyan fool di wisest of women. Di thing now is to get yuh outta a sticky situation. An Na'tan an

131

Sam are di good ones to do et. Now stop your worrying and finish your pie."

As Sue took another bite, Sam said, "We've done some figuring, and if you're agreeable, on the days you work late, I'll watch Danny after play practice—"

"Play practice?" Sue looked over at her son's gleaming face. "What's this?"

"I got the part of Captain Von Trapp in *The Sound of Music*," Danny replied with a grin.

"I didn't know you were going to audition for a play."

"Me either," Danny said, "but it was lots of fun. My teacher says I have a great voice."

"That's wonderful," Sue said. "Your daddy used to sing in the church choir. I'm glad you're taking after him."

As Sue ran her hand down her son's cheek, Sam leaned forward and said, "My church is next to Danny's school. On weeknights, I oversee a youth gathering he can attend. I'll walk him home afterwards and stay with him when you work late."

Sue gave Sam a smile. "I can't believe this! I was praying for help last night, and here it is, falling into my lap...but are you sure it isn't too much of an imposition?"

"If it was, I'd say so. I—"

"Don't worry," Mr. Jacobson said. "Sam can handle it. Even though he's a bachelor, he's awfully good with children. If you're worried about his abilities, I'll give you a list of parents you can call for references."

"That won't be necessary," Sue replied. "If Sam wasn't trustworthy, his misdeeds would be all over the front page of the paper. Reporters love to discredit ministers."

"That's true." The old man nodded. "My grandson prides himself on his reputation. He has a good character—no one can say different." Putting his elbows on the table, he said, "A few nights a month, Sam works at the homeless shelter. When he's busy, Danny can stay with me. I used to be a cook during the war. I'll teach him the tricks of the trade. Sound good, Danny?"

"You bet!" the boy replied.

"If you need help on a weekend, there are enough of us to fill the gap. We'll all step up and see you through."

"Thank you—all of you—thank you," Sue said. "I promise it won't be for long. I'll have a full-time position at the hospital by Thanksgiving. When my schedule changes, I can quit waitressing and be home in the evenings."

"That's what neighbors are for."

Sam cleared his throat. "What about Rick? When are you going to tell him to stay away?"

"At lunch tomorrow."

"I'll be at the diner in case he tries to make trouble. Will he be there at noon?"

"More like 12:30. I'll talk to him during my break." She hesitated. "I appreciate your willingness to help, but Rick's always been friendly to me. I don't think he'll make a fuss in a public place. It's Danny's safety I'm worried about."

"You need to worry about yourself too," Sam said grimly. "If a man abuses a child, he could harm a woman as well. You shouldn't use his past behavior as a reliable guide."

"I suppose not. Truthfully, I'm not sure how he's going to react."

Nathan spoke up. "That's why Sam needs to be at the diner. If things get bad, he can pretend to be your fella. Lots of times when a troublemaker knows another man's in the picture, he'll get the hint and drift away."

Feeling Sue's gaze, Sam's eyes twinkled. "Don't worry, I promise not to hold you to the relationship."

"I didn't think you would," Sue said. "I'm just not sure any of this is necessary."

"I don't think we should take that chance."

"If you think it's so important, I won't argue."

"*Good.*" Feeling unusually relieved over her answer, Sam crossed his arms over his chest. He didn't know why Sue's safety should matter so much to him, but it did. "I'll arrange for someone else to be in charge of the church's activities, so Nathan and I can be at your house when school lets out. If Rick tries to hurt Danny, we'll be there to stop him."

"Thanks so much. Where Danny's safety's concerned, I'm more than willing to be under obligation."

Mr. Jacobson gave Sue's hand a pat. "Now, honey, don't fret. My grandsons will handle Rick if things turn nasty. If I was younger, I'd be happy to send Rick on his way myself. You may not believe it, but I was a boxing champ in the Navy."

Danny looked at the old man in obvious awe. "Can you teach me a few moves?"

"Sure, I taught Nathan and Sam." Mr. Jacobson slapped his hands on his knees and looked over at Nathan's wife. "Zara, can you and Nathan spend the night tomorrow?"

Zara nodded. "'Ow 'bout ef I mek pumpk'n chicken soup for suppa?"

Mr. Jacobson smiled. "Sounds wonderful! I've been hankering after it. Danny can come over, and I'll show him how to throw a few punches and make sourdough rolls Navy-style." He turned to Sue. "What's your schedule? Can you come for supper?"

"Actually, I'm not sure," Sue replied. "After my shift at Stubby's, I'm on-call at the hospital. I'll either be working until 10:00 p.m. or not working at all. I won't know until 2:00."

"Either way, you can come over for supper, even if it's a late supper. When you get here, we'll discuss things and decide if we need to take further action."

"I'd like that…as long as Zara's okay with having two more mouths to feed?"

"Dohn mind a bit. Soup's one of di easiest things to mek. Doesn't matta ef it's fah two or six. It all goes inna di same pot."

Looking at the clock, Sam said, "Now that everything's settled, how about playing a game? Unless Danny has some homework to do…?"

The boy grinned. "Nope. Got it all done plus some make-up assignments."

"Do you and your mom know how to play Chicken Foot Dominoes?"

As Danny shook his head, Sue said, "We don't know the rules, but a game sounds nice."

"Don't worry, it's easy to pick up. I'll explain the rules as we go along." Sam's blue eyes twinkled as he opened a cabinet and pulled out a box of dominoes. "I'll have you know that I'm a magnificent teacher. I'll have you up to speed in no time."

As Zara opened a bag of tortilla chips and set a bowl of homemade salsa on the table, she said to Sue, "I know we just ate, but games seem to bring pon di ragin' munchies."

"I know what you mean," Sue replied with a laugh as she dipped a chip. "Munchies and games just go together."

TWENTY

TWO HOURS LATER, Mr. Jacobson smiled as Sue sat casually with one blue-jeaned leg tucked underneath her and won her second game in a row. His smile grew as Sam moaned expressively and offered Sue the last chip in the bag.

"This has been so much fun," Sue said, scraping up salsa with the chip. "I feel like a new woman."

"A new woman with sharp Chicken Foot skills," Sam said with a chuckle. "It took me a month to win my first game. You're either a smart pupil or a former Chicken Foot champion living incognito. You're such a natural I'll have to teach you Double Bergen."

"Mo chips?" Zara asked. "There's anodda bag inna di pantry."

Sue shook her head. "I can't eat another bite."

"'Ow 'bout yuh, Sam? You've dun di number on di pineapple salsa tonight."

"No, thanks. If I eat anything else, I'll be popping antacids."

As Sam leaned closer to Sue and helped her turn over her dominoes, Mr. Jacobson caught Zara's eye and raised an eyebrow. Zara nodded and winked. Seeing the way Sam was allowing his arm to rest lightly against Sue's, Mr. Jacobson's grin widened. As Sam and Sue reached for the same domino and their hands brushed, Mr. Jacobson's grin turned into a satisfied smirk. Glancing back at Zara, Mr. Jacobson began to feel alarmed—the island beauty was looking way too smug. Fearing that an imprudent comment might stop whatever was starting, he gave Zara a tiny kick beneath the table. Unfortunately, he missed his target and Nathan yelped.

"Sorry about that," Mr. Jacobson said sheepishly. "Must've had a muscle spasm. How about another game?"

At Mr. Jacobson's words, Sue looked up at the clock and reluctantly shook her head. "I'd love to, but we should be going. Danny has school tomorrow." Rising from her chair, she said, "Thank you for a lovely evening and for everything your family's doing to help us."

"Think nothing of it," Mr. Jacobson replied.

As the group stood to their feet, Zara pulled Sue aside and handed her a dish of leftovers. When she protested, Zara whispered in a conspiratorial way, "Tek it, sugar. I made brawta."

"Brawta?"

"Extra. I'm planning pon having anodda piece of pie at 2:00 a.m. That's mi favorite time to eat. I wan yuh and Danny to be all set inna case yuh get di midnight munchies too."

Sue laughed. "That sounds wonderful. I'll think of you when I'm indulging."

As Zara packed the leftovers in a bag, Sue saw Sam talking to Danny. "Don't worry about tomorrow," Sam said. "I'll watch over your mother."

"Thanks so much," Danny replied. "I've been awfully worried about her."

137

"That's understandable. You did right in asking for help. Some things are too big for a man to handle alone."

"I'm glad you believed me."

"Like I said, you have an honest face."

As Sue smiled gratefully at Sam, she was drawn into a flurry of well wishes and goodbyes. With friendly farewells echoing in her ears, she and Danny started home. Suddenly, Sam bounded up behind her. "Sue, wait up. You forgot your purse."

"Thanks, I don't know where my head is tonight. I usually don't misplace things."

"Don't worry about it. You have a lot on your mind." He gave her a mischievous glance. "It's not every day a woman gets saddled with a new boyfriend."

Blinking in a startled way, Sue studied Sam's face. Seeing his peek-a-boo dimple, her eyes began to twinkle. "That's true. And not a common 'boyfriend' at that. You're a minister to boot. Talk about *intimidating*."

"You'll get used to it." He chuckled. "I'll see you tomorrow, and remember, if it comes down to it, I'll be honored to pretend to be your fella. Besides helping you, it'll raise my standing in the community to be seen keeping company with such a pretty gal."

As she laughed, Sam said, "Plan on seeing me at noon. I'll be the mysterious stranger with the smoldering stare. Shall I wear a white rose in my button hole?"

"You nut, I can recognize you without the flower. But by all means, if it tickles your quirky sense of humor, go right ahead."

Winking broadly, Sam called over his shoulder, "Until tomorrow."

"Bye, Sam," Danny yelled. "See you later, alligator!"

Sam's laughing reply carried back through the darkness. "After awhile, crocodile."

Running gentle fingers over her son's cowlick, Sue began humming a happy tune. Filling the air with music, she admitted to herself that she'd thoroughly enjoyed Sam's company. His lighthearted jokes had kept her in stitches.

"Whatcha humming?" Danny asked.

"Am I humming?" Sue smiled. "I guess I am, aren't I? It's a lovely song called *Some Enchanted Evening*."

"Sing it to me?"

Thinking of the lyrics, she blushed and shook her head. "It's a mushy love song. After you get tucked into bed, I'll sing you something else."

"I don't mind love songs. I'm not a little kid anymore."

"I guess you're not, are you?" she said softly, kissing the top of his head.

As Sue and Danny went into their house and closed the door, an engine sprang to life across the street. Headlights pierced the darkness as a pickup emerged from the shadows and slid toward Mr. Jacobson's house. Keeping his engine running, Rick turned off his headlights and waited. Fifteen minutes later, Sam stepped onto his grandfather's porch. Rick tightened his grip on the steering wheel. His eyes narrowed into smoldering slits as Sam began to whistle and walk down the block toward his house.

The pickup crept forward. One tire stole onto the sidewalk and then stopped abruptly as Sam cut across his lawn and unlocked his door.

When Sam's kitchen lights flicked on, Rick gunned his motor and flipped a sharp U-turn. When he was level with Sue's house, he rolled down his window and threw a beer bottle at her door. The bottle hit the oak tree by the porch and shattered. As the broken pieces fell into a pile of raked leaves, Rick careened down a side street. For a moment, the sound of squealing tires filled the air. Long after the sound faded, the faint smell of burning rubber lingered behind in the chilly autumn breeze.

TWENTY-ONE

WASHING HIS FACE with a cheerful gusto that splashed water onto the floor, Danny listened to his mother's singing. Suddenly, he realized that he hadn't seen Gil for quite a while. Running into his bedroom, he found her sitting on the floor beneath his window, writing in a journal.

"Where have you been?" he demanded.

"Missed me?" Gil asked. "Everything was going so smoothly that I slipped away to do my homework. I'm supposed to make journal entries on your progress, and you made lots of progress today. In fact, so much progress I have writer's cramp. By the time this exam's over, I'm gonna have permanent nerve damage to all my itty-bitty fingers."

"Come on." Danny laughed. "Seriously, when'd you come home?"

"Around 9:00. It seemed like the game was gonna last awhile. Was it fun?"

"Sure was. Sam's gonna teach me Nertz tomorrow. It's gonna be a blast hanging out with him." He scratched his head. "But how'd you get in here? The house was all locked up."

"I came in your window. You left it unlocked when you made your hasty exit yesterday."

"You should be a cat burglar." He sighed and smiled. "Oh, Gil, I had so much fun. You were right about the Jacobsons. They're terrific."

"They sure are. Dr. Ableman told me that neighbors can be a big help, and he was right." Gil tossed her journal into her backpack and yawned. "Do you wanna talk to the docs tonight or go straight to bed?"

"What do you think?"

She grinned. "If I was you, I wouldn't miss it either. Are you done with the bathroom?"

Danny nodded.

"In that case, I'll scoot in and get ready for bed." Her lopsided dimple danced. "Should I wear a green facial when we contact the lab?"

"I don't know." He smirked. "How far do you wanna press your luck?"

Gil threw her pillow at him and struggled to pick up her suitcase. "There must be an easier way," she groaned. "Maybe next time, rather than one large suitcase, I should pack a dozen smaller ones."

"Maybe you should pack lighter."

"But I *need* all my clothes. It takes work to represent the future in a respectable manner."

"I think you should stop worrying about your looks and start worrying about your back. You're gonna end up in traction if you keep lugging that monster bag of yours."

"Oh, shush up, you little squirt," Gil said with a giggle, dropping her suitcase to the floor. "You need to learn to respect your elders."

"If you want respect," Danny chortled, "you shouldn't walk around in fuzzy bunny slippers."

$\backsim$

Twenty minutes later, Gil, in her bunny suit and curlers—but without her green facial—sat with Danny and put *Extreme Exam* into the PlayFest console. Immediately, a blue glow filled the room. Across the wave, she could see Dr. Moosly glaring at William. Obviously, her transmission had interrupted an argument between the two men.

Dr. Nelson smiled through the portal. "Right on time, Gil. How are things going?"

Before Gil could respond, Dr. Moosly blustered, "I still say it's highly irregular to include a child in—"

"I know you do," William interrupted. "You've been saying it for the past ten minutes straight." Turning his shoulder on Dr. Moosly, he said to Gil, "Well, look who found a washcloth. It's nice to see your face."

"You're one to talk," she said with a snort. "What are you hiding beneath your beard? A weak chin or dimples?"

William gave a bellow of laughter. "I'll have you know, my chin's fine. However, I'll make you a deal. I'll shave off my beard when you pass your field exam as long as you throw away your green facial. When I saw you last night, I thought you'd started to mold."

"Tossing a jar will be a small price to pay to finally see your chin."

Dr. Moosly glowered. "Enough of this nonsense! We need to get down to business."

"Regretfully, I agree," Director Matthews said, moving closer to the Staging Platform. "Danny, as you requested, we've looked into your mother's suicide, and we've found some troubling inconsistencies."

"What's inconsistencies mean?" Danny whispered in Gil's ear.

"Things that don't add up." Giving Danny's hand a reassuring squeeze, Gil peered through the blue wave. "What did you find?"

"It's what wasn't found that concerns us most. Sue's body wasn't discovered until three days after Danny's arrest."

"W-where was she?" Danny asked in a jerky voice.

"Hanging in the shed in your backyard."

"Did she suffer?"

Seeing the director hesitate, Gil said softly, "Hanging isn't a pleasant way to die, Danny, but let's focus on the facts that can prevent her death, okay?"

As the boy nodded, the director continued, "Although an autopsy confirmed Sue died the same day Rick was stabbed, a more accurate time of death was never pinpointed."

"Is that usual?" Gil asked.

"In this case, it was gross negligence. When Danny was arrested, he told Charlesberg police Rick had murdered his mother, but no one took him seriously. That oversight directly led to his harsh sentencing."

"I don't understand."

"The inconclusive autopsy was used to refute the idea that Danny was acting out of self-defense against the man who killed his mother. Sue's death was simply ruled a suicide. A timely autopsy would've made a world's worth of difference to his future."

William leaned forward. "Gil, Rick will attack Sue within the next twenty-four hours. You'll need to keep an eye on her as well as Danny. Have you found neighbors who can help?"

"We've made contact with the Jacobsons. There are two strong men in the family who'll assist me in protecting the Winstons."

"Even though you have help, you'll need to be very careful. If you get hurt, obtaining medical aid will be extremely difficult."

"You can say that again," Danny murmured. "How can a doctor operate on an invisible woman?"

Knowing the boy's mood needed lightening, Gil nudged him and whispered, "Hey, can you imagine a doctor trying to put a thermometer between my toes instead of in my mouth? How do you think he'd respond to being told I was upside down?"

Giving her a wobbly grin, Danny replied in his fake British accent, "Upside down? You don't say, old chap, how ever can you tell?"

Laughing, Gil gave Danny's shoulder a little bump with hers.

"All joking aside," Dr. Nelson said, "do be careful. Things may be more dangerous than we thought. We don't want to say anything prematurely, but do you have anything that might contain a sample of Rick's DNA?"

"I wish we hadn't been so vigilant about throwing away the beer bottles," Gil moaned. "The trash truck came today, didn't it, Danny?"

He nodded, but then he jumped up and exclaimed, "Hey, we didn't clean the garage! A while back, Rick was out there working on something. I'll bet beer bottles are all over the place. Would a bottle work, Dr. Nelson?"

"That'd be great. Can you grab one for us? Hold the bottle close to the bottom and don't touch the top where Rick's mouth went."

Nodding, Danny left the room at a quick gallop.

"Gil," William said in a tense voice, "let me reiterate not to take Rick lightly. Tomorrow, look *before* you leap."

"Looking before leaping is foreign to my nature," she replied. "Stop worrying. I *do* have common sense, even if it's rusty from lack of use."

Before William could respond, Danny came bounding into the room holding a half-empty beer bottle. "This stuff sure stinks," he said with a wrinkled nose. "It smells like dog pee. What do we do now? Do you want me to empty it?"

"No," Director Matthews replied, "that could compromise the sample."

As William grabbed a box of latex gloves and began to distribute them, Dr. Moosly stepped back and blustered, "I'm not getting splashed with filth again."

"Have it your way," William replied. "We don't need you for this anyway."

"Now, Danny," Director Matthews instructed, "I want you to toss the bottle carefully through the time portal, but before you do, are there more bottles if we break this one?"

Danny shook his head. "The rest were busted up in pieces. Rick must've thrown them against the wall."

"Then we'll just need to catch this one on the first try. Are you ready?"

As Danny nodded, Dr. Moosly scuttled hastily to one side and crossed his arms.

Gil watched as Danny gently threw the bottle. Inside the lab, William caught it easily without spilling a drop.

"Great job, Danny!" William crowed. "You should go out for baseball."

Gil smiled and said to the director, "When will you have the DNA results?"

"Around noon tomorrow. For sure by 1:30."

She turned to Danny. "After lunch, can I leave you at school so I can contact the lab?"

The boy nodded. "If we can pin something on Rick, I'm all for it."

"Gil," William said firmly, "I want you to be careful tomorrow. You too, Danny."

"You bet," chirped the boy. "We got so many aces up our sleeves, we can't lose."

Seeing that William was about to launch into another lecture about safety, Gil gave him a cheeky wave. "Signing off until tomorrow afternoon."

Before he could respond, she severed the GAP connection. As the wave dissipated, Danny laughed. "He wasn't done talking yet."

"If he wasn't, he should've been," Gil said. "I really like Dr. Ableman, but sometimes he can be a real windbag. Time for bed, young man. We have a busy day of *not* murdering coming up tomorrow."

As Danny grinned and nodded, Gil rummaged through her suitcase and found her green facial. "First things first," she said decisively, pitching the jar into the trashcan. "You can tell Dr. Ableman I've thrown the green goo away. He's not gonna weasel outta this one. His beard's gonna finally bite the dust."

"That green glop sure was nasty."

"That's why I don't mind tossing it. It clung to my nose like concrete last night. I thought I was gonna have to use sandpaper to get it off. Besides, I have a purple facial I like much better. I'll just use it instead."

"Is that fair?"

"Sure it is. Doc didn't say I had to throw away *all* my facials— just the green one. And what he doesn't know won't hurt him."

TWENTY-TWO

D-DAY DAWNED BRIGHT and clear. When Danny woke up, he could hear Gil singing off-key in his bathroom. Grinning to himself, he threw back the covers. Today was gonna be a wonderful day! If he could get through today, he'd be in the clear. He was *sure* he could do it.

As the first rays of dawn pierced the lab windows, Director Matthews rubbed his tired eyes and sighed. Tests had been completed on the beer bottle, and GAP had pieced together some disturbing information. In light of the data, he'd refused to go home—running GAP scenarios throughout the night. As he waited for the next batch of data to be compiled, he rubbed the back of his neck, willing the computer to work faster. He was finding results— more results than he liked—and GAP was still discovering additional, alarming information.

William paced in his office, clenching and unclenching his fists. He'd spent the night wandering the halls, trying not to imagine the worst. As he paced between his desk and office door, he kicked at balloons on the floor—remnants of a student prank. He looked at the clock. The hands hadn't moved. He'd been hoping D-day would pass uneventfully, but in light of the upsetting new data, that seemed unlikely.

He looked back at the clock and groaned. *Would the blasted hands ever move?* Peering down at his watch and seeing it was five minutes slower, he tore it from his wrist and flung it to the floor.

In Charlesberg, Danny pelted to the bathroom door and knocked. "Gil," he called softly, "you big bathroom hog, get a wiggle on! Hurry up, will you?"

Opening the door a crack, Gil peeked out wearing a purple facial. "Sorry, do I have a minute, or should I get out now?"

Danny hopped on one foot. "That depends on your definition of a minute!"

As the clock in Danny's cozy living room chimed the hour, across town in the seedy trailer he called home, Rick was lying on his unmade bed surrounded by empty beer bottles. An arm with a tightly clenched fist was thrown up over his face, and his lips were moving, muttering angry things no one could hear.

As a dog's frantic barks filled the air, Rick got up and walked to his dresser. Seeing his reflection in the mirror, he punched the glass just to hear it shatter. After a long moment, he reached into a drawer and pulled out a long red cord…

Later that morning, with the delicious smell of Sue's pancakes wafting through the air, Gil sat cross-legged on the floor of Danny's bedroom and marked some verses with a ribbon.

"Whatcha doing?" Danny asked, licking his buttery fingers as he came into the room.

"I've marked a Bible passage for your mom to read. It's one of my favorites."

"Cool! I'll hurry and brush my teeth."

"Make sure you wash your face. You've got a bit of egg on your nose."

"You sound just like Mom."

"That's 'cause I care."

Pulling a face, Danny rushed into the bathroom.

While he brushed his teeth, Gil bowed her head. "Dear Lord," she whispered, "it's D-day. Please protect us. Help me know what to do and when to do it. I've come to love this family. I don't want them hurt…" As her eyes filled with tears, her whispered words stumbled to a halt. Sitting in silent submission, she began to feel God's peace stealing its way into her heart.

As Danny came back to the bedroom, Gil watched with a smile as he picked up his Bible and flashed her a grin. She followed a few paces behind as he loped into the kitchen and tackled his mom with a hug.

"I've got a passage for us to read," he said excitedly. "A friend of mine says it's one of her favorites."

"Let's read it then," Sue said, sitting down and opening to Isaiah 43:1-5. *"Don't be afraid for I have ransomed you; I have called you by name; you are Mine. When you go through deep waters and great trouble, I will be with you. When you go through rivers of difficulty, you will not drown! When you walk through the fire of oppression you will not be burned up—the flames will not consume you...you are precious to Me and honored, and I love you. Don't be afraid for I am with you."*

When Sue finished reading, Danny asked, "Does that mean God's gonna help us today?"

"That's *exactly* what it means." Sue smiled, thumbing through his Bible. "I have a passage for us to read too. I want us to study the Book of John. Let's read chapter one, okay?"

Danny nodded.

After reading the chapter and answering Danny's questions about Jesus and John the Baptist, Sue took her son's hand and prayed over their day.

When Danny was ready to leave for school, Gil watched as he paused and said hesitantly, "Mom, you'll be extra careful today, won't you? You won't take any chances?"

Sue bent down and put her cheek next to her son's. "I promise with the very best promise I can make. You have nothing to worry about. The diner's a public place, and Sam's promised to be there."

"I know," Danny said, "but what about afterwards, when Sam leaves?"

"I'll probably be working at the hospital, but if not, I'll come home and lock the doors."

"I don't want you alone t-today," Danny said with a catch in his voice. "I have a bad feeling."

"If you're that worried, I'll go to Mr. Jacobson's if I'm not needed at the hospital."

"That's good," Danny said, giving her a hug. "I love you so much it hurts!"

"I don't want you in pain." Sue laughed. "You can love me less and keep your health."

"No, I can't. You mean the world to me."

"That makes two of us then," Sue said. "Now, no more worrying. We've made our plans as best we can, and we've prayed. All that's left is to face today with courage and a smile."

Gil moved away from the wall and gave Danny's arm a gentle squeeze. "Come on, trooper, let's get to school. Everything's gonna be fine."

As Danny shouldered his backpack and went out the door, Gil murmured beneath her breath, "Here we go. Ready or not. It's D-day."

TWENTY-THREE

WALKING TO SCHOOL, Danny saw Slim running toward him. Cringing a little, he braced for confrontation, but for the first time in weeks, Slim didn't harass him. Instead, Slim waved and asked, "Hey, do any kung fu last night?"

Danny gave a relieved smile. "Nope, did you?"

"Nah, but I did watch a movie about a Japanese warrior who teamed up with a cowboy. He wasn't as fast as you, but he had some great moves." Slim paused. "Hey, Danny, will you tell me how you moved so fast?"

"It's hard to explain," Danny replied, looking over at Gil. "But someday, I might. You won't believe me though."

Slim tossed Danny a candy bar. "Try me sometime."

As the bell rang, they rushed into school and shouted a quick so-long. Glancing at Slim over his shoulder, Danny gave a satisfied sigh. D-day, or not, things were going just fine.

William balanced two cups of coffee as he entered the lab. Putting a steaming mug by the director's elbow, he asked as calmly as he could, "What have you found, Peter?"

The director picked up the mug and took a long sip. "About Danny or about Rick?"

"Both."

"Neither one is good."

Hearing the gruffness in the director's voice, and knowing it was due to lack of sleep, William said, "Take another drink and explain."

Director Matthews nodded and rubbed his eyes. "It's worse than we assumed. This assignment should've been conducted by a professional, not a student cadet."

"Gil was perfect for this job."

"It doesn't matter. The information I'm digging up about Rick Olsen is staggering. When Gil reports in, she needs to be warned that Rick's extremely dangerous—and I mean *extremely*."

"Gil doesn't pay attention to warnings."

"She has to!" the director exclaimed. "If she doesn't use extra caution, we won't get her back. I've never lost a cadet yet, but she could easily be my first."

Feeling his stomach churning, William clenched his hands. "What about Danny? What's GAP saying about the boy's future? Is the risk to Gil worth it?"

"Right now, it's running straight up fifty-fifty. Half the time, GAP says Danny dodges D-day. A few seconds later, it has him back on death row. I don't know what to say. These are the most inconsistent predictions I've ever observed. I can't call it."

Sue walked downtown to hustle through some errands before her shift started at the diner. As she entered Wiseman's Jewelry Emporium to replace her watch battery, she began to hum *Some Enchanted Evening*. She smiled softly. Sam was taking up a lion's share of her thoughts. She hadn't felt so comfortable around a man since her husband passed away.

It was funny how life worked. When she'd started her job at Stubby's, another waitress pointed out Sam as the nicest man in town. After that, she'd kept a casual eye out for him. From the diner's windows, she'd seen him carrying groceries for elderly ladies and helping tourists with directions. Walking home from work one day, she'd spotted him helping a little boy search for a lost puppy. And from her desk in the emergency room, she'd watched him comforting people in pain. It seemed that everywhere she went she caught a glimpse of "the nicest man in town." She'd never expected to meet him, of course. But now that she had, she'd freely admit he was more wonderful than rumor reported.

Still humming, she wandered over to the counter and noticed a man in his eighties buying jewelry.

"You sure know how to pick 'em," the clerk said as he handed the old man a couple of ring boxes. "That sapphire's a beauty."

"It has to be. It's going on the hand of the most beautiful woman in the world. My wife and I will be celebrating our Sapphire Anniversary next week." The old man put the velvet cases in his pocket and turned around. When he saw Sue, he smiled.

Sue smiled back at him. "Congratulations, I overheard you saying your anniversary's coming up."

"Thank you, miss, I'm blessed indeed. I have the best wife in the world."

"Forty-five years is quite an accomplishment."

"True, but I had wonderful parents who set a grand example. They celebrated over fifty years together. My siblings and I have kept the tradition. All our marriages have lasted."

"What's your secret?"

Twinkling, the old man whispered in her ear, "Lots of love and separate bathrooms!"

Sue threw back her head and laughed.

Across the street from the jewelry store, Rick stood in an alley, watching Sue laughing with the old man. Grinding his cigarette out against a brick, he spat contemptuously. She had no right to be happy. No right at all. *Sue Winston was nothing but a cheap, two-timing tramp.*

As the relentless sun forced itself through his bedroom curtains, Sam began to pray. He kept waiting for God's peace to come, but when it didn't, he went to the bathroom to splash water on his face. As he scrubbed the back of his neck, he groaned and peered at his reflection. His face was haggard—it was obvious he hadn't slept. Truth be told, he'd been thrown off balance by Sue, and his emotions were all over the map.

Roughly rubbing his cheek with the back of his hand, Sam sighed. He wondered if Sue knew how her eyes sparkled when she smiled and just how pretty she looked in blue. As he pictured her face, his breath caught in his throat.

Tossing the washcloth in the sink, Sam set his jaw. He couldn't afford to get close to a woman—it simply wasn't a good idea. If Sue was going to have such an effect on him, he needed to take precautions. Keep things formal. Business like. He may like Sue, but dating her wasn't worth the risk. He had too much to lose.

"I want you to read Philippians 2:7."

Sam froze. He knew the Lord's voice when he heard it. Going back to his bedroom, he picked up his Bible and flipped to the verse. *"But Christ made Himself of no reputation…"*

Sam stopped reading and peered at the ceiling. "What are you trying to say?"

The Lord's voice came again, soft and still inside his heart, *"Christ put aside His reputation, and so must you."*

Sam squirmed. When he graduated from seminary, the woman he'd been dating had spread nasty rumors after they broke up. Since then, he'd steered clear of women. It didn't take much to set people talking, and he hated to be the topic of malicious gossip. In fact, he hated it so much that guarding his reputation had become an obsession.

"I want all of you," the Lord's voice said, *"not just the parts of your life you're willing to share. I want you to trust Me with the things you hold most dear."*

"But God," Sam protested, "my sterling reputation is honoring to You. I like Sue, but if I get too close to her, the gossips will be marrying us off before we have our second date. And if we break up, it could hurt my ministry. It's wise for me to keep separate from—"

"Look up 1 Corinthians 3:19."

Hunching a shoulder, Sam opened his Bible. *"For the wisdom of this world is foolishness with God."*

"By trying to be wise," the Lord said gently, *"you are being a fool."*

Sam stared at the ceiling in confusion. "I don't understand what You want from me. I'll help Sue. I'll be nice to her. But I'm not getting involved beyond a certain point. Living a single life is a sacrifice, but it's better than—"

"1 Samuel 15:22."

Giving a gusty sigh, Sam turned to the verse. "...Obedience is far better than sacrifice." Tossing his Bible on the bed, Sam shouted, "What do You want from me?"

"I've already told you. I want you to yield your reputation. I want your obedience. I want you to listen to Me rather than your own fears."

"But what about the gossips? If they—"

"Think about Christ."

Knowing that God's words were a command and not a suggestion, Sam mentally reviewed the life of Jesus. As he did, he realized that Christ wasn't swayed by people's opinions. He also realized that Christ didn't spend His time trying to squelch gossip.

"I think I understand," Sam said, "but why are You telling me this?"

The Lord's voice came again, "You'll find your answer in Jeremiah 29:11."

"I don't need to read that verse. I can quote it," Sam said. "For I know the plans I have for you, says the Lord. They are plans for good and not for evil, to give you a future and a hope."

"Knowing doesn't always mean understanding. Look it up."

Sam flipped through the worn pages of his Bible. When he found the verse, he blinked in astonishment. Taped over Jeremiah 29:11 was a note from his brother.

"Read what Nathan has to say," the Lord prompted softly.

With a shaking voice, Sam read the note, "Brother-of-mine, God has great plans for your life, and I believe a wife is one of them. Put aside your fears, and open your heart. The love of a good woman is one of God's greatest gifts."

Sam felt a lump rising in his throat. "What are you trying to tell me, God? Are You saying Sue and I are meant to be together?"

"I'm saying that if you will trust Me with your reputation, you will allow Me to do something wonderful. Never let the fear of people's opinions rob you of the blessings I have in store."

Humming to herself, Sue glanced at her watch and turned toward the diner. The rest of her errands would have to wait or she'd be late for work. Suddenly, she felt a prickling on the back of her neck. Fearing she was being watched, she turned and looked. Rick wasn't in sight.

Hastening her step, she crossed the street. The feeling of being watched came again. She swung around. Rick wasn't behind her—at least not where she could see him. Flinching at shadows, she made short work of the walk to the diner, and when she reached it, she sighed in relief. Giving a customer a wobbly smile, she grabbed a polka dot apron from beneath the counter. Seeing the way her hands were shaking, she chided herself for her fear. After all, there was no reason to be anxious.

No reason at all.

Rick had always been kind to her. He certainly wasn't following her. She'd just been imagining things...

TWENTY-FOUR

CRYSTAL STARED AT a note taped to the door of Hertz Lecture Hall. Spinning on her heel, she collided with someone standing behind her. As her head crashed into the man's chin, her backpack fell and her glasses slipped and hung by one ear.

"Careful, Cris," the man said, grabbing her elbows and steading her.

Hearing the voice, Crystal groaned inside. Straightening her glasses, she mumbled, "Sorry, Marc. Didn't see you."

"So I gathered." He pointed at the note. "Is Doc cancelling the recapitulation session?"

Crystal nodded. "The note says our graded finals will be mailed to us."

"So that's it? The semester's over?"

"I guess so." Pushing her owlish glasses further up on her nose, she said in a worried voice, "I don't like it."

"What's not to like? Summer vacation, here we come!"

"That's not what I meant," she muttered. "Doc *never* cancels *anything*. Last year, he held classes even though he had double pneumonia. Something's wrong."

"Don't be dramatic."

"I'm not! Something's up!"

"Just because Dr. Ableman cancelled one measly review session?"

"No, because Dr. Nelson cancelled her classes too. I'm going to wander over to the lab and see if I can figure out what's happening."

"It won't do you a bit of good," Ryan said, coming up behind them. "TEMCO's locked down tighter than a drum. Only those with Alpha-Blue clearance are being allowed onto the second floor of Hawking Hall."

"Are you serious?" Crystal said, pushing at her glasses. "That's never happened before, has it?"

"Not to my knowledge."

"Do you think it's a drill?" Marc asked.

Ryan shook his head. "I doubt it. I ran into Dr. Nelson in the parking lot. It looked like she'd been crying."

Marc blinked. "That woman's cool as a cucumber. I've never seen her upset."

"I told you so!" Crystal exclaimed. "Something's going on, and it's not good.

Entering Stubby's diner, Sam saw Sue cleaning syrup from the floor. As his heart rate increased, he wondered if this was how Isaac felt when he first saw Rebekah. He couldn't believe how pretty Sue was, even in her silly uniform that seemed designed to make a woman look frumpy. She actually made the uniform look good, and that was saying something. He watched as Sue gave the floor a final swipe with a dishcloth. As she stood to her feet, he waved to catch her attention.

Sue smiled and walked to his side. "I'm glad you made it. So far, no trouble to report."

"Hopefully, there won't be any," he said. "Where do you want me to sit?"

"How about that booth in the corner? It has a good view of Rick's usual table, but it's concealed by plants, so you shouldn't be conspicuous."

"Good plan."

"No white rose in your buttonhole? Decide against it?"

Sam grinned. "I figured it didn't quite fit the bill, and I couldn't find a white carnation."

Sue blinked and laughed. "White roses represent new beginnings, and white carnations mean *alas, my poor heart*. What type of message are you trying to send?"

"Know the language of flowers, do you? Next time, I'll have to wear a lavender rose."

Sue chuckled. "If you're the victim of love at first sight, I'll eat my dishrag."

Giving her a smile, Sam changed the subject. "How's Danny holding up?"

"He was worried about me being home alone. He made me promise to go to your grandfather's if I don't work this afternoon. Will that be all right?"

"Sure, Grandpop loves company. Besides, it'll give me a chance to recoup my dignity at dominoes—that is, if you'll let me challenge you to a rematch?"

Sue nodded and smiled. As Sam smiled back, time seemed to slow down. Sue was so focused on him that Sam could see himself reflected in the pupils of her eyes. For a moment, they were conscious only of each other.

"Sue! Order up!" Stubby bellowed.

Sue took Sam's hand and gave it a squeeze. "Thanks for everything."

Sam felt himself blush. He didn't mind at all that her hand came with a dirty dishrag. What amazed him more was he didn't mind that Deacon Pruette was sitting in a booth staring at him.

"I've got to go," Sue said breathlessly. "I'll bring you a cup of coffee in a minute."

"I'll look forward to it."

As he watched Sue gracefully weaving around tables, Sam realized that Deacon Pruette was grinning and elbowing his wife in the ribs. Smiling at them, and feeling more than a little dazed, Sam went to his designated booth in the corner. He looked over at Sue. She was humming a tune from *South Pacific* and glancing his way.

As time went by, Sue kept coming to his table to refill his coffee cup. Sam dutifully drank the coffee down. After all, the quicker he drained his cup, the quicker she was back at his side. He was enjoying the morning, but as the clock crept past noon, he noticed that Sue's humming had stopped and she was watching the door with increasing anxiety.

Outside Hertz Hall, Crystal watched as Ryan brushed a lock of dark, wavy hair from his eyes. "What do you think's going on?" he asked.

"I think Gil's in trouble," she replied. "She's the only cadet still out in the field. I memorized the surf manifest."

Marc rolled his eyes. "Of *course* you did."

As she winced and stared at her shoes, Ryan asked gently, "Why'd you memorize it?"

"Boredom," Crystal mumbled. "A few weeks ago, I was waiting to talk to the director and the manifest was posted by my chair." Raising her eyes, she glared at Marc. "I don't see why memorizing the manifest is so strange. You memorize football statistics, and if that isn't a complete brain-dead waste of time, I don't know what is—" Crystal choked back her words, realizing they revealed her interest in Marc.

As Marc grinned, she squirmed. Before she could think of a pithy comment to put Marc in his place, Ryan asked, "Is the manifest the only reason you think Gil's in trouble?"

She shook her head. "Dr. Ableman's her advisor, and he didn't go home last night. His car's parked where it was yesterday."

"He could've parked in the same place this morning," Ryan pointed out.

"His left rear tire has a bald spot that's in the same place it was last night. If his car had been driven, the odds of the bald spot still being an inch above the pavement are astronomical."

Marc's lips twitched. "Don't tell me you pay attention to tires."

Crystal pushed at her glasses. "I happen to notice things. I don't sleepwalk through life like some people I know."

"Meaning me?"

"Meaning that if you'd pay more attention maybe you'd learn a few things."

"Like who has bald tires? I think I can survive without—" Marc's voice came to a halt as a convertible purred up to the curb. Quick as a flash, he turned away from Crystal and sauntered over to the car. "What are you doing here, Molly?"

The woman in the driver's seat perched her sunglasses on top her head and said in a flirty voice that set Crystal's teeth on edge,

"Looking for you, *silly*. How about ditching your boring old review session and going for a drive?"

As Marc gave Molly a dazzling smile, Crystal's hands curled into tight fists. Molly was *everything* she wanted to be. Beautiful. Exotic. Alluring. Crystal gazed at Molly's glossy black curls and fingered her own messy bun. As Molly fluttered mascaraed lashes and began to talk in an animated fashion, Crystal sighed. Molly was so gorgeous that her face belonged in an ad campaign for French perfume. A perfume like *Desire*, or *Passion*, or *Longing*. Something sensual and slightly sinful. A scent that she herself would never dare to wear.

As Marc hopped over the passenger-side door and into the convertible, Crystal studied the way Molly's flawless olive skin was set off by a tailored, white blouse.

The woman definitely knows how to dress.

Crystal tugged at her baggy shirt and frowned. Molly was a knock out. She was everything a man would desire. Everything *Marc* would desire. There was no way anyone else could compete. No way anyone else should even *think* of competing.

Crystal's eyes fell, and she miserably contemplated her sensible brown shoes. As Molly gave a rippling laugh and drove away with Marc, Crystal sighed again. Suddenly, she caught Ryan looking at her with such compassion in his eyes that she didn't know whether to burst into tears and ask for a hug, or snarl at him to mind his own business. She did neither.

"What do you say to an ice cream cone?" Ryan asked softly. "My treat."

"No, thanks. I don't like eating too much sugar."

"In that case, how about a salty pretzel?"

Crystal gave a weak chuckle. "Are you trying to make me fat?"

"Heaven forbid. But we should do something to celebrate the start of summer vacation. After all, it's been a tough semester."

"It sure has." Crystal shouldered her backpack and started down the sidewalk. "I can't imagine what senior year's gonna be like."

"Let's let next year worry about itself," Ryan said, swinging in beside her. "Right now, let's go get that pretzel."

"I don't know…" Crystal mumbled, giving Hawking Hall a concerned glance.

"Leave the worrying to the higher-ups," Ryan said, giving her shoulder a friendly bump with his. "After all, there's nothing you can do."

At 12:45, Rick strolled into Stubby's and sat at his usual table. Taking a deep breath, Sue picked up the coffee pot and slowly walked toward him.

TWENTY FIVE

SITTING BENEATH A tree on the lawn of Fairfield Middle School, Danny watched as Gil unwrapped a TEMCO energy bar. As she took a bite and made a face, he laughed. "Maybe if you plug your nose it'll go down easier."

"Maybe," Gil said with distaste. "I knew these things were bad, I heard rumors about them from my old classmates, but I thought I'd get used to them." She took another bite and gagged. "Honestly, I might as well be munching on kitty litter! Do you mind if I dunk it in your barbeque sauce? Maybe it'll make it taste better."

"Dip away as long as no one can see you."

"Thanks, you're a life-saver—or should I say a palate-saver?" Gil looked around, dipped her bar in the barbeque sauce, and quickly brought it to her mouth. "Umm. Barbeque-coated kitty litter. Much better."

Danny jumped as a voice spoke behind him, "Mind if I eat with you?"

Turning around, he saw Slim standing next to the tree with a tray. "Sure, what's up?"

167

"Can you explain how you moved so fast?" Slim asked, sitting down and opening his milk carton. "I still can't figure it out."

Picking some grass stems and crushing them between his fingers, Danny peered over at Gil. She was looking helplessly at him. She obviously didn't know what to advise.

"Look, I know I was a jerk," Slim said, "but it's driving me crazy. How'd you do it?"

"Maybe the floor was slippery, and you just fell."

"We both know that's not what happened." Hanging his head, Slim mumbled, "I guess if I was you, I wouldn't tell either. I've been pretty mean."

"It's not that. It's just that you wouldn't believe me if..." Danny's words stumbled to a halt as he realized Slim was no longer listening. He was looking with horrified fascination at a blob of barbeque sauce floating a few feet in the air. As the barbeque sauce hung suspended and then disappeared completely, Slim jumped to his feet and rubbed his eyes.

"Gil!" Danny hissed, smacking her knee.

Gil stopped chewing and looked so guilty that Danny had to laugh. "You absent-minded nut, what were you thinking?"

"I'm sorry! I wasn't thinking at all. I forgot he couldn't see me."

Shaking his head, Danny motioned for Slim to sit down. "It's not as bad as you think."

"I d-don't know what to think," Slim stammered, sinking down on the grass.

Peering over at Gil, Danny softly hissed, "What do I do now?"

Gil grimaced and shrugged her shoulders.

Leaning close, he whispered, "You should've read the manuals! Am I gonna blow up the world if I tell?"

"Stop basing everything on movies," she whispered back. "The world won't explode, but Slim might think you're lying and start harassing you again." She groaned. "None of my classmates described this predicament, but then, they probably weren't stupid enough to eat in front of anyone."

"Don't worry about it," Danny said. He turned to Slim. "I'm gonna tell you the truth, but I don't expect you'll believe me."

Still staring at the spot where the barbeque sauce had disappeared, Slim mumbled, "I just might."

Sue sat down across from Rick with a cup of tea. Briefly closing her eyes, she prayed silently, *Dear Lord, somehow get me through this.*

"So that's what's going on," Danny said, after speaking for ten minutes straight.

"Are you on the level?" Slim asked. *"Time travel?"*

Danny nodded and watched as Gil threw caution to the wind and began dipping her energy bar into the barbeque sauce with wild abandon.

"If there's a girl from the future sitting beside you," Slim said, watching the moving dots of sauce with obvious awe, "have her do something to prove it."

"What do you want her to...?" Danny's voice trailed away as Gil jumped to her feet and tugged on Slim's sleeve.

With his arm dancing wildly in the air, Slim sputtered, "W-what's going on?"

"Cut it out, Gil!" Danny demanded. "You're freaking him out."

Slim began to laugh. "Actually, she isn't. This is awesome! I can't believe you have your own super-bionic chick from the future. Where do I get one?"

Punching Slim's shoulder, Danny said with a relieved grin, "So you believe me?"

"You bet, this is totally cool! It's better than anything I could imagine. It's even better than Jackie Chan." Slim laughed and pointed at the grass stems bending beneath Gil's weight as she sat down. "Hey, Danny, is this Gil-girl pretty?"

Smirking impishly, Danny chortled. "Compared to what?"

Danny saw Slim's eyes widen as a wad of grass was plucked up and tossed by an invisible hand. Picking the grass out of his hair, Danny said, "Yah, she's really pretty."

"What's she like?"

"You really want to know?"

"Sure—tell me everything."

"In that case, she hogs the bathroom, sings off-key, and couldn't find her nose if it wasn't fastened to her face. But other than that she's—" His words came to an abrupt halt as Gil lunged forward and tickled his ribs. "Uncle! Uncle! I take it back! You sing like an angel." As the tickling stopped, Danny gasped out, "But you *do* hog the bathroom!"

As another wad of grass was tossed, Slim peered at the mysterious patch of air and asked, "If I try, can I touch her?"

"Sure," Danny said, "but you can't see her, so you might poke her in the eye—how 'bout if she touches you? Hold out your hand."

As Slim held out his hand and Gil shook it firmly, Danny said, "Gil says she's pleased to meet you."

Licking his lips, Slim replied, "I'm glad to meet you too, Gil. Thanks for not kicking my butt more than you had to the other day." He turned to Danny. "This is unbelievable. I can feel her hand, but I can't see it. This is off the charts *wicked*. It's the biggest thing that's ever happened to me. Thanks for telling me. I promise I'll keep your secret."

"Friends then?"

"Friends? We're gonna be more than just friends. I ain't gonna ever leave your side."

∽つ

Sue watched with an anxious knot in her stomach as Rick used a roll to mop up the last of his red-eye gravy.

"What time shall I come over tonight?" he asked causally.

Nervously licking her lips, she looked over Rick's shoulder and focused on Sam's steady blue eyes.

"I asked you a question," Rick murmured with narrowed lids.

"Actually, you don't need to watch Danny anymore," she replied. "I've trespassed on your good nature for too long. You were kind to help me out of a pinch, and both Danny and I appreciate it, but it's time we stand on our own." As she spoke, she saw the pretense of friendliness fall from his face.

"I'm coming over tonight," he hissed. "I've earned that right."

His icy voice sent a chill racing down her spine. In spite of her fear, Sue looked him straight in the eye. "You haven't earned any rights that would give you free rein of my home. I think you have the wrong idea about us."

"Really? I asked you out to dinner last week."

"And I said no. My answer's still no. I never wanted to be in a romantic relationship with you. I believe I made that clear when you asked me out."

Rick's eyes turned into molten pools of fury. "Does this have anything to do with that pretty-boy preacher you were with last night?"

"What?" Sue's mind whirled, trying to figure out how he'd seen her with Sam.

"I asked you a question."

171

"This has nothing to do with him," Sue replied, shuddering at the naked hostility in Rick's eyes. "I never should've accepted your help."

"Why did you then?" A muscle jumped in his jaw. "Why did *Little Miss Perfect* let me watch her *brat* of a son?"

"Danny's not a brat. He's—"

"I want an answer!" Rick spat. "Why did you let me hang around if you weren't interested in me? Were you using me? Just stringing me along?"

Sue bit her lip. "I thought you wanted to help. I misread your intentions."

"Liar!" A torrent of profanity spewed from Rick's lips. "You knew what I wanted and used me as free daycare! Admit it!"

"I'm s-sorry." Sue stuttered. "I was in such a hard spot that I didn't think about your side. Can you forgive me?"

Rick slapped Sue's cheek. "Darlin', I don't forgive. I get even."

Behind Rick's back, Sue saw Sam leaping to his feet. As she shook her head at him, Sam reluctantly sat back down. Even though he'd obeyed her request, Sue could see anger blazing in his eyes. She knew the situation was about to explode.

"Baby doll," Rick murmured, grabbing her wrist and squeezing it painfully, "I'm gonna rain a whole heap of trouble down on you, and on your boy, and on that preacher. *No one* makes a fool outta me."

Sue shivered at the sight of Rick's face. It was so contorted with malice that it barely looked human. As he squeezed her wrist even tighter, tears welled in her eyes. She lowered her lids to keep Sam from seeing her tears and coming over regardless of her wishes.

Rick's mouth twisted into a cruel smile. After a moment, he released her wrist and slowly drew an X on her forehead with his finger.

172

"What are you doing?" she asked in an unsteady voice.

"X marks the spot," he replied in an eerie tone that was more frightening than his anger. "I'll be seeing you *real* soon. You can count on that."

As Rick threw some money on the table and left the diner, Sue stood on trembling legs. She took one step toward Sam and wobbled. As her vision blurred with tears, she saw Sam leaping to his feet and pushing past a table full of his parishioners. She watched as he ignored their greetings and grabbed for her hands. As she winced, Sam looked down and saw her bruises.

"Oh, Sue," he murmured, gently stroking her injured wrist, "why didn't you let me come? One glance from you, and I would've knocked him flat."

"He was looking for a fight. It would've made things worse—at least, I think it would've."

"Are you okay?"

"No," she admitted in a shaky voice. "Danny was right. Rick wants to hurt us—and you too. I don't know how, but he saw us together last night." Her voice broke as she said softly, "I'm frightened."

"Shh," he whispered, taking her gently into his arms. "God as my witness, I won't let anything happen to you or Danny."

Rick glanced over his shoulder at the diner's windows and saw Sue in Sam's arms. A guttural noise of pure rage ripped from his throat. Swinging around, he punched the side of his pickup with such force that he split his knuckles and left a deep dent in the metal.

TWENTY SIX

TAKING A BITE of pretzel, Ryan looked over at Crystal and asked, "So what are your plans for the summer? Doing anything fun?"

Crystal nodded. "In July, I'm visiting my grandparents in Massachusetts."

Ryan gave her a sideways glance. "What are you doing until then?"

She shrugged a shoulder. "Staying in D.C."

"Sounds boring. Why don't you fly to California with me?"

Crystal's jaw dropped. "Are you s-serious?"

He nodded and took another bite. "My parents are hosting a week-long family reunion. Having you along will help me get through it."

"Would there be room for me?"

"Sure. I'm gonna be camping in the backyard along with a host of cousins I hardly remember. I'll pull a few strings and make sure you get my old bedroom, but you may have to share it with a few of my great-aunts."

"I wouldn't mind the roommates, but I'd hate to horn in on a family gathering."

"Believe me, you'd be doing me a favor. If you come, I'll have an excuse to get out of some of the obligatory 'family togetherness.' We'll sneak away, and I'll show you the sights." He smiled and took a sip of iced tea. "I'll teach you how to surf."

"That'd be an absolute blast!"

"So you'll come?"

Crystal's grin wavered and fell. "I'd love to, but I can't. My apartment lease is up soon, and I don't want to renew it."

"I thought you liked your place?"

"I like the location but not the paper-thin walls. If I'm gonna survive senior year, I need to find a quieter apartment—preferably one not associated with student housing. But that's gonna be easier said than done."

"Having trouble finding a place that'll accept pets?"

Crystal gave an unhappy sigh. "I'm not taking my pets with me. As far as animal adoption, I've been out of control."

"I don't see how. You only have two cats and a dog."

"Five cats, three dogs, four birds, twenty-one fish, six hamsters, a rabbit, two ferrets, and an overweight gerbil."

Ryan gave a shout of laughter. "What happened?"

She shrugged. "I'm just a soft touch. When an animal needs a home, I can't say no."

Ryan ripped a piece off his pretzel and popped it in his mouth. "I'll admit your number of pets is unorthodox, but if you're enjoying them, I don't see the problem."

"That's because you don't know my landlord. I've been living in dread every time the doorbell rings for fear he's found me out. It's ripping my heart to give my animals away, but I'm starting to feel like Noah."

"You'll never be able to live pet-free. You'll see an abandoned kitten meowing pitifully in a puddle, and you'll melt and take it home."

"I will not!"

As Ryan quirked a doubtful eyebrow at her, he saw her lips twitch.

"Well, maybe I would," she admitted. "That's why I'm renting an apartment that won't allow pets. It'll be easier to be self-controlled if I don't have a choice in the matter." Ryan watched as she gave him a calculating glance. "*You know*...statistically, people who own pets live longer."

He grinned. "The way you've been going, you'll beat Methuselah."

"True," Crystal gurgled. "But now that I've discovered the secret to longevity, I'd *love* to share the health benefits. Would you like to adopt a deaf kitty who loves to chase yarn balls, or a feisty Chihuahua with a limp, or a rascally ferret who enjoys getting into the toilet paper, or a big fat gerbil named Tom-Tom, or a—?"

"My apartment won't accept pets," Ryan interrupted with a laugh.

"Convenient excuse."

"It sure is, and it's the same excuse you're trying to get for yourself."

"Only temporarily, and only until my willpower has a chance to recharge." She gave a fierce frown. "I'm out of control, and I *can't stand* to be out of control in *any* area of my life."

Hearing the harsh note in her voice, he laid a gentle hand on her arm. "Give yourself some slack. I think you're pretty terrific just the way you are."

Crystal blinked at him through her owlish glasses. "You do? Really?" As he smiled and nodded, she said, "That's *awfully* nice of you to say. I hoped to find a few friends when I came to D.C., but I never expected to find a brother."

Ryan gave her a startled glance. "B-brother?"

She nodded. "You and Zeke are the big brothers I've always wanted but never had. Thanks for being such a nice friend."

Turning away, Ryan stared at the cars in the parking lot and took a slow, painful breath. "You think we're friends?"

"Of course I do! Don't you?"

Hearing the puzzled note in her voice, Ryan flashed her a smile. "Sure I do. Good friends."

Gil put her hand on Danny's arm. "It's after 1:00. I need to find out what TEMCO's learned about Rick."

"Sure, Gil," Danny replied.

"What'd she say?" Slim asked.

"She's gonna go talk to the folks in the future."

Slim whistled. "This is *so* unreal!"

Keeping her hand on Danny's arm, Gil said firmly, "I'll plan on being back before school's over, but if things with TEMCO take longer than expected, go straight to Mr. Jacobson's—don't set a single toenail inside your house."

"What about Mom?"

"Sam's looking out for her, and I'm looking out for you. Remember, it's D-day. Let's be smart about it. There's no way you and Rick can fight in your kitchen if you're not even in your house. Go straight to Mr. Jacobson's, you hear?"

"Loud and clear."

"What's she saying?" Slim asked.

"She's giving me instructions about after school. Actually, she's shouting them. You're lucky you can't hear her. You'd be going deaf."

"Wisecracker," Gil said affectionately, tousling his hair. "Have fun in PE. I'll try to be back before science is over, okay?"

"Sure, see you later. Come on, Slim. Let's hotfoot it before bionic-chick goes ballistic!"

As the boys waved and ran toward the school, Gil smiled affectionately after them. They were going to be quite a pair. A dynamic duo indeed—

Gil's happy musings came to an end as her stomach grumbled loudly. She grimaced. She had to get something to eat besides those blasted kitty-litter bars. Hoping to raid the Winston's refrigerator before contacting the lab, she walked quickly to Danny's house. When she arrived and saw the wealth of goodies in the kitchen's "magic box," she began singing an off-key rendition of *Food! Glorious Food!*

Ryan watched as Crystal nibbled her pretzel. After a moment of silence, he said, "Since you and I are such good *friends* would you mind if I gave you some *brotherly* advice?"

"Not at all."

"You need to come to Bible study again."

Crystal jolted, her elbow knocking over a saltshaker. "I can't."

"Why not?" he asked, bending over to retrieve the shaker.

"If you don't know," she mumbled with red cheeks, "you can guess."

"Even if Marc's there, you can still come."

"I'd end up making an idiot of myself. Marc doesn't know I exist, and it's better that way. I'd never have a shot with him anyway."

"Can't you just forget him?"

"Believe me, I'm trying."

"Try harder," he grumbled. "I miss you."

Crystal gave a spurt of laughter. "You see me practically every day."

"It's not the same. After summer vacation, will you come to Bible study again?"

"I will if I can get Marc out of my system. I can't avoid him during class, but I don't have to spend my free time with him."

Ryan stared out the window at the sunlight sparkling on the car windshields in the parking lot. He felt like punching Marc or punching himself for inviting Marc to Bible study in the first place. The whole situation smacked of some grotesque Shakespearean love triangle, and he was sick of it.

As if reading his thoughts, Crystal grimaced. "Don't you *dare* call me Titania."

Ryan's lips twitched. "But, Cris, Marc's the personification of Bottom the weaver."

"I know! Donkey's head and all!" Rolling her eyes, she grumbled, "And me '*enamored*' with him. I'll tell you one thing though, I'm not about to '*pluck the wings from painted butterflies to fan the moonbeams from his sleeping eyes.*'"

"*Midsummer Night's Dream*. Act III. Scene I."

"See," Crystal groaned, "you and I are in sync. Why couldn't I have a crush on you?"

Ryan's laughter froze. "I don't know. Why couldn't you?"

"Probably because I'm a simple-minded idiot with no taste at all." She smiled at him and finished her pretzel. "Well, if I'm Titania and Marc's Bottom, who are you? Oberon?"

Ryan's heart twisted, but he knew she wasn't being deliberately cruel. He cleared his throat. "I've never thought of myself as the matchmaking King of the Fairies type. I think I'd better settle for a role like Puck."

Crystal gave a gurgle of laughter. "You're way too tall to be a wood imp." Her eyes twinkled. "However, there is something a bit *puckish* about you at times."

Ryan struck a pose. "'*Thou speakest aright; I am that merry wanderer of the night!*'"

"*Midsummer Night's Dream.* Act II. Scene I."

"Exactamundo. How about splitting another pretzel, *cankerblossom*? My treat. I'm still starving."

She twinkled at him. "And if I say no?"

He laughed. "Then you'd better hope your legs are as long as Helena's, so you can run away before I pick you up and carry you. After refusing to go to California, the least you can do is walk to Phil's Pretzel Stand."

"Lead the way. Another pretzel sounds absolutely fab-u-lous. Of course," she said ruefully, "I'm gonna have to run it off on the treadmill."

As they stood to their feet, Crystal stared at the distant silhouette of Hawking Hall. Seeing her worried frown, Ryan asked, "Wondering about Gil?"

She nodded. "I hope she's okay."

For a moment, they stared in silence at Hawking Hall. When they turned to go into Student Union, Ryan asked, "Did you sign-up to help with summer shutdown?"

"You bet I did," Crystal replied. "I hope I'm able to work with the techs backing up GAP's memory core. I think I'll die if I get assigned some boring old job like collating files. Do you think the lockdown will be over by then?"

"I hope so. If it isn't, there's more going on than either of us realize." Giving her a smile, he asked a bit awkwardly, "After the pretzel, how about a movie?"

"I can't," she replied, staring at Hawking Hall. "I have some things to do this afternoon."

Sam stayed in his booth for the rest of Sue's shift. Rick's threats had shaken her, and he couldn't imagine leaving her. In fact, he hardly took his eyes off her—guarding her with an intensity that left him feeling surprised. When Sue's shift was finally over, he watched as she sat down next to him and gave him a smile that trembled around the edges.

"Did the hospital call?" he gently asked. "If you have to work, I'll go with you."

"What about Danny?"

"I phoned Nathan. He'll be at your house to watch him. So how about it? Are we headed to the hospital?"

"They never called," she replied. "But if they had, you could've sat by my desk." She gave him a shaky smile and teased, "It's by the coffee maker which would've come in handy."

"Have some pity and don't mention the 'C' word," he said with an exaggerated groan. "I don't know how many cups of coffee I drank today—I lost count—but I never want to look a coffee bean in the eye again."

"Beans have eyes? Are they blue or brown?"

"Neither." Sam grinned. "They're amber-speckled green."

"If you were Danny, I'd say you had a big imagination."

Sam's blue eyes filled with tenderness. He knew she was frightened, but she was doing her best to keep things light. With a gentle hand, he brushed a tumbled lock of golden hair away from her face. "Rick won't get to you, you know," he said in a calm, serious voice. "You or Danny. He'll have to go through me first."

"I know," she whispered. "That's what I'm afraid of."

TWENTY SEVEN

GIL GAVE A satisfied sigh, basking in the afterglow of a good meal. After putting away her last dish, she went to Danny's room and took *Extreme Exam* out of her backpack. As she sat down in front of the TV, she felt her jeans digging into her stomach.

Groaning a bit, she undid the top button and pulled her shirt down to hide the gapping waistband. Taking a third helping of spaghetti had been a big mistake. She was in danger of bursting the seams of her blue jeans, and the prospect wasn't pleasing. Seeing it was 1:30 on the dot, she slid the game into the PlayFest console and tried to avoid looking like she'd eaten a week's worth of calories in one sitting.

As a blue glow filled the bedroom, she looked through the portal at William and Director Matthews. Her heart missed a beat. She didn't know what was going on, but judging by the men's tense expressions, it wasn't good.

"Hi, guys, what's up?" she asked in a deliberately casual tone.

"We're thinking of pulling you from the field," William replied.

"What?"

"Rick's more dangerous than we thought."

"I don't care if he's Jack the Ripper," she said flatly. "I'm staying."

Director Matthews picked up a handful of printouts. "He isn't Jack the Ripper, but he might as well be. I've found evidence that he's killed at least ten women."

"I don't care."

"You're facing a serial killer," William said. "You must realize the seriousness of the situation."

"I *do* realize it. You don't. Today's Danny's D-day. If I abandon him, he's gonna die on death row. I love that kid, and I'm not about to let his life be destroyed. Where's Dr. Nelson? She'd agree with me."

"She said it was our decision," the director replied.

"It's my decision too, and I'm not about to abandon—"

"It's not abandonment," William interrupted. "GAP's only predicting a fifty percent chance that it'll make a difference to Danny's future if you stay. Regardless of your hard work, Daniel Winston may be destined for death row. We're not risking your life over a hopeless—"

"There's *no way* you're getting me out of here! If there's a fifty percent chance that Danny can be saved, I'm taking that fifty percent chance. It's my life I'm risking. Not yours."

William ran a hand over his face. "We're all risking a lot."

"I don't care. I'm not—"

"Enough of this!" William said harshly. "Let the director speak. When he finishes, we'll discuss things."

"If that's how you want it," Gil said with lightly veiled hostility.

"That's how it's going to be. Tell her the facts, Peter."

"Here it is, Gil," the director said. "Bald facts. Fact number one: Rick's a serial killer. He strangles women with a red cord and hangs their bodies to mimic suicide. He does his murderous work so well, that unless a coroner's an expert, the homicide is missed. At this time, it's impossible to know how many murders Rick's committed.

"Fact two: Rick's meticulous and methodical—that means he's dangerous. He's undoubtedly been planning to kill Sue for weeks. He'll already have things set in motion.

"Fact three: GAP's predicting a 98.8 percent chance that if you stay, you *will* be hurt. Since Danny has only a fifty percent chance of escaping death row, you'll be risking your life on a gamble."

Gil sat quietly for a few moments. "I've heard what you've said and understood it. Will you respect my decision?"

"Yes," William replied. "It's your decision to make."

"Then my answer's the same as it was from the beginning. I'm staying. Now, give me all the information you can about what I'm facing, and please do it fast. I don't have much time, and I need all the help I can get."

Outside Stubby's diner, Sam gave Sue's pale face a searching glance. He knew the confrontation with Rick had taken a toll. "Where's your car parked?" he asked softly. "I'll follow you home."

"I don't have a car."

He blinked in surprise. "You walk to work? It's over two miles to your house."

"That's not far. Walking keeps me in shape."

"Well, you're not walking today."

Gently taking her elbow, Sam steered her toward his car. Thinking of the snowstorm they'd had a few weeks ago, he winced. He hated to think of the battle she must've fought with icy sidewalks. He wondered if he'd ever driven past her—unaware of her need. The thought made him feel sick inside.

As he started his car and pulled away from the curb, he asked, "How do you get to the hospital? It's seven miles away. Surely you don't walk that far?"

"Of course not, I take the bus."

Sam's jaw tightened. *The bus stop is a three-mile walk from her house.*

"Don't worry," she said in a plucky voice, "the walk's not bad."

He shook his head. "It's not safe either. You've been walking alone—at times, close to midnight. That's *way* too far and *way* too dangerous."

"I haven't had much choice," she replied. "I meant to buy a used car when I came to Charlesberg, but the move was more expensive than I anticipated and my refrigerator didn't survive the trip. When things didn't pan out at the hospital, I couldn't cover all my bases. But honestly, it doesn't matter. I've almost saved enough money to buy a bicycle and then I'll ride to Stubby's and the bus stop in style. Besides, as long as it's not snowing, I enjoy the walk."

Sam stopped at a red light and said grimly, "Winter's just around the corner, and walking alone isn't safe for you, especially right now. Grandpop has an old Plymouth he'd be happy to lend you. I'll tune it up this weekend."

"Thank you, but I can't accept your offer. I don't have a driver's license."

"You let it lapse? That's all right, we'll get it renewed."

"No, Sam, I've never had one. I was planning to take a driver's education class when I moved here, but there wasn't any point when I couldn't afford a car."

Silence stretched before Sue answered the question he was too polite to ask. "I suppose it seems strange that I don't have a license, but when my father left my mother, he took the car. Our money never stretched enough to buy another, and later when Bill and I married, the same was true. Getting a driver's license just wasn't a priority." She sighed. "I suppose with my transportation issues, I should've found a house closer to the hospital, but I wanted Danny to grow up next to the woods. I loved wandering around the forest when I was his age."

Sam suddenly pulled into a deserted parking lot. Without a word, he got out and walked to Sue's side of the car. When he opened her door, she looked at him in surprise.

"Scoot over," he said in a firm voice.

Sue blinked. "What?"

"Scoot over. We have some time before Danny gets home, and you're getting your first driving lesson."

Sue blinked again and chuckled. "Don't I need a learner's permit first? Are you getting ready to break the law, Pastor?"

"I sure am. Scooch."

As Sue slid behind the wheel, Sam sat beside her and asked, "Have you driven before?"

"Does a bumper car count? I *ruled* at bumper cars when I was a kid."

Sam's blue eyes danced. "The concept's a tad different. On the road, one tries to *avoid* cars—not run into them."

"But what's the fun in that?"

Gil watched through the portal as Director Matthews picked up a stack of files and enclosed them in an expandable folder. "Gil, get ready to play catch," he said. "I'm sending you information about Rick's homicides."

"What kind of information?" she asked.

"Crime-scene photographs, case notes, and DNA evidence collected from the bodies of Rick's victims. I've also enclosed a copy of Rick's fingerprints and DNA profile. They can be matched against the serial killer's. Are you ready?"

As Gil nodded, the director tossed the bundle through the portal. The folder slipped through her fingers and hit the floor with a solid thunk. "Sorry," she said. "What's next?"

"I'm sending back the beer bottle. The police can use it for additional testing."

"I hope I don't drop it."

"Me too..." Gil watched as the director passed the bagged bottle to William. "You throw it. You have the better arm."

William nodded and gently tossed the bag to Gil. When she caught it easily, she crowed, "Maybe I'd better go out for baseball too!"

"Say the word," William smiled, "and I'll sign you up for TEMCO's softball team."

The director cleared his throat. "Gil, tell Danny to give the evidence to Nathan."

"But shouldn't he give it to a Charlesberg police officer?" she asked.

Director Matthews shook his head. "Nathan's Westfield Precinct has an impeccable reputation. The Charlesberg Precinct is negligent and corrupt. The evidence *must* get into the right hands."

"But how will Nathan be able to see the files? After all, they're coming through a temporal portal like I did."

Gil watched as Director Matthews peered at William with a raised eyebrow.

"Tell her," William said. "She can be trusted."

The director turned to Gil. "The inventor of GAP has been working on a top secret device that will enable people in the past to see an object from the future without being subjected to temporal scans. Considering the circumstances, a verbal go-ahead has been given to use the technology on the files. This will be the prototype's first field test."

"You actually spoke to the Wonderful Wizard?"

"Pardon me?"

"That's what the cadets call the inventor of GAP—the Wonderful Wizard of Oz, because he's in charge, but none of us has seen him. We have a betting pool about his identity." Gil smirked. "And I'm gonna win it!"

"Oh?"

"Yep, it's Dr. Moosly. He's a dead ringer for an eccentric inventor."

"You may be right, and you may be wrong," the director said, "but now's not the time to get into a guessing game. It's enough for you to know that the inventor wishes to remain anonymous, but is willing to help. Now, do you have any more questions about the files?"

"How should I transport them?" she asked. "If I put them beneath my sweater, will they be hidden to the people on the street?"

"You didn't read the manuals, did you?"

Gil lapsed into shamed silence.

"Anything wrapped in your clothing will be as invisible as you are."

Feeling relieved that she hadn't received a lecture, Gil quickly changed the subject. "Can you tell me anything else about Rick?"

The director nodded. "Autopsy photographs show he's careful not to leave bruises on his victims' bodies. When he strikes, he strikes fast. There won't be a long struggle when he attacks Sue today. You won't have much time to save her."

"What else?"

"It takes several days for the bodies of Rick's victims to be discovered."

"Why's that important?" she asked.

"Because his victims lived in small towns where domestic disturbances are usually reported. No one hears his attacks. He takes his victims by surprise and prevents them from screaming."

"That's bad, isn't it?"

"Extremely. The lack of crime-scene evidence shows he's a planner. He probably has things hidden or set up around Sue's house to expedite his attack."

Exhaling slowly to calm her nerves, Gil asked, "Anything else I should know?"

The director looked grim. "I've tried to find instances in which women have escaped a red-cord strangler, but there aren't any. If Rick gets his hands on Sue—or on you—the chances are high the outcome won't be favorable."

Gil swallowed the lump in her throat. "What about Danny? How do I increase his odds of escaping death row?"

"All I can suggest is keeping him out of his house and away from knives. I'm afraid I can't be more helpful. Events are changing on a second-by-second basis, and GAP's acting so erratic that if it were a person, I'd say it was experiencing a psychotic break. Danny's fate may rest on a split-second decision, and I don't want to lie to you—from what GAP's telling me, that decision may cost you your life."

Looking down at her hands, Gil said hesitantly, "If I don't go through with this—if I come home now—what will happen to everyone?"

"Danny will end up on death row, Sue will be murdered, and there's a 99.2 percent chance that Sam will vanish, and years later, his skeleton will be found in the forest behind Sue's house."

"That's what I was afraid of."

"Technically," the director said, "Sam and the Winstons met their fate almost a quarter of a century ago. There's no shame in coming home. In fact, I think it's highly advisable."

"Maybe so," Gil said quietly, "but I'm staying here regardless."

"I can't change your mind?" As Gil gave an adamant shake of her head, the director said, "In that case, Godspeed and good luck. I'll be praying for you this afternoon. And for what it's worth, if you succeed, you won't have to worry about journals or review boards, you'll have your Time-Counselor License."

"Really?"

The director smiled. "Absolutely. And, Gil, it'll be a Class-One Alpha-Blue License. If you make it through this, you'll have a position on staff."

Sam peeled himself off the dashboard and sat back down next to Sue. "That was a good stop, but next time, don't press the brake so hard. If you ease into a stop, you won't feel a jolt."

Sue nodded. Her brow was furrowed, and she was biting her bottom lip in concentration. Sam smiled at the sight. She looked *incredibly* cute.

"Let's try it again," he said patiently. "Drive in a circle around the light poles and park by that dumpster over there. Ready?"

She nodded.

"Slowly step on the gas," he instructed.

The car lurched forward.

"See that light pole? Go around it. That's right...you're doing great."

"Am I going too fast?" Sue asked anxiously.

Sam swallowed a chuckle. She was going three miles per hour. "Your speed's fine. When you get comfortable you can increase it...okay, you're getting close to the dumpster. Gradually start to slow—"

Sue tromped on the brake and Sam ended up glued to the dashboard again. "That was better. Still a little hard, but you're doing fine."

"Liar," she groaned. "If I was doing fine, you wouldn't look like a bug squashed on the windshield." As Sam settled into his seat, she chided, "You need to wear your seatbelt."

He shook his head. "I want to be able to grab the wheel if I need to. Besides, we aren't going fast enough to be dangerous."

"It feels like we're going eighty miles an hour."

"Trust me, it's more like five. You'll get used to it. You have natural aptitude."

"Really? How many people have you taught?"

"Counting you?" he asked.

She nodded.

"One."

Sue looked at him and began to laugh. As Sam smiled, he grabbed a flashlight out of the glove box and set it on the floor behind her heel.

"What's that for?" she asked curiously.

"It'll help you judge your stops. If you stop too fast, the flashlight will hit your heel. If you stop gradually, it'll stay in place. Now, let's try again. Circle the parking lot and park by that brick wall."

Sam watched as Sue anxiously bit her lip and swung the car around in a wide circle. "You've mastered the art of steering," he said encouragingly. "Your form couldn't be better."

"Really?"

"You bet. You're the best pupil I've had today. Okay, get ready to stop—slowly."

Sue nodded and gently stepped on the brake. As she approached the brick wall, the car slid to a controlled, perfect stop. The flashlight stayed in place—so did Sam.

"See?" he said jubilantly. "What'd I tell you? Natural aptitude!"

"I think I'm getting the hang of this."

"I knew you would."

Sue smiled and took her foot off the brake. Immediately, the car lurched forward and hit the brick wall with a thud. Sam chuckled as Sue looked over at him in guilty disbelief.

"What'd I do?" she gasped.

His lips twitched. "You forgot to put it in park."

"What do I do now?" she asked in a nervous voice.

"Put it in reverse and go around the parking lot again. This time, park next to that tree."

"But your car...did I break it?"

"You only gave it a love tap. That's what bumpers are for. It's about time I got my money out of mine. Come on, Sue, let's try it again."

Gil jumped as the GAP computer began to beep. "I have to go," the director said hastily. "That's information about red-cord related suicides."

As the director moved out of earshot, Gil looked through the portal at William. Seeing his tense posture, she said softly, "You've been awfully quiet. What are you thinking?"

William brushed a shaking hand over his face. "That I'm proud of you, but I'm terrified for you. I wish I knew if you're putting yourself in danger for nothing."

"It's my decision," she said gently. "You have nothing to do with it."

"I have more to do with it than you realize."

"You may've recommended me for this assignment, but it was my decision to come—just as it's my decision to stay. If I went home now, I'd never forgive myself."

"I know, but please be careful. I've arranged for a portal to be fixed to your temporal position. If things get out of control, you can use *Extreme Exam* to surf home without waiting for lab authorization."

"I didn't know GAP could do that," she said.

"There's much you don't know. If you're in danger, don't hesitate—just come home!"

"You sound like you're anxious to see me."

"I am," he replied, giving her a crooked smile. "But until then, stay invisible and don't play with knives."

"Fair enough." She laughed.

"Contact us at the usual time—sooner if needed. We'll be in the lab until D-day's over."

Hearing the concern in his voice, Gil said softly, "Oh, Doc, everything's gonna be fine. God hasn't brought us this far to drop us. He—" Her voice came to an abrupt halt.

"What's wrong?" William demanded.

"I don't know," she whispered. "Did you hear that noise?" Her body tensed as she stared at the bedroom door. "There it is again...I gotta go. Someone's in the house."

With a swift movement, Gil stopped *Extreme Exam* and flattened herself against the wall.

TWENTY EIGHT

WILLIAM STARED ANXIOUSLY at the Staging Platform. Since the connection between the lab and Charlesberg was still viable, Gil had obviously forgotten to turn off power to the gaming console. He knew the connection would fade quickly, but at least in a tentative way he was still with her. Suddenly, he heard a sharp sound coming from beyond Danny's bedroom, and as he did, the blue light surrounding the Staging Platform began to dissipate.

As the timewave swirled and vanished, Director Matthews put a hand on his shoulder. "We knew it would come down to Gil's decision, and her decision alone. There's still a fifty-fifty chance, and that's worth fighting for."

William took a shuddering breath. "I keep thinking there's something we overlooked—some other way to handle things. The risk to Gil is too great. I should've brought her home."

"She wouldn't have come."

"Then I should've gone in after her!"

The director shook his head. "GAP's indicated with one hundred percent certainty that if you involve yourself in D-day, Danny will die by lethal injection and Gil will die at Rick's hands."

Beads of sweat rolled down Gil's forehead as her heart hammered in her chest. Knowing she should discover where the sounds were coming from, she tiptoed to Danny's doorway. As she cautiously peeped around the corner, she saw Sue and Sam talking in the entryway. Gil sagged against the wall in relief.

Sue smiled at Sam and tossed her purse on the couch. "I can't believe we survived."

"Don't sell yourself short," Sam replied, twirling his car keys. "You did great. When I drive you to work tomorrow, we'll get your learner's permit and a manual."

"Is the written test hard?" she asked.

"Not if you study. Don't worry, I'll help you prepare. You'll ace it."

"What about the driving part of the exam?"

"That's a different kettle of fish, but you'll do fine. All you need is practice. After your shift tomorrow, we'll drive some country roads—you've graduated from parking lots."

"Even though I dented your bumper and scratched your paint job?"

Sam's eyes twinkled. "A few dents and scratches just give a car character."

"I still say that light pole moved," she groaned.

"It's possible. I've heard poles can sprout legs. But cheer up, tomorrow you won't have to face light poles, just cows."

"I hope I don't flatten one."

"I wouldn't worry about it." He grinned, putting his keys in his pocket. "At the speeds you travel, even a blind, arthritic cow should have plenty of time to meander out of your way. And if it doesn't, it's dumb enough to deserve to be road kill." As Sue gave a bubbling spurt of laughter, Sam asked, "What time should I pick you up tomorrow?"

"7:30, but you really don't have to drive me to work."

"Yes, I do. *Safety first* is our new motto. Speaking of which, now that you're sure the coffee pot's off are you ready to go to Grandpop's?"

"Can I have a minute to freshen up?" she asked, fingering her messy braid.

"Of course," he replied. "But let me search the house first. I don't want you out of my sight unless I know you're safe."

"If the house is getting searched, we're doing it together," she said firmly, opening the hall closet and handing Sam a baseball bat. "I'm not letting you face danger alone."

"Plucky, aren't you," he asked with a smile.

Sue curtsied and shouldered a broom. "When's Nathan arriving?"

"Any moment. When he and Zara get here, we'll discuss restraining orders and other steps we can take to keep you and Danny safe."

Sue nodded. Together, they went through the house, making sure the doors and windows were secure. Side-by-side, they looked behind the furniture, under the beds, and in the closets.

"No one here but us," Sue said in relief. Walking past the hall mirror and seeing their reflection, she laughed. "How ridiculous we look!"

Sam grinned and flourished the bat. "Regardless, I'm glad we did it. I'll go outside and patrol the grounds while you freshen up. Don't take too long. I'll be lurking on the curb, and I'm liable to be picked up for loitering if you go all typical female on me."

"Don't worry." She laughed. "I'll hurry."

Sue felt her heart race as Sam brushed her fingertips and picked up her phone.

"I'll make my cell number speed dial one, so you can reach me at a moment's notice," he said. "If you need me, call."

As she watched him programming her phone, her eyes clouded. "All right."

"Hey, what's wrong?" Sam asked softly.

Sue hesitated and raised her eyes to his. "Why are you being so helpful?"

"What do you mean?" he asked, looking startled.

"I appreciate everything you're doing, but you're going way beyond the call of duty—even pastoral duty. I got into this mess because I didn't question Rick's motives. I don't want to make the same mistake again."

Sue watched as Sam began to blush. "For now," he said, "why don't we chalk it up to Christian charity?"

She shook her head. "I don't believe Christianity has anything to do with it."

His blush became even more pronounced. "That's funny, neither do I."

"Why, then?"

"I think we both know why," he said softly, "even though it's too soon to put it into words. Trust me, my intentions toward you are pure."

Sue's face turned rosy pink. "I'm sorry I questioned you, but I had to know."

"No problem," he replied, "but turnabout's fair play. Are you only spending time with me because you're afraid of Rick?"

Silence fell.

Sue felt her blush deepen as Sam coaxed softly, "Come on, Sue. Tell me why."

Looking up at him from beneath her long lashes, she gave him a glance that was both shy and teasing. "How else am I gonna learn how to drive a car?"

Sam roared with laughter. "I hope it isn't just my driving ability you're enjoying."

"I also like beating you at dominoes."

"How about my company?" he asked. "Do you like that too?"

She grinned and tipped her head to one side. "Well, maybe just a *little*."

"Glad to hear it." After a moment's hesitation, Sam gently put his arms around her and pulled her into a tender hug.

Laying her cheek against his chest, Sue sighed. "I really should get ready."

"Don't get too gussied up—if you get any prettier, you'll have an unfair advantage at dominoes. That blue blouse you had on last night made you look so lovely I had a hard time keeping my mind on the game. Give a guy a decent break and put on a potato sack, will you?"

As Sam held her close, Sue's heart began to flutter. She held her breath as he gently kissed her forehead and murmured against her hair, "Not that a potato sack would make any difference. You'd be a beautiful distraction no matter what you put on."

Sue tried to speak, but couldn't manage it. As Sam smiled at her, she was captured by the gentleness of his eyes. When she was growing up, her mother told her to be on the lookout for people with Jesus eyes—people whose kindness, compassion, and decency could be seen through the windows of their soul.

Sam has Jesus eyes, Sue thought in amazement. *He really does.*

Stepping back a pace, Sam cleared his throat. "I'll see you in fifteen minutes, all right? Fifteen minutes, or I'm coming in after you. I want you safe at Grandpop's." As she nodded, Sam stepped onto the porch. "Lock the door behind me, and call if anything worries you."

"I'll be fine," she murmured, flashing him a smile and closing the door.

Sue put her eye to the peephole and watched as Sam walked to the curb and scrutinized the street. She smiled.

He looks awfully handsome.

For a moment, she allowed herself the luxury of reliving the memory of his lips on her forehead. Her heart fluttered and beat faster. The last thing she'd expected to find in Charlesberg was love. Truth be told, she hadn't looked at a man in a romantic way since her husband died. It felt strange to be looking now, but she couldn't seem to help herself.

She wondered what Bill would say about the situation. Suddenly, she smiled—she knew exactly what he would say. He'd tell her to go for it. Kicking off her shoes, she began singing *Some Enchanted Evening* as she strolled to her bedroom.

As Sue passed Danny's doorway, Gil smiled at the woman's obvious happiness. Knowing that at the moment everything was under control, Gil went to Danny's hideout to examine the files. The first file she grabbed covered the homicide of a woman named Jenny Lou Parklyn. Gil quickly flipped past the crime-scene photos, but then she turned back to them, studying the pictures despite her squeamishness.

Sue pulled bobby pins out of her hair and tossed them in a tumbled heap on her dresser. Singing little snatches of song, she opened her closet and thumbed through the hangers. She paused when she saw a lovely purple dress. She knew if Sam thought she was pretty in blue, she'd knock his socks off in purple. She contemplated the dress. It was made of light, airy material that was ultra-feminine, but casual enough to be appropriate for a neighborly visit. Other than her hideous uniform, she hadn't worn a dress in years and the only reason she'd do so now would be to catch Sam's attention. She hesitated, smiled, and then hung the selected dress in her doorway. Singing cheerfully, she went to her bathroom to touch up her makeup. Fifteen minutes wasn't much time to get ready to dazzle a man, but she thought she could manage it.

As Sue vanished into the bathroom, the bush outside her window began to quake. The branches parted, and Rick's face appeared behind the glass. He stood for a moment, staring into Sue's bedroom, and then he expertly inserted a knife between the window and sash. Quietly and patiently, he worked with the blade until he was able to open the lock. At his touch, the well-oiled window slid up with barely a sound. Listening to Sue's singing, he drew on black leather gloves—he'd learned from experience that women, just like cats, liked to scratch…

TWENTY NINE

FEELING NERVOUS ABOUT the possibility of being caught, Crystal walked "nonchalantly" across campus. She was going crazy with curiosity and worry, and she was sure it wouldn't hurt anything to snoop a bit. Taking a deep breath, she pulled open the door to Hawking Hall.

NSU's Genetic Research Division occupied the ground floor of the building, and as usual, it was full of activity. Mingling with the crowd, Crystal made her way to the marble staircase leading to TEMCO's Center of Operations.

Seeing that the stairs were empty, a feeling of intruding washed over her. That feeling intensified when she reached the second floor and saw a heavy metal door blocking her way. She knew TEMCO was capable of high-security lockdown, but she hadn't envisioned vault doors and retinal scanners as being part of the process. She descended the stairs with a heavy sigh. Suddenly, a briefcase bounced past her.

"Blast and botheration!" Zeke's voice exploded.

Looking up, Crystal saw Zeke trying to descend the staircase carrying a teetering stack of papers, three laptops, a backpack, and a canvas bag. His thick-lensed glasses were sliding down his nose, and his hair was sticking up in unruly tufts. As she stared at him, his papers started to slide. He grabbed at them, almost dropped a laptop, and nearly pitched down the stairs.

"Hey, can I give you a hand?" she asked, running to his side.

"Cris, you're a sight for sore eyes. Grab the laptop, will you?"

Crystal nodded and took it from him as he stumbled down the steps.

"Thanks. Can you shove it under my arm and hand me my briefcase?"

"I'll do better than that," she said as he tried to readjust the pile of papers and ended up dropping the canvas bag. "I'll help you carry things. Where are you headed?"

"Student Union. The director asked me to substitute for him. I'm giving his *Computer Theory and Technology* class its final."

"How on earth are you gonna do that? That exam's taken on TEMCO computers."

"The dean gave us permission to use the supercomputer in the basement of Student Union. I'll link it to the GAP computer core. The sophomores won't be able to access the majority of GAP's files, but they'll be able to access enough of the computer to take their exam."

"Would you like some help setting things up?"

"That'd be great. Substituting wasn't on my radar today, and I feel totally unprepared."

"Glad to do it," she replied, taking his canvas bag and another laptop. "I didn't realize Student Union's supercomputer could be linked to the lab."

He flashed her a smile. "That's because it's never been done before."

"Stop walking a minute, will you?"

"What for?"

"Cosmetic imperative." Pushing Zeke's glasses back up on his nose, Crystal smoothed down his hair with her fingers. "You look like you ran through a bush backwards."

Zeke blinked. "I didn't realize."

"Your students would," she replied, straightening his collar and twitching his jacket into place.

"Thanks." He chuckled. "Better?"

Giving him a critical glance, she nodded. "Now you look like you ran through a bush *forwards*—it's a vast improvement."

As he laughed and shifted his papers, she asked in a deliberately casual tone, "By the way, can you tell me what's going on?"

"No."

"Oh," she replied in a deflated voice. "I don't have high enough clearance?"

"*I don't*. The second floor's open to Alpha-Blue, but the hallway leading to the lab is locked to almost everyone. I don't know what's happening any more than you do."

"I thought Alpha-Blue had full access."

"It does—mostly. I guess this is the exception to the rule. Only a handful of people really know what's going on, and I'm not one of them."

"Can't you tell me *anything*?"

"Only that whatever's happening is serious. When he talked with me just now, the director looked awful. I don't know what's taking place, but it's big."

As soon as he spoke, Zeke looked conscience-stricken. Seeing his troubled expression, Crystal pulled him to a stop. "Hey, what's wrong?"

"I shouldn't have said what I did."

"But you didn't say *anything*. I wish you'd talk with me." When Zeke didn't reply, she sputtered, "You can at least tell me what you're thinking, can't you?"

He paused for a moment. "I'm thinking that your curiosity's a good thing when it comes to scientific research, but in cases like this, it's a character flaw."

Feeling as if she'd been slapped, Crystal gasped and tried to decide if she was offended. Zeke was like her big brother, and she knew he'd never deliberately hurt her. If he saw a flaw in her, it was probably because it was there.

Hunching her shoulder, she asked slowly, "Do you really think so?"

He nodded. "I don't mean to be harsh, but TEMCO's locked down for a reason—a good reason. Even if we don't know what's going on, we can trust the people in charge to do what's best for the program—and for us."

"Just asking a few questions won't hurt anything."

"That's not true, at least not when it comes to our line of work. TEMCO deals with people's futures. It's not like we are researching butterflies or examining mold in a petri dish. If we mess up, people die. The people in charge don't need your interference. After all, some mysteries are mysteries for a reason."

"I think you'll do," Sue murmured to her reflection as she finished reapplying her lip liner. Blowing herself a kiss in the mirror, she went to her bedroom and slipped her dress off its hanger. She couldn't wait for Sam to see her in purple.

"Hi, baby doll."

Hearing Rick's voice, Sue gasped and spun around. The dress fell from her hands as she lurched back toward the closet and asked in a frightened voice, "H-how did you get in here?"

"Through the window. I removed your screen weeks ago for an opportune time just like this." His eyes turned cold. "I saw that preacher of yours searching the yard. As a protector, he leaves a lot to be desired. He forgot to check all the bushes."

Sue backed up another step. "What do you want?"

"What do you think?"

She watched with frightened eyes as Rick slowly—like a snake uncoiling—moved away from the wall and took a long, red cord out of his pocket. As he twisted the cord around his hands to shorten its length, he smiled the same smile that had once made her think he was kind.

"You know, darlin', considering our history, I'm gonna enjoy this a bit more than usual."

Sue tried to scream but couldn't get a single sound out of her throat.

Suddenly, Rick lunged toward her. Darting out of the bedroom in her stockinged feet, Sue ran down the hall.

Thinking she heard a noise, Gil glanced up from the coroner's photo of Jenny Lou Parklyn. She paused and listened, but the house was quiet, so she turned back to the file.

Rick ran behind Sue as she sprinted toward the front door. Swiftly, he threw his red cord around her neck. "Let's take this nice and slow," he whispered, dragging her back toward the bedroom. "I could kill you quick like the others, but what's the fun in that? After all, this is special day for me. In a way, it's my thirtieth anniversary. You make number thirty, you know."

Rick smiled as Sue frantically scratched at his gloves. His smile faded when she reached back further and viciously dug her nails into his neck.

"That isn't very ladylike," he growled, jerking his head away. "And after all I've done for you. Why, just today, I called the hospital and told them you were sick, so you could come home and play with me." Smiling at her fear, he slowly tightened the cord. "Where's my thank you?"

Seeing she was about to black out, he loosened his grip and let her catch a partial breath. "You know," he murmured, "a man has to be an expert in something, and I've perfected this. The main thing is the kill, and in order to keep killing, you can't get caught. Some killers choose their victims first. I choose the towns. Did you know, sweet babe, that your little town of Charlesberg has the lowest arrest rate in Colorado? I had this town all picked out before I met you—you were just a special bonus. The day I came to town, there you were in the diner—just as pretty as a picture—all ready to serve me eggs with a smile. The perfect date for my anniversary."

Rick tightened the cord. Sue beat urgently against his hands. Pressing his lips to her temple, he whispered, "After we play a while, we'll go out the backdoor to the shed. Last week, I installed a shiny steel rod in your honor. There should be someone hanging from the rafters—clicking her heels—when a special party's underway. I think it's fitting that we finish our business while your preacher's standing like an idiot on the curb."

Rick loosened the cord, and when he felt Sue getting ready to scream, he tightened it again. Sliding his mouth down her cheek, he hissed, "People talk about the joys of motherhood. A strange thing that—a bloody cord being used to give life. People say life and death are in God's hands—*that makes me God*. I take life with my red death-cord, and soon you'll be swinging on the end of it."

Seeing Sue starting to faint, Rick loosened the cord and shook her. "Hey, none of that! I want this one to last a while."

When Sue began to struggle again, he twisted the cord and hissed, "Women are like cats, I think. I used to practice on cats when I was little. Cut into them while they were still alive and try to see the spirit inside. They taught me there's nothing inside but blood and bones. No spirit. No worth. Just blood and bones. They also taught me patience. Cats like to scratch too."

Rick put his lips to Sue's ear—his hot breath curling around the side of her face. "Women are so vain. Always grooming. But secretly so desperate for a little attention. That's what always gets them in the end. That's how I used to catch my cats, and that's how I catch my women. Just show a woman a little kindness, and she'll follow you right to the hangman's noose. You were like that. So tired. So troubled. Just wanting a little love." Rick gave the cord an angry twist. "Well, you found love, didn't you? But not with me. I wasn't good enough for you, was I? You snuggled up with that preacher!"

Rick spat his words against Sue's neck. "If you were a cat you wouldn't be a Persian or a tabby—you'd be a Siamese. Inscrutable and traitorous. You didn't let me touch you, but you let *him* touch you. The Siamese—so proud and clean—waiting for her preacher to save her. Well, he won't save you. He doesn't even know you're in trouble."

Rick violently tightened the cord. "Preachers are worthless. They're fish, opening and closing their mouths with nothing really to say. Thumping their little fins against the current. They're yammering parrots. Speaking things they've heard, but don't understand and pecking incessantly at your mind. They're annoying, but powerless." Grabbing Sue's hair, Rick yanked her head around to face him. "*You're a fool*. You chose a fish over a tiger, and now the tiger's gonna show you the improvements to the shed."

Putting Sue into a headlock, he began dragging her toward the back door.

THIRTY

THE HOUSE WAS deathly quiet. *Too quiet.* Setting the gruesome photograph of Jenny Lou Parklyn on the floor, Gil stood to her feet. *When had Sue stopped singing?* Cautiously tiptoeing to Danny's doorway, she peeked around the corner and saw Sue struggling against Rick—a red cord wrapped tightly around her throat.

Gil gasped and ran full tilt into the grappling couple. As they fell to the floor, Gil grabbed Rick's head and slammed it against the wall. Before he could recover, she kicked him in the stomach, causing him to temporarily lose his grip on the cord. Gil watched as Sue frantically scrambled on all fours and knocked the phone to the floor. As Sue reached for the receiver, Rick seized her ankles and pulled her back toward him. Sue's fingers scrabbled fruitlessly along the floorboards as Rick flipped her onto her back and straddled her.

Gil beat against Rick's back, but he ignored her. She could see Sue trying to scream, but Rick had his thumbs pressed to the tender hollow of her throat, cutting off the stillborn sound. As Sue scratched wildly at his gloves, Rick rammed his thumbs down even harder, chuckling softly as Sue's mouth widened into a gaping, silent scream. Gil watched in horror as Sue's eyes rolled back until only the whites were showing and a trickle of foaming saliva trailed down her chin.

Knowing that Sue was out of time, Gil kicked Rick again. He whipped around and grabbed at the air, catching her foot and tossing her off balance. As she fell, Gil hit her head on the living room doorway. Lying in a huddled heap, she stared at Rick. She knew he couldn't see her, but he obviously wasn't thrown by having an invisible adversary. If she'd been afraid before, she was terrified now.

Feeling sick and more than a little shaky, Gil rose to her feet. As Rick started dragging Sue toward the back of the house, Gil picked up the phone and pressed speed dial one. On the other end of the line, she could hear Sam saying hello. Knowing that he couldn't hear her if she spoke, Gil began banging the receiver against the wall. Through the line, she could hear Sam yelling Sue's name. Within seconds, he was lunging against the bolted door.

Gil shuddered at the horrible gurgling sound coming from Sue's throat. Dropping the phone, she grabbed a vase and swung it at Rick. He dodged to one side and dove at the vase, hitting Gil in her midsection. The vase fell from her hands and shattered.

"I don't know what you are," Rick snarled as he found Gil's throat and squeezed, "but get outta my way!"

Rick hurled Gil like a ragdoll against the wall. As she fell, she saw Sue trying to crawl away. Rick kicked Sue's head and shoved her face against the floor. As he rewrapped the cord around her neck, Sue clawed at the floorboards with broken, bloody nails.

As Sam continued to throw his weight against the door, Gil struggled to her feet. Seeing Sue's fingers splayed outward and trembling in taunt desperation, she grabbed fistfuls of Rick's hair and yanked. Letting go of the cord, he swung around and jerked Gil's feet out from under her. When he had her down, he threw a punch that sent her sliding down the hall on her back. As Rick rolled on top of Sue and tightened his cord, Gil scrambled to her feet and sprinted to the door. Quickly unbolting the locks, she jumped out of the way as Sam burst through.

Gil heard a sound of pure rage bursting from Sam's lips as he dove at Rick and knocked him away from Sue. With a roar, he crashed his fist into Rick's mouth. Sam's punch slammed Rick's face into the wall, leaving a large smear of blood trickling toward the floor.

"Not a fish, not a parrot," Rick mumbled as he fell to his knees.

Gil leaned against the wall and tried to catch her breath as Sam tore the cord from Sue's neck. "Sue," he said, "are you all right?"

Sue nodded and pointed wildly at Rick who had taken the clock from the wall and was swinging it at Sam's head. Ducking, Sam threw a punch that sent Rick reeling.

"So you wanna play?" Rick said, wiping blood from his mouth. "Don't you want to quote a few scriptures and pray a while like a good little minister?"

Sam advanced and said in a menacing voice, "Do you know who David was? He was a man after God's own heart, but he was also a warrior."

Sam flew at Rick and punched him violently in the face with a fast uppercut and cross combination. Rick stepped back and threw a hard punch into Sam's midsection. To Gil's eyes, Sam was so angry that he didn't even notice.

"The unique thing about David," Sam snarled, "was that he wrote praise songs to the Lord while at the same time showing no mercy to his enemies. When he met an enemy, he ground him to dust and scattered the dust in the wind."

Sam lunged at Rick, driving his shoulder into Rick's stomach and flinging him into the wall. Drywall collapsed beneath Rick's weight. The hall mirror fell to the floor and shattered. Gil ducked as glass showered around her. Down the hall, Sam leapt into the air with a roundhouse kick that connected with such force Rick doubled over and spat blood.

Taking Rick by the hair and putting him in a chokehold, Sam growled, "The thing about following in David's footsteps is you have to know who your enemy is. But from where I'm sitting, that looks pretty clear. Your mistake about preachers is that you never read the Old Testament."

Gil watched as Rick threw an elbow into Sam's stomach and thrust his head against the side of Sam's face. With blood streaming from a gash on his cheek, Sam threw Rick violently against the wall. Hunks of plaster fell as the drywall caved away.

As Sam stepped purposefully toward him, Rick drew a knife out of his pocket. With light flickering along the blade, Rick snarled and lunged—hate contorting his face until he barely looked human. As Sam pivoted to one side, Gil winced. Sam's pivot was a wise move, but it put Rick between him and Sue.

Gil stumbled forward, trying to protect her. At the same time, Sam shouted, "Sue, go lock yourself in the bathroom and don't come out until I call!"

Sue scrambled to her feet, nearly running into Gil. Instead of hiding in the bathroom, Sue stumbled to the hall closet and grabbed the baseball bat. Down the hall, Rick slashed again, trying to drive his jagged blade through Sam's stomach. Dodging, Sam kicked the knife out of Rick's hand, sending it flying into the living room along with Rick's glove. As Sam delivered a flying roundhouse kick to his jaw, Rick flew back toward Sue. Sue took aim and swung. The bat hit Rick and knocked him into the window by the front door. The glass shattered. Choking on blood, Rick threw a chair as hard as he could at Sue. As she fell, Sam rushed to her side, shielding her with his body from further attack.

Seeing Rick making a break for the door, Gil stuck out her foot and tripped him. As he fell down the steps and landed in a heap on the sidewalk, she grabbed his legs. Rick kicked violently. His blow connected with Gil's nose and sent her sprawling. As Rick ran down the sidewalk, Gil sat weakly on the top step and gingerly touched her nose. The pain made her wince. Rolling her eyes, she groaned. She didn't know what a broken nose felt like, but she had an *awful* premonition that it felt exactly like hers did now. Looking inside the house, she saw Sam gently cradling Sue.

"Are you okay?" Sam asked, smoothing the hair away from Sue's face.

Sue smiled weakly and tried to brush the blood from Sam's cheek with her thumb. "Sure I am—he barely touched me."

Sam laughed and laid his cheek against Sue's hair.

"Score one for our side!" Gil shouted wildly, pumping her fist in the air.

THIRTY-ONE

AS ZARA AND Nathan drove down Paradise Avenue, Zara saw a bleeding man running down the sidewalk. "Na'tan," she exclaimed, "is dat de bad mon?"

"It sure is!" Slamming on the brakes, Nathan pulled out his gun. "Honey, take the wheel and drive back to Westfield. Call my department and tell them I need backup. Don't come back until I phone you. Get out of here now!"

As Nathan jumped from the car and ran after Rick, Zara put the car in reverse and peeled rubber. She knew when Nathan spoke in that voice not to question but to simply obey. Turning a corner, she frantically dialed Chief Rogers's direct line.

Crystal watched as a group of sophomores filed into the basement of Student Union to take their exam. The link-up to the lab had gone well, but she wanted to stick around in case the connection failed. As the students settled into chairs, Zeke began passing out exams. Crystal knew he was out of his element—he

215

hated teaching—but he was handling things well. She doubted the students were picking up on his nervousness.

She smiled. She admired Zeke more than anyone she'd ever known. He had a tragic past, but that didn't stop him from trusting God and believing in other people.

As Zeke interrupted her thoughts by launching into instructions about the exam, Crystal frowned. He was using the same tone he'd used when lecturing her about curiosity. It was true she was only a junior cadet, but she knew she could help if those in charge would let her. Crystal balled her hands into fists. Regardless of her lowly status at the moment, someday she was going to be Alpha-Blue, and when that day came, *nothing* was going to stop her from making a difference.

Nathan ran swiftly, closing the gap between himself and Rick. "Rick Olsen," he shouted, "you're under arrest! Stop or I'll shoot!"

Rick swerved off the sidewalk and sprinted into a neighbor's yard. Nathan winced and ran faster. The yard belonged to a family with two preschool girls. He hated the thought of a child being taken hostage. As Rick jumped over a tricycle, Nathan weighed his options. There weren't many. Without knowing where the girls were, he couldn't discharge his weapon.

Nathan followed close behind as Rick broke through a stand of bushes and sprinted into the forest. Dodging between trees, Rick raced to the rim of a canyon and pulled a rifle from behind a log. Nathan stumbled to a stop as Rick turned and shot a volley of bullets.

Inside Sue's house, Sam jumped at the sound of gunshots. "Sue, stay here," he said. "I have to see what's going on. Nathan may be in trouble."

She grabbed his arm. "I'm coming with you."

"Are you able?"

Tossing him the baseball bat, she nodded firmly.

A smile tugged Sam's mouth as Sue shouldered the broom, but when she took a step toward the door and wobbled, his smile faded. "I don't think this is wise."

"Look," she replied, slipping on her shoes, "we're wasting time. Stop arguing."

Seeing the resolute tilt of her chin, Sam knew he'd met his match. As they ran out the door, more shots rang through the autumn air.

With bullets whizzing past his ear, Nathan dodged behind a tree and returned fire. Rick responded by sending another torrent of bullets his way. As Nathan took cover, Rick turned and raced down the canyon. Nathan saw a pickup parked at the bottom. Pebbles flew in all directions as Rick jumped into the driver's seat and drove off in a swirl of dust.

Bolting to the edge of the canyon, Nathan took aim at Rick's tires. He shot and missed. He shot again as the pickup careened around a bend. Falling to his knees, Nathan wiped blood from his brow—his heart thumping wildly in his chest. After a few moments, he rose to his feet and hiked back to the subdivision. In the distance, he could hear police sirens drawing near. He knew that Zara had relayed his message and that help was on its way. When he reached the tree line, he met Sam and Sue running toward him.

"I feared the worst when we heard shots," Sam gasped. "I knew it was time for you to show up, and I was afraid for you."

"You had a right to be," Nathan replied, showing his brother the jagged cut on his brow. "Rick had a rifle hidden in the woods."

"Were you shot?" Sam asked in a horrified voice.

"Nah, a bullet clipped a tree. Some bark splintered off and hit me, but Zara's gonna have a fit. She'll start pestering me to quit the force and open a bakery."

Sam laughed. "I'll back her up. The world needs more bakers."

"You wouldn't say that if you tasted my last batch of bread." Inspecting Sam's injuries, Nathan said, "You look kinda battered yourself, but Rick looked worse."

"Between us, Sue and I managed to fend him off."

As the sirens grew louder, Nathan put a gentle hand on Sue's throat to examine her bruises. Seeing the extent of the damage, he shot Sam a quick look. There was a pulsing anger burning in Sam's eyes. It was a type of anger that Nathan had never seen in his brother before. In the face of such fury, he knew Rick had better run the other way if he met Sam again.

"I can hear my backup arriving," Nathan said. "We need to go. Zara has my phone, and I need to tell them which way Rick went. I don't want him getting away."

As Sue swayed, Nathan took her broom and Sam put a gentle arm around her waist. Together, they ran back to Sue's house as police cars from the Westfield Precinct sped into the driveway.

Jumping out of the lead car, Chief Rogers called, "What's the status?"

As Nathan explained the situation, he looked at Sue in concern. Her face was pasty white, and she was trembling like a leaf. As an APB was called into dispatch, Nathan turned to Sam. "Do you want to give your statements at Sue's house or Grandpop's?"

"At Grandpop's," Sam said firmly. "Sue's house isn't secure. She'll sleep at Grandpop's tonight. I'll help her pack a bag, and we'll meet you next door."

"What about Danny?" Sue asked in hoarse voice. "Is he safe?"

"We'll make sure he is," Nathan replied. He motioned for a policeman to join them. "This is Officer Donnly. He'll assist with your packing."

As Sam nodded and helped Sue into the house, Chief Rogers handed Nathan a cell phone. "I'll assign protection to the Winston boy while you call your wife. When she phoned me, Zara threatened to cut off my supply of coconut cookies if you didn't call her as soon as possible—and that's one threat I can't afford to ignore."

Grinning, Nathan began dialing.

Thirty-Two

WITH HIS ARM around Sue, Sam carefully picked his way down the hallway—his feet crunching over shattered glass and hunks of plaster. As Sue tripped over the broken frame of her mirror, Sam steadied her and asked if she had any suitcases.

Shaking her head, Sue stared with glazed eyes at the smears of blood on the wall. "We used boxes for the m-move."

Hearing her voice break, Sam knew reaction was setting in. Gently leading her to the bedroom, he had her lie down while he propped pillows beneath her feet.

"When's the medic arriving?" he asked Officer Donnly in a worried undertone.

"Soon. There's one in route. What can I do?"

"Guard her—don't take your eyes off her."

As Donnly stood by Sue's bed, Sam ran to the garage and grabbed boxes. When he returned, he asked, "Do you want to tell me what to pack or do I use my best judgment?"

"I trust you, Sam," Sue replied. "Surprise me. Just don't f-forget our toothbrushes."

Nodding, Sam went to the dresser and tripped over a dress on the floor. As he put it on a hanger, he saw a tear sliding down Sue's cheek.

"I was going to wear that t-tonight," she said, wincing with pain.

Sam bit his lip. Sue had been through so much, he was afraid she was going to fall apart if he didn't do something quick. Holding up the dress, he whistled softly and long. "Susie-Q, if you'd worn this I wouldn't have just been distracted at dominoes, I'd have been distracted clear-clean out of breathing! Talk about taking unfair advantage of a man. I'm just mortal, don't you know."

Sue blinked and gave a shaky laugh. "Throw it in the box, and watch me take your breath away."

Carefully folding the pretty dress, Sam knelt beside her and gently wiped her tears. "Susie-Q," he whispered, "you already *have* taken my breath away."

Gil watched as Sam pulled clothes from Sue's dresser. He was doing a good job of packing, but when he went to Sue's bathroom he was at a loss. Gil choked back a giggle as Sam picked up an eyelash curler and scratched his head. She saw his confusion increase when he spotted a bowl of leg-waxing cubes. After gingerly rolling a cube around his palm, he shrugged and placed the lone cube in the box. Gil's giggle broke free as he carefully packed a luffa. He obviously didn't know what a woman considered essential, and he wasn't thinking clearly enough to figure it out. When he turned his back, Gil tucked Sue's makeup in the box.

After Sam packed for Danny, he swaddled Sue in a blanket and carried her to his grandfather's house. As Officer Donnly followed with the boxes, Gil went to Danny's room and put the files inside her pillowcase. Clutching the bulky bag to her chest, she ran down the sidewalk toward Danny's school.

❧

Sam watched anxiously as a paramedic examined Sue. "You're a lucky lady," the medic said. "You don't need to go to the hospital unless you'd prefer it."

Sue looked at Sam. "I'd rather stay here, is that okay?"

Sam, who hadn't let go of her hand since they'd entered the house, nodded.

As the medic wrapped Sue's wrist with a bandage, there was a screech of tires outside. Zara's agonized voice echoed, "Yuh deh policeman, where's mi Na'tan?"

Sam watched as Nathan sprinted to the door, and Zara collapsed in a soggy heap in her husband's arms. "Yuh *wretch!*" She sobbed, her worry making her Jamaican accent more pronounced. "Dohn yuh evva go jumping outta di car telling mi to drive wey fram you! I won't dweet again! Not evva! Yuh hear?"

Nathan hugged his wife. "Don't worry, honey, I hear."

"You'd betta! Telling mi to drive wey an leave you running afta dat bad mon!"

"I'm sorry," Nathan murmured. "The chief's here. Do you wanna say hello?"

Sam watched with amusement as his sister-in-law went to Nathan's boss and kissed his cheek. "Yuh beautiful mon!" she said. "I gi yuh *many* cookies for keeping mi Na'tan safe!"

As Nathan tried to restrain his wife's exuberance, Sam saw Sue removing her oxygen mask. When he tried to reposition it, she shook her head. "I need to be able to talk. Is Danny safe?"

222

Chief Rogers spoke from across the room. "There's an officer guarding him. He's fine."

As Sue smiled in relief, Sam replaced her oxygen mask and gently brushed her hair away from her forehead.

Gil walked swiftly through the halls of Fairfield Middle School, but when she saw a policeman posted outside the science room's open door, she froze. She knew the officer couldn't see her, but her shoes were squeaking against the linoleum and she wasn't sure if he'd be able to hear the racket. Feeling disgusted at herself for neglecting to read the manuals, she slipped off her shoes and tiptoed past the policeman in her socks. Sneaking up beside Danny, she tapped his arm. The boy looked up with a smile, but when he saw her bloody nose, he gasped.

"Oh, Danny, I'm sorry!" she moaned. "I forgot how I look. Don't worry, everyone's fine. Rick made some trouble, but Sam and your mom *clobbered* him! Unfortunately, he got away, so there's a policeman guarding you."

Seeing Danny turn to look, she grabbed his arm. "Sit still! I need to talk to you, and I can't if you attract attention."

Danny settled back in his chair and neatly folded his hands on his desk.

"Wisecracker," she said affectionately, "you can cut the golden-cherub act. I know you too well. Now, are you ready for some payback? I have info linking Rick to some murders."

"Cool!" Danny said.

"Hey, watch out!" Gil exclaimed. "The teacher's glaring at you." As Danny focused on the chalkboard, she said, "You'll need to give the information and Rick's beer bottle to Nathan."

Seeing Danny's smirk, she rolled her eyes. "Yes, I *did* catch the bottle, smarty pants. Pay attention, you insolent bug!"

As Danny's lips twitched, she answered the question she knew he was dying to ask. "The evidence is solid. It'll put Rick behind bars, and I say good riddance! The stupid jerk broke my nose. How am I supposed to win *Miss America* with a broken nose, I'd like to know?"

Hearing Danny turn strangled gasps of laughter into a cough, she said, "I suppose you're right. My pageant goals are a bunch of moonshine. I'd never make it past the embarrassing swimsuit competition. Can you picture me trying to walk in a bikini and high heels? But a girl can dream, can't she?" Seeing his quirked eyebrow, she chuckled. "Let's forget my pageant dreams and focus on Rick. I *loved* watching that creep get his face rearranged by Sam."

As Danny's quirked eyebrow rose further, she admitted, "All right, it wasn't just *watching* I enjoyed. Pulling Rick's hair and kicking him as hard as I could was great! In fact, I more than enjoyed it—I *relished* it." Tilting her head to one side, she allowed her eyes to twinkle. "I never knew I had such a propensity toward violence. It's quite disturbing. I may need to seek counseling when I get home."

Seeing Danny cough down another chuckle, Gil got back to business. "But enough about that. We need to get the evidence out of my pillowcase and into your hands without being noticed. I can't do it now, and after class you're gonna be surrounded. We'll need a distraction. Any suggestions?"

Danny chewed his pencil eraser. After a moment, he wrote, *Can Slim help?*

"That's it!" she exclaimed. "Write Slim a note asking him to create a distraction when you open your locker."

When the note was complete, Gil stuffed it under her sweater and went across the room. She smiled when she saw how intently Slim was staring at Danny. She knew he was watching for signs that the super-bionic chick was back. Her suspicions were confirmed when she laid her hand on his, and rather than jumping, Slim wrote on a scrap of paper, *Is that you, Gil?*

Squeezing his hand, she slipped the note on his desk.

While Danny's teacher explained the mysteries of chlorophyll, Sue finished giving her statement. She knew Chief Rogers was trying to make the process easy, but reliving Rick's attack was a nightmare. As she spoke, Sam's family sat beside her in a unified show of support.

"Na'tan," Zara exclaimed, "I tek bak wah I said, I dohn wan yuh to be baker like mi fadda. I wan yuh to arrest dat bad mon and put him inna prison wid big nassy rats!"

As Zara's impassioned words broke the tension in the room, Sue felt herself relax. "Chief Rogers," she said, "there's something else I should tell you, but it'll sound strange."

"Believe me, I've heard it all."

Sue hesitated and then said in a rush, "When Rick attacked me, something ran into him."

"That was me," Sam said. "I pulled him off you."

"No, Sam, it happened before you broke through the door."

Leaning forward, Nathan gave her arm a pat. "When you're being attacked, it's easy to get confused."

"I suppose that's true," she replied, "but a series of strange things happened today."

"Like what?" the chief asked.

She shifted uncomfortably. "Something picked up the phone and dialed it."

Sam blinked. "You didn't call me?"

"Rick had me pinned to the floor. I couldn't reach the receiver. I'm telling you, bizarre things happened before you arrived. A vase swung itself at Rick, and the door miraculously unlocked." Sue turned to the chief. "I know it sounds crazy, but I'm not making this up."

The chief nodded and closed his notebook. "If you want a logical explanation, strangulation often causes hallucinations due to oxygen deprivation."

"Do you really think that's what it was?" she asked doubtfully.

Chief Rogers laid a gentle hand on her shoulder. "Officially, yes. But unofficially, I believe God intervened."

"I'm glad you spoke up," Sam said, giving her hand a reassuring squeeze. "It shows God was watching over us."

"I'm glad you don't think I'm crazy."

A teasing light gleamed in Sam's eye. "Well...I never said *that*."

As Sue chuckled, Sam leaned forward and, in view of his matchmaking family, kissed her brow. The tenderness in his eyes was unmistakable.

Clearing his throat, Chief Rogers said, "If I have further questions, I'll call you."

"Isn't this crime outside your jurisdiction?" Sam asked.

"Technically, yes. But I've received permission to conduct the investigation since it involves one of our officers."

"That's no surprise," Nathan said with a snort. "If Charlesberg PD took the case, they'd actually have to work."

"Quite," the chief said briefly. "Go pick up Danny. I'll be next door if you need me."

After Chief Rogers left, Sue said, "He's kinda gruff, but the chief's nice, isn't he?"

Zara nodded and said with emphasis, "Dat mon's worth more dan cookies. I'm gwine bake him special cake wid butta-crème frosting too!"

THIRTY-THREE

AFTER SAM AND Nathan left to get Danny, Sue caught Zara looking at her with a twinkle in her eye. "So, sugar, yuh 'ave Sam on di hook. 'Ow yuh intend pon reeling him inna?"

Sue blinked and began to laugh. Instead of trying to tell Zara she was mistaken, she simply said, "I brought a pretty dress."

"Dat do fah startas, but I suggest yuh sidle up to mi brother-in-law an gi him a smooch."

Sue gurgled. "Sam and I just met, it's too soon for kissing."

"I kissed mi Na'tan di night wi met, but yuh be right—Sam moves ahwful slow. If yuh go kissing him, yuh scare di poor mon to pieces." She gave Sue's knee a pat. "I haven't seen Sam wid a girl since I marrid mi Na'tan."

"Sam doesn't date much?"

"Much?" Zara snorted. "Over di years, I've seen women trying to ketch his eye, but he wouldn't look der way. When I ask him 'bout it, he told mi some fool-fool story 'bout wanting to live di solitary life focused solely pon di Lord. Sam's flying inna di face of nature, an it's 'bout time he gat di wakeup call." Zara began to

228

chuckle. "Unless I'm mistaken, you're jus di gyal to dweet. Wah color is dat dress of yours?"

"Purple."

"Dat should dweet. Purple mek your eyes go glossy-shine. Let's get bizzy! I help yuh git ready, and we mek Sam tek notice!"

⌒⌒

A few minutes before school was dismissed, Danny saw Sam and Nathan slipping into the back of the classroom.

"The guys are here," Gil whispered. "I'll get in place by your locker."

Danny nodded and watched as Gil tiptoed out the door. After the bell rang, Sam and Nathan approached and told him about Rick's attack. Trying to give Gil and Slim time to prepare, Danny asked questions and then began "accidentally" dropping his notebook.

"Why don't I carry that for you?" Sam said, picking up papers for a fourth time. "I know hearing about your mom was upsetting, but I promise she's fine. Are you ready to go?"

Looking at Gil standing beside his locker with her hand in her pillowcase, Danny shook his head. "I need to get something out of my locker first."

"That's fine," Sam said, putting his hand on Danny's shoulder. "When you're finished, we'll go play dominoes with your mom. Sound good?"

Danny nodded in a distracted way. There were so many people around his locker he knew Gil couldn't maneuver. Praying silently for Slim's distraction to work, he twirled his combination lock. As the locker opened, an air horn blasted behind him. Although he'd been expecting something of the sort, he dropped his books and whirled around.

"Give a shout-out for our football team!" Slim yelled. "Go Lions!"

Danny smiled. He had to admire Slim's ingenuity. The distraction was loud and effective, but it wouldn't get him into trouble. After all, no matter how loud the air horn, Slim could hardly be punished for showing school spirit after school hours. Danny's grin widened. Everyone was so focused on Slim that no one was looking Gil's way.

When Slim winked and sauntered down the hall, blasting his air horn, Danny turned and saw that Gil had stowed the evidence by his backpack.

"Don't give Nathan anything in front of that Charlesberg policeman," she hissed in his ear. "Wait until you're in the car."

Nodding briefly, Danny picked up the folder. As he grabbed the beer bottle, Sam shot him a concerned look. "What are you doing with beer?"

"It's a science experiment on the dangers of drinking," Danny glibly replied. "Don't worry, I didn't sip any. It smells like the boy's bathroom."

A few minutes later, as Nathan put on his seatbelt, he felt surprised as Danny handed him a large folder. "Why are you giving me your science experiment?" he asked.

When Danny shrugged, Nathan opened it. Seeing the contents, he turned shocked eyes onto the boy. "Where'd you get this?" he demanded.

"A stranger," Danny replied.

Nathan eased a sheaf of papers out of the folder. A gruesome crime-scene photograph fell onto his lap. Covering it with his hand,

Nathan commanded gruffly, "Sit back, Danny, and close your eyes."

"But I wanna see."

"Do as I say!" Nathan ordered, using the same tone that had sent Zara speeding away with screeching tires.

When Danny obediently sat back and shut his eyes, Nathan passed the sickening photograph to Sam and began thumbing through the papers.

Peering down at the gory image of a blonde woman strung up with a red cord, Sam murmured, "You can tell she suffered."

"She wasn't the only one," Nathan whispered, passing him a similar photo of a brunette.

Sam took the photo with shaking hands. Closing his eyes against the horrific image, he asked, "How many?"

"Ten."

Glancing over his shoulder at Danny, Sam whispered in a low undertone, "Rick boasted twenty-nine."

"This is the start we'll need to prove it." As he glanced through the files, Nathan found Rick's DNA profile. Cocking an eyebrow at his brother, he murmured, "What do you wanna bet his DNA's all over the bottle?"

"It'll be all over the house too," Sam said in a steely voice. "I clocked him good—his blood's on the wall."

"I need to get this evidence to the chief. Can you drop me off before you take Danny to his mother?"

"Can I open my eyes yet?" Danny asked plaintively from the back seat.

"No!" both brothers shouted in unison as a photo of a strangled redhead fell to the floor.

As Danny slumped in his seat, Nathan pushed the papers back in the folder. When the pictures were out of sight, he said over his shoulder, "You can look now."

"What was it?"

"Something ugly that you didn't need to see—something that'll put Rick on death row."

After dropping off Nathan, Sam walked into his grandfather's house with Danny. He was in mid-sentence, but when he saw Sue in her purple dress, the words died on his lips. He blinked, stumbled over his feet, and stood perfectly still and gazed at her.

"Sam," Danny said, looking at him strangely, "what's wrong?"

Sam didn't reply—he couldn't reply. Sue's golden hair was curling around her shoulders in luxurious waves. Her blue eyes were sparkling, and the rich purple of her dress was making her skin seem luminescent. Sam's eyes drank in the delicate beauty of her features and the soft curves of her figure. He swallowed hard.

"You look awful funny, Sam," Danny said. "Are you feeling okay?"

Nodding briefly, Sam walked slowly to Sue. She began blushing under his steady gaze.

"Di cat 'ave your tung, Sam?" Zara teased.

Still not speaking, Sam took Sue's hand and gave it a squeeze.

Zara began to laugh and slap her knee. "Sure nuff picked di right dress. Dat mon's clean dead-an-gone. A speechless mon is di caught mon!"

THIRTY-FOUR

THAT NIGHT, GIL hovered in the background as Mr. Jacobson taught Danny how to make Navy-style rolls. She sniffed the air appreciatively. The combination of the yeasty rolls and Zara's pumpkin soup was marvelous. She turned her attention to the conversation and chuckled when Danny asked Zara to recite some nursery rhymes because he liked the sound of her accent.

After dinner, Sue was given icepacks and relegated to the couch with Sam by her side. Trying to keep out of the way while the dishes were done, Gil followed them to the living room. Sam and Sue were talking like old friends, but as time passed, their banter transformed into a breathless exchange of stolen glances.

Feeling slightly bored, Gil started wandering back to the kitchen just as Nathan popped his head in the living room. "The chief just called. Rick's truck was spotted over the state line."

"So we're safe?" Sue asked, reaching for Sam's hand.

"At least for now," Nathan replied. "Rick's too far away to get back before morning."

"In that case, how about some Chicken Foot?" Sam said, rising from the couch. "I could use a little innocuous entertainment before bed."

"I 'ave di dominoes set up aredy," Zara called from the kitchen.

"I think you married a mind reader," Sam said, elbowing his brother in the ribs.

"You have *no* idea." Nathan chuckled. "Did I ever tell you what my sweet little wife did on our—"

"Stop all di chit-chat!" Zara loudly admonished. "I 'ave pulled a batch of spice chip cookies from di oven—come quick ef you wan to eat dem warm."

Gil watched in envy as the group played several games of Chicken Foot and ate multiple gooey cookies. Later that night, as everyone went to the bedrooms Mr. Jacobson had prepared, Danny cuddled up on the couch, and Gil stretched out on the floor next to him. All around her, the house fell quiet as everyone drifted to sleep.

At 11:16 p.m., Gil woke up. She'd been sleeping in a draft, and her knee was aching. Sighing a little, she got up to walk out the cramp. As she paced around the living room, dark shadows loomed as the wind shook the trees outside. She looked at the shadows and shivered. Something was nagging at her mind, and she couldn't figure out what it was.

Suddenly, she groaned and clapped her hand to her mouth. She'd forgotten to check-in with TEMCO, and worse than that, *Extreme Exam* was still plugged into Danny's running PlayFest console! Closing her eyes, Gil tried to remember Dr. Nelson's instructions about cartridge care. She knew there was a limit to how long *Extreme Exam* could be in a gaming console before it overheated. Nibbling a fingertip, Gil tried to do the mental math.

Sue had come home at 2:30. Right now, it was 11:20—that meant the game had been in a running console for nine hours.

Gil groaned. *Nine hours!* That was *way* too long. She was probably toast—big black burnt toast with no marmalade. She couldn't put off retrieving the game. If it was fried, she'd be stuck in the past.

As she slipped on her tennis shoes, Danny stirred on the couch. "What's going on?" he whispered in a sleepy voice.

"Shh!" she said, buttoning her sweater. "Go back to sleep."

"Not a chance," he replied, tossing his covers aside. "Where are you going?"

"Oh, Danny," she moaned. "I blew it! I left *Extreme Exam* at your house."

"So what? It's been so busy they'll understand if you don't make contact."

"That's not what I'm worried about. I left the game in your PlayFest console. Don't you see? I may've fried the stupid thing. If it's not ruined already, it'll be ruined for sure by morning. I have to go get it."

Danny pulled on his shoes. "Then I'm coming with you."

"Oh, no, you're not!" she said firmly. "It's still D-day, and it will be for forty more minutes. I'm not sure you'll be safe over there."

"If I'm not safe—you're not safe."

"Look, I'm sure Rick's across the state line, but I can't take any chances. My whole surf will be for nothing if you two tangle. I'll be back in less than ten minutes."

"Please stay here," Danny said, clutching her arm.

"If I do that, I won't be able to go home."

"Is that so bad?" Danny started to blush. "In eight years, I'll be old enough to marry you. I'll take care of you, just like you've been taking care of me."

Blinking rapidly, Gil said, "That's so *sweet* of you, but I can't marry you."

"Why not?" he asked in a hurt voice. "Don't you like me?"

"Of course I do, but I'm too old for you. In eight years, I'll be in my thirties."

"Who cares?" he grumbled.

"I do, and so should you. Do you *really* think you'll want a wife in her thirties when you're eighteen?" She gave him a tiny smile. "Why, I might be wrinkled as a prune."

"I'd still think you were beautiful! I love you every bit as much as Mom."

"Regardless, it wouldn't be fair to you. Besides, think of the complications. Can you imagine our wedding? People would think you were nuts and lock you in a padded room."

"I wouldn't care."

"But I would," she said softly. "I can't marry you, but I'll always treasure the fact that you asked me." She gently wrapped a blanket around his shoulders. "I have to go home if I possibly can — and you, my fine young friend, have to stay here until D-day's over."

"But if you get in trouble, no one will know. No one can hear you but me. I could wait on the steps and —"

"You're not going," she said firmly. "I came here to save you, and I'm not gonna risk all our hard work because I was too stupid to turn off a blasted machine." When he started to protest, she shook her head. "You're not leaving this house tonight. Got it?"

"But what if something happens to you?"

"If I'm not back in ten minutes, wake up Sam and tell him you saw someone next door. Now, where's your house key?"

"Promise you'll be careful," he said, retrieving the key from his backpack.

"I promise. Can I borrow the flashlight Mr. Jacobson lent you? I may need the light."

Danny reached beneath his pillow and handed it to her.

"I'll be back before you know it," she said, giving him a smile. "I won't test the game. I'll just bring the stupid thing back, and we'll get some more sleep."

Without waiting for Danny's reply, Gil left the house and ran through the shadowy darkness. As a storm brewed above her, the wind whipped branches and sent autumn leaves flying. When she reached the Winston's porch, she glanced back at Mr. Jacobson's house and saw Danny standing by a window with his nose pressed against the glass. Even though fog from his breath was clouding the glass, she could tell he was worried. Giving him a reassuring wave, she ducked under the police tape and went inside.

Danny's house was pitch black and very cold. Gil turned on the flashlight and walked down the hall. Broken glass and bits of plaster popped beneath her feet. She shuddered as she remembered the afternoon's struggle. It had been close—way too close.

Shaking off the memory, she quickened her step and entered Danny's room. She waved the flashlight at the window, knowing Danny was watching and could see the light. Turning around, she focused the beam on the running PlayFest system. *Extreme Exam* was still inside the console. Muttering beneath her breath, she pulled the cartridge out. It was hot. *Really* hot. As she blew on the game trying to cool it down, a breeze touched her neck. She froze and swung around. Danny's bedroom window was open.

"Well, if it isn't the little ghost," a voice hissed from the shadows. "It seems my net did catch a fish."

Gil frantically turned her flashlight toward the voice. Rick's face gleamed evilly in the light as he pulled a butcher knife from his pocket. Gil gasped and stumbled.

"When I made arrangements for my pickup to be taken out of state, I was hoping Sue would come home, so I could finish with her. I guess you'll have to do instead."

Clutching her flashlight, Gil backed slowly toward Danny's hideout.

"You cheated me out of my anniversary present and now you're gonna pay." Brandishing his knife, Rick slowly advanced toward her. "I don't know what you are, but if you can hold a flashlight you have a body—*and anything with a body can be hurt.*"

As Rick lunged toward her, Gil threw the flashlight at his head. Rick laughed and dodged to one side. As the flashlight hit the wall, Gil dashed across the floor with the game in her hand.

"I see you," Rick hissed as he gave chase.

Realizing the game was giving her away, Gil dropped it as she sprinted into the hall. The broken rubbish on the floor crackled beneath her feet, making her easy to find. Grabbing at her, Rick tossed her into the kitchen. She fell against the sink and reached for the window. She tugged on it until she realized it had been nailed shut. Shrinking back against the counter, she knew with sudden clarity that Rick had made the kitchen a trap with only one exit—an exit he was blocking. Standing absolutely still, she forced herself to calm her rapid breathing. She had to be quiet, *very* quiet. Sooner or later, Rick would leave the kitchen doorway, and when he did, she would sneak past him.

"All ye, all ye, outs in free," Rick sang in an eerie voice that sent chills racing down her spine. "Come out, come out, wherever you may be."

Gil shivered and choked down a whimper. She saw Rick's eyes flicker. Peering from side-to-side, he whispered, "Why don't you come out and play?"

With baited breath, she watched as he slowly advanced. She knew he was trying to draw her out. If she moved prematurely, she'd give away her location. Her muscles tensed and a mist of perspiration beaded her brow. As he made his way deeper into the kitchen, she made a sudden lunge for the doorway.

Hearing her footsteps, Rick grabbed her as she ran past. "Got ya!" he said triumphantly.

Gil struggled wildly as Rick dragged her over to the counter. From the dish drainer, she picked up a frying pan and hit him across the face. He grunted and spat blood. She swung the pan again and knocked the butcher knife out of his hand. It skidded across the floor to the doorway. Rick's fingers bit into her skin like a vice. His cruel strength was frightening. Gil tried to swing the pan again, but he knocked it away.

"Naughty, naughty," he crooned, tightening his grip. "Let's see what you look like, shall we?"

Gil tried to wiggle away as he picked up the flour canister and dumped it over her head. Gil gasped, inhaled flour, and sneezed uncontrollably. As the flour sifted down her body, she shook herself and sent flour flying in all directions. Suddenly, her blood froze. The flour was *on* her body. It wasn't encapsulated *in* her body or hidden by her clothes. Could he see her now? Were the flour-coated parts of her visible? She wished desperately that she had read the manuals.

Rick put her doubts to rest by laughing softly. "So you're a woman. I get my anniversary present after all. Sue would've made a wonderful number thirty, but you'll be even better. Since you can't be seen, I don't have to be careful about leaving evidence—I can do whatever I want to your body." Leaning close, he whispered, "And since we're in a house protected by police tape, we have all night to have some fun. I haven't heard you talk yet—*I'll bet no one will hear you scream.*"

As a crescent moon rose over the NSU campus, and the minutes slowly ticked down to midnight, Director Matthews watched as William restlessly paced the floor. Across the room, Dr. Nelson huddled in a chair, looking as if she were collapsing inside. Anxiously peering at the clock, the director roughly rubbed the back of his neck. He had no comfort to give. No advice or suggestions. He'd finally given up trying to run calculations. No matter what he did, GAP continued to show a fifty percent probability that Danny was dying on death row. He could only wait for midnight to arrive and for D-day to be resolved one way or the other. There was no way to predict the outcome of Danny's fate. There was no way to know what was happening to Gil.

Gil flung herself around—thrashing and trying to get free. Rick didn't seem to notice. He chuckled as he held her tightly and opened the drawer containing Sue's cooking knives. He leisurely selected a wicked-looking knife and then, in a rough movement, backed her up against the counter. Her groping fingers reached behind her and found a coffee cup. She grabbed it and swung. Dodging the cup, he slapped her. Her lip split as he slapped her again and brutally pushed the side of her face down against the counter. She tried to move, but couldn't. Her mouth filled with the acrid taste of blood.

"I used to do things to cats when I was little," Rick whispered in her ear. "I've never tried them on a person before." He chuckled softly. "Maybe tonight, I will."

Pressing the knife to Gil's forehead, Rick carved a big X. As blood rolled down her face and pooled on the counter, Gil felt panic rising to choke her.

"You've got my mark, little ghost. That means you belong to me."

Rick put the knife to her flour-covered cheek and made a long gash. Gil willed herself not to scream. Danny would hear if she did, and she couldn't afford to let him hear. She bit her lip and tried not to cry as Rick slowly slashed her forearm.

"This is interesting," he said conversationally. "I know I'm cutting deep enough, but I don't see blood. Do you bleed, little ghost? Do you feel pain?"

As Rick shifted his weight, Gil quickly kneed him in the groin. Grunting in pain, he punched her face with such force that it left her stunned. Throwing her to the ground, he straddled her body. With his weight pinning her down, she couldn't move. He pressed the knife to her neck. Chuckling, he slowly slid it down her chest, leaving a trail of blood.

"Well, little ghost," he whispered, "shall we cut you open and see if you have a spirit inside?"

Peering through the blood streaming down her face, Gil looked across the room and saw Danny standing in the kitchen doorway. Her heart lurched. She watched as Danny grabbed Rick's butcher knife from the floor.

"No!" Gil shouted wildly. "Drop the knife, Danny! It's D-day! This is it! This is the moment! This is why you stab Rick!" Writhing in agony as Rick began to make the small incision to her chest deeper and longer, she cried, "Go get help!"

Danny raised the butcher knife and took a step forward.

"Drop that knife, and get out of here!" Gil shouted with venom in her voice. "I don't want to be saved this way! If you kill him, I'll *never* forgive you! I'll *hate* you! Do you hear me? *I'll hate you forever!* Go get help!"

Danny dropped the knife with a clatter. Rick looked up and saw him. Danny ran for the door as Rick jumped to his feet. Gil grabbed desperately at Rick's legs. As he fell, she saw Danny making it safely outside. Gasping in pain, she scrambled for the frying pan and hit Rick's head. Clutching her wounded chest, she staggered to the hall and picked up *Extreme Exam*. As she lurched toward the door, Rick ran into her from behind. Their combined weight fell against the door, slamming it shut and sealing her inside.

THIRTY-FIVE

SPRINTING INTO MR. JACOBSON'S house, Danny screamed for help. All around him, he heard feet hitting the floor. With his shoulder holster slung over one arm, Nathan came barreling down the stairs, pulling on his pants as he ran. Sam, in bare feet and blue boxer shorts, wasn't far behind. Above them, Zara appeared. She ran down the stairs, colliding with Sue and Mr. Jacobson.

"Danny," Sam gasped, pulling on a T-shirt. "What's wrong?"

"It's Rick. He's next door. He's killing her. He's cutting her open!"

"Who?" Nathan asked, zipping up his pants.

"My friend, Gil. Rick has her in the kitchen. There's blood everywhere!"

Nathan pulled his gun from its holster. "Sam, grab Grandpop's rifle and come with me. The rest of you stay here. Zara, call the chief. Tell him—"

"No!" Danny objected. "We can't have police."

"If Rick's attacking a girl, we need them," Nathan replied. "They'll—"

243

"No!" Danny shouted almost hysterically. "We gotta do this alone. *Please!*"

Nathan gave Danny a sharp glance and then slowly nodded. "Okay, no police—at least not yet. Zara, toss me my phone. If I need you to phone the chief, I'll let you know."

"But Na'tan—!"

"The boy's earned our trust."

"Den I'm coming wid yuh!"

"So am I," said Sue.

"No!" both brothers shouted in unison.

Danny tugged frantically at Sam's hand. "We gotta go *now!* He's killing her!"

Unzipping the golf bag in the corner, Zara tossed Sue a club. "Grandpop, mon di phone. We'll let yuh know if wi need yuh to call di chief."

Mr. Jacobson nodded, and the whole cavalcade, in their bare feet and pajamas, poured out the door. Danny led them through the darkness, pulling Sam by the hand and running as fast as he could.

Inside Sue's house, Gil tried to get away, but Rick grabbed her by the hair and slammed her face against the wall. As the cartridge flew from her grasp, she flipped around and dug her fingers into his eyes. Turning his face away, Rick yanked her arm violently. Gil gasped in pain as something popped and her arm went dead. Rick punched her, knocking her into the door leading to the garage. With her good hand, she grabbed a ballpoint pen from the hall table and stabbed him in the shoulder. When he fell back, she staggered down the hall, cradling her arm. Hoping to open a time portal, she picked up the game as she ran.

Suddenly, Rick caught her from behind and pulled her into a chokehold. "You keep grabbing that game," he hissed. "Is it something special?"

Snatching *Extreme Exam* out of her hand, he threw it to the floor. Gil heard the plastic snap and break. With panicked thoughts swirling through her brain, she began to bite the arm pinning her. As she drew blood, Rick roughly pushed her away. A wave of nausea engulfed her as her injured arm hit the edge of Danny's doorway. When she slumped against the wall, Rick punched her brutally in the stomach. Doubling over and gasping for air, she saw Rick reaching down and picking up the butcher knife Danny had dropped. Keeping her eyes on the knife, she slowly backed into Danny's room.

Suddenly, Rick came at her, slashing. She raised her good arm to protect her face, and the knife went deep. Rick slashed at her body, laughing as the knife cut rapidly and randomly. Gil stumbled backwards, tripping over the corner of Danny's bed and falling to the floor. Picking up a skateboard from beneath the bed, she knocked the knife out of Rick's hand as he straddled her.

"So, you want to do this the old fashioned way?" he snarled. "I can handle that."

Rick closed his hands around her neck and squeezed. Gil scratched at his face, but he just laughed and squeezed harder. Blood pounded in her ears. She beat frantically at Rick's hands, but soon it got harder and harder to move—and then she stopped moving altogether.

Sam ran through Sue's house, flipping on lights as he ran. Entering Danny's bedroom, he saw Rick kneeling over a messy pile of laundry. Anger rushed over Sam in a powerful wave. "In here!" he shouted, lunging forward.

Rick grabbed the skateboard and flung it at him. It bounced off Sam's shoulder as Rick bolted out the window. Sam tried to follow, but tripped over the pile. As he fell, he realized the bundle wasn't laundry—it was the body of a woman. She was lying in a crumpled heap, and she wasn't moving.

"Where'd he go?" Nathan shouted, entering the room.

"Outside," Sam said baldly, looking in horror at Gil's flour-covered form.

Nathan doubled back and ran out the door as Zara cried in dismay, "Is dat di gyal?" She clutched the wall and retched. "Dat monster has cut her completely inna half!"

"No, he hasn't," Danny said, kneeling by Gil's body. "You only see what's covered by flour, but I see the rest. It's there. She's from the future and can't be seen by anyone but me. Mom, can you see the blood?"

"I only see flour," Sue replied in a choked voice.

"There's lots of blood," Danny said in a panicked tone. "She's covered in it."

"Gyal from di future? Invisible blood? I just dohn understand."

"Look! We're wasting time," Danny yelled. "I don't know if Gil's breathing."

"Move, Danny," Sue said, putting her face next to Gil's flour-covered mouth. Grabbing Gil's wrist, she said to Sam, "She's not breathing, and I can't find a pulse. Do you know CPR?"

Sam looked at the messy mound of flour. "Yes, but I can't see most of her body."

"You don't need to see her legs to do CPR, do you?" Danny asked tearfully.

Sam ran a shaking hand through his hair. "No, I guess not."

He knelt down and began compressions as Sue said to her son, "Get some T-shirts and wrap them around her wounds. Put pressure where she's bleeding most."

"Wah should I do?" Zara asked.

"Look for a PlayFest game called *Extreme Exam*," Danny replied in a shaky voice as he rifled through his dresser. "We gotta find the game to get Gil home."

As Sam continued CPR, he heard a clock chiming midnight.

At TEMCO, William, Dr. Nelson, and Director Matthews began cheering. GAP had just indicated with one hundred percent reliability that Danny wasn't ending up on death row.

Holding a wadded shirt to Gil's chest wound, Danny watched as Zara stooped to scan the rubble on the hallway floor. "Are yuh sure di game's outa here?" she called.

"No," Danny replied, "but it's not in my room. The hall's my best guess."

Zara began shifting clumps of drywall. Suddenly, she shouted, "Yeh, mon, I've found it!"

"Give it here, and take my place," Danny said as she ran to his side. "This is the worst wound. Hold the shirt tight."

Taking the shirt, Zara made a shocked sound. "I can't see di blood, but I sure feel di warmth an stickiness."

Sprinting to his hideout, Danny carefully put the shattered cartridge into his PlayFest system. When he turned on the console, broken blue bars and wavy black lines filled the television screen. Dimly, in the background, he could see the mangled outlines of people and hear happy voices cheering.

"Is anyone there?" he shouted. "I got an emergency! Gil's hurt. She's not breathing! We gotta get her home!"

Through the portal, Danny could hear the cheering stop. He saw the distorted, wavy image of William rushing toward him. "D—ny? What did—say?"

"Gil's dying! You gotta help!"

Extreme Exam began to crackle and spark. As the cartridge sent out an acrid puff of smoke, the image of the lab died away.

Danny pulled the cartridge from his gaming console and dropped it as it burned his fingers. "Guys," he shouted, "I think we're on our own."

William looked in dismay at the empty Staging Platform. Although Danny's words had been garbled, the message was clear enough. Ripping off his suit jacket, he ran across the lab.

The director grabbed his arm as he flew past. "What are you doing?"

"It's after midnight," William said, shaking off his hand. "I'm going in!"

"Gil requires more help than you can give. We need the Facilitator."

Continuing to put pressure on Gil's wounds, Danny looked up as Nathan ran into the room. His bare chest was glistening with sweat, and he was breathing hard.

"I lost Rick in the woods," Nathan said, gulping for air. "He had a car by the creek."

"Did you get the license number?" Sam asked, administering compressions.

"I couldn't get a good look at it. I wasn't able to keep up with Rick in my bare feet. It was stupid of me not to put on shoes. I kept tripping."

Danny saw Zara's face filling with concern. "Na'tan, yuh be fine?"

"Sure, honey. I'm not hurt. I came back as quickly as I could to see about the girl. How is she? Have you called an ambulance?" Looking down at the mangled mass of flour, Nathan gasped. "What on earth's that?"

"It's Gil," Danny replied. "She came from the future to help us with Rick."

Danny watched as his mother's eyes found Sam's. "My invisible helper," she whispered.

As Sam nodded, the doorbell rang.

"Stay here," Nathan said. "I'll get it."

Holding the T-shirt tight, Danny strained to hear what was happening. There was a low murmur of voices and then Nathan returned, stumbling as he stepped on glass.

"Yuh, okay?" Zara asked in a worried tone.

Catching his balance, he nodded. "Fine, honey, I just wish I had shoes."

"Wah yuh 'ave inna your hand?" she asked.

"A package for Danny," he replied, holding up a brown box. "The deliveryman said it was a matter of life-and-death. But who delivers packages at midnight? It doesn't make sense."

"Take over for me," Danny said urgently. "It makes perfect sense."

When Nathan knelt beside Gil, Danny ripped open the package. Inside was a new game cartridge and a note that read, *Play me now. Move out of the way.*

249

Running to his hideout, Danny slid the game into his PlayFest console. As he turned it on and backed away, the TV glimmered with blue light. Immediately, a bag was thrown through the screen. A scant second later, William sailed through the portal in a running nosedive. He landed heavily on the beanbag, causing the seams to split and stuffing to skitter across the floor.

Danny plucked frantically at William's shirt. "You gotta help Gil! Hurry up, she's dying!"

William picked up his bag and sprinted across the room. When he approached, Zara and Nathan stared at him with open mouths.

"Give me room," William ordered, kneeling beside Gil and unbuttoning her shirt. Taking a long, wicked-looking needle from his bag, he plunged it into her chest.

"What are you doing?" Danny yelled, trying to push William away.

"It is adrenalin," his mother said, grabbing his hands. "He's helping. Leave him alone."

Danny watched as William took another needle and inserted it into Gil's vein.

"You did well," William said. "You got through D-day. Death row's gone."

"It won't matter a bit if she dies," Danny cried, trying to clutch Gil's arm.

"Stay back," William ordered harshly, taking paddles out of his bag and placing them on Gil's chest.

When Danny backed away, William administered a shock. Danny started to cry as Gil's body jolted violently. He watched with a sick stomach as William checked for a pulse, and not finding one, administered another shock.

Suddenly, Gil gave a ragged breath. As she started to cough, William took an oxygen mask out of his bag and put it on her. After starting an IV, he grabbed a unit of blood and passed it to Sam. Sam scrambled to his feet and hung the bag on the back of a chair. William took rolls of gauze and began binding up Gil's bleeding wounds.

"Is she gonna be all right?" Danny asked in a shaky voice.

"Only if we get her to medical aid," William replied, adjusting Gil's oxygen mask with blood-covered hands.

"You mean back through GAP?"

William shook his head. "Her cartridge was destroyed, and mine isn't calibrated for her. We need to take her to the Facilitator and his wife."

"Who are they?" Danny asked.

"They're the ones who mail the games. They're from further into the future than I am."

Suddenly, Danny noticed that everyone could see William. "Hey, why can everyone see you if you didn't scan their brains? Did you—"

"If you want to help," William barked, "stop asking questions!"

Danny nodded and backed toward his mother.

William bandaged Gil's chest wound and said gruffly, "I'm sorry, but we don't have time to talk. We need to move fast to save Gil and keep you all safe."

"This is unbelievable," Nathan muttered.

"Unbelievable or not, it's happening. I need you to deal with it." William began winding gauze around a hideous wound to Gil's stomach. "In twenty minutes, there's a 94.9 percent chance that Rick's going to enter Mr. Jacobson's house with a gun."

Danny watched as William locked eyes with Nathan. "You and Zara need to get your grandpa and go to Westfield. Take Maple Lane to Highway 33—no other route. Check into the Cunningham

Hotel under an assumed name and park your car in their covered garage."

As Nathan nodded, William continued, "After you get on the road, call Chief Rogers and tell him that Rick's back and that Sam and the Winstons are staying with friends in the country."

William stared over his shoulder at Zara. "You and Mr. Jacobson need to remain in the hotel *at all times*. If you do, there's a one hundred percent probability factor that you'll be safe. If you leave the room, your odds go down to 5.2 percent. Do you understand?"

"Yeh mon, wi won leave di room."

William handed Nathan a folder. "You're going to need this. We've discovered more of Rick's victims—women whose red-cord hangings were pronounced suicides."

Nathan gasped. "The files Danny gave me came from the future? How did—"

"That's not important!" William rolled gauze around Gil's forehead. "You only have fifteen minutes before Rick arrives. Get your grandpa and come back here. Now move!"

As Zara and Nathan ran out the door, William wrapped a six-inch gash on Gil's thigh and said to Sam, "Go to Grandpop's and load Sue and Danny's boxes in your trunk. Pack some of your grandfather's clothes for yourself. Call your associate pastor and tell him he'll be taking over for a while. When you're finished, drive back here and park close to the door. Now move!"

Sam hesitated. "Will Sue and Danny be safe if I leave?"

William checked his watch. "Only if you're back within thirteen minutes."

Sam raced out the door, and William turned to Sue. "Grab your photo albums, the cedar chest your husband built, your orange shoes, and your jewelry box. Set them by the front door. Call the

252

hospital and Stubby and tell them you'll be missing work for a while. Call Danny's school and leave a similar message. You have twelve minutes."

Sue scurried away, and Danny watched as William focused on him. "Put your Bible and the framed photo of your dad in your pillowcase."

As Danny obeyed, he heard the low murmur of his mother's voice as she made her calls. He looked over at William—his hands were shaking as he wrapped another layer of gauze over Gil's chest wound. "Anything else I should pack?" Danny asked.

"Your father's pocket watch. It's in your dresser under your blue jeans."

Danny heard cars coming to a screeching halt outside the house as William bandaged Gil's lacerated hands and put her arm in a sling.

"Sue," William bellowed, "put your things and Danny's pillowcase in Sam's trunk."

When Sam and Nathan entered the room, William turned to Danny. "Show the guys Gil's luggage. They won't be able to see it, but they *will* be able to feel it."

Danny smiled for the first time in what felt like years. "Now I know why you wanted them to come back."

"Hey, I'm no dummy," William replied with half a smile. "Have you tried to lift that suitcase?" As Danny chuckled, William said, "After showing them the luggage, grab some wet wash clothes and a few bath towels. Get into the backseat of Sam's car and put my bag on your lap. You have five minutes. Now scoot!"

After the trunk was loaded, Danny watched anxiously as Sam and Nathan laid Gil in Sam's backseat with her head on William's lap.

"Keep her feet elevated on my bag," William said to Danny. "She's in shock."

As Danny nodded, William shouted out his window at Nathan, "You have less than two minutes to get your family off this street. Keep Zara and your grandfather inside the hotel!"

Nathan nodded and ran over to his car where Zara was trying to calm Mr. Jacobson.

"Sam," William said tersely, "go to Ozark Street and turn left. You have only one minute and twenty seconds to get us out of here."

Behind him, Danny could hear the squeal of Nathan's tires as he turned onto Maple Lane and into GAP's predicted safety zone. Sam punched the accelerator, and in less than a minute, they turned onto Ozark.

"Pull into the driveway of the green house on your left and turn off your lights and engine," William ordered. "Everyone, lie down in your seats and be still."

As Danny crouched down, he heard the soft whisper of tires passing behind him. He held his breath as a car halted at the stop sign and turned onto Paradise Avenue.

"Start the car, Sam," William whispered, "but don't turn on your lights for another block. Go down Ozark and take a right onto Hunnington. I'll feed you more directions as we drive."

"Where are we going?" Sam asked.

"To a private estate. You can turn on your lights now, but don't speed. If you do, we have a 66.2 percent chance of being pulled over, and that'll delay us too much for Gil's sake."

The car filled with tense silence. The only sound was Gil's labored breathing.

As Sam turned onto Hunnington Avenue, Danny whimpered. "Is she gonna make it?"

William looked him in the eye. "Gil said you liked things straight. Is that true?"

Danny hesitated and then nodded.

"She has a fifty-four percent chance."

"That's not good, is it?"

"No," William said with a crack in his voice, "it's not good at all. But you only had a fifty percent chance earlier tonight, and you made it. Gil had faith in you despite the odds, and we're going to have faith in her." Taking a wet washcloth, William began to wipe the blood gently from Gil's face. "She's going to live," he murmured in a choked voice. "*She has to!*"

As Danny gave a watery sniff, William asked, "What stopped you from stabbing Rick?"

Wiping his nose with the back of his hand, Danny mumbled, "I was gonna stab him. He was on top of Gil, cutting her. She was all bloody and couldn't move. It was awful. She kept telling me to drop the knife, but I wanted to save her. Then Gil yelled that if I stabbed Rick, she'd never forgive me. She said she'd hate me." Danny put his hand on William's arm. "I couldn't have her hate me—I love her. She was so mad. I never heard her sound that way before."

"I know the tone of voice you're talking about. She used it on me this afternoon."

"Do you think she's still mad?" Danny asked tearfully. "Do you think she hates me?"

William pulled him close. "I can promise she doesn't."

Danny's voice became thick with tears. "It's all my fault. I put her in danger."

"It's no one's fault but Rick's. Gil said what she did to get you out of harm's way and to keep you off death row. Rick belongs there—not you. When she wakes up, she'll be proud of you. You kept your head and brought help. Not only that, you helped her pass her exam. She's earned an Alpha-Blue License—the best TEMCO offers. She's graduating with honors."

"She deserves it," Danny said, brushing tears from his face. "She's the best."

As a road sign flashed past Danny's window, William stiffened. "Sam, our exit's coming up. Get off the highway and turn onto Timberfield Lane. Head west for sixteen miles and turn left onto County Line Road."

"Sixteen miles is so far away," Danny moaned. "Are we gonna make it?"

"We're going to try," William replied. "That's all we can do."

Twenty-five minutes later as the car was heading deep into farming country, Gil began to groan. Leaning down eagerly, William whispered, "Gil, can you hear me?"

"Doc," she said weakly as her eyes fluttered open. "I knew you'd come. Is Danny safe?"

"I'm fine," the boy replied. "I didn't stab Rick. We won!"

"Good," Gil said in a slurred voice. "I knew we would."

Leaning down, William brushed her forehead with a kiss. "I'm so proud of you."

"Brillo pad," she whispered.

"What?" he asked softly, cradling her face with his hands.

"Brillo pad or a wire brush. You *gotta* get rid of that beard."

"What a thing to say at a time like this." William chuckled, stroking her cheeks gently with his thumbs.

As Gil smiled into his eyes, she began to cough—deep coughs that shook her entire body. Her face turned ghastly white. "It hurts," she whimpered. "Doc, it hurts so much."

"I know," he said in a tortured voice. "Just hold on. I'm taking you to meet the Wizard."

"The Wonderful Wizard of Oz? Everyone's gonna be so jealous."

Suddenly, Gil's body began to shake. Her eyes rolled up in the back of her head. A trickle of blood slipped out of her mouth and slid down her chin.

"Gil!" Danny shrieked.

"Quiet!" William barked. "Hand me a towel."

William put pressure on the fresh blood pouring from Gil's chest wound. "Step on it, Sam! We have to speed now, or we won't make it. In a few miles, we'll come to Country Road 7. It's a dirt road by a big barn. Sue, help him look for it—we can't afford to miss the turn. Danny, take over for me. Keep the towel firm."

The car picked up speed. William held onto Gil's flour-covered form as it shook wildly in the backseat. "I want you all to start praying. We're going to make it! We have to!"

As everyone prayed beneath their breath, Gil's shaking slowly stopped. William held onto both sides of Gil's face as tears flowed from her eyes and her breathing became shallow.

"Please don't leave me," William whispered tremulously, brushing her hair away from her forehead. "Just concentrate on breathing. I know you can be pig-headed and stubborn as a mule. Please, be stubborn about this."

Giving a wobbly smile, Gil put a hand to his cheek. "I'm not pig-headed. I'm focused."

Taking her hand in his, he murmured, "Be focused then. *Very* focused."

"There!" Sue shouted. "There it is!"

"Sam, turn right," William said, keeping his eyes locked with Gil's. "Sue, watch for the second road to the left. It's called Painted Pony Drive, but it won't have a marker."

"Doc," Gil whispered, "I'm sorry."

"You've done nothing to be sorry about."

"Yes, I have," she said with a faint smile. "I filled your office with balloons last week."

"That was you? You minx, I'm going to take it out of your skin later."

Gil smiled. Her eyes slowly rolled back and closed.

"What's wrong with her?" Danny asked anxiously.

"She's lost consciousness again. Keep the towel firm."

"There!" Sue yelled. "There it is!"

As Sam turned onto the road, William said in a tense voice, "Go down the third driveway to your right." Stroking Gil's hair, he whispered in her ear, "Hold on. Please, just hold on."

THIRTY-SIX

WILLIAM CLUTCHED GIL to his chest as Sam's car bumped through an orchard. Minutes later, the dirt road forked. At William's instruction, Sam turned left onto a paved driveway.

"Get as close to the door as you can," William urged as they reached a large house.

Sam nodded, pulling onto the sidewalk and parking in a flowerbed.

William and Sam eased Gil out of the backseat as Sue sprinted to the porch. Before Sue could ring the doorbell, an elderly woman with white, candy-floss hair and twinkling eyes popped the door open.

"Come in," the Facilitator's wife said. "We've been expecting you." She turned around and shouted to someone inside, "Get ready, Poppa. They're here."

As William carried Gil into the house, he could hear Sam and Sue gasp.

The old woman chuckled. "You can see Gil now, can't you? That's because of a Scan Emitter set on wide-beam emanation. We—"

"Where do you want her?" William interrupted in a gruff, worried voice.

"This way," the Facilitator's wife replied. "We're set up down the hall." She led William through a large living room with a vaulted ceiling. Motioning to a bedroom, she said, "In there, Dr. Ableman. Please lay her on the bed."

When William placed Gil on a state-of-the-art hospital bed, the Facilitator's wife took the unit of blood from Sam and hung it on a pole. Without speaking, she attached Gil to monitors.

William stood helplessly. Although his body was still, the agony in his eyes belied his calm. He clenched his hands as a spry old man in his early eighties entered the room.

"How does it look, dear?" the Facilitator inquired, washing his hands in a basin.

His wife peered at the monitors. "Not as good as we hoped, but better than we expected."

Grunting, the old man took a syringe from a tray of instruments and plunged the needle into Gil's arm. Taking another syringe full of golden liquid, he slowly injected it into the side of her neck. Both he and his wife watched the numbers changing on the monitors. After a minute, William saw them looking at each other and smiling.

Moving away from Gil's side, the old woman said, "We're going to take good care of your friend, but now it's time for you to leave."

"Wait," Danny said anxiously. "What's wrong with her?"

"Besides her lacerations and a dislocated shoulder, she has a punctured lung and a perforated bowel. We'll need to operate to repair the damage." She motioned everyone to the door. "I won't see you until tomorrow. If you go past the kitchen, you'll find prepared guest rooms. Get yourselves a snack and go to bed. There's nothing more you can do."

As the Facilitator's wife pushed him gently out the door, William grabbed her arm. "Tell me straight—I have to know. What are Gil's chances? Is she going to live?"

The woman smiled and tapped his cheek. "Her odds are up to eight-four percent since you did so well with emergency care. She'll be fine. I feel it in my bones. Now, go get some food. You look like a walking corpse. When the little lady pulls through and sees you, you'll scare her to death. Go on now," she said, giving him a push. "Shoo!"

As the door shut behind him, William leaned his forehead against the wall and covered his face with trembling hands.

"Did that woman say Gil's gonna be okay?" Danny asked in a scared voice.

William nodded and put an arm around the boy. "She said she felt it in her bones."

"That's what Gil always said," Danny mumbled. "That she felt things in her bones."

"Then we'll take it as a sign and believe Gil will be fine."

"Who was that old man?" Danny asked.

"That was the Facilitator," William replied with a wobbly smile. "You're a lucky boy. Not many people get to see him—at least not see him and know his identity."

"Is that why you call him the Wizard of Oz?" Sam asked.

William nodded. "Like the Wizard, he keeps behind the curtain." Clearing his throat, he requested in an unsteady voice, "Sam, will you lead us in prayer for Gil's surgery?"

Sam nodded, and everyone held hands as he prayed. When Sam was finished, William felt more at peace. As Sue sent her son into the bathroom to clean up, William went with Sam to bring in the luggage.

"What does Gil have in here?" Sam groaned, picking up her suitcase. "A set of encyclopedias?"

William shook his head. For some things there were just no words.

Several hours later, the Facilitator gave a tired sigh and left Gil's bedroom. As he and his wife entered the living room, he saw William propped up in a chair. Sam and Sue were sitting on the couch with Danny lying across their knees. They were all in clean pajamas, and they were all fast asleep.

Putting his arms around his wife, the Facilitator chuckled. "And after all the trouble you went to making up the beds."

His wife slapped his shoulder. "Wasn't any bother at all. I don't remember you being able to go to bed during a crisis either."

"I suppose not," he said, kissing her cheek. "Look at them, will you?"

"Dear people, each of them. I'm glad we were able to help."

Moving into the room, the Facilitator gently shook everyone awake. Seeing their anxious faces, he said, "The surgery went fine. Gil will live. Now, off to bed. You're all exhausted."

William passed a trembling hand over his face. "Thanks for your help."

"Not at all," the Facilitator replied. "You did right to call on us."

As Sam stood to his feet and introduced himself, the old man's eyes twinkled. "Glad to meet you, stranger. Call me Poppa. Everybody does."

"And call me Twinkles," his wife said. "Poppa's called me Twinkles for more decades than I'd care to admit—and I just love it."

William stood and asked in a shaky voice, "Can I see Gil?"

"Me too?" Danny asked.

"You can peep in the doorway, but that's all," Poppa said firmly. "I don't want her disturbed."

Together, the group walked to Gil's doorway and peeked in. She was breathing normally and had better color.

"We won't clean her up until later," Twinkles said. "Sue, maybe you can help me bathe her when the time comes?"

As Sue nodded, William asked, "When will she regain consciousness?"

"I'm not sure," Poppa replied. Seeing the fearful look in William's eyes, he said gently, "Stop worrying. She's doing splendidly, and she'll mend fast. I expect her to make a complete recovery except for some residual nerve damage in her shoulder. She'll be her wisecracking, spunky self in no time at all. Remember, our medicine is more advanced than yours. Tomorrow, I'll let you sit by her, but I want you to go to bed now. Twinkles and I will watch her tonight."

THIRTY-SEVEN

THE NEXT AFTERNOON, Crystal sat on a bench by Broglie Hall and glanced casually at the quad where Marc was playing an impromptu game of football with his friends. As the ball sailed back and forth, a group of women sitting on the grassy sidelines cheered. The men hammed it up, and the women cheered even louder. Crystal scowled and opened a thick book on quantum field theory. Trying her best to concentrate, she read: *The propagation of Gaussian wave packets adjusted to a—*

The cheering intensified. Crystal glanced up and saw Marc stripping off his shirt and tossing it to Molly. His muscles rippled as he picked up the ball and threw it to Ryan. Muttering beneath her breath, Crystal hunched a shoulder. Ignoring the game, she peered down at her book: *—transparent spectral region much lower than the resonance of—*

"Toss it here, Marc," Kyle called. "I'm open!"

Crystal peeked up from her book in time to see Marc throwing a perfect low slant into Kyle's arms. Molly jumped to her feet and cheered wildly while Jill and June booed and yelled for Wade and Jake to get off their duffs and sack the quarterback.

Crystal pushed at her owlish glasses and watched as Marc's team huddled to discuss their next play. She sighed. Marc was starting to sweat, and he was doing it in a *particularly* gorgeous way. It amazed her how a little bit of sweat on a man's chest could make her feel so strange.

Making an exasperated sound in her throat, Crystal squinted down at her book and forced herself to read: —*the inverted multi-level atomic medium exhibiting superlumination may...*

She tried to concentrate, but she couldn't. Against her will, she looked up as Marc prepared to throw the ball. The muscles in his back were undulating in a mesmerizing way. The wind stirred the pages of her book as she cupped her chin in her hands and stared at him. She wanted to get through the chapters on Gaussian wave packets, but she supposed that allowing herself a brief indulgence in the study of human physiology wouldn't be too amiss—after all, one should be well-rounded in all of one's academic endeavors.

Marc launched the ball and stood outlined against a backdrop of blue sky. Seeing his masculine pose, Crystal gave another gusty sigh. Suddenly, she noticed Molly looking at her with a sarcastic grin. Blushing hotly, Crystal put her hand on the book's fluttering pages. Her eyes skipped over the text reading at random: *In an inverse Fourier transform...each separate wave phase-rotates in time...there is an overall normalization factor...*

As she read, churning thoughts filled her brain. She couldn't believe she'd been caught staring. Her cheeks burned as she cautiously peeked up. She began to breathe easier when she saw that Molly's attention was back on the game. Mumbling beneath her breath, Crystal thumbed through her book, trying to find her lost place.

Suddenly, a groaning gasp went up from the crowd of women. Glancing quickly at the quad, Crystal saw Wade Kingston slamming into Marc with the force of a freight train. Jill cheered wildly for Wade as Marc lost the ball and it bounced across the grass. Jake swooped in and ran for a touchdown. As Jake triumphantly loped back to center field, June ran up to him and gave him a spectacular kiss. Ignoring them, Crystal stared at Marc in concern. He was still down and he wasn't moving. Biting her lip, she rose slowly from the bench.

"Are you all right?" Molly called, running toward Marc's crumpled body.

When Molly got close, Marc reached up and pulled her down beside him. "A guy could die out here before anyone noticed." He laughed. "What took you so long?"

Molly giggled and pulled away. "You big fraud! Leave me alone. You're all sweaty." As she pulled him to his feet and he swooped in for a hug, Molly pushed him away and purred, *"Not now, silly!"* She pointed at Crystal who was standing like a stone statue. "We have an audience."

As Marc stared over at her, Crystal's face turned bright red.

Giving a cruel smile, Molly laid her hand possessively on Marc's bare chest and said in a honey-toned voice that was calculated to carry, "Poor girl, pressing her nose up against the glass. I think she likes you."

As Molly's tinkling laugh filled the air, Crystal picked up her book and walked away as quickly as she could.

The afternoon was edging its way into a windy evening as William studied Gil's pinched, white face in concern. Very gently, he stroked her matted bangs away from the stitches in her forehead. His heart twisted painfully in his chest. She looked awful.

"What do you think, Poppa?" Twinkles whispered in the hallway.

William tensed at Twinkles's words. With his breath catching in his throat, he blatantly eavesdropped on Poppa's reply.

"I don't like it," the old man murmured. "She should be conscious by now."

William felt his stomach tightening. He ran a finger over Gil's eyebrow.

"If she doesn't wake up soon," Poppa whispered, "something's definitely wrong."

"Is she bleeding internally?" Twinkles asked.

"I don't know," Poppa replied. "I can't tell."

"What about William? Should we tell him what we suspect?"

"He's worried enough as it is. Has he eaten anything yet?"

"Not a bite," Twinkles replied. "He won't leave her side long enough to come to the table. He's awfully worried about her."

"He should be," Poppa murmured. "There was a tremendous amount of damage to her intestines. Hopefully, we didn't miss one of the wounds. I don't like the idea of exploratory surgery. I'm out of my depth, and I..."

As Poppa's words faded into the distance, William gently traced Gil's pale cheek with a trembling finger. A few minutes later, he heard Twinkles entering the room.

"Here you go, love," Twinkles said, putting a tray of food on his lap.

William looked up in confusion. "Thank you, but I didn't ask for this. I'm not hungry."

"Nonsense," Twinkles said in a militantly cheerful voice. "You didn't have breakfast or lunch. Trust me, you're starving."

As William sighed and ran a weary hand over his eyes, Twinkles gave his shoulder a motherly pat. "Eat something," she coaxed. "Starving yourself won't help Gil. In fact, she'd think it was an extremely silly thing for you to do."

When the old woman left the room, William put the tray on the floor and took Gil's hand in his. Giving it a gentle squeeze, he said, "It's time to wake up. Can you open your eyes?"

Outside the room, he could hear murmuring voices as everyone gathered for supper. He was glad for some peace. Sam, Sue, and Danny had taken turns keeping vigil by his side, but he preferred to be alone with Gil. It was exhausting to keep up a cheerful front for their benefit. As Sam's voice rose in prayer over the meal, William studied the strained lines etched around Gil's mouth. Even though she was unconscious, she was obviously in pain. The knowledge tore his heart.

"You're safe," he murmured, brushing a feather-light kiss on her brow. "There's nothing to fear. I have you. Please open your eyes. Can you do that?"

Peering down at her unresponsive face, William felt a tear sliding down his cheek. As he moved to brush it away, it fell onto her broken nose. He gently wiped it away with his thumb as a sob rose in his throat. "I'm so sorry, darling. This is all my fault."

As another tear slid down his cheek, he buried his face in her shoulder and prayed brokenly, "Dear Lord, I don't know how to help her—only You can. Please heal her and put her mind at peace as she sleeps." Pressing his lips fervently to her forehead, he whispered, "Please, bring her back to me. I need her. I love her so."

Hearing Gil give a gentle sigh, William slowly raised his head. As he peered down at her, he gasped. The tension lines were gone from her face, and her cheeks had a healthy pink color. He watched as she sighed deeply in her sleep and began to smile. For the first time since Rick's attack, her face was serene and peaceful.

As William breathed a thankful prayer and nestled his head on Gil's shoulder, Marc helped Molly out of his car and walked her to her door. "I enjoyed tonight," Marc said softly as he looked up at the silvery moon. "It was perfect."

"Which part?" Molly asked in a flirty voice. "The meal or the company?"

"Both."

"Do you want to come in for a while?" she murmured seductively, glancing at him from beneath her lashes.

He shook his head. "It's getting late."

"What does that have to do with anything?"

When he didn't reply, Marc felt her fingers brushing his leg. He stepped away.

"I could make you a cup of coffee," she whispered, slipping a hand under his jacket.

He shook his head. "What time do you want me to pick you up tomorrow?"

"Seven will be fine." She sighed, giving him an exasperated glance. "Did you rent a tux?"

"In a manner of speaking. I decided to purchase one this time."

"Oh?" She pulled her keys from her purse. "That seems extravagant."

"Not really." He chuckled. "Tomorrow will be the third black-tie dinner we've attended in as many weeks. It's wasteful to keep renting."

"Planning on being invited to more fancy dinners in the future?"

"You tell me," Marc replied with a laugh. "You're the one who works for a senator."

Molly put her key in the lock of her door, fumbled, and gave an exasperated mutter.

"Problems?" he asked.

"It's this silly key—it keeps sticking."

Putting his hand over hers, he said softly, "Let me."

Molly nestled close as he jiggled the key and opened the door. As he stepped back, she grabbed his arm and whispered, "Surely, you aren't going home without giving me a kiss?"

Marc hesitated and then pulled her into his arms. "I think I can manage that."

"I thought that you might," she murmured in a sultry voice.

As he lowered his head and kissed her, she melted her body into his. After a few moments, he started to pull away, but she clung to him and deepened their kiss. Marc felt blood pounding in his ears as the kiss continued. He tried to back away, but Molly grabbed his shirt and pulled him inside.

In Charlesberg, Rick struck a match and looked at the trail of gasoline leading to Sue's back door. Giving a smile, he dropped the tiny flame and watched it zip its way into the house.

Suddenly, the world exploded around him. The force of the blast knocked him flat. Lying in the grass, he stared at the writhing flames twisting across the night sky. It was like looking into the face of hell.

Car alarms blared and people began pouring into the street. Rick jumped to his feet and sprinted into the forest. He knew the police would be arriving soon, and he couldn't afford to get caught. Standing behind a tree, he paused for a moment and looked at the raging inferno. Sue may have run away, but he could still hurt her. And when he found her again, he'd make sure she suffered…

THIRTY-EIGHT

A FEW DAYS later, Sam glanced out Twinkles's living room window and saw Danny sitting alone on the grass. Seeing the depressed slump of the boy's shoulders, he grabbed a jacket and headed outside. When he reached Danny, he sat beside him and said, "Poppa says Gil's vitals are strong. Even though she hasn't opened her eyes yet, I'm sure she's gonna be fine."

Danny didn't reply.

"Poppa bragged about your singing. He says you've got *Edelweiss* nailed. And your mom told me you finished your last make-up assignment today."

Danny shrugged a shoulder.

"I've heard rumors that Twinkles is planning a party tonight to celebrate your hard work. Grilled steaks and strawberry cupcakes are on the menu."

As Danny stared at the grass, Sam said gently, "What's wrong, buddy?"

"Me." Turning to him, Danny said in a tight voice, "Is it wrong to hate?"

Sam paused, choosing his words carefully. "Hate's a normal human emotion, but it's also destructive. Hate doesn't harm the person who hurt you, it only makes you feel terrible inside. God can take away your hate if you ask Him."

"I *have* asked, but my hate gets bigger every day. I don't know what to do."

Sam put his hand on the boy's shoulder. "In Matthew 5:44, Jesus said to combat hate by doing the opposite of what it wants you to do. When you're mad at someone, pray for them. That kind of behavior helps you get rid of your anger."

"Do you really think that'll work?"

"It always works for me." Sam peered up at the clouds. "You know, Danny, you remind me of David."

"The guy who killed the giant?"

Sam nodded. "David tried to live a God-honoring life, but even though he was doing his best, King Saul tried to murder him."

"You mean like Rick tried to kill me and Mom?"

"I sure do. When David escaped, Saul hunted him. It would've been easy for David to hate Saul, but he didn't let himself. He even refused to kill Saul when he had the opportunity."

"Why didn't he slaughter the jerk?"

"I'm sure David thought about it, but he knew murder would destroy his future. David showed Saul mercy—even though by man's judgment, Saul deserved to die."

"So the big jerk got away with it?"

"Not for long. Saul died in battle. He got what he deserved, but not through David's hands. And because David did what was right, he became king in Saul's place. I know Rick hurt you, but hating him won't make you feel better. It'll only make you feel worse."

"I'm not mad at Rick—at least not at the moment."

Sam blinked. "Then who…?"

"Dr. Ableman. *I can't stand him.* Whenever I visit Gil, he's always there holding her hand. This is the first time he hasn't been in her room, and that's only because he got kicked out while she's having a bath." Danny glared over at William who was pacing in the orchard. "He never leaves her. He's a big, fat, selfish hog!"

"That's because he loves her," Sam said gently.

"But I love her too! Before he came, she and me did everything together. Now I can't even sit by her without having him there too. It's not fair!"

Sam glanced across the lawn at William. His head was down, and his hands were clenching and unclenching. It was obvious that he was praying as he was pacing. "You know, Danny," Sam said, "sometimes loving people means sharing them."

"I don't wanna share Gil! I wanna have her all to myself."

"I know, but think about what Gil would want. She likes the doc." Sam gave Danny a smile. "If you give him a chance, I'm sure you'll like him too."

"Maybe," Danny grumbled, "but I wish he'd give me some time alone with her. Even though she's not awake, I wanna talk to her. I wanna tell her I'm sorry she got h-hurt..."

As the boy's voice cracked and faded away, Sam said softly, "After Gil has her bath, I'll make sure you get some time alone with her, okay?"

"You'd do that?"

"Of course." Clearing his throat, Sam said, "Speaking of sharing, there's something we should discuss man-to-man. How would you feel if your mother and I started dating?"

"It doesn't matter how I feel," Danny mumbled, glaring at the grass.

"It matters to me. I'm not doing anything without your permission."

"You mean it?" Danny blinked, looking up at him.

Sam nodded. "I want you to feel comfortable having me in your lives."

"What happens if I say no?" Danny asked, blowing a ladybug off his hand.

"I'll be disappointed…after all, I really like your mother, but I'll understand. I'll still be friends with you both, but I won't ask her out on a date."

"And if I say yes?"

Sam smiled. "Then you can help me decide where to take her. I was thinking about that new Italian place across from Stubby's, but I'd like your advice first."

Looking up from beneath his bangs, Danny grinned. "Forget Italian. Her favorite's Chinese. And if you really wanna please her, take her out for frozen yogurt afterwards, and don't forget to spring for extra sprinkles."

"Does that mean you approve?"

"She needs a good man in her life, and I happen to like you."

"I like you too," Sam said with a relieved smile. "In fact, I like you a lot."

"I never imagined the mess blood and flour could make stuck in someone's hair," Twinkles groaned as she and Sue finished bathing Gil. "I sure needed your help."

"It's the least I could do," Sue replied, tucking the covers around Gil. "Everyone's done so much for us. I still can't believe I'm surrounded by people from the future."

"Why not? Time travel's nothing special. For me it's old hat— boring in some respects."

"How far into the future do you come from?"

Twinkles put her head to one side and did mental math. "Let's see, starting from this moment in time, it'd be over sixty-nine years."

"I can't even imagine that," Sue said, smoothing a wrinkle from Gil's bedspread.

"Oh, my math's quite accurate. Gil traveled twenty-four years into the past to counsel your son, and I'm from forty-five years further into the future than she. That makes sixty-nine."

"How many times have you time traveled?" Sue asked.

"Mercy, I have no idea. I lost track *years* ago. Poppa and I worked as time counselors, and we took on more cases than I can remember."

"I thought Dr. Ableman said your husband invented GAP?"

"That didn't stop him from participating in the program. Poppa and I were partners, and good ones at that. We had the top success rate of any team until my daughter and her husband broke our record. Poppa and I had grand times together. We fell in love on my first assignment."

"That must've been romantic."

"It was." Twinkles chuckled. "At first I thought Poppa was kinda reserved, but when we started dating, I discovered he has more romance in his little finger than most men have in their entire bodies." She looked at Sue in a conspiratorial way. "Can I tell you a secret?"

Sue nodded with a grin. "I wish you would."

"Poppa writes me love poems. When we were courting, I asked him to write me one and he's been writing them ever since. He hides them and I find them unexpectedly. It's a delightful game that keeps our marriage happy. After all, what woman can get angry at a man for leaving the toilet seat up when there's a love poem about her eyes taped to the bathroom mirror?"

"I suppose that's true."

"Yes, but it has its downside. One time, when we were entertaining our pastor, I opened a tin of cookies and one of Poppa's love notes fell onto the reverend's plate. It wouldn't have been so bad, but it was a rather *warm* little missive describing the beauty of my curvy derrière."

"Oh, my goodness," Sue said, gasping with laughter. "How *embarrassing*."

"Poppa was mortified, but I kinda like people knowing that my husband thinks I'm desirable. Would you like to see one of his poems?"

When Sue nodded, Twinkles grinned and took a book from her sweater pocket. "I used to keep Poppa's poems in a cedar box, but last Christmas my youngest boy had them typed and bound." As she thumbed through the pages, she gave a happy sigh and read to Sue:

My heart beats softer when you draw near
So soft, I can hear the approaching footsteps
Of the invading love lights of your twinkling eyes
Coming to capture my heart, mind, soul, and body.
Sweet tender invasion of ecstasy.
I am content.

Sue whistled. "You're one lucky woman."

"Don't I know it! I've always said the greatest aphrodisiac is a well-turned phrase when the man saying it means it with all his heart."

In Washington D.C., Marc stood in front of the TEMCO lab and straightened his tie. The lockdown was over, but things were far from normal in Hawking Hall. The tension on campus was thick, and those "in the know" weren't saying anything. Speculation was running high, and the fact that Gil and Dr. Ableman had dropped off the face of the planet wasn't helping matters. Some said the couple had eloped. Others said Gil had died during her exam, and Dr. Ableman had committed suicide. The most logical rumor was that Gil had flunked, and Dr. Ableman was campaigning for her to be reinstated. Whatever was going on, the director was visibly stressed and Dr. Nelson was walking around like a zombie.

With things so unsettled, Marc thought the summer closing of TEMCO would be postponed indefinitely, but he'd received a message telling him to report to the lab to get his assignment. He knew he was overdressed, but he wanted to look his best when the pictures were taken. Photos spanning every summer closing since the establishment of TEMCO adorned the walls of the main office, and this was his first chance to be in one.

Taking a nervous breath, Marc opened the lab door. Immediately, he was engulfed in well-organized chaos as techs moved around in a fluid dance and cadets ran to-and-fro. In the far corner, Director Matthews and Dr. Nelson were sitting at a table, studying a pile of printouts. When Marc approached, the director shoved the papers into a folder.

"Mr. Kerry," the director said, "you're right on time."

"Am I going to be working in the lab?" Marc asked hopefully.

The director shook his head. "The archives."

Marc's heart sank. TEMCO's archive was built like a huge maze, and the last thing he wanted to do was spend any serious time in the dusty old place. Biting his lip, he objected cautiously, "But I don't have Alpha-Blue clearance, how can—"

"I've programmed the vault to recognize your retinal scan. Another student is already up on the third floor, and she'll fill you in on what needs done. The job will take several days, so you'd best get to it."

Groaning inside, Marc nodded and left the lab.

∽

"I'll bet Poppa dreamed up an extremely romantic way to propose, didn't he?" Sue asked.

"Of course he did," Twinkles replied, "but he had *lousy* timing. The night he proposed, I hadn't been expecting him. I had curlers in my hair and was painting my toenails." Twinkles gave Sue a long-suffering look. "Why a man can't understand that a woman likes a *little* notice is beyond me. Surprises are fun and all that, but I like to be prepared for them, especially when they show up at my front door."

"I totally agree," Sue replied, breaking down into helpless giggles.

"I still remember the chagrin I felt, toddling toward Poppa in a beat-up bathrobe with my toes separated by cotton balls. I don't think any woman could've looked more unromantic than I did, but he just kissed me soundly and said he'd be back in thirty minutes."

"You only had thirty minutes to dress?"

"Wasn't that *ghastly* of him? But it's amazing what a girl can do when she senses a proposal's in the wind. I dried my toenails with a hairdryer while I brushed my teeth, and when Poppa came back I looked like a dream in a red silk dress. And Poppa..." Twinkles sighed and smiled. "Well, he seemed to approve. We took a carriage ride to a lakeside restaurant and had a candlelight dinner eaten to the sound of violins. As the evening progressed, Poppa gave me roses, quoted poems, and had singers serenade us."

"Oh," breathed Sue. "How romantic."

"Yes it was, but..." Twinkles looked at Sue and laughed. "Poppa was looking so scrumptious in his suit that all I really wanted him to do was propose quick, so we could go somewhere private and have a little kissing time—after all, Poppa's an *exceptional* kisser."

"So did he propose after you finished eating?"

Twinkles shook her head. "He took me for a stroll by the lake. The moon was full—count on Poppa to wait for a full moon—and the stars were out. After we walked for a while, he took me to a canoe and paddled us to the center of the lake."

"And then..." Sue asked, leaning forward.

"And then, under the shining stars, he gave me my ring." Twinkles held out her diamond cluster for Sue to admire.

"That's a lovely story."

"Yes, it is, but it isn't over. After he gave me my ring, Poppa leaned in to kiss me, and as our lips almost touched, his best friend sent up a fountain of fireworks. The fireworks startled me so much I jerked my head up and hit Poppa square in the nose. He fell backwards and overbalanced the canoe. We fell headfirst into the freezing water—me in my red silk dress and Poppa in his suit.

As Sue gasped, Twinkles chuckled. "Most men would've been mad at a girl for messing things up, but Poppa just laughed. He told me not to worry about it and then he kissed me as we clung to the overturned boat, and you know, I think that kiss was even better than if everything had gone as smoothly as planned." Twinkles sighed and smiled. "It's a *wonderful* thing to be loved by the right man."

∾

As Marc left the lab, Dr. Nelson raised her eyebrow and said, "That was cruel, Peter. Marc obviously wanted to be in the lab when the photographs are taken."

"He needs to think less about his ego and more about his job," the director replied dryly.

"True, but I don't know why you assigned him the archives. You've already given that job to Crystal, and she and Marc don't get along. He's always making fun of her, and she's all thumbs whenever he's around. They drive each other crazy."

"That's exactly why I'm doing it." The director steepled his fingers. "Marc and Crystal are top-notch cadets, and when they finish their training next year, I'd like to put them on staff, but that'll be impossible unless they can find a way to work together."

"So this is a test run?"

"You could say that. If they can't team up during a simple project, there's no way I can trust them to team up during something as crucial as a professional time surf. If they botch this assignment, I'll need to cut one of them from the program."

"That seems harsh."

"Would you rather have a staff you can't rely on?" the director asked. "If we've learned anything the last few days, it's that time surfing puts lives on the line. If employees can't check their personal conflicts at the door, they aren't any good to us."

"If they make a mess of things, which of them will you keep?"

"There's really no contest." The director pushed a folder over to her. "The Junior Class IQ scores came back yesterday."

Opening the folder, Dr. Nelson exclaimed, "Is this accurate?"

"I've had her tested twice, Laura, there's no mistake. Crystal's IQ breaks the chart. We can't afford to lose her."

"Raw intelligence is one thing, but having exceptional interpersonal skills is definitely another. Although he can't seem to get along with Crystal, Marc gets along well with everyone else. He's going to make a great counselor if he gets the chance."

"True, but I don't appreciate the way he treats Crystal. Besides, look at this..." Director Matthews opened another folder and took out a handful of papers covered with complicated equations. "Crystal came to me with ideas about how to make time portals larger. She also had some rudimentary ideas about portable Staging Platforms."

Dr. Nelson thumbed through the papers and blinked. "How *on earth* did a third-year cadet come up with these formulas? Could she have broken into the safe?"

"She hasn't seen the research, I assure you. Crystal Stuart is just *that* smart. If time travel hadn't already been invented, she would've invented it."

"I guess you're right." Dr. Nelson sighed. "TEMCO needs her. I just wish Marc's neck wasn't on the line. He's the most promising counseling recruit since Gil and Zeke."

"If he can find a way to work with Crystal, I'll hire him. But if he can't, it's better to find out now rather than later."

"When would you cut him?" she asked.

"After he takes his practicum field exam. For Zeke's sake, we need him in TEMCO for at least that long. I'll let Marc earn his degree, but I won't put him on staff."

"That doesn't seem fair."

"Life often isn't. However, it may not come to that. It's possible Marc and Crystal can work out their differences."

"I hope so." Dr. Nelson nervously twirled a pen between her fingers. "What about Charlesberg, Colorado? Have you heard from William?"

"Not since the last time you asked."

She dropped her pen and sighed. "Am I being a bother?"

The director reached across the table and gave her hand a squeeze. "Not at all."

She bit her lip. "I can't believe William hasn't contacted us. I wish he'd let us know what's going on."

"You and me both."

Dr. Nelson took a steadying sip of coffee. When she put her mug down, a small grin tugged at her lips. "So, how's Iggy?"

The director groaned. "I don't know how William talked me into babysitting his pudgy, pampered lizard. Last night, the stupid thing climbed up my bathroom shelves and dropped into my bathwater. I thought I was going to have a heart attack. If he pulls that prank again, Iggy's going to become a flashy pair of boots."

"So what type of counseling cases did you and Poppa handle?" Sue asked.

"Mercy, all kinds," Twinkles replied. "We even stopped a big school shooting over in Barrville, Texas."

"I don't remember a shooting in Barrville."

"That's because for you it never happened, and a good thing too. Fifty-two eighth graders and six teachers were killed. After we counseled the shooters, one ended up becoming a CEO and the other a Navy SEAL. Poppa and I had all kinds of adventures in the old days. I even gave birth to our first child on an assignment."

"You mean during the shooting case?"

"No, during a case in Smithtown, Wyoming. Little Jay came early, and Poppa had to deliver him. I can still see Poppa with his hair all messed up and his eyes all wild. I had to slap him, *actually slap him*, to calm him down. You'd never believe a man could get into such a tizzy over a little thing like childbirth. Poppa said it was my fault the baby came early, but I still say that riding a motorcycle over a bumpy field had nothing to do with it. A baby will come when a baby will come, and the girl I was counseling was running away. I couldn't let her give us the slip, could I?"

Sue smiled and shook her head. "Where was Poppa?"

"He was right there," Twinkles replied. "If he'd been faster, he could've jumped on the Harley with me, but he was busy picking up apples."

"Apples?"

"Yes, dear, apples spilled all over the road. Now tell me, why will a man concentrate on spilled apples when something much more important is going on?"

"I couldn't say."

"Well, I can. It's a man-gene. It's the same gene that'll make a supposedly intelligent man meticulously dust the living room blinds when you call and ask him to clean up the house quick because you're having unexpected company. *Dust the blinds!* And yet leave the clothes to be folded in a heap on the couch, the dirty dishes strewn on the kitchen counter, and his wet raincoat sitting in a soggy wad on the floor."

As Sue laughed, Twinkles gave a gentle smile. "Truthfully, I can laugh over those blinds and the apples with a grateful heart. If that type of thing is all I can complain about after so many years of marriage, I'm a blessed woman indeed."

Marc climbed the marble stairs of Hawking Hall, grumbling beneath his breath. Working in the archives was going to be anything but easy. The shelves twisted in a strange configuration that was *way* beyond his grasp. Of all the summer-closing assignments, this was the last he would've chosen.

Reaching the vault door, he put his eye next to the retinal scanner. A few seconds later, huge bolts began pulling back and the thick metal door swung open. Sighing, Marc stepped inside and called, "Hello! Anybody here?"

As the door swung shut and locked behind him, a blonde head peeped cautiously from behind a shelf. Marc groaned when he saw who it was. He honestly hadn't thought things could get worse, but he was wrong. Working in close proximity with Crystal was gonna be a nightmare.

As Crystal walked toward him, she stumbled over her feet and said, "I thought I was doing this alone."

"I guess the director thought you needed help." Hanging his suit jacket over a chair, Marc asked, "So what are we doing?"

Crystal pushed at her glasses. "Putting this year's file boxes onto the shelves."

"That doesn't sound too bad."

Crystal laughed. "Look behind you."

Glancing over his shoulder, Marc sputtered, "You've *got* to be kidding!" Staring at the huge pyramid of boxes leaning haphazardly against the wall, he moaned, "Didn't *anyone* put *any* boxes away this year?"

"I guess they were leaving it for summer shutdown."

Marc cracked his knuckles. "Surely there haven't been *that* many counseling assignments this year."

"Sure there have. Two semesters' worth of senior field exams plus an innumerable number of professional cases would make quite a pile. Each case has its own box and—"

"For Pete's sake, stop explaining things," he grumbled, yanking off his tie. "I'm not your student, and I'm not stupid."

Crystal's face turned bright red. Marc watched as she ducked her head, picked up a hand-held scanner, and scanned a small conical code on the lid of a box.

"Why are you using a scanner?" he asked. "Aren't the boxes shelved alphabetically?"

Crystal shook her head and mumbled, "For confidentiality reasons, case subjects' names aren't on the boxes. A conical code and lid number are our only means of box identification."

Marc blinked as he picked up the box she'd just finished scanning. It felt like it was full of bricks. Crystal picked up another box and swung it easily onto her hip.

As he raised an eyebrow, she stuttered, "My b-box is pretty light. It's probably a cadet's field exam—a suicide prevention by the feel of it. If criminal activity were involved, my box would be heavier."

He gave a noncommittal grunt.

"If you want," Crystal said awkwardly, "we can trade boxes."

"I'm not a ninety-pound weakling. I think I can manage to lug a box."

"That's not what I meant. I just want to be fair..." Her voice trailed away. After a moment she said, "From the look of things, I'd say the case subject of your box was someone who was *very* bad or someone who's going to be *very* important."

"Any other deductions, Sherlock?"

She nodded. "I'll bet a professional time surfer handled the case."

"Where'd you come up with that idea?" he asked as they walked toward the shelves. "Just by the weight of my box?"

She shook her head. "Before you came in, I put four other boxes with the same fourteen-digit identification number up on the shelves. Any case subject with five whole boxes dedicated to their case is important enough that they wouldn't be assigned as a student's field exam."

Marc shifted the box in his arms. It was seriously heavy. "Where does this monster go?" he grunted. "I hope it's close, or I may end up applying for workman's comp."

∽

"So, did you and Poppa work cases year round?" Sue asked.

"No, dear. Only during NSU's school year. We'd go on mission trips during the summer. I'd teach and Poppa would sing. My hubby's a wonderful singer. He supported himself in college by giving lessons. He had Jay singing before he was three."

"Who's Jay again?" Sue asked.

"Our eldest boy. In a few weeks, he'll be singing in Milan at the Teatro Alla. Jay's one of the best tenors in the world, and I'm *not* being maternally prejudiced. Recent reviews are likening him to Enrico Caruso."

"I'll bet you're proud."

"I sure am." Twinkles gave Sue's knee a pat. "Your boy's also remarkably musical. Poppa's enjoying training his voice. You must be as proud of your son as I am of mine."

"I couldn't be prouder, but I can't take any credit for his talent. Danny inherited his musical abilities from his father. I can't carry a tune in a bucket."

"Me either, but that's okay." Twinkles laughed. "We need to let our menfolk do some things better than us or they'll feel insecure. Men have such fragile egos, you know."

THIRTY-NINE

CRYSTAL FROWNED AND tried to calm her breathing. No matter how handsome Marc was, he was just a simple bipedal mammal, and a bad-mannered one at that. She needed to get a grip.

"So where does my box go?" Marc groaned as he shifted the heavy box in his arms.

"XCVI-Lambda-Violet-S³-18," Crystal replied, peering down at the scanner. "It's a code."

"I've figured out that much, Einstein. Explain it."

"I thought you didn't want me to explain things?" When Marc didn't reply, she blew a curl out of her face. "XCVI refers to the ninety-sixth row of shelves."

She watched as Marc stared at the rows surrounding them. "Are you telling me we've gotta count each row?" he groaned. "There must be thousands of them."

Crystal shoved at her glasses. "Actually, there are only one hundred. The veins in the marble floor show the roman numeral of each row. The design is easy to miss. It was created by introducing a…" Her voice trailed as Marc gave her a pointed glance.

288

They walked in silence to row ninety-six. As the row split in six different directions, Crystal saw Marc shifting his box again. "What's next?" he grunted.

"Except for a few exceptions, there are six sub-rows in every main row," she replied. "From left to right, they're called Epsilon, Lambda, Mu, Pi, Phi, and Chi."

"Are you on the level?"

"Just listen, okay? Each Greek number corresponds with a Nobel Prize category: economics, literature, medicine, peace, physics, and chemistry. Your box belongs in sub-row lambda-slash-literature."

As they turned down the aisle, and the sub-row began to twist and turn, Marc grumbled, "This whole place is a huge maze."

"I know," Crystal said in a sparkling voice. "Isn't it terrific?"

Marc rolled his eyes. "So we're in sub-row lambda-slash-literature, what's next?"

"Each shelf's assigned a hue in the visual spectrum. The top shelf is violet. The next is—"

"For Pete's sake, I *do* know the colors of the rainbow."

Wincing at his sarcastic tone, Crystal said in a brittle voice, "Your box is assigned violet. It goes on the top shelf. The shelves in this row are separated into seventeen subsections. We're looking for sub-section S^3."

"That's as clear as mud."

She hunched a shoulder and said awkwardly, "In 1996, Wislawa Szymborska was awarded the Nobel Prize for Literature. Szymborska has seventeen letters in her name—three of which are Ss. We're looking for the third S. *Id est*—S^3. *Ab uno disce omnes*."

"Quit speaking Latin!"

"I didn't know I was," she mumbled. "It's my knee-jerk reaction to stress."

"What do you have to be stressed about? I'm the one locked in the archives with a Latin-speaking know-it-all."

Crystal swung around and gave Marc a withering glance. "You're a real jerk! Or should I say, *es a rudi homine?*"

Marc gave a crack of laughter. "Okay, I deserved that. I hope you know how to find S³ because I sure don't."

"The clues are right in front of you if you'd take the time to look," she grumbled.

"Sure they are, Sherlock."

Crystal stopped walking and pointed at the top shelf. "The middle grouping of bolts in each section are braille letters spelling out Szymborska's name. If you look at the bolts, you can tell what section you're in." She stood on her tiptoes and ran her fingers over the bolts. "Two dots, no dots, and one dot left. That means we're in section M—four sections away from S³." She peered over at Marc. "I'll write the braille alphabet out for you, if you'd like."

"I can't believe you know braille," he muttered.

"Why wouldn't I? It's a blast to close your eyes and read a book in it."

"I suppose you were bored and thought pretending to be blind would be fun?"

"There's nothing fun about blindness," she said. "And it isn't something to joke about."

"You're the one who enjoys reading braille for kicks."

"I just like figuring things out," Crystal said, hunching a shoulder. "Louis Braille was a genius, and I respect his work."

Reaching section S³, she set her box on the floor and took a computer pad from her pocket. "Here are the names of all the Nobel Prize winners from 1901 to 2001. You can use the list. I don't need it."

"Don't tell me you memorized a hundred years' worth of Nobel Prize data."

Crystal glared at him. "I get bored a lot, okay? What's it to you?"

"Don't you do anything besides study?"

"Of course I do," she snapped.

"Yah, right. I'll bet you're just a walking encyclopedia with no social life."

"I have a social life, it just doesn't include *you*."

"I'll bet on Friday nights, you cuddle up with a cat on your knee and read Oedipus Rex in the original Greek."

Crystal felt herself blush. "Why don't you drop it?"

"Scared of what I might think?"

"No, too bored to care." Crystal pointed at the eighteenth space on the top shelf. "That's where your box belongs: XCVI-Lambda-Violet-S^3-18."

"What kind of mind thought up this ridiculous system?"

"A brilliant one. The boxes are impossible to find unless you know the code key."

"You've got that right." Shoving his box onto the top shelf, Marc muttered, "I don't see why TEMCO needs an archive. GAP has this information in its memory core."

"What if GAP came down with a computer virus?" she asked. "Having a paper copy will insure the preservation of TEMCO's history."

"You're putting a lot of faith in a bunch of paper."

"Under the right conditions, paper's surprisingly durable. Centuries after we're dead and turned to dust, TEMCO's alkaline, lignin-free, cellulose paper will remain. It could easily last over five-hundred years."

"Fascinating," Marc said dryly.

"Isn't it? Five-hundred years is a long time, but if TEMCO would do more calcium carbonate buffering and experiment with different paper fibers, we'd be able to increase that time frame exponentially. After all, the wrappings of Egyptian mummies have lasted for over *five-thousand* years and…"

Her voice trailed away as Marc gave an exasperated sigh. Embarrassment washed over her in a sickening wave. She wished she would've held her tongue. *Guys like Marc didn't want lectures on the chemical makeup and history of paper—who would?*

"Egyptian mummies," Marc mumbled. "That's fascinating. Truly riveting. But I still don't see the point. GAP has firewalls. Maintaining an archive is a waste of time."

"What if a Time Tsunami occurred? A Cataclysmic Failure could destroy GAP."

"The people in charge are too smart to let that happen."

"Intelligence has nothing to do with it. Time's a tricky thing to mess with, and these records are too important to lose." Crystal looked at the boxes sitting primly on their shelves and her resolution to watch her tongue flew out the window. Turning to Marc, she said with glowing eyes, "These boxes are testimonials to TEMCO's success. Think of it! Thousands of boxes representing thousands of lives transformed for the better. Tragedies averted. Lives saved. Families healed. Happy endings! And all because of us! I don't like office work, but when I visit the archives, I feel glorious inside, just like I do when I hear a choir singing Händel's *Hallelujah Chorus*."

As she smiled at Marc and saw his expression, her face went white. He was laughing at her—not out loud, but silently—in the way that hurt her most. Taking a hasty step backward and tripping over the box by her feet, she fell heavily against the shelves. As the shelves rocked and crashed toward her, she screamed and threw her hands over her head.

∽

"It sounds like you've had a busy life," Sue said.

Twinkles chuckled. "You can say that again! Poppa and I tried retiring, but we couldn't settle down to the old golf-cart-and-shuffleboard routine. So, since Poppa's in charge of TEMCO, we made ourselves a new job and became Facilitators."

"And what does that entail?" Sue asked.

"A little bit of everything, but mostly delivering the games and smoothing out the bumps time counselors experience during their travels."

"It's amazing you've had time for a family."

"You make time for what's important. Our children—Jay, Deleena, and Will—were always our priority. In fact, Poppa refused to let me time surf for *three months* before Lena was born. I thought that was excessive, but he wasn't taking chances after delivering Jay by himself."

"Is Deleena a singer like her brother?"

"Merciful heavens, no! She inherited my voice, the poor girl. She followed in our footsteps and became a time counselor. She placed second in the Martial Arts World Tournament in Busan City, South Korea a while back. She looks like a delicate angel, but she has a fist of iron."

"Does she have a family?"

Twinkles nodded. "She married her partner. Their courtship was *most* amusing to watch. Lena was determined not to ruin a good business relationship by dating, so her partner took my advice and used some underhanded tactics to win her over. The whole thing had me in stitches."

"I can imagine." Sue laughed. "What about your youngest? What's he like?"

"Of all my children, he takes the most after his grandfather. He and his wife have four kids, and their youngest girl looks just like I did when I was her age."

"Do people call her Twinkles too?"

"Of course they do." The old woman smiled. "I've loved my work and my role as a wife and mother." She peered over at Sue. "How about you? Do you like motherhood?"

"I love it. You're lucky to have three children. I always wanted a houseful of kids, but it wasn't meant to be." Sue looked down at her hands. "I had complications when Danny was born, and my doctor told me I wouldn't be able to have another baby."

"Yes, dear, I know. But that isn't necessarily true. Two more children are in your future. A girl and a boy."

Sue's mouth dropped open. "What do you mean? Is that just a guess?"

"My dear, I'm a time surfer. I don't guess. I know. And they'll both look remarkably like Sam."

"Watch out!" Marc shouted, pushing Crystal to safety.

As Marc grabbed the shelving unit and steadied it, he heard an ominous scrapping sound. Looking up, he saw the heavy box from XCVI-Lambda-Violet-S³-18 sliding toward him. Before he could move out of the way, the box smashed against his upturned face and sent him to his knees. As the box hit the floor, the seal broke and a snowstorm of papers swirled around him.

"Marc!" Crystal cried. "Are you okay?" Springing toward him, she slipped on a piece of paper and fell on his lap. Her head slammed against his chest, and the injured side of his face hit the shelves with a resounding smack. The pain made him wince.

"Will you be careful?" he snapped. "What are you trying to do, kill me? Can't you go five seconds without an accident? What's the matter with you?"

"I'm so—"

"Don't say it! I'm sick of your sorrys! If you were really sorry, you'd get off my lap and stay away from me!"

Giving a choking gasp that sounded suspiciously like a sob, Crystal slid off his legs. Marc winced as her knee scraped over his ankle. As she huddled by his feet, he fingered his throbbing eye and glared at her. She looked so remorseful that it made him feel like a heel. Uttering an exasperated sigh, he tried to remind himself that he was the injured party.

As Crystal made another choking sound, Marc grumbled, "Oh, for Pete's sake, don't start blubbering."

"I'm not crying," she spat, looking at him with swimming eyes. "You couldn't move me to tears if you tried."

"I'm not trying, but why the dickens can't you watch where you're going? Do you have an inner-ear imbalance?"

Instead of answering, Crystal mumbled, "Your nose is bleeding."

As Marc reached up and tried to brush the blood away, she took a tissue from her pocket and handed it to him. "Thanks," he muttered grudgingly.

"Let me look at your eye."

"It's fine," he said quickly, backing away.

"If it was fine, you wouldn't be clutching it."

"I said it's fine and it is!"

"Don't be such a baby," she chided, scooting forward. "Let me see."

"I'm not a baby," he grunted, "and you're kneeling on my hand."

Blushing wildly, Crystal raised her knee.

Snatching his hand away, he raised the tissue to his nose. "Leave me alone, will you?" As she ignored him and gently pried his hand away from his face, he flinched and said crossly, "I mean it. I don't need your help."

"Shh."

When Crystal carefully touched his cheekbone, Marc stared at her in surprise. Her fingers were amazingly gentle. As she continued to examine the damage, he gradually allowed himself to relax. For some reason, Crystal's soothing touch seemed soft and tender—almost loving. He sighed and closed his eyes. She gently smoothed the rumpled hair away from his forehead and trailed her fingers down the side of his face.

As the air conditioner switched on and a lock of her hair wisped lightly against his chin, an electric bolt of energy ripped through his body, leaving him shaken. His eyelids quivered as her hair continued to tantalize him. It was soft as silk, and it felt heavenly against his skin. His breath caught, and his heart began to race. Golden ripples vibrated down his spine, filling him with an unbearable aching pain. She was so close that he could feel her breath on his cheek. She smelled wonderful. Like apple blossoms. Like springtime.

"The side of your face is already swelling," she murmured, "and your eye's black-and-blue. Open it, will you? I want to check and see if you have a concussion."

Marc slowly opened his eyes and looked at her. As he did, all his dreamy castles shattered. She might smell like apple blossoms and have a touch that could turn his knees into goo, but she was still plain-old Klutzy Crystal, the dowdy campus joke. He peered at her hair. It was shiny and clean, but it was perched on top her head in a messy bun and there was nothing attractive about the style. He studied her owlish glasses and hideous clothes. She looked like a frumpy bag lady. As she touched his cheek again, he stiffened and jerked away. There was no way he could be attracted to someone like *Crystal Stuart*. The thought was ridiculous.

Crystal peered into his eyes, and as if sensing what he was thinking, she quickly backed away. As she tried to scramble to her feet, she slipped on a piece of paper and fell hard on her backside. Marc stared at her. Her bun was falling down, and her cheeks were bright red. As confusing emotions engulfed him, he felt himself becoming angry. He didn't like being off balance, and he didn't like Crystal.

As she tried to get up and fell against his leg, he barked, "Will you be careful? You're gonna kill us both if you keep this up."

Crystal ducked her head. "I'm not clumsy on purpose." When he didn't reply, she mumbled, "Your eyes are dilating properly. You don't have a concussion."

"I could've told you that," he snapped, feeling far more shaken by their close encounter than he cared to admit. He roughly rubbed his cheek, trying to erase the magical feel of her fingertips. "You didn't need to put on a Florence Nightingale act."

"I was worried about you."

"If you were really concerned, you'd be more careful."

"I try. Honest, I—"

"Obviously not hard enough. You're a walking disaster zone. I'll be fine as long as you don't keep pummeling me with heavy objects." Clutching his eye, he grumbled harshly, "Just keep away from me, okay? That's all I ask. Stay away and leave me alone. My life's at risk every time you say hello."

As he watched, Crystal's face went completely white. "You don't want me around?"

Knowing he was stepping over the line, but feeling too shaken to care, he glared at her. "Why would I? The last thing I need in my life is someone like *you*."

"That's just fine with me," she spat. "From now on, I'll stay far away. It doesn't take two people to carry one box. We'll get finished faster if we work separately."

"That's the most sense I've ever heard you make."

Crystal drew her knees up to her chest. "Your nose is bleeding again. You'd better go take care of it."

Marc glanced at the blood speckling his best dress shirt and grumbled beneath his breath. Trying to dab at the spots with the bloody tissue, he muttered, "I'll go to the restroom and see if I can get my nose to stop gushing while you pick up the papers."

"You're just smearing the blood with that tissue. Try washing the spots out with cold water. If your shirt's ruined, buy another and send me the bill."

"I wouldn't do that," he said, standing to his feet.

"Why not? It's my fault your nose is bleeding."

"I wouldn't say that."

"You did a minute ago," she said. "I may be a klutz, but I have a good memory. I can remember everything you've said in graphic detail."

Marc shifted uncomfortably. He never stayed angry for long, and he was beginning to regret some of his harsh words.

"What are you waiting for?" she asked with a hint of tears in her voice. "Go on! Get out of here! Who needs you anyway? I sure don't."

Something in her tone made Marc hesitate. "I'm sorry, Cris. I didn't mean—"

"Yes, you did! You meant every word! Don't deny it."

He stared at her. Her hair was wisping around her face, and her eyes were dewy and brilliant. For one brief moment she actually looked pretty.

"Are you deaf as well as dumb?" she hissed. "I told you to get out of here, and I meant it. I don't need someone with the IQ of an orangutan slowing me down."

"Cris—"

"Just do what I ask. You're dripping blood all over the papers."

Making an exasperated sound, Marc stood up and walked away. He got about ten feet before he turned and looked at her. She was sitting in a huddled heap with her head down on her knees. Biting his lip, he started to retrace his steps, but then, changing his mind, he simply walked away.

Rick tossed the contents of Sam's closet on the floor and kicked at the clothes in frustration. He'd been over every inch of Sam's house and still hadn't found a clue to Sue's location.

Picking up Sam's Bible from the nightstand, he flung it across the room. He couldn't believe a *pastor* had stood up to him. Grabbing a can of spray paint, he began writing obscenities on Sam's bedroom wall. The angry orange words spilled out into the hall and into the living room. After defacing a picture of Christ, Rick looked at Sam's cheap furniture and sneered. He wondered how Sue was going to enjoy being the girlfriend of a poor church mouse.

Crystal heard the vault door closing behind Marc as she brushed the tears from her face. Marc may not want her in his life, but that was fine, she didn't want him in hers either. In fact, outside of work, she'd never talk to him again.

As she grabbed a handful of papers and began sorting them into piles, she came across a case subject's name embedded in the text: *Andrew Hamilton*. Crystal blinked rapidly. *Everybody* knew Andrew Hamilton. He was the most famous man on the eastern seaboard. Heisman trophy winner, entrepreneur, one of the richest men in the nation, and one of the most handsome. As her eyes scanned the papers, she realized that Andrew Hamilton was Andy—the teenage boy Zeke had just finished counseling.

Shuffling through the papers, she found a red file labeled the *Poppa Report*. Her eyebrows rose. She'd heard rumors of a man named Poppa, but she hadn't believed he existed. She knew she shouldn't open the red file, but she couldn't help herself. After reading a few paragraphs, she gasped. The file was full of information about the future.

As she read what Andrew Hamilton was going to accomplish, she realized why his file was marked *Condition Gold*—the information about him was dynamite. If anyone wanted to derail America's future, all they had to do was assassinate Andrew before he rose to power.

She slammed the *Poppa Report* shut. She knew beyond a shadow of a doubt that she shouldn't be reading the file. It was more than just confidential—it was dangerous. Shame washed over her in a sickening wave. Zeke had been right. Her curiosity was a character flaw. She'd have to confess to the director and make sure Andrew's box was resealed and put in a different location.

Quickly shoving the papers back in the box, she stood on her tiptoes and pushed it onto the top shelf. As she looked at the five boxes dedicated to Andrew Hamilton, she whistled silently. At least now she knew who to vote for when the time came.

Hearing the vault door opening, and the sound of a cell phone ringing, Crystal grimaced and skittered down sub-row Lambda. She recognized Marc's ring tone, and she didn't want to be anywhere near him. Not now. *Not ever.*

∽

Being sure to observe the speed limit, Rick drove through the suburbs of Westfield, Colorado. Turning left into a well-kept cul-de-sac, he raised his eyebrows and smirked. It was obvious which of the cookie-cutter houses belonged to Nathan and Zara. They had the American and Jamaican flags painted on their garage door.

Tapping his fingers against the steering wheel, he made his plans. He'd enter through the back and see if Nathan's wife was home. If she was, he'd make her tell him where Sue had gone. He smiled. He'd never attacked a policeman's wife before. He thought it'd be quite amusing.

FORTY

WILLIAM STOOD BY Gil's bed as Poppa and Twinkles examined her.

"We should start skin regeneration," Twinkles said, leaning over Gil's unconscious form. "There'll be scarring if we wait, and she won't want scars, especially on her face."

Poppa nodded. "Her vitals are strong enough. Pass me a regenerator."

"What are you doing?" William asked in a worried voice as he grabbed Gil's hand. "What's regeneration? Will it hurt her?"

"Not at all," soothed Twinkles. "Regeneration speeds the healing process, so cuts don't scar. We didn't want to stress Gil's system by doing it sooner, but best results are seen during the first seven days." She turned to Poppa. "What about her nose? Is it too late to straighten it?"

"I might have to rebreak it. She can live with a bent nose."

"No, I can't!" a voice objected. "I wanna be Miss America."

William jumped and gave a shout of laughter. "Gil, are you awake?"

Gil didn't answer. William could see that she'd slipped back into a peaceful dreamland.

∽

Marc tossed his jacket over his shoulder and emerged from the corridors of Hawking Hall into the warm twilight air. As he strolled toward the parking lot, he grimaced. Crystal was avoiding him like the plague, and it was *really* getting on his nerves. She was making him eat more humble pie than he cared to admit, and he didn't like the taste one bit.

On his left, he saw Ryan hurrying past Hertz Hall. "Hey, Ryan, wait up!" he shouted.

Ryan slowly turned around. "Hi, Marc, what are you up to?"

"I was gonna ask you the same thing. I haven't seen you for days. I tried to call, but all I got was your answering machine."

"Sorry about that. I've been...busy."

"Do you want to catch a movie tonight?" Marc asked.

Ryan hesitated and looked uncomfortable. "Don't you have plans with Molly?"

Marc shook his head. "So, how about that movie?"

"Sorry," Ryan said abruptly. "I'm taking Kailee to a concert."

"Since when are you two an item?"

"We're not. She's trying to make Tim jealous."

Marc laughed and finished closing the distance between them. He caught Ryan looking at his black eye and grinned. Ryan never gossiped and never pried. No matter how curious he was, Ryan didn't snoop. It made him a comfortable friend to have around.

"So how did Kailee manage to rope you into a concert?" Marc asked.

Ryan shrugged. "She's a friend. You do things for friends." Ryan's voice took on a strained note. "All the women around here seem to view me as their big brother."

"The kiss of death." Marc slapped Ryan's back. "With your looks, I'd think women would be falling all over you."

As Ryan gave a noncommittal shrug, Marc looked over his shoulder at Hawking Hall. Crystal was just leaving the building. Turning around to avoid being caught staring, he asked, "So what assignment did the director give you?"

"I'm sending acceptance and rejection letters to the freshman recruits."

"Were there many acceptances?"

Ryan shook his head. "The number's way down from last year."

"Why? Is interest in the program declining?"

"Not at all," Ryan replied. "We had more recruits than ever, but admission requirements are becoming stricter. No one's getting in without an undergraduate GPA of at least 3.85. If you didn't graduate summa cum laude, you might as well not apply."

Marc whistled. "I'm glad I applied when I did."

Ryan grinned. "You and me both."

Marc glanced back at Hawking Hall. Crystal caught him looking and ostentatiously turned the other way. His jaw tightened. "So did the cute girl with golden freckles make it in?"

Ryan nodded. "Phoebe Reynolds was accepted, but I don't see why you care. You already have a girlfriend."

Marc shifted uncomfortably. "Not anymore."

"What on earth happened? I thought you and Molly were doing great."

"Apparently too great," Marc mumbled. "When I took Molly home the other night, she made it clear that she wanted to take our relationship to the next level."

"She proposed?"

Marc bit down a laugh. Ryan might look like a Hollywood heartthrob, but he was rather naïve when it came to women. Ryan was what his mother would call a sweet, innocent lad and what Kyle would call a buttoned-up preacher-type.

Marc's grin faded. With his own reputation, no one would call him innocent or preacher-like. He wondered how long it'd take before his reputation was as spotless as Ryan's. He felt his stomach tighten. If he could take back the last few years, he'd do it in a heartbeat.

As fading beams of sunlight broke through Colorado clouds, Gil began to stir. Feeling sunshine on her face, she slowly opened her eyes. She awoke to find everyone standing by her bed praying for her. Smiling, she said cheerfully, "Anybody care to say hello?"

"Gil!" Danny yelled, lunging toward her. As Sue shouted a quick warning, the boy stopped his headlong progress. "Are you okay?" Danny asked quietly. "You've been asleep for days. I thought you'd *never* wake up."

"I'm fine," Gil said, opening her arms wide. "Come here, squirt."

"Will I hurt you?"

"Not a chance." As Danny hugged her, she said, "You did good on D-day. I'm awfully proud of you."

"But it's my fault you got hurt," he mumbled.

"That's silly," she said, looking him in the eyes. "If it's anyone's fault, it's mine because I was too stupid to remove that silly game from your PlayFest console. You, my young knight, are the one who got me out of a pickle of my own making."

As Danny's smile dawned huge and bright, Gil pumped his hand in an exaggerated handshake. "You're a fine fellow," she said with a British accent, "and I'm glad to know you!"

Danny laughed and said in his own British imitation, "Jolly good and right-o." Smiling, he said excitedly, "Guess what? My school work's all caught up!"

"That's wonderful!"

"Twinkles made me cupcakes to celebrate. I saved you one. Do you want it?"

"Maybe later," Gil replied, shifting painfully on the bed. "Keep it safe for me, okay?"

Nodding, Danny said with a tremor in his voice, "It was really scary when you weren't breathing. Mom and Sam gave you CPR and then Dr. Ableman arrived. He sailed through the TV like a rocket."

Gil looked over at William with interest. "Like a rocket, huh?"

Danny nodded. "He came so fast that I was almost squashed flat. He broke my beanbag."

As William cleared his throat and blushed under her intent gaze, Gil murmured, "Go on, Danny. What'd the doc do next?"

"He got to work fixing you up and barking orders." The boy's voice became gruff in imitation. "Nathan, do this and this. You have ten minutes. Move! Sam, do this and this. You have six minutes. Move!"

Gil's lips twitched. "He sounded just like that, huh?"

"Oh, much worse," piped Danny. "He was so ferocious to look at, and so ferocious to hear, we just upped and did whatever he said. We were afraid not to."

"And it's a good thing we did, young man," Sue said. "He saved Gil's life."

Gil reached out her hand to William. When he stepped quickly to her side and took her hand in his, her eyes began to shine. "You *do* care, don't you, Mr. Rocket Man?"

Smiling tenderly, William chuckled. "Are you just figuring that out?"

Gil laughed and squeezed his hand.

Marc fingered his black eye. It was throbbing again.

"I knew Molly was crazy about you," Ryan said as they walked past the library, "but I didn't know she was thinking about marriage."

"She wasn't," Marc replied dryly. "She was making a different type of proposal."

Ryan looked blank for a moment and then his face turned fire-engine red. "I didn't think she was that type of a girl."

"I didn't think so either."

Silence fell. Marc shifted uncomfortably.

"You don't have to tell me what happened," Ryan said quietly.

"I know, but you're my accountability partner." Marc took a deep breath and plunged in. "I thought it was safe to kiss Molly, but I was wrong. One moment we were kissing on her porch, and the next, she was dragging me inside. When I realized what was happening, I told her that regardless of my reputation, I wasn't sleeping with any woman unless I was married to her."

"What'd she say?"

"She didn't say anything, she just laughed at me."

Ryan grimaced. "I'm sorry."

"I deserved her skepticism. My past isn't spotless, and it keeps rising up to haunt me."

"Give it time. You've only been walking the straight-and-narrow for a few months."

Marc sighed. "And every day's been a challenge. You don't know how close I came to giving in to her."

"She kept pressuring you?"

He nodded. "She whispered that a woman you could touch was far more fun than a God you couldn't see. When I backed away, I tripped over a chair and fell flat. By the time I'd gotten to my feet, she had her blouse off."

Ryan blinked. "Talk about temptation."

"You aren't joking. Getting out of that house without sleeping with her was the hardest thing I've ever done." Marc swallowed. "When I was living apart from Christ, I used to pride myself that I wasn't living in a way that'd become addictive. I avoided too much alcohol and refused party drugs, but I never imagined that a woman's touch could be as addicting as any chemical." Marc cracked his knuckles. "I wanted Molly. I wanted her badly."

"What stopped you?" Ryan asked quietly.

"When she slid off her skirt, I had a vision of myself spitting in Christ's face. I knew if I slept with her I'd be shaking my fist at God. I just couldn't do it."

"I'm proud of you."

"I'd be prouder of myself if I hadn't been so close to caving in."

"You got outta there," Ryan said, thumping his shoulder. "That's what counts."

"I did get out, but not gracefully. When she started unbuttoning my shirt, I ran for the door. I knew if she kept touching me, I was gonna be sunk. I felt like an idiot running away like that, but I didn't dare stick around."

"Don't feel foolish. You did exactly what Paul advised in 1 Corinthians 6:18. Although *flee fornication* was probably meant to be taken figuratively, a literal interpretation works too."

"I *literally* fled all right. Oh, how I fled!"

"How'd she take it?"

"She threw a flowerpot at my head, does that give you any clue?"

Seeing the way Ryan was staring at his black eye, Marc chuckled. "Molly isn't the one who gave me this—not that she didn't want to."

As Gil smiled at William, Sue said to her, "I can't thank you enough for all you've done."

"Don't try," Gil ruefully replied. "I did so many things wrong that I'm convinced God stepped in and straightened them out. I thought Danny would be in the clear when we threw away the kitchen butcher knife. When I saw Rick's butcher knife, I felt so stupid that I wanted to beat myself up. Unfortunately, Rick beat me to it."

Seeing William shudder and turn pale, Gil squeezed his hand. "So, did we get him?"

"Not yet," William replied. "But Nathan says the police are closing the net. Rick's been leaving quite a trail. He ransacked Danny's school, then Sam's house, then Nathan's."

"Not Sue's?" As William hesitated, Gil's eyes narrowed. "What aren't you telling me?"

William sighed. "I didn't want to tell you yet, but Rick burned down Sue's house."

Gil gave a dismayed gasp.

"It's not as bad as it sounds," Sue said quickly. "I brought my most precious possessions with me. Nothing was destroyed that can't be replaced."

"I don't care a bit about the house," Danny said, leaning against her pillow. "Mom and I are gonna live with Mr. Jacobson. He called the night of the fire to invite us. Mom says we'll only stay until we get our feet under us, but I hope we live there forever. I *like* Sam's family."

As Gil smiled and started to reply, Twinkles came bustling into the room. "That's enough talking for now. Gil needs another nap."

William squeezed Gil's hand and followed the others out of the room.

Twinkles pulled down the shades and murmured, "Go to sleep, dear. Everything's fine. Everyone's safe. You have nothing to worry about."

Deciding that the advice sounded perfect, Gil yawned and closed her eyes.

༄

"So it's over between you and Molly?" Ryan asked, as they cut across the grass.

Marc grimaced. "For me it is...for her, not so much. I told her we're through, but she showed up at my door to renew her offer. When she kept insisting it wouldn't matter if we slept together, I told her that according to Hebrews 10:26-29 there's a big difference between an accidental slipup and a willful sin." Marc started to blush. "I hoped she'd get the point, but she just grabbed my rear and said sex isn't sinful—it's natural."

Ryan gave a bark of laughter. "How do you like being on this side of the fence?"

"The irony isn't lost on me," Marc replied, tugging his collar. "When I told her sex belongs within the bonds of marriage, she called me a stuffed shirt."

Ryan's lips twitched. "Seems to me that when we had the same talk, you called me a prudish holy roller who didn't know how to have fun."

"I remember. I also remember how close you came to getting my coffee tossed in your face." Marc cracked his knuckles and sighed. "Molly says anyone with a reputation like mine won't reject her forever...I'm starting to wonder if she's right."

"She isn't," Ryan said firmly. "You're stronger than you—"

Marc's cell phone rang. As Marc took it out of his pocket and looked at the number, he winced. "It's her again. She keeps calling."

"Don't pick up. You can't say anything you haven't already said."

As the phone rang again, Marc asked, "Shouldn't I try to convince her to live for God? You didn't give up on me when I had questions."

"That's because you weren't trying to sleep with me," Ryan replied. "We'll ask Kailee to invite her to church. You need to stay away. Remember Delilah and Potiphar's wife. Sometimes, the best way to handle a woman like Molly is to sever all ties before she destroys you."

Letting the call go to voicemail, Marc gave Ryan a shaky grin. "You're probably right. It just makes me feel like a coward to keep running from her."

"It's not cowardly, it's self-preservation."

Silence fell.

"Actually," Marc said uncomfortably, "Molly's the reason I wanted to go to a movie with you tonight. I know she'll be waiting at my apartment when I get home." His voice lowered self-consciously. "And it's getting harder to refuse her. I had a dream about her last night." Marc's voice cracked. "It's been torture, and what makes it worse is I know I'm being an idiot. She isn't hurt that I won't sleep with her—she's peeved. She's not interested in a relationship anymore. She just wants me to break my purity vow. If I sleep with her, I'm gonna be a sinner *and* a fool."

"Well, you're not going to be available to her," Ryan said firmly. "I'm cancelling on Kailee, and we're going to that movie. Afterwards, you're coming to my place. In fact, you're temporarily moving in with me. My kitchen needs remodeling, and there's nothing like cold showers and hard work. By the time we've finish installing my kitchen cupboards, Molly will have moved on to someone else."

"And if she hasn't?" Marc asked as they reached the parking lot.

"Then how would you feel about participating in an Adam's family reunion in California?"

Marc grinned. "Will Gomez and Morticia be there?"

"Sure. Cousin It and Pugsley too."

"I knew I could count on you."

"Don't mention it," Ryan said, pulling out his car keys. "You'd do the same for me. None of us are above temptation, especially *that* kind."

Marc's phone rang.

"Give it here," Ryan said, taking Marc's cell and turning it off. "You can use my phone for the next several days, and I'll use yours."

Feeling a bristle brush on her face, Gil awoke to find William kissing her forehead. She felt like swatting his scratchy beard away, but she liked William enough to let it stay. Besides, his lips were warm and tender, and he was murmuring *lovely* things in her ear. She began to smile and then giggle.

"Gil," William murmured tenderly, "are you awake?"

"Awake enough to realize you should've been a poet rather than a professor," she said with heightened color.

William ran a gentle finger down her cheek. "You inspire me."

"Really?" she said, looking up anxiously. "Are you sure? Am I an ugly fright now?"

"You're just as lovely as ever, you vain little peacock."

"What about my nose?" she asked. "Did you go to bat for me? Did they fix it?"

"We've entered you in the next beauty pageant."

"Good," Gil sighed, snuggling down on her pillow. "It'd be a shame if years of using green goo went to waste."

"What about the purple goo?" William asked with a laugh.

"How'd you know about that?"

"I also know about the blue gunk you smear on your eyebrows," he said with a twinkle.

Gil thought about tossing her pillow at him but decided it'd take too much energy.

William's smile turned serious. "Honestly, how are you? Are you okay?"

Squeezing his hand, she answered truthfully, "I'm sore as the blazes, but I'm feeling stronger."

"What can I do to make it better?" he asked, gently stroking her hair.

"I'm starving," she replied. "I could eat the hide off an elephant without using salt or pepper."

"Why didn't you say so?" William chuckled. "I have a TEMCO bar right here."

Making a face, Gil pushed his hand away. "You awful man! No kitty-litter bars. I want Sue's pancakes. The smell of them drove me *crazy* at Danny's house."

"How about lime gelatin and a side of broth instead?"

"Just try it, mister! Poppa's cleared me for solid food, and I want pancakes!"

"Okay." William laughed. "Pancakes it is. Anything else?"

"Don't stint on the syrup. I want 'em *drowning* in maple syrup. And butter. Lots of butter. And peanut butter. And powdered sugar. And a big glass of ice-cold milk. And that cupcake Danny's been saving for me."

"Anything else?" he asked, bending down and kissing her forehead.

"Yes! For pity sake, shave off that *horrible* beard!"

Later that night, as he and Marc stood in line at the movie theater, Ryan shuffle-stepped forward and asked, "What job did the director assign you?"

Marc groaned. "I've been stuck in the archives with Crystal. I don't know which is worse—the assignment or the company of the campus klutz."

Ryan's lips tightened. "You shouldn't make fun of her."

"Why not? She brings it on herself."

"That doesn't matter. Gossiping about someone's shortcomings is just as sinful as sleeping around."

"For Pete's sake," Marc grumbled, "just look at my eye! Crystal dropped a box on my face. I've never met a more awkward, frumpy—"

"You're being cruel," Ryan said harshly, "and I don't appreciate it."

"And I don't appreciate having a busted face! She's a menace! She's—"

"I don't want to hear it! God doesn't make a distinction between sins. If you're gonna commit yourself to Him, you need to watch your mouth as much as your zipper."

Marc rolled his eyes. "You sound like you're in love with her."

The muscle in Ryan's jaw worked overtime.

Marc gasped. "Are you?"

Ignoring him, Ryan pushed some bills across the counter. As he accepted his ticket and moved aside, Marc said reproachfully, "I told you about Molly."

"Look, it wouldn't matter if I was in love with Cris. She doesn't see me that way. Drop it, will you? I don't want to talk about it. And definitely not with you!"

Marc purchased his ticket in silence and then said dryly, "I can see why you avoid the topic. Crystal's about as alluring as a hairball. You'd be nuts to be attracted to her."

Ryan ground his teeth. "You're blind as Samuel, aren't you?"

"What do you mean by that?"

"If it'd been up to him, Samuel would've anointed David's brother, Eliab, as king. But God told Samuel it's more important to look at someone's heart rather than their appearance." Handing his ticket to the usher, Ryan said gruffly, "And for your information, Crystal has a beautiful heart."

"As opposed to a beautiful face?"

"Her face is beautiful too—if you look at it."

"If you like her so much, why don't you ask her out?" Marc asked.

"Don't you think I've tried?" Ryan replied explosively.

"She turned you down?"

"She was clueless that I even asked."

315

"But what if you'd—"

"Forget it," Ryan grumbled. "Whatever you're suggesting, it wouldn't work."

"How can you tell? Maybe if—"

"Look, I've prayed about a relationship with Crystal, and I've received an answer. Cris isn't the woman God wants for me, but the man who wins her will be blessed indeed. She's a fascinating woman. You shouldn't make fun of her, you'd be lucky to have her as a friend."

"I don't think that's an option," Marc said. "After the box incident, I told her to keep away and now she won't talk to me."

Ryan gave a sharp laugh. "I'll bet that's a new experience for you."

Marc narrowed his eyes. "I'm not worried. She'll come around eventually."

Ryan shook his head. "Once Cris makes up her mind, she sticks to it. It's all or nothing with her. If she's determined to ignore you, you haven't got a shot."

"Wanna make a bet?" Marc asked as they found their seats.

"It's no fun to gamble when there's no risk involved. If Crystal's determined to cut you out of her life—you're out."

"And you're in?"

"I haven't a shot with her either, and I know it." As the lights began to dim, Ryan turned to Marc and said grimly, "For the good of our friendship drop it, okay?"

Forty-One

BEFORE BREAKFAST THE following day, Sam and Sue took cups of coffee and went outside to watch the sunrise. As they settled into the garden glider, Sam wrapped his arm around Sue's shoulders, being careful of her bruises. They slowly glided back and forth, sipping coffee and watching the clouds turning from red to gold as the rosy morning light kissed the treetops.

"Sue," Sam said gently as she snuggled back against him, "please tell me about Bill."

"What do you want to know?" she asked quietly.

"Whatever you're willing to share."

Sue took a sip of coffee. "Bill was my first love. We were high school sweethearts, and we got married right after graduation. Billy was a foster kid. He never had a real home life, so he wanted to make the best home he could with me—and he did."

"You were happy?"

"Very." Sue took another sip of coffee. "Bill worked at the plant outside of town while I made our little house as cozy as possible. We didn't have much money, so I did my decorating with glue and

317

a sewing needle." She laughed. "Our end tables were wooden crates covered with material. Billy thought they were lovely. Every month, we'd save up and buy something for the house. He'd get more excited over buying a spatula than most men would get over buying a sports car. Billy thought it was a grand adventure to set up housekeeping…"

As her voice trailed away, Sam prompted gently, "Go on."

"Our main outings were to church and choir practice." She turned and smiled at him. "I can't sing—I was just a warm body to fill the choir loft—but Billy had a marvelous voice. He led the Sunday worship service. I was awfully proud of him."

"He sounds like a wonderful man."

"He was. When Danny came, Billy was over the moon. He read every book on parenting he could get his hands on. I think he got more mileage out of my pregnancy than I did. He actually swore he got food cravings. In the middle of the night, I'd wake up and catch him feasting on peanut butter and pickled beet sandwiches. I can still see him eating by the light of the nightlight—his hair all tousled and his eyes twinkling when he caught me watching from the bedroom doorway. He'd motion for me to join him, and I'd sit on his lap and snuggle down against him. As he munched away, I'd listen to his heartbeat and the sound of the kitchen clock ticking away. I've never felt safer than I did wrapped in his arms."

"It sounds as if your house was full of love."

"It was, and we couldn't wait until Danny was born to add to that love." Her smile faded. "My pregnancy went well, but there were complications with the delivery. Although Danny was fine, my doctor told me I'd never have another baby."

Sam's heart lurched. "I'm sorry," he said quietly.

Sue was silent for a moment. "I had to keep down for a while, so Bill took care of the baby. He loved doing it. He didn't even mind

318

changing diapers. I was just starting to hobble around when my mother got sick. She moved in with us and died two months later."

"Oh, Sue!"

"It was a hard time, but Billy was a rock. After a while, things got better. Bill got a promotion and I took care of Danny. We still didn't have much money, but we did have lots of fun. Our favorite thing was to pack up Danny, grab a picnic lunch, and go for a hike in the woods. Bill could make even a simple walk seem like a grand adventure."

"You loved him very much," Sam said, looking off into the distance.

"Yes," Sue quietly replied. "I did."

Sam looked back at her. "And then…?"

Sue took a shuddering breath. "And then he got sick. It started slowly. I'm not even sure when it first started. Bill would get tired playing with Danny, but we didn't think much of it at first—we thought he was just working too hard. But I started noticing he was losing weight. I was worried, but Bill brushed it off. I wanted him to go to the doctor, but he didn't want to spend the money. In the end, he went more to please me than because he felt worried, but…"

Sam gently tightened his arm around her and waited.

"It was cancer."

Sam brushed away the tear sliding down her cheek. "I'm sorry."

They sat in silence, gliding slowly back and forth. After a moment, Sue cleared her throat. "The final two years were a nightmare—and a treasure. Bill was weak from his treatments, but he stayed upbeat. Every day, he tried to show me how much he loved me. When he quit his job, I found work at the plant while he watched Danny after school."

"Danny mentioned his dad reading the Bible to him."

Sue nodded. "Bill was determined to teach our son all about God. He became so frail that he had to lie on the couch, but he'd have Danny cuddle up with him and they'd read the Bible together. Eventually, Bill couldn't hold the Bible, so Danny turned the pages for him."

"He sounds like a wonderful father."

"He tried to be, and he was."

"And a wonderful husband?"

"Yes."

"I'm sorry for your pain," Sam murmured, taking her hand.

"I was more numb than in pain. I'd never worked outside the home before, and suddenly, I was pulling full-time shifts to pay for massive doctor bills, taking care of a sick husband, running a house, and raising a child. Even though Bill's health kept deteriorating, I was certain God would heal him. I refused to let Bill talk about funeral plans. I wasn't in denial about his type of cancer—we both knew it was terminal—but I was convinced God would give us a miracle. I had the deacons anoint Bill and pray over him, I fasted and claimed his healing, I taped healing scriptures all over the house, I put Bill on prayer chains, I played worship music in every room, I even Jericho marched around the house, but…"

Sam held her close and remained silent.

Sue cleared her throat. "At the funeral, one of the deacon's wives told me that if I'd had more faith, Bill would've been healed. Another person said Bill must've committed a secret sin or all the prayer would've worked."

"*Oh, Sue!*"

"I stopped going to church after that. I was hurt and angry, but most of all, I felt betrayed by God. Billy was a *good* man. He did his best to serve God. And I *did* have faith. I *did!* I believed so much in

320

Bill's healing that when I discovered he wasn't breathing...it was a shock."

"I'm so sorry," Sam said gently.

"So am I," Sue muttered. "Bill's death was senseless and it hurt."

Sam nodded and gently rubbed her shoulder. "I don't know what it feels like to lose your soulmate, but I understand the pain of losing someone you love after praying for them. When my father died, it hit me hard. I don't know why God sometimes chooses not to heal."

"I don't know either," Sue mumbled, her voice thick with tears. "But I do know that it wasn't because Billy was sinful or because I wasn't praying hard enough."

Holding her close, Sam said firmly, "Those people at the funeral were wrong—*horribly* wrong. It's our job to pray for healing, but it's God's job to decide whether or not to do it. We can't hope to understand the scope of God's plans."

Sue shifted in his arms. "Before I moved here, the deacon's wife visited me. I didn't want to talk to her, but I didn't know how to get rid of her without being rude. Over tea, she brought up Bill's death. She said since Jesus healed everyone He met it was obviously my fault or Billy's that things hadn't turned out differently."

Sam made a disgusted sound in his throat. "That's the cruelest type of heresy! Granted, there were some instances in the Bible when Jesus healed everyone present at a particular time, but there were also instances when He deliberately avoided healing. In John chapter five when Jesus healed the man at the pool of Bethesda, there were lots of people waiting to be healed, but Jesus didn't heal any of them. Only God knows why. Only God sees the big picture. Humans can't begin to understand why some are healed and some aren't."

"It just feels awful to be ignored by God."

"He didn't ignore you," Sam said, gently stroking her cheek. "He just said no."

"Even though I know you're right, it still hurts. I felt like God was playing games with me—that's why I walked away from Him. I didn't want anything to do with a God who'd let me experience such pain. I couldn't understand why God let Billy die."

"I felt the same after Dad passed away. I believe it's the *why* that drives a person crazy."

"It was the *why* that kept me up at nights."

Leaning down, Sam picked up a stick. "When Dad died, I was so angry at God that I wrote the word *why* over and over on a piece of paper. As I did, I began to see a truth." With the stick, Sam drew a W in the dirt. "When we're in pain and start to ask *why*, it's as if we're traveling through the word itself. At first, we come to the W. We embark on a crooked path full of downs and ups. We struggle with who we believe God is. We struggle with how we'll respond to Him in light of our pain. We hate God. We run to God. We hate God. We run to God. We're traveling in the W."

"That's how I felt," Sue said. "I wanted to run to God with my pain, and at the same time, I wanted to punish Him by ignoring Him. I felt so confused."

"That's the W. Confusion. Crookedness. Ups. Downs." Sam drew an H on the ground. "The devil loves to take advantage of us when we're confused, so after the W, we come to H—the place of entrapment. Satan loves to whisper lies in our ears. Soon, he has us trapped between false ideas about why God let us be hurt."

"I did feel trapped in my pain. I didn't understand why Bill wasn't healed."

Sam retraced the *H*. "When I was angry at God, the two things the devil kept telling me was either God wasn't powerful enough to stop Dad's death, or else—"

Sue spoke up quickly, "—or else God was mean."

Sam nodded. "The devil had my mind running back and forth between those possibilities. *God isn't powerful. God is mean.* My mind felt like a ping-pong ball hitting two walls. I was stuck in the H."

"So what did you do?" Sue asked.

"Well, after the H, you come to the *Y*." Sam drew a *Y* on the ground. "In the Y, you start at the bottom and work your way up. You acknowledge that God's tugging at your heart and you reexamine your faith. You decide if you're going to believe that God is real and that He's personally interested in your life. You look at what the Bible says and decide if you're going to trust it. It's as if your old faith was made of building blocks that have come tumbling down, and you inspect each block and decide what to do with it."

"My faith did feel like a pile of toppled blocks," Sue said softly. "But even while I was trying to ignore God, little things kept drawing me to Him...I just kept resisting."

Sam smiled. "I think God shows His love best when we, as His children, throw a temper fit and He calmly waits for us to stop kicking so He can hug us again."

Sue slowly nodded. "I knew God wanted to help me with my pain, but I was too angry to care. I thought if God had done things *my* way, everything would've been fine."

Sam squeezed her shoulders. "I think everyone feels that way at times—if they'll admit it. I know I did. But when I stopped fighting, I came to the crossroad at the top of the Y. After you reexamine your beliefs, you'll either deny God and throw away your faith in Him, or else—"

"—or else you'll accept the fact that even though you don't understand why things happened, God is still *God* and He loves you."

"Exactly." Sam retraced the *why* in the dirt. "There'll come a time in every Christian's life when they have to walk through the *why* and decide to follow Christ even when life seems unfair."

Sam sighed and looked at a hawk wheeling in the sky. "I never understood what a *sacrifice* of praise meant until the first time I worshiped God after my father's death. I was in such turmoil that singing was the last thing I felt like doing, but after I gave my sacrifice of praise, I felt God's peace enveloping me again."

"You were pretty upset, weren't you?" Sue asked.

"Truthfully, I was so angry that I accused God of lying in Hebrews 4:15."

Sue frowned. "I don't think I'm familiar with that verse."

"It says that Jesus suffered in all things just like we do."

"And you didn't think that was true?"

"I thought it was a bald-faced lie. I told God that Jesus never had anyone die on Him except Lazarus. And since Jesus raised Lazarus from the dead, it didn't count. As I was yelling, I heard a sorrowful voice deep within my spirit say, 'What about Joseph?'"

Sue blinked. "I never thought about him."

"Me either, but I did some research and learned that Joseph probably died when Jesus was young. Being the eldest boy, the support of Jesus' family likely fell on His shoulders. Mark 6:2 says He worked as a carpenter. Jesus knew the pain of death, and He knew the pressure of finances. Not only that, He knew betrayal by His own family. When He began His ministry, His brothers and sisters didn't believe in Him. His hometown rejected Him. The religious leaders accused Him of being drunk and demon possessed. The gossips tore His character apart and twisted His words. He was lied about, misunderstood, and tossed out of towns. One of His best friends betrayed him to the authorities. He was arrested on false charges and beaten. He died a horrible, humiliating death. And worst of all, while He was dying on the cross, He felt completely forsaken by God. The miracles surrounding Jesus are only one side of the coin. The other side is full of suffering and pain. If we want to follow Jesus, we'll experience both sides of the coin—not just one."

"What exactly do you mean?" Sue asked, looking startled.

"Jesus said the servant is not above his master. Since Jesus experienced trials, temptations, and troubles, so will we. I think people get tripped up in their faith because they expect a wonderland existence in a world wracked with sin and pain. They expect the road to be smooth, and when they hit the bumps, they get mad at God. I know I did. We live in a fallen world, and we're in a spiritual battle with evil. Denying that truth gets us into trouble and tricks us into getting angry with God when He's the one we should be running to for shelter."

"That's a sobering thought," Sue said, biting her lip.

"Yes, but it's reassuring to know that although Jesus thought God had forsaken him—God hadn't. Our feelings, and the pain we're in, can make us feel as if we're separated from God, but in reality He's always right by our side. To me, it's comforting to know that Jesus understands our confusion when bad things happen. He's experienced grief and pain first hand."

Sue sighed and snuggled back into Sam's arm. "I'm glad God's big enough to handle our problems and our doubts as well."

Sam nodded. For the next several minutes, they sat in silence, sipping coffee as the sun appeared in a golden blaze above the treetops. Breaking the silence, Sam said, "Thank you for telling me about Bill. He sounds like a wonderful man."

"He was wonderful," Sue whispered, turning toward him, "and Sam, so are you."

Sam's breath caught as Sue brushed back a lock of hair that had tumbled down on his forehead. As she smiled, the morning sunlight seemed to intertwine with her hair, turning it into burnished gold. Her beauty seemed almost too much for him to bear, and at that moment, Sam realized that Sue had completely captured his heart. Barely breathing, he gently took her hand, and the glance that passed between them was as tangible as a gentle caress.

Marc yawned and rolled over on the lumpy futon in Ryan's living room. As the morning light cast dim shadows over the furniture, he sighed. Ryan had barely spoken after the movie, and he knew he owed him an apology—he just hated admitting it. His opinion about Crystal hadn't changed, but he shouldn't have teased Ryan about liking her.

Flinging back the covers, Marc rose from bed and stubbed his toe on the cupboards sitting on the floor. Stumbling back, he fell against the coffee table and knocked over a jar of nails. As the nails clattered across the floor, Marc bit back an oath and began scooping them up. The bedroom was suspiciously silent. It was obvious that Ryan was still mad. If he wasn't, he'd be shouting out a laughing comment—after all, the nails hadn't exactly been silent.

Leaning down, Marc inspected the cupboards Ryan had built. Woodland animals were cunningly carved into the oak doors. He gave a silent whistle. He knew Ryan was an artist, but he hadn't realized the extent of his talent.

Wading through sawdust, Marc went to the kitchen to brew a pot of coffee. As the rich aroma filled the air, Ryan emerged from his bedroom and leaned against the table. Shifting uncomfortably,

Marc rinsed a couple of mugs in the sink. He'd been hoping to ignore the situation, but seeing the anger in Ryan's eyes, he knew he couldn't.

"I'm sorry," Marc said awkwardly as he gave Ryan some coffee. "I was a jerk last night."

Ryan blinked and remained silent.

"I shouldn't have pestered you about Cris. I was angry that you didn't want to confide in me, but you have the right to keep your personal life private."

Ryan blinked again and slowly smiled. "I'm sorry too. As far as Christianity goes, I have just as much to work on as you. The way I handle my anger is anything but godly."

"I wouldn't say that," Marc replied with a grin. "You didn't slug me."

Ryan's lips twitched. "Maybe I was afraid of your right hook."

As Marc laughed and poured himself a cup of coffee, Ryan dropped a sugar cube in his mug and sighed. "I need to apologize for more than bad temper. A few days ago, God told me to seek you out, but I pulled a Jonah. I unplugged my phone and avoided you like the plague."

"Why'd you do that?" Marc asked in a startled voice.

"I was upset about Cris, but that's no excuse. If I'd done what God asked, you would've been at my place days ago and avoided some of the trouble with Molly. I'm sorry."

"Don't be," Marc replied, taking a sip of coffee. "I'm here now, and I'm grateful."

Ryan gave half a grin. "Grateful enough to start installing my cupboards?"

"Don't push it." Marc laughed. "Those things look heavy."

"Why'd you think I invited you?"

"My stellar company?"

"Don't flatter yourself." Ryan chuckled, pushing a box of chocolate-frosted donuts toward him. "I need your brawn. I tried lifting the cupboards myself and nearly broke my back. Next time I do some carving, I'm gonna use balsa wood."

Rick sat in his car and glared at the Cunningham Hotel. Nathan and Zara hadn't been home for days and a hotel was the logical place to look for them. Unfortunately, they must've registered under an assumed name. The Cunningham was the last hotel on his list, and the parking lot was restricted and covered. Since he couldn't search for their car, he'd spent hours watching the lobby and pool, but he hadn't seen a trace of Nathan's Jamaican wife.

Rick slammed his fist against the dashboard. *The Cunningham was another dead end.* Revving his engine, he drove away and didn't look back.

Forty-Two

MORNING LIGHT STREAMED into Gil's bedroom as Twinkles and Poppa began detaching her tubes and wires. Seeing what they were doing, Gil gave a whoop. "Freedom at last!"

"Are you sure she's well enough to be off the monitors?" William asked anxiously.

"Quite sure," Twinkles assured him. "Look at her, she's turned the corner."

William bit his lip. "But she's so pale. What if—"

"Trust me, my boy," Poppa said gently. "I know what I'm doing."

As William nodded and brushed back her bangs, Gil watched as Poppa detached her IV. Suddenly, she blinked. "Poppa, have we met before?"

The old man smiled. "You were the best waitress I ever had."

Gil squealed and turned to William. "Poppa's the mystery man who gave me my scholarship to NSU!"

"I didn't know that," William said, adjusting her blanket and offering her some water.

"Stop hovering like a worried old granny, and I'll tell you all about it!"

As William chucked and sat beside her, she said, "You know my parents died my senior year of high school, but what you don't know is that after their funeral our house was sold to cover debts. I didn't have any money left for college. Any money left for anything really. I rented a grubby little apartment and waitressed at Bubba's Bonanza to make ends meet." She bit her lip. "Money was so tight, sometimes I had to choose between food or electricity."

"I'm sorry," William said, squeezing her hand. "I didn't know it was so hard."

She shrugged a shoulder. "It's not something I like to remember, but luckily it didn't last long. One day, Poppa came into Bubba's and ordered a Beefy Burger with fries. After he left, I cleared his table and found a cookbook with an envelope inside. A note said I could have the envelope's contents if I promised to master all the cookbook's recipes."

Seeing William's quirked eyebrow, she laughed. "I thought the cooking part was strange too." Her eyes glowed. "But inside the envelope was a full-ride scholarship to NSU."

Gil smiled over at Poppa. "There wasn't any contact information, so I couldn't thank you. But your gift changed my life!"

"No one deserved it more," the old man replied.

She gave Poppa a dimpled grin. "I kept my promise—I have the cookbook memorized."

Poppa chuckled and changed the bandage on her hand. "Good, I knew you would."

"I always wondered why you gave me the scholarship," she said slowly. "It was such a huge gift, and—"

"Stop wondering," Twinkles said firmly, giving Gil's shoulder a pat. "Poppa and I have more than enough money to spread around. Investing some in you was pure pleasure."

Crystal sat outside the director's office and anxiously wrung her hands. She'd tried to confess her infraction earlier, but the director hadn't been able to talk with her. By the time he'd arranged to see her, she'd worked herself into a nervous tizzy.

Crystal looked up in shock as raised voices came from the director's office. As the argument continued, she heard enough to realize that someone was upset about Gil's time surf. Trying to ignore her curiosity, she began to hum *The Banana Boat Song*. She was giving her *Day-Os* extra oomph when the director's door flew open.

"I don't care what you say," Dr. Moosly growled, stomping past Crystal's chair. "It's unforgiveable that I've been left out of the loop. When I get to the bottom of things, I won't be silent about what I find!"

Leaning up against the wall, Director Matthews said in an expressionless voice, "I'll take that under advisement."

"You'd better! I'm compiling a report on Dr. Ableman's infractions, and I'm starting one on you too!"

"By all means, go ahead."

Dr. Moosly shook his finger in the director's face. "Something's going on!"

"Perhaps it isn't what you think," Dr. Nelson said softly, emerging from the office.

"Perhaps it's *exactly* what I think!" Dr. Moosly shouted, slamming the hallway door.

Crystal watched as Dr. Nelson looked at Director Matthews and raised her eyebrows. The director gave a noncommittal grunt. "Miss Stuart," he said, "I'm sorry to have kept you waiting. We're ready for you now."

Rising from her chair, Crystal said uncertainly, "If this is a bad time...?"

"Not at all," the director assured her. "Do you mind if Dr. Nelson joins us?"

Crystal hesitated. "Does she know about *Condition Gold?*"

Nodding, the director motioned for Crystal to enter his office. When the door was closed and they were seated, he said, "Now, what exactly is the problem?"

Crystal took a deep breath. "I had an accident in the archives. One of the boxes broke open and some papers spilled out."

The director steepled his fingers. "The box belonged to a *Condition Gold* case subject?"

Crystal nodded.

"Which one?"

Hesitating, she looked pointedly at Dr. Nelson.

The director smiled. "You may talk freely."

"It was A-Andrew H-Hamilton's box." Crystal gulped.

"I see," he said. "How much did you read?"

"Enough to know that I shouldn't be s-seeing what I s-saw." Crystal's face turned bright red. "At first, I only read enough to put the papers in order, but then I started to get curious." Looking up at the director, she confessed, "I read three pages of the *Poppa Report* on purpose."

"You didn't read it all?"

She shook her head. "I realized that what I was doing was wrong. Mr. Hamilton's box needs to be sealed again. I think all five of his boxes should be assigned a different place in archives."

"Five boxes? How do you know there are more than one?"

Crystal pushed at her glasses. "There are five boxes with the same fourteen-digit identification number on their lids. I assume the number's Andrew Hamilton's name in Prinkleton's numerical code—but that's just a guess of course."

The director raised his eyebrows. "It's a good one. You're the only person other than the designers of the archives to make the Prinkleton connection."

Crystal shifted uncomfortably beneath his scrutiny. "I didn't try to break the code on purpose. The solution just popped into my head while I was brushing my teeth."

"I understand, but don't mention the Prinkleton connection to your classmates."

"Of course." Crystal bit her lip. "So you'll take care of the box?"

The director nodded. "Information about Mr. Hamilton is too important to mishandle."

As the director stared at her, Crystal squirmed. "I know I was wrong to read the *Poppa Report* without permission. I'm willing to accept any disciplinary action you deem fit."

"Any action?"

Nodding slowly, she said in a scared voice, "I deserve to be punished, but I hope my punishment isn't expulsion—I'd hate to be expelled."

Giving a ghost of a smile, Director Matthews said gently, "I think we can forgo discipline as long as you promise not to do it again."

"Oh, I do! I *really* do!"

As relief flooded Crystal's face, the director said in a deceptively mild voice, "Did Mr. Kerry read the files as well?"

She shook her head. "Marc was there when the box fell, but not when I picked up the papers. He didn't see anything."

"Good." Crystal watched as the director began rolling a pencil between his thumb and index finger. After a moment, he asked, "So, are you and Mr. Kerry working well together?"

Crystal bit her lip and remained silent.

"Miss Stuart, I asked you a question. Answer it."

"Marc's a hard worker," she said in a brittle voice. "I couldn't ask for a more conscientious colleague. He grasped the concept of archival filing quickly. He does his duties well. We've gotten through a tremendous amount of work."

Crystal saw the director looking at her with narrowed eyes. "Are you enjoying him as a coworker?" he asked.

"Like I said—Marc's competent."

"How competent?"

"Extremely," she said baldly.

The director's lips twitched. "How do you feel about him personally?"

Raising her eyes, she said slowly, "I don't see how that's relevant."

"It's relevant if I say it's relevant."

Crystal's eyes took on an angry glint. "I choose to disagree. My personal feelings are of no consequence. Marc and I may never be best friends, but as long as we can work together, that's all that matters."

"I see." The director put the pencil down on his desk. "Do you feel you could work with Mr. Kerry in the future?"

"Of course I do. We're professional enough to do our jobs."

The director inspected his fingernails. "If I decided to cut Mr. Kerry from the program how would you feel? Relieved?"

"No," Crystal said forcibly. "I'd feel as if you were making a grave mistake. I may not be the head of Marc's fan club, but I'm smart enough to see he's going to be a top-notch time counselor. If you let him go, you'd be a brain-dead fool!" Biting her lip, she said in a subdued voice, "Of course, I mean that statement most respectfully, sir."

A choked chuckle escaped the director's lips. He cleared his throat and said mildly, "Of course." Handing Crystal a file folder, he said, "On another subject, here's something I'd like you to analyze over the summer."

Crystal opened the folder and thumbed through several pages of formulas.

"Do you understand what you're reading?" the director asked.

She nodded and pushed at her glasses. "Someone's obviously trying to create a portable GAP computer. I thought a portable Staging Platform was theoretically possible, but I never envisioned anything on this scale. If this would work, it'd render the TEMCO lab virtually obsolete. Timewaves could be harnessed by the surfers themselves..." Crystal's voice trailed as she reviewed the equations. Suddenly, she bit her lip.

The director leaned forward. "What do you see?"

"It's what I don't see," she said in an uncomfortable voice. "These formulas are visionary, but there's a notable gap in them. I see two glaring errors right off hand."

"Show me."

Laying the folder in front of the director, she pointed. "Here and here. See?" As he nodded, she said awkwardly, "I'm sorry to point them out, but they are rather obvious."

The director's lips twitched. "Quite." He smiled at her. "Actually, there are twenty-two mistakes in all—see if you can locate them. Next fall, we'll get together and talk."

"Is this a test?" she asked curiously.

"Let's just say it's a door of opportunity. If you can locate all the errors, perhaps I'll show you the current revisions of the formulas."

Nodding, Crystal tucked the folder in her backpack.

"Even though the formulas are flawed, Miss Stuart, they're to be kept secret."

"I won't breathe a word," she said.

"Good. Now, if there isn't anything else, I believe there are some boxes in the archives waiting for your attention."

Turning to leave, Crystal said hesitatingly, "And Andrew Hamilton's boxes...?"

"I'll personally take care of them today."

"Thank you," Crystal said.

As she left the office and the door started closing behind her, she heard Dr. Nelson saying in amazement, "It took us five months to find the two errors that Crystal just pointed out."

Crystal stopped dead in her tracks. She heard the director chuckling. "I told you she was smart."

As the door clicked shut, Crystal smiled and shouldered her backpack. Maybe being intelligent wasn't so bad after all.

In Colorado, Sue held Sam's hand as Poppa and Twinkles led them into a room filled with brightly wrapped packages.

"What's all this?" Sue asked in surprise.

"Why don't you peek in a box and find out?" Twinkles said in a mischievous voice.

Obediently, Sue unwrapped a package containing an exquisite tea set. "Oh, how perfectly lovely!" she breathed.

The old woman smiled. "I'm glad you like it. It's yours."

"Mine?" Sue asked in a startled voice.

"Call it a dowry, dear. Technically, these things will be yours and Sam's."

As Sam gave a sudden bark of laughter, Poppa said, "Twinkles, you're getting ahead of yourself."

"Pshaw! We all know which way the wind's blowing. Why beat around the bush?"

Shrugging his shoulders, Poppa laughed. "She's right, you know."

Sue's discomfort grew as Twinkles said briskly, "Sue, dear, your things were burned in that awful fire, and Sam's only set up for rough housekeeping, so we decided to give you two an early wedding present."

"B-but S-Sam and I aren't getting married," Sue stuttered.

"Of course you are! Of all the silly nonsense!"

Sue blushed wildly. "B-but Sam hasn't proposed. We just met."

"Fiddlesticks!" Twinkles said firmly. "Who needs formalities? Proposals are just fussbudget verbiage. From my viewpoint, you two have celebrated your fiftieth wedding anniversary—and lots more anniversaries after that. Of all the silly blathering. *Of course* you're getting married! Now, open another box—you too, Sam."

"I'm not sure..." Sue said hesitatingly.

"What's to be sure about?" Twinkles demanded. "Here, open this one."

Obediently, Sue and Sam began opening presents. Every time Sue tried to stop, Twinkles pushed another box in her hands.

"It's too much," Sue protested, opening a set of gold-rimmed dishes. "Way too much."

"Nonsense." Twinkles laughed. "And that's not all. There's a rental truck out back. The king bed we bought you is simply *scrumptious.*"

Sue winced and glanced over at Sam. He was standing with his mouth slightly open.

"Now don't worry, Sam," Twinkles said, "we researched the dimensions of your house. All the furniture will fit—even the pool table Poppa insisted on buying. I didn't see much use in a pool table, but Poppa said you'd like it."

"I will," Sam said in a voice quivering with laughter. "Thank you."

"No need to thank us," Twinkles burbled. "We had lots of fun picking out the furniture. Besides, the best wedding present you'll be getting is Sue. She's gonna make you a perfect wife. There isn't a nicer girl around, don't you agree?"

Sue squirmed at Twinkles's demanding tone. As Sam nodded, the old woman tapped Sue's shoulder. "See that? Sam thinks you're wonderful. I'll bet you think he's special too."

Blushing vividly, Sue remained silent. As she opened the last gift—several sets of silk sheets—her face turned pale, and she refused to meet Sam's eyes.

"Come on," Poppa said, giving his wife a grin. "These youngsters need some time alone."

As Sue quickly crammed the sheets back in their box, she saw Poppa pressing a tiny velvet case into the palm of Sam's hand. As Sam looked at it in surprise, Poppa winked. Feeling completely mortified, Sue knelt and started repacking a set of pots and pans. Behind her, she heard the door close and Sam's footsteps as he approached.

"Can I give you a hand?" he asked.

Ignoring him, she continued packing the box.

Laying a hand on her shoulder, Sam said softly, "Hey, what's wrong?"

Keeping her eyes on a frying pan, she replied in a tight voice, "I could just die—that's what's wrong! I've never been more humiliated in my life."

Sue felt Sam flinch. As he slowly drew his hand away, she looked up—his face was pale. "Are you embarrassed at being paired with me?" he asked quietly.

"*Of course not!*" she exclaimed. "I could never be embarrassed of you."

A glad, gleaming light sprang into his eyes. "That's a relief." He chuckled. "It'd be a shame for you to spend the next fifty-some years married to someone you didn't even like."

"It's not nice of you to tease."

"Probably not, but you have to admit there's quite a bit of humor in the situation."

"Not for me!"

His smile died. "I can see that," he said gently. "Can you tell me why?"

She shifted uncomfortably. "I'm sure you never expected your kindness to mushroom into something like this." She pointed accusingly at a crystal serving dish. "As lovely as these things are, you can't deny they're wedding gifts."

Sam nudged a coffeemaker with his toe and grinned. "I was kinda tipped off by the white wrapping paper and silver bows."

Covering her face, Sue squirmed. "And them buying us a bed! I know they meant well, but I could die! Die right here on the spot! I promise I didn't put them up to this."

"I never thought you did. I'm glad you don't think I set it up."

"You're way too honorable to think up a scheme like this." She hunched a shoulder. "I can't believe the way they were tossing me at your head. When they asked us to follow them in here, I never dreamed they were going to give us wedding gifts."

"I know, me either."

"I never even *hinted* to Twinkles that I thought you might propose. Twinkles did some hinting herself, but I never said a single word. I promise."

"I don't think Twinkles needs hints. I think she sees things clearly for herself."

As Sue blushed and turned away, Sam knelt beside her and said, "I know what they did was unorthodox, but you don't need to feel shy or embarrassed with me—not ever."

Sue looked up with a flushed face and troubled eyes. "But you've been so good to Danny and me. I'm sorry you're being pushed and bothered like this."

Tenderly cupping her chin with his hand, he murmured, "Susie-Q, do I *look* like I'm being pushed or bothered?"

Looking deeply into Sam's blue eyes, Sue saw that there was no annoyance in them, only love—lots of love—with a tiny bit of laughter around the edges. Her blush deepened. "No matter how many gifts they've given us, we don't have to be anything more than friends. I'll let you out of this relationship."

"Do I look like I want out of it? Do you?"

As Sue slowly shook her head and lowered her gaze, Sam ran his hands down her arms and gathered one of her hands in his. "I don't feel pressured—I feel blessed." His voice caught and shook. "You're my pearl of great price—an unexpected treasure that I never hoped to find. You and Danny—it's like we've always been together. I don't want my life to be without you."

"Are you sure? You don't have to—"

"I *want* to." He gave her a smile full of love. "I happen to think you're pretty terrific."

As Sue reached up and slowly stroked his cheek, Sam's eyes searched hers. "I know it's awfully fast," he whispered, "but would you consider...? Would you be willing...?"

Watching a deep red blush climbing up his neck, she murmured softly, "What are you trying to say?"

Sam's blue eyes filled with tenderness and laughter. "I'm saying what Twinkles and Poppa knew all along I was going to say. They knew it when they put us in this room together."

"And that is...?"

Sam trapped her hand within his own. "I'm already down on one knee if that gives you any hint."

"Stop hinting. Spell it out for me. Regardless of Twinkles's opinion, I happen to like fussbudget verbiage."

Sam threw back his head and laughed. "In that case, Susanna Winston, will you marry me?"

She gave him a wobbly smile. "I'm not sure."

"You minx." He laughed. "Do you want me to beg?"

"No, just give me a good reason why I should say yes. After all, I never planned on marrying again."

"I never planned on marrying at all."

"Then why should we get engaged?" she asked.

"Other than the fact we have it on good authority that our marriage will be a resounding success and last a lifetime?"

"Besides that," she replied with a smile.

"I'll give you two reasons," he said, putting a finger beneath her chin and tipping her face up toward his. "I love you with all my heart, and I know you love me. I can see the love shining in your eyes, and I can feel it in your touch."

"But we haven't known each other for long. We're practically strangers."

"So were Isaac and Rebecca."

Sue pulled slightly away. "I'm not interested in having an arranged marriage."

"Neither am I," he said, moving closer. "Our marriage will be based on love. You're everything I've dreamed about and more." Rubbing her hand with his thumb, he asked, "Can you picture yourself with someone like me?"

"Truthfully," she admitted, "that's all I've been picturing for the last few days."

Sue saw Sam's eyes gleam as he leaned closer. She put a restraining hand on his chest. "But what about Danny? Are you willing to have a ready-made son?"

He nodded. "I know Danny's part of the package, and I'm glad he is. He's a good boy, and I'll do my best to be a good father. I'll make sure your—*our*—son feels happy and loved."

"I know you will. You're that type of man."

Searching her eyes, he said softly, "So it's settled? You'll marry me?"

"I don't know," she said slowly. "I'm not sure I'd make a good pastor's wife. I can't play the piano or sing."

Sam started to grin. "The church has a pianist and the choir loft is full."

Seeing his smile, Sue sputtered, "Don't you *dare* laugh! This *isn't* funny! Would the Ladies Auxiliary expect me to lead prayer?"

"Probably," he said with twinkling eyes. "But you can handle it."

"I'm not good in Easter productions. The one time I was in a church play, I tripped against the scenery and made the walls of Jerusalem fall on the choir."

Sam's lips quivered. "I own a hammer. I'll nail the scenery securely to the floor."

Sue didn't return his smile. "I can't do so many things—I wouldn't be useful to you."

A droopy curl fell onto his forehead as he gave her a wicked grin. "I happen to have lots of *uses* in mind for you—none of which involve music or church dramas."

Sue blushed hotly. "I'm being serious."

Sam's voice lowered to a husky murmur. "So am I."

As he reached for her, she put out her hand to stop his advance. "I know we'd like to let our emotions take over, but we should think this through. Besides being tone deaf and clumsy, I feel faint whenever I talk in front of a crowd."

"It's a good thing I'm the preacher then."

"Regardless, I'm not a churchy type of person—I'd rather wear blue jeans than dresses."

"Me too," he replied solemnly. "I don't look good in nylons."

Refusing to laugh, she muttered, "I hate sitting on front pews, and I'd be expected to."

"Susie-Q," he said, scooting closer, "if seating arrangements are all that's keeping you from accepting my proposal then we'll sit on the back pew."

"You couldn't do that!" she objected in a scandalized voice.

"Why not? If I'm sitting behind Edward Pruette, he won't feel safe enough to doze off during services. Besides, walking down the aisle when it's time to preach will make me feel important. I'll enjoy the attention."

As she fell silent, he smiled and reached for her. "So that's it then? No more objections?"

Pushing his hands away, she said in exasperation, "Sam, you're just not looking ahead! You should marry a woman who can help you at the church—not someone like me. A pastor's wife should be the epitome of Proverbs 31."

"Honey," he chuckled, "I'm looking for a wife, not an associate pastor—and I'm definitely *not* looking for Ms. Proverbs 31. She'd intimidate the life outta me and likely be boring to boot. I don't care if you lift a finger at the church. All I want is your love."

Sue bit her lip and focused on the pulse beating rapidly in Sam's throat. "It's just such a big step," she whispered, "and I'm not pastor's wife material. I've struggled in my walk with God, and—"

He interrupted with gentle firmness. "Your struggle will help you relate to those who are hurting and confused. My congregants will love you just as much as I do."

"But—"

"Shh! No more buts. Marry me and I promise to do my best to make you the happiest woman in the world."

As he cupped her face and murmured tender words of love, Sue's heart flipped over and danced. This time when he reached for her, she allowed herself to be gently pulled into his arms.

"I already *am* the happiest woman in the world," she breathed against his chest. "You've made me that."

"So you'll be my wife?"

Nodding slowly, she said, "But only if you're certain you want me."

"I've never been more certain of anything in my life." Pressing his lips to her forehead, he whispered, "But how about you? You're pretty enough that you could have any man in the world. Are you really willing to marry a backwoods preacher like me? I'll probably never be rich or famous."

"I don't care," she said. "I've never had much money, and the thought of being married to someone famous makes me shudder."

"Will you be content living in Charlesberg? I have no desire to move to a bigger city, but if you—"

"I love small towns and enjoy being by the forest."

"So do I." He trailed a finger down her cheek. "I can't believe you're willing to marry me. You're so lovely, and I'm not very good looking."

Sue gave a sputter of laughter. "You're so handsome that you make my knees go weak. Whenever I'm around you, I feel like I need to be using crutches."

"I have a pair in my attic," he said, chuckling with delight. "I'll lend them to you."

As Sue gave a gurgle of laughter, she saw his eyes suddenly cloud. After a moment, he said in a troubled voice, "You loved Bill very much, didn't you?"

"You know I did." She pulled back a little. "I loved him with all my heart—just like I love you. Is that a problem?"

"Love's never a problem," he said slowly. "But I may not measure up to your memories. I can't replace Bill—I wouldn't know how."

Sue swiftly took his face in her hands. "I wouldn't want you to try. Comparing you to my first husband would be silly."

"I don't want you to be disappointed. You deserve the best."

"You *are* the best!" Nuzzling his chin with her cheek, she whispered, "I'm not trying to find a substitute for Billy—I want you for *you*." Seeing a faint hint of insecurity in Sam's eyes, Sue leaned close and murmured, "I happen to think you're pretty terrific."

As she echoed his own words back to him, Sam smiled. "Are you sure?"

"Positive. Billy was special, and I loved him dearly, but, Sam, you're..."

"I'm what?" he coaxed.

Blushing wildly, she whispered against his chest, "Being with Billy was like being with a comfortable friend, but when you hold me I can hardly breathe. I've never felt..."

As her voice came to a smothered, breathless halt, she saw a pleased smile passing over Sam's face. Kneeling in the tissue paper jungle, he raised her blushing face and lowered his trembling lips to hers. Their first kiss was gentle at first—like a summer breeze—and it was full of such sweet promise that it brought with it an aching pain and a sense of wonder and delight. As their breath mingled, a peaceful feeling of harmony enveloped Sue. Sam held her even closer and slowly deepened his kiss. As her body began to tremble, he brought their kiss to a close.

Pulling back a little, Sue gazed into Sam's eyes. Seeing that he was looking slightly dazed, she giggled softly. "I make your knees go weak too, don't I?"

"You turn my bones into liquid goo." As she cuddled close, his blue eyes twinkled. "I think I could get used to this. Is marriage just as nice as being engaged?"

"With the right person, marriage is *even better*."

As Sue reached up and smoothed the droopy curl away from his forehead, Sam handed her the velvet case Poppa had given him. "This may not be what I think it is, but open it and let's find out."

Lifting the hinged lid, Sue gasped. Inside was a beautiful engagement ring with a large diamond surrounded by clusters of amethysts. Looking at Sam with laughing eyes, she said, "Twinkles and Poppa think of everything. It's even my favorite color." Her smiled deepened. "The night we met, Nathan said you were a slowpoke with women, but you certainly proved him wrong. Talk about a whirlwind romance! I didn't know a man could move this fast."

"If I remember right, Nathan also said that some enterprising girl was gonna have to light a fire under me to get me moving."

"Is that what I did?"

Sam gently traced the contour of her lips with his thumb and whispered, "You not only lit a fire under me, you set me completely ablaze."

Drawing her close, he kissed her again. Their kiss grew more passionate and demanding until the room seemed to spin. When Sam moved his lips to her neck, Sue shivered in delight. Snuggling down against his chest, she sighed in happy contentment.

Sam took the ring and slowly slid it onto her finger. "I never expected to fall in love. In fact, I was determined to stay single. I'm so glad God stepped into my life and brought me you. I love you, Sue."

"I love you too," she whispered softly. "I love you so *very* much!"

At her words, Sam gathered her tightly in his arms, and after they had kissed once more, they stood as if in a dream. Leaving the mounds of tissue paper behind them, they went to find Danny to tell him the good news.

FORTY-THREE

"EXCUSE ME, MISS," Rick said politely to the teenager sitting behind the reception desk at Fairfield Middle School.

Looking up from her magazine, the girl stretched and yawned. "Can I help you?"

"I hope so," Rick said, looking over his shoulder at the police filling the principal's office. He pulled his baseball cap lower over his face. "What's going on around here?"

"I'm not supposed to say."

Rick smiled. "I won't tell. I promise."

"Sure, you won't." The girl rolled her eyes. "Regardless, I can't see why secrecy matters. What's happened is all over the *Charlesberg Gazette*."

"Care to fill me in?"

"Some jerk broke into the building a few nights ago and rummaged through student files. It's been a gigantic pain in the neck putting things back in order."

Rick leaned his elbows on the counter. "But why are the police still here?"

"Heightened security or something. Seems like a lot of bother over some stupid files, if you ask me." She yawned again and snapped her gum. "Is there anything else you wanted to know?"

"I have an unusual request."

"Well, lay it on me," she replied, tossing her magazine aside and twisting the class ring on her thumb.

Focusing on the ring, Rick said in a charming voice, "I see you're a woman in love."

The girl blinked. "I've got a boyfriend if that's what you mean."

"It is." Keeping his face turned away from the police, Rick said softly, "I'm in love too, and I need an angel to help me out."

Rolling her eyes, the girl said in a bored voice, "Cut the malarkey. Whatcha want?"

"My high school sweetheart just got divorced. She's staying with some friends while her house is fumigated, and I can't track her down."

"What's that got to do with me?" the girl asked, blowing a bubble.

"She's awfully careful about her son's schoolwork. I'm sure she's been calling for his assignments while they're out of town. Do you think you could check?"

"Maybe. What's her son's name?"

"Daniel Winston."

Turning to a stack of papers on her left, the girl nodded. "I have his assignments right here. His mom called a few minutes ago to get them."

"What's her phone number?" Rick said eagerly.

"She didn't leave one." As Rick's face fell, the girl smirked. "But she was my last phone call—her number's in the Caller ID."

349

"Can you write it down for me?" he asked, glancing at the principal's office. It looked like the conference was winding down. He needed to get the number and get out—he was out of time.

"Whatcha gonna give me if I do?" the girl asked slyly.

"How about my undying gratitude?"

"How 'bout twenty bucks?"

Rick nodded and pulled out his billfold. As the girl wrote the number down, he passed her the cash. "If Sue Winston calls again, don't mention me. I want to surprise her."

"No problem." The girl yawned, picking up her magazine.

Rick turned swiftly and went down the hallway. He began to smile. All he needed was Internet access and he'd be able to turn the number into an address. And once he had that...

His smile grew.

A cheer went up from the crowd in the living room as William came out of the sick room with Gil in his arms. As he placed her gently on the couch, Danny rushed to cover her knees with a blanket. Seeing the way the boy was grinning, Gil knew something had happened.

"I got a surprise for you!" Danny shouted, confirming her suspicions. "A good one!"

"What is it?"

"I'll show you," he replied, running over to his mother and picking up her hand.

"Oh!" Gil gasped as the diamond in Sue's ring sparkled and shot a fire of rainbows into the air. "I'm so happy for you all!"

"I'm pretty happy for us too," Sue said, grinning widely.

Sam chuckled. "When time travelers tell a couple they're meant for each other, the couple had better listen. After all, who are Sue and I to stand in the way of fate?"

"Who indeed?" Gil laughed. Turning to Danny, she said, "You told me your mom needed a new husband. I think we got her a good one."

"You bet! Sam's the best! And guess what? Mom getting a husband means I get a dad!"

As Sam smiled and put his hand on Danny's shoulder, Sue laughed. "It generally works that way."

Danny gave a little hop. "Sam's gonna teach me martial arts, and pool, and baseball. Life's gonna be terrific!"

"I'm sure it will be," Gil said, feeling heart-glad at Danny's pleasure.

"That's not all the surprises for you, lovey-girl," Twinkles said, crossing over to the piano. "The guys have been working on another one."

Poppa, William, and Danny went and stood beside Twinkles. The old woman struck three notes, and they began to sing *The Hills are Alive with the Sound of Music* in a beautiful three-part harmony. As their acapella voices blended flawlessly, Gil began to cry. Danny was singing the same song that she'd heard Death Row Daniel singing in his prison cell—it was the same song that had touched her heart and convinced her to pick Daniel Winston as her case subject. When the last note was sung, Gil clapped until her hands stung.

Running into her arms, Danny asked, "Did I do good? Are you proud of me?"

"Proud? I'm *way* past proud!" Giving Danny another hug, she glanced over at William. "You've been holding out on me. I didn't know you could sing."

"I'm not sure you can call what I do singing," he replied. "Compared to these two, I just warble along. However, I enjoyed Poppa's lessons."

Twinkles gave Gil's hand a pat. "When you were unconscious, we had to rope the doc into singing lessons. The poor man's pacing was wearing a hole in my carpet."

As Gil laughed, the oven timer went off. "That's my cue," Poppa said. "I hope everyone's hungry. I made lasagna for lunch."

"It smells *marvelous*," Gil replied as her stomach rumbled.

Twinkles gave her husband an affectionate swat on his rear as he walked past. "Poppa's lasagna is *better* than marvelous. He's a wonderful cook."

"Thank you, love," Poppa replied as he went to the kitchen. As he took the bubbling lasagna out of the oven, a heavenly aroma filled the house.

While the men were busy talking in the kitchen, Twinkles whispered to Gil and Sue, "Poppa's a wonderful cook *now*, but you've *never* tasted anything as *ghastly* as his lasagna when he first started making it. Just thinking about it gives me indigestion. His parents and I used to think of ingenious ways to dispose of his leftovers. We never actually buried any of his culinary attempts in the backyard—but we were *mighty* tempted."

"Surely it couldn't have been that bad," Gil said with a laugh.

"It was worse! You'd never believe a man with Poppa's IQ would have such a hard time figuring out which spices went with which foods. I had quite a battle convincing him that cinnamon and cayenne pepper couldn't be added to every dish."

That afternoon, William went into Gil's room to carry her outside for some fresh air. The minute he walked through the door,

Gil gasped and stared at him with wonder in her eyes. "Your beard!" she exclaimed. "The bristle brush is gone! Let there be dancing in the streets."

Blushing a little, he asked, "Is my chin nice enough looking for you?"

Her lopsided dimples peeped out. *"Well..."*

"Come on, I haven't been without a beard for years. Do I look okay?"

"Tell me truly," she said mischievously, "did it take hedge clippers or a weed whacker to get rid of that ghastly thing?"

"Gil—!"

"More than hedge clippers? You *poor* man. Did you have to get someone to pull it out by the roots like a stubborn old onion bulb?"

"I used Sam's razor, okay?" He laughed. "Stop fooling around, and tell me what you think."

Giving him a smile, she said, "I think you look *scrumptious*. I don't know why you hid that *gorgeous* chin. I'd tell you just how handsome you look, but then you'd get a big head." As his blush deepened, she crooked her finger. "Come here, Doc."

Crossing the room, he stood by her side and looked down into her eyes.

"Closer," she murmured.

He leaned closer.

"Closer."

William's breath began catching in his throat as he bent down some more.

Sitting up swiftly against her pillows, Gil pulled his head down even more. Nuzzling her cheek against his, she gently pressed her lips to his chin and whispered, "That's *so* much better. I'm glad you shaved."

William gave an unsteady chuckle. "If I'd known this would be the result, I would've shaved yesterday."

$\sim$

"Hurry up," Marc said, bracing himself against the counter and trying to shout over the noise of Ryan's electric screwdriver. "I'm gonna drop this beast on your toes if you don't—it's slipping."

As Ryan nodded, Marc shook the sweat out of his eyes and tightened his grip. When the cupboard was firmly attached to the wall, he dropped into a chair and rubbed his sore biceps. "I'm glad that's the last of them."

"It's the last for now," Ryan said with a grin, pushing a bag of chips toward him. "But after summer break, I'd like to make more cupboards and cover the east wall too."

Marc gave a groaning chuckle. "I might've known. I'll give you a hand when it's time to install them, but we need to recruit more help. I bet Kyle would volunteer if we sweetened the pot with dinner at Dos Maracas."

"Good idea." Ryan went to the fridge and grabbed some sodas. "How much time do we have until we need to report back to NSU?"

"About fifteen minutes. Remind me to avoid taking long lunches with friends with ulterior motives. I've been sweating so much that I need to change before we go."

"You and me both. I don't want to show up in the main office looking like this."

"With the director overseeing your work, I don't blame you," Marc grumbled.

"I don't know why the director makes you so nervous. He isn't a bad sort."

"I know, but he has a way of staring at me that makes me feel two-inches tall." Marc shrugged and took a chip. "The funny thing is, I think he'd make a great friend if you could get to know him."

"Well, I'm not gonna be the one to find out. Even though I'm working in the office, the director's been in the lab most of the time. I hardly see him."

Marc grunted. "So how many more letters do you need to send out?"

"None, I finished them yesterday. I have some filing to do, but I'll be done with that today." Ryan handed Marc a soda and sat down at the table. "How about you? How are things going with Crystal?"

Marc took a drink. "She still won't talk to me. It's like I'm invisible."

FORTY-FOUR

THE BIRDS WERE singing in the orchard as William carried Gil into the sunshine. Gil secretly knew she could walk on her own—and she suspected William knew it as well—but she was enjoying the closeness they were sharing too much to mention it. When they came to the glider, William sat down and perched Gil on his lap. She nestled her head against his chest. As he tightened his arms around her, contentment wrapped itself around her heart. She gave a soft sigh as happy thoughts flittered through her mind.

Suddenly, Gil felt something wet hitting her forehead. Pulling back, she looked up at William. Shock rippled through her when she saw tears in his eyes. William had always seemed so reserved and emotionally controlled. She couldn't believe he was crying.

Grabbing his hand, she asked in concern, "Hey, what's wrong?"

"Things that can't be changed." William traced the fading scar on her forehead with his finger. "You paid too high a price to save Danny, and it's my fault."

"I don't see how," she gently chided. "I distinctly remember ignoring you when you wanted to pull me out of the field."

"I never should've allowed you to go in the first place."

Putting her hands on either side of William's face, she said softly, "I *wanted* to go."

Tears welled in his eyes. "I've never been as frightened as I was during D-day. I thought I was losing you."

Putting her head down on his chest, she listened to his thudding heartbeat and whispered, "It's okay. I'm right here."

He held her close. "Sitting in the lab waiting for midnight to arrive was the hardest thing I've ever done. I wanted so badly to come and save you."

"You did save me," she murmured. "You came when I needed you most."

"I'm sorry this happened," he whispered. "I'll spend my life making it up to you."

Gil's dimples peeked out. "Now *that* sounds like something I can work with."

"I'm being serious," he said, looking intently into her eyes.

"So am I," she grinned. "If you *insist* on feeling responsible, I can milk your guilt for all it's worth." She tipped her head. "Now, what should I ask for? Pearls? Dinners? Shall I demand to be serenaded?"

"Gil—"

"I can think of a thousand things, but none of them are necessary. D-day wasn't your fault. You're being rather silly, you know."

Moving her gently from his lap, William stood and turned his back to her. "You don't understand—there's no way you could."

Hearing the distress in his voice, Gil stopped grinning and rose to her feet. Putting her hand on his shoulder, she said quietly, "Please turn around."

As William slowly turned and faced her, Gil blinked rapidly. She'd seen him angry. She'd seen him worried. She'd never seen him looking like this.

"What's bothering you?" she asked gently.

He opened his mouth, but couldn't seem to speak. "Look at me," he finally said. "Tell me what you see."

"I could do that all day," she lightly replied, trying to make him smile. "You're rather easy on the eyes, especially since the tumbleweed growing off your chin's gone. Do you want me to catalogue the features I like best?"

"I want you to look past the obvious."

"Fishing for compliments, are you?"

"Please stop joking. Tell me what you see."

Hearing the urgent note in his voice, she nodded and gently cupped the side of his face. As his breath caught at her touch, she smiled. "When I look at you, the first thing I see is your eyes—I've never seen such kind eyes before. They're gorgeous, but more importantly, they're full of love. If eyes are windows to the soul then yours tell me everything I need to know."

"What else do you see?" he whispered.

She trailed her finger slowly up his cheek and over his forehead. As he shivered at her touch, she murmured, "Your brow's wide and thoughtful. It shows dignity and honor."

William's breath was coming in controlled gasps as she moved her finger down to slowly trace his mouth. "Your lips are tender and warm," she said softly. "They're swift to speak encouraging words and to participate in shared laughter."

"Look at me," he said in a choked voice. *"Please, look at me."*

"That's what I'm doing," she said in confusion.

"Look harder! Tell me what you see!"

"You vain man," she chortled, "just how many compliments do you need? Do you *actually* want me to keep going?"

William nodded with troubled eyes.

"In that case, you have an *awfully* cute schnoz." She gave his nose a playful tweak. "It's perfectly wonderful, in fact." She tweaked it again. "It isn't broken for one thing—it's nice and straight like I like 'em."

"Please stop joking. This is important."

Her smile faded. Putting a finger beneath his chin, she inspected his clean-shaven jaw from every angle. "Your chin has a bit of a tan line, but that'll fade. You have a strong, firm jaw. It's a jaw that belongs to a *real* man in the truest sense of the word. A man a woman can love and respect. A man a woman can feel honored to be loved by..." As her voice came to a smothered halt, she smiled and cleared her throat. "All in all, I think it's a perfectly lovely jaw, especially the cute little freckle right here."

As Gil kissed the heart-shaped freckle, her body froze. Stepping back two paces, she looked at William with shocked eyes.

"You know, it's funny," she said in a tight voice, "we've known each other for years, but I don't know your first name. William's your middle name, and you've always had your students call you Doc or Dr. Ableman. Please tell me your first name."

"Gil, I—"

"Tell me!"

"I think you know it," he said softly, his eyes never leaving her face.

"*Danny?* It can't be!"

William—Danny—gave her a wobbly smile. "Can't it? You told me I'd grow up big and handsome. What do you think?"

359

Gil stepped forward and put a hesitant hand to his cheek. "Danny?"

"It's Dan actually. I haven't gone by Danny since high school."

"But your last name's Ableman—not Winston. I don't understand."

"Oh, Gil," he said tenderly. "You overlook the simplest things. Sam married my mother."

"But Sam's last name is Jacobson—not Ableman."

He shook his head. "Sam's mother was Mr. Jacobson's daughter. She married a man named Ableman, and I took the Ableman name after Sam and Mom married."

"I'm such a dunce," Gil moaned, touching his freckle. "Your identity was right in front of me."

Dan grabbed her hand and held it next to his chest. "Can you understand my guilt now? It *is* my fault. Every bit of it. I'm the reason you had to come to Charlesberg."

"But how's that even possible? I *saw* Death Row Daniel. You were in the same room with him."

"Oh, Gil," he replied with a shaky grin. "You really should've read those manuals."

"I know," she mumbled, rolling her eyes. "Stop rubbing it in and explain."

"If you'd done your homework, I wouldn't have to."

"Quit being an obnoxious cheeseball"—she laughed—"and start explaining."

"Okay, here's the short version. Normally, timewaves travel individually like ocean waves skimming toward the beach. I want you to get a clear picture of an ocean wave in your mind—it has a circular motion that isn't perceptible until it gets closer to shore. We harness that circular motion with GAP. Now picture a piece of driftwood caught in the wave. When a time surfer is sent back to change the past, the surfer is essentially changing the position of a piece of driftwood. The location of the driftwood has no bearing on the motion of the wave—correct?"

"I guess so," she replied.

"Most time surfs follow that innocuous pattern. A surfer makes a small change, but nothing so major that it interrupts the circular flow and forward motion of the wave. However, when something goes terribly wrong during a time surf, a Cataclysmic Failure is initiated that's destructive to the timewave being manipulated. This causes the timewave to split apart and create two separate timelines. The two halves of the timewave will travel simultaneously toward the temporal shore in a massive Time Tsunami. As the tsunami travels, the two halves of the wave intersect at various junctions."

"Oh, for Pete's sake," she grumbled. "I never did understand this split-wave mumbo jumbo when you brought it up in class."

"Why didn't you ask me to explain it better? I would have—gladly."

"I know. I just didn't think it was relevant. I wasn't planning on anything going wrong during my time surfs."

As Dan raised an eyebrow, Gil put her hands on her hips. "Look, don't give me static. I'm asking you to explain it now, okay? Quit going all professorish on me."

"Professorish?" Dan chuckled. "Is that a word?"

Gil smacked his shoulder. "If it isn't, it should be. Stop being a smarty pants."

"Okay," he smiled. "Let's look at it differently. A split timewave resembles two pieces of string tangled together. As they cross, intersecting junctions occur. A tangled timeline needs to be straightened out. The confusion gets worse the longer it's left."

"How do you straighten it?"

"It takes a third timeline acting as a mirror image of one of the previous two timelines to dissipate the split."

"Are you talking about the *Canceling Rule of Threes?*"

He quirked an eyebrow. "So you were paying attention in class?"

"Partially," she replied, refusing to rise to his bait. "I know the term, but I don't understand the concept."

"It's simple. The third timeline, being identical or extremely similar to one of the timelines in the split wave, will merge with its duplicate counterpart. Once they merge, they gather strength and wash over the differing timeline and cancel it out." Dan's eyes searched hers. "This is actually the third time Gil Montgomery has traveled through a temporal portal to little Danny Winston, even though from your point of view, it's the first."

"Are you serious?"

He nodded. "The first time Gil Montgomery went through GAP, her surf failed and produced Death Row Daniel. The second time Gil went through GAP, her surf succeeded and produced me. As little Danny, I can remember Gil's second surf clearly, even though you cannot. You—the Gil Montgomery you are now—was a toddler when I was ten-year-old Danny."

"I think I understand, go on."

"Your third surf—the one you just completed—was a success, so it underlines the successful second surf that produced me and cancels out the failed first one that produced Death Row Daniel. Your second surf and third surf have merged together and formed one single timeline. Does that make sense?"

"I think so," she said slowly. "But how could you and Death Row Daniel be in the same room together?"

"The prison was where our timelines intersected. The junction was a dead giveaway that the timeline was tangled. A third surf had to be completed to erase one of the Daniel Winstons. It was fifty-fifty for a while which timeline was going to win out. If your current surf had failed, I would've been erased from existence rather than him."

"That was quite a gamble."

Dan shook his head. "It wasn't a gamble—it was a necessity. I have the memories of ten-year-old Danny. I knew about Gil Montgomery's time surf. That's why I had to find you and convince you to train for TEMCO. Your surf would lead to a final outcome, one way or the other. It would cause one of the grown-up Daniel Winstons to be erased."

"That's why you feel so guilty."

"Yes." His voice was ragged. "The decision to send you to Charlesberg knowing what you'd face was hell—pure hell." He put a shaking hand to his forehead. "For years, I drove myself crazy trying to find GAP scenarios in which you didn't have to go back and save little Danny—but there weren't any. It was Danny's love for you, and your love for him, that made the surf a success. It was love, more than anything else, that won D-day. It had to be you who went back. No one else would've had the same impact."

As she stood silently, he looked intently into her eyes. "I tried to find another way—I promise—but all I found were dead ends. I calibrated a game cartridge, so I could surf in at a moment's notice, but GAP predicted disaster if I used it before midnight. I thought about ignoring the tangled timeline, but the tangling was getting worse on a daily basis. GAP was melting down, and all of the violence TEMCO's prevented was in danger of reoccurring. If it'd just been my life on the line, I never would've sent you, but other lives were going to be destroyed. I can't ask you to forgive it, but please understand it. Sending you back, knowing what you'd face, was the hardest thing I've ever done."

"But you tried to pull me from the field. What would've happened if I'd come home?"

"The minute you passed through the time portal, I—Dr. Ableman—would never have existed and TEMCO would've been destroyed."

"Then why'd you give me the option?"

He shuddered. "I realized I'd made a horrible mistake in sending you." His eyes searched her face. "When I was a boy, the adults shielded me from most of the details of Rick's crimes. When I was training you, I thought my childhood memories of your injuries were exaggerated, but I was wrong. When Director Matthews uncovered data showing how vicious Rick was, I couldn't believe I'd put you in such danger. I thought I'd rather disappear and have TEMCO collapse, than have you go through all that pain—pain that I realized would be *every bit* as horrible as I remembered. What kind of a man sends a woman to face such agony? It was unforgivable of me to involve you in D-day."

As Dan trembled and turned away, Gil pulled on his shoulder. When his guilty eyes met hers, she said quietly, "It's not unforgivable."

When he began to protest, she laid a restraining finger on his lips. "No matter what you think you orchestrated, I *chose* this profession. I wanted to help Death Row Daniel, and I'd have *chosen* to help him even if you hadn't been my adviser. I made my choice to stay and face D-day knowing all the facts. Knowing Rick was brutal. Knowing that facing him could mean my death. I *chose* it. And now, looking back and remembering everything Rick did to me, and every bit of pain I experienced, I can tell you without hesitation that I'd choose to do it again."

As hope began to fill Dan's eyes, she said firmly, "You don't need to feel guilty anymore. I understand and forgive you. More than that, I'm grateful to have been involved. This surf has been the most fulfilling experience of my life."

Dan gave a gasp and bowed his head. Gil watched as a strong tremor ran through his body. When he raised his head, the worry lines that had been etched into his face were gone.

She laughed lightly. "Is that why you grew that silly beard—for camouflage?"

Dan ran a trembling hand over her hair and nodded. "The heart-shaped freckle on my jaw was a dead giveaway. GAP predicted if you recognized me as Danny, it'd lead to disaster."

Her eyes twinkled. "That beard was *horrible*. Couldn't you come up with something else? A Halloween mask or heavy makeup?"

"Either option would've been far better. I hated my beard even more than you did. It was a bristly mess that looked awful and felt worse."

"You should've tried some hair tonics."

Dan began to blush.

"You didn't!" She laughed. "Not after teasing me about my facials."

His blush deepened. "I tried everything—even slathering it with raw eggs and papaya."

Her eyes widened. "Is that what you were doing when I picked up the violet?"

He chuckled and nodded. "I nearly had a heart attack when you rang the doorbell."

Gil gave him a swat. "You pig! You actually had me feeling sorry for you when you told me about your *blender accident*. You're such a little liar!"

"Hey, I didn't dare admit to trying a hair care tip gleaned from a ladies magazine. I knew you'd never let me live it down."

"You can bet I wouldn't." She laughed. "And I still won't! You can never, *ever* call me vain again, or make a single comment about my beauty products. I guarantee none of them made me look as weird as you did in that egg-papaya mess."

"Fair enough," he replied with a smile.

Gil looked at Dan's clean-shaven chin. "All humor aside, you don't have to worry about your looks anymore. I never knew how much perfectly good face a handsome man could hide under a terrible-looking beard."

"I'm glad you like my looks now that you can see them. That goes a long way toward soothing my ego. It was bruised pretty badly by that ghastly beard."

Gil laughed and bobbed her head. "Glad to oblige ya." Touching his freckle with her fingertip, she smiled. "So, what exactly should I call you now? Doc, William, or Dan?"

"I've been waiting for over twenty years to hear you call me Dan," he replied softly, taking her hand.

"Dan it is then," she said a bit breathlessly, looking down at their clasped hands.

As Ryan turned his car into the parking lot nearest Hawking Hall, he saw Marc drumming his fingers.

"Something bothering you?" Ryan asked, turning off his blinker.

"I don't want to face the frigid blast when I go to the third floor. Cris hates me."

"She's too kind to hate anybody."

Marc grunted. "That's what you think. I'm tempted to cut and run. Do you think your parents would mind if I arrived in California a few days before you did?"

"They wouldn't care a bit. But if you want a place to bolt, why not South Dakota? Wouldn't your parents like a visit?"

Marc hunched a shoulder. "Maybe, but my dad and I aren't exactly speaking. In his opinion, a deacon's son shouldn't live the way I've been living."

"You're not living that way anymore."

"It doesn't matter. He's disappointed in me, and I don't want to face him."

"I know," Ryan said, pulling into a parking space, "but maybe you should. After my family reunion, we could swing by South Dakota so you could mend a few fences. Having me at your initial meeting with your dad might dispel some of the tension."

"You'd do that for me?"

Ryan smiled. "What are friends for?"

Marc sat silently for a moment. "Do you think Dad would actually forgive me?"

"If he's a true Christian, he will. Either way, it'd be good for you to take the first step toward reconciliation—even if it doesn't lead anywhere."

As Marc nodded, Ryan fished beneath his seat for a hat and gloves.

"What are those for?" Marc asked, looking at the winter gear in confusion.

"To fight off the archive artic chill. We need to get to work or we'll be late."

Acutely aware of their clasped hands, Gil asked softly, "Dan, can you tell me why the first surf—the one that led to Death Row Daniel—failed?"

Dan's eyes became serious. "When I first met the Death Row Daniel version of myself, I asked him that very question. He said his Gil wasn't able to stop Rick from killing Sue, and when she tried, Rick attacked her. The child version of Death Row Daniel walked in on the fight after school. He stabbed Rick, but he didn't know how to stop Gil's bleeding. She died in his arms."

Gil shuddered. "No wonder he wouldn't tell me what happened."

"What could he say? That your death haunted him as much as his mother's? He begged me to find you more help."

"That's why you told me to contact Sue's neighbors?"

Dan nodded and gently brushed a strand of hair away from her face. "I knew obtaining help would be pivotal to your success—so did Death Row Daniel."

Gil's eyes filled with tears. "His story's so sad."

"It was tragic. He knew if we succeeded, he'd cease to exist, but he pleaded with me to end his timeline. He said his life was agony. In prison, he made you a locket. I promised to give it to you after your surf succeeded, but when Danny won through on D-day, the locket vanished."

"I won't need a necklace to remember him," Gil said softly. "I know he made some awful choices, but he was unforgettable in many ways."

"It looks as if your life has been touched by all three of the Dannys."

"You could say that. All three of you are very dear to me." Gil paused. "But, Dan, what started everything? Why was I sent back to Danny in the first place?"

"If you'd read the manuals, you'd know the triggering event of a tangled timeline is usually never identified."

"You mean it acts like a Temporal Black Hole?"

He shook his head. "Temporal Black Holes are a different phenomenon—one I don't understand myself. This is more like progressive fading. Trying to discover a triggering event after three surfs is as difficult as finding meaning in distorted shadows in the moonlight. Unless Poppa can shed some light on it, we'll never know how our story began—only how it ends."

Hearing the subtle meaning behind his words, Gil glanced at Dan and caught him gazing at her with such love that it took her breath. Breaking eye contact, she stepped away from him and picked a flower. Keeping her eyes averted, she began stroking the pink petals.

Dan moved to her side. Gently taking her hand, he inquired softly, "So, how is our story going to end?"

Gil didn't speak for a moment, and when she raised her eyes to his, she was blushing a deeper pink than the flower she held. "You know," she said slowly, "I've had an *awful* crush on my teacher for more than a year and a half now."

Dan smiled a smile that made her heart flip over. "You know," he murmured in a husky voice, "I've been in love with you for a lot longer than that."

"Why, Dr. Ableman," she exclaimed in mock horror. "I'm surprised at you! NSU frowns on professors and students fraternizing in a romantic manner."

"Frowns upon, but doesn't forbid," he replied. "Besides, my *dear* Miss Montgomery, you've passed your field exam. You aren't my student anymore."

Taking a brazen step forward, Gil put her arms around his neck. "In that case," she whispered, "what are you waiting for? Are you ever gonna shut up and show me what you got?"

Dan smiled softly and gently put his arms around her waist. As he drew her close, Gil held her breath and tipped her face up toward his. Slowly—ever so slowly—Dan lowered his warm, tender lips to hers.

FORTY-FIVE

INSIDE THE HOUSE, Twinkles stood at a window next to Poppa and watched Gil and Dan kissing in the garden. As Twinkles leaned back in her husband's arms, Poppa grinned and nibbled the nape of her neck.

"Aw, *nuts!*" a voice next to them grumbled.

Startled, Twinkles looked down and saw little Danny glaring out the window.

"I might've known she'd end up with him," the boy mumbled, scuffing his feet.

Bending down, Twinkles said softly, "Who'd you want her to end up with?"

"Me!" Danny scowled. "I don't care if Gil's older than me. I'll love her *forever!*"

Twinkles gave the boy's shoulder a squeeze. "I believe you."

Giving a gusty sigh, Danny stared at the kissing couple in the flower garden. "I know Doc will take good care of her, but I wish she could've belonged to me."

Poppa gave Twinkles a wink and looked Danny straight in the eye. "Maybe she can belong to you both."

Briskly, Twinkles drew the drapes. "Let's give those two some privacy. I have Rocky Road Brownies in the oven. How 'bout I make you a brownie sundae with hot-fudge sauce?" Seeing Danny's frown, she coaxed, "I'll put maraschino cherries on it."

"Okay," the boy grumbled. "I guess a fella can have a broken heart and a homemade hot-fudge sundae too. Nothing says he can't."

In the garden, Gil felt her heart summersault as Dan raised his lips from hers and murmured, "I've been waiting to kiss you for twenty-four years—you've always been the only woman for me. I've tried hard to become the man you'd desire for your husband."

Gil smiled and snuggled close. "You've succeeded." Flirtatiously, she peeped up at him through her lashes. "Was our kiss worth a twenty-four year wait?"

"It was worth every second," he replied, tightening his arms around her.

"I'm glad. I enjoyed our kiss too, but..." Gil let her sentence trail away.

"But what?" he asked in concern.

"Even though it was enjoyable, I once had a wise professor who said everything gets even better with practice."

"You little rascal." He laughed. "Are you using my own words to flirt with me?"

Gil's dimples came out to play. "I'm just giving you something to think about."

"It's an interesting thought, indeed." His eyes sparkled. "Shall we put in some more practice and go for kiss number two?"

Grinning mischievously, she turned her face away. "I don't know..."

Dan laughed. "You're gonna be quite a handful, aren't you?"

"Of course, I am." She twinkled up at him. "But if you want another kiss, you'd better give me an *awfully* good reason for giving you one. I'd hate for my lips to get all chapped for nothing."

"How's this for a reason? We belong together, you and I. I love you, and I always will."

Gil smiled and cuddled close. "I love you too—more than you could imagine."

Dan gently tipped her face toward him. "So how about that practice?"

"I thought you'd never ask."

After a few swiftly passing—yet delightfully slow—minutes, Dan moved his lips to her ear to whisper endearments. Smiling happily, Gil ran her fingers through his silky hair. Nuzzling his chin, she murmured, "Why was your beard so bristly when you have such soft hair growing out of your head?"

"I don't know." He chuckled. "It's a mystery of life. But is hair care what you really want to discuss right now?"

"Not really," she whispered as he kissed her earlobe. "But I do have a question."

"Mmm?"

"You said you wanted to be my husband. Does that mean you just proposed?"

Gil felt the quickness of his heartbeat and the soft rumble of his laughter as he replied, "Honey, if you remember, I already asked you to marry me and you refused."

She gasped with laughter. "You rat, that didn't count! You were only ten."

Dan chuckled and looked at her with glowing eyes. When she started to speak, he suddenly became very occupied with kissing her neck. The touch of his tender lips sent shivers of pleasure cascading through her body. A bit breathless, she pulled back and said, "Don't try to distract me. I asked you a serious question."

With a smile, he tightened his arms around her. "When you were a little girl, I'll bet you peeked in the closet to find your Christmas presents."

"What does that have to do with anything?"

"Stop trying to spoil your surprise. I've had twenty-four years to plan my proposal and you're going to love it. Besides, do you really want to skip dating and go straight to being engaged?"

Gil laughed. "Not a chance! I plan on playing hard to get." Pulling his head down, she nibbled his heart-shaped freckle and whispered, "So what exactly would you call the state of our relationship right now?"

One corner of his mouth twitched up into a grin. "I'd say we were extremely engaged to eventually become engaged."

As his eyes captured hers, time seemed to slow down. She held her breath as he gently brushed a lock of hair behind her ear and gathered her close. A wave of incredible sweetness washed over her as his lips found hers for kiss number three.

After a few moments, Dan raised his head and murmured, "Even though today isn't our engagement day, it's still very special. Do you know why?"

"That depends on what date you're talking about." Her voice held a quiver of laughter. "Back in Washington D.C. it's June fifteenth, but here in Charlesberg, it's October twenty-sixth. With time travel clouding the issue, you need to be more specific."

"Seeing we're currently in Colorado, I think we'll stick with the Charlesberg calendar." He smiled. "So do you know what's significant about today?"

Nestling her cheek against the hand that was caressing it, she shook her head.

Dan tilted her face toward his. "October twenty-sixth is the day Gillyflower Meadowlark Deleena Rosemarie finally discovered the true identity of Daniel William Winston Ableman. It's the day they understood each other and declared their love at last."

"I can live with that. I'll mark it on my calendar with a giant red heart and a big, fat, sparkling star." With a twinkle, she pulled his head down and whispered, "Come on, let's go for number four."

Seeing Dan's smile, she knew he was more than happy to accommodate her wish.

Marc peeked out from behind a shelf at the dwindling stack of boxes. As he watched, Crystal quietly picked up a box and scanned it. Rejecting it, she scanned another. Rejecting that box as well, she scanned a third and struggled to swing it onto her hip.

Marc's brows snapped together. He'd wondered why his boxes had been easy to shelve—now he knew. Crystal was taking the heavy boxes that belonged deep in the complicated heart of the maze. He blinked rapidly. If she disliked him so much, why was she making his life easier?

As he watched, Crystal's heavy box slipped and she struggled to stabilize it. When she turned around, he whipped his head behind the shelf. All women were complicated mysteries, but Crystal Stuart was a mystery that might as well have been written in Chinese. He'd never figure her out.

FORTY-SIX

WHEN GIL AND Dan came in from the garden and wandered into the kitchen, Twinkles met them and offered them a brownie. Looking at the gooey squares, Gil hesitated, calculating the potential calories in her head.

"Go ahead and treat yourself," Dan said with a chuckle, leading her to the table. "I'll still think you're beautiful even if you look like a stuffed apple barrel."

As Gil gave his shoulder a swat, he handed her a brownie. "If you think you're overdoing it, we'll swim an extra lap at the pool when we get back."

"Oh?" she said as Twinkles disappeared into the pantry. "Are you actually planning on swimming with me again? Has your chlorine allergy miraculously cleared up?"

"The chlorine never bothered me," he replied.

"Then what did? You never told me why you stopped swimming."

"For Pete's sake," he sputtered. "Don't you own a mirror?"

"What's that got to do with anything?"

"You really don't know?" When she shook her head, he blushed. "I guess I have a confession to make. I used to plan my trips to the pool to coincide with when I knew you'd be there. I only stopped going when the sight of you in that little red swimsuit got to be more than I could handle. Watching you frisk around in that sizzling suit was *torture*, and I loved every minute of it."

Gil choked on her brownie. "I'm shocked at you!"

Looking into her twinkling eyes, he replied, "You should be. I'm shocked at myself."

"I've got a confession too," she giggled. "I don't even enjoy swimming."

"You don't?"

"I hate it. I only swam to be near you. The sight of you pulling yourself out of the pool would make me go weak in the knees. It was the absolute highlight of my day. You have gorgeous muscles, and when they're glistening with water — *mercy!* When you stopped coming to the gym, exercise lost all its zing!"

"You actually thought I was handsome? Even with the beard?"

"I thought you were a major hunk. Emphasis on *major*."

He grinned. "I thought I was just a stodgy, old professor in your eyes."

"You were," she said impishly. "You just happened to be in excellent shape."

As Dan laughed, Gil smiled and nibbled delicately at the brownie she held in her left hand. She stifled another giggle. Dan was holding onto her right hand underneath the table, and his thumb was beginning to do *amazing* things to her palm. As she looked over at him and grinned, his thumb began to work double-time.

Twinkles bustled back into the room and began pouring coffee. "I take it you're both on cloud nine?"

"We're way past cloud nine," Dan replied. "We've sailed right to the moon."

As Dan continued caressing her palm, Gil said to Twinkles, "Being from further into the future, I assume you know that Dan is little Danny all grown-up. I still can't believe it. Life seems inside out and upside down—but in a good way of course."

Twinkles gave Gil's arm a pat. "Time travel has a tendency to do that. Its unexpected whimsy makes strange things happen every day." Suddenly, she jolted. "What time is it?"

"A bit after 2:00," Gil replied.

"Be exact, dear. What time *exactly?*"

"It's 2:11 p.m.," Gil said, peering at the clock.

"More exact."

Gil looked at her strangely. "It is 2:11 p.m. and thirty-two seconds."

"Ahh," said Twinkles. "Excuse me, I have something to do."

As the old woman hurried out of the room, Gil helped herself to another brownie. "How 'bout we swim two extra laps? These are really yummy."

"I know something even yummier," Dan murmured, crooking his finger suggestively, beckoning her to come closer.

"Who's the flirt now?" She laughed, quirking an eyebrow.

As Dan motioned again—more instantly this time—her eyes gleamed. Slowly, she leaned toward him and hovered with her lips a scant inch apart from his. Dan stared at her lips. She heard his breath beginning to catch. Seeing the effect she was having on him, she whispered in a low, sultry voice, "Not yet. Wait until I finish my brownie."

Blinking rapidly, Dan threw back his head and laughed. "You little tease! Life with you is never gonna be dull, is it?"

Gil's eyes twinkled. Running a deliberately provocative finger over his lips, she murmured, "Peace is overrated."

Pulling her close, Dan chuckled. "Honey, you can say that again."

⌒⌒

Fifteen minutes later, Twinkles emerged from the study and went to the living room to find Sam. He was sitting on the couch with Sue, listening to Danny's singing lesson.

"Sam," Twinkles said, "I left my book in the rental truck. Can you get it for me?"

Sam rose to his feet. "Sure, where's the truck?"

"In the barn. You're sure you don't mind?"

"Why would I? I'm glad to help."

As Sam moved to the door, Twinkles tugged on his sleeve. "Speaking of help, I was playing *Bible Trivia* with Poppa and two questions stumped us. What does 1 Corinthians 16:13 say?"

Sam thought for a moment. *"Be on your guard; stand firm in the faith; be men of courage; be strong."* He smiled. "What was the other question?"

"How did the Israelites tell the King of Edom they'd travel on the road?"

"They said they'd turn neither to the right nor to left."

Twinkles tilted her head to one side. "You know, even though those verses are talking about different things there's a lesson if you take them together."

"How so?" Sam asked, opening the door.

"Standing firm and not going right or left is good advice for our spiritual life and sometimes for our physical life as well. Don't you agree?"

"I suppose so," Sam replied.

"Take it from an old time traveler, applying those words to your life will keep you safe. Now, go get my book like a good boy. I'll give you a brownie when you get back."

Giving Twinkles's cheek a lightning-fast kiss, Sam went out the door.

Twinkles walked quickly to Gil's bedroom where Dan was tucking Gil back in bed. Peeking around the door, Twinkles said, "Dan, can I borrow you for a moment?"

"Sure," Dan replied, kissing Gil's forehead.

"Do you have to go?" Gil asked, grabbing his hand.

"I won't be gone for long," he replied, combing her bangs with his fingers. "And when I get back, maybe we can *practice* some more."

Gil's eyes twinkled. "I think I could squeeze it into my schedule."

As Dan left the room, his grin faded. Looking at Twinkles, he asked quietly, "Is it time?"

She nodded and handed him a black box. "Sam's on his way to the barn."

"Watch after Gil for me," Dan said, clipping the box to his belt. "And whatever you do, don't let her out of the house."

Forty-Seven

WHISTLING HAPPILY, SAM walked down a grassy lane toward the barn. He was smiling to himself as he thought about Sue. She was an incredible woman and he couldn't wait to marry her. His grin grew. Actually, he didn't *want* to wait to marry her. If she'd agree, he'd like to be married in a few weeks' time. The gossips would talk, but he simply didn't care. What he cared about was getting his new family under his roof and starting their life together.

Joyously kicking a stone and sending it cartwheeling down the path, he continued to plan. He'd ask Danny to be his best man—it'd please the boy to pieces, and Nathan would understand. As he kicked the stone again, he chuckled. Zara was gonna flip about the wedding. He was sure she'd bake the wedding cake. He hoped so. He loved her buttercream frosting.

Sending the stone sailing, he began to plan the perfect honeymoon. His thoughts became so absorbed he hardly noticed reaching the barn. Sighing at the interruption of his daydreams, he swung open the barn door and looked at the rental truck parked inside. It was bigger than he'd expected. Obviously Poppa and Twinkles had bought more furniture than they were admitting.

Entering the cool shade of the barn, he caught a whiff of dusty hay and sneezed. Making his way through dim shadows, he opened the truck's passenger-side door and found a biblical concordance resting on a coil of rope. Wondering if the concordance was Twinkles's idea of light reading, he slung it awkwardly beneath his arm. Feeling it slip, he clutched it against his chest.

Suddenly, Sam heard a loud noise and felt a heavy blow striking his chest. Crashing back against the truck, he groaned and tried to catch his breath. Blinking against the pain, he looked down and saw a gaping hole in the concordance. His mind felt paralyzed as he realized that he was looking at a bullet hole. The bullet was embedded in the book.

As he spun around and peered through the darkness, an eerie voice hissed, "Missed you, did I? Well, this one won't miss."

"Who's there?" Sam shouted, squaring his shoulders despite the pain.

"Who do you think?" Stepping out of the shadows, Rick raised his gun. "I'm gonna enjoy shutting up your psalm-singing mouth for good."

Inside the house, Sue was listening drowsily as Danny and Poppa sang. As a gunshot rang through the air, she jumped violently. Sick with fear for Sam's safety, she ran toward the door.

Watching as Rick raised his gun, Sam remembered Twinkles's words: *Stand firm; don't go right or left.* Knowing their talk couldn't be a coincidence, he stood his ground.

"All right, preacher," Rick said venomously, "let's see if you can be a dog groveling on the ground."

Sam didn't answer. Looking into Rick's hate-filled eyes, he remained motionless.

"Did you hear me? Grovel! Beg for your life." As Sam stood still, Rick began to curse. Droplets of spit flew from his mouth. "You're a dog! A cur! Get down and beg!"

When Sam didn't reply, Rick shot his gun wildly. The bullet shattered the truck's windshield, spraying Sam with glass.

"Beg!"

Rick shot again, this time at the dirt in front of Sam's feet. Sam didn't move. He regarded Rick steadily and stood firm.

Bolting out of her bedroom, Gil narrowly missed crashing into Sue. She ran frantically to the front door, but Twinkles was blocking it. As she and Sue tried to get past, Poppa moved swiftly to his wife's side, barricading the door even further.

"Let me through!" Sue shouted. "Sam's out there!"

"I think the doc is too!" Gil cried. "I've got to go find him."

"Ladies," Poppa said calmly, "what's going on is out of your hands."

"Let me by," Sue demanded.

Twinkles shook her head. "If you go out there, you'll just mess things up. Sit down and have a brownie."

Gil tried to push past Poppa, but he laid a restraining hand on her arm.

"Poppa, *please*, I gotta go!"

He firmly shook his head. "Would you change anything that happened on D-day, seeing the results it brought?"

"No," she said, trying to pull away, "but what's that got to do with anything?"

"Dr. Ableman feels the same way about what's going on right now. Like Twinkles said, go have a brownie. You and Sue can't do anything but wait."

∽

Inside the barn, Rick sent a bullet sailing past Sam's arm. "Beg!"

Sam flinched, but refused to speak.

"*Beg!*" Rick shot at the air next to Sam's head.

Hearing the bullet as it whistled past his ear, Sam held absolutely still.

"If you won't beg then it's time to die. I'll give your regards to Sue. I'll bet she'll beg."

Sam's eyes blazed, but remembering Twinkles's words, he remained motionless.

"What? No fancy speech? I thought you loved to hear yourself talk." Rick raised his gun and aimed it at Sam's heart. "Any last words?"

With half-formed prayers running through his mind, Sam stared at the gun and tried to prepare himself for what was about to happen. He pictured Sue's face, wanting it to be the last thing he remembered.

As Rick pulled the trigger, Sam saw his arm jerking to the left. The bullet flew astray and hit a bale of hay. Rick pulled the trigger again. His arm jerked right. The bullet flew wide and hit a wall.

Sam saw Rick narrowing his eyes. Looking sideways at an empty patch of air, Rick lunged and grabbed at something invisible. Holding onto it, he purred, "So the little ghost has come back to play. Naughty! Naughty!"

Suddenly, as if a switch had been flipped, Dr. Ableman appeared. "Wrong!" he growled. "It's the little ghost's boyfriend!"

Sam watched in shock as Dr. Ableman twisted free and punched Rick with a brutal blow. As Rick fell back, Dr. Ableman kicked the gun from his hand, sending it spinning through the air toward the door.

Snarling with uncontrollable rage, Rick lunged. Dr. Ableman stepped to one side, and using Rick's momentum against him, threw him against the wall. As Rick spun around, Dr. Ableman threw three fierce blows in rapid succession—each sending Rick reeling across the floor. As Sam watched with dazed eyes, Dr. Ableman leapt in the air with a jumping spin-hook kick that sent Rick crashing to the ground.

Scrambling to his knees, Rick grabbed a handful of dirt and threw it into Dr. Ableman's eyes. As Dr. Ableman pawed at his face, trying to clear his vision, Rick rolled to his feet and looked for his gun. Realizing that Dr. Ableman was in danger, Sam sprang forward. All of the minister's pent-up rage broke free as he gave a powerful round-house kick to Rick's belly. As the blow connected, Rick hit the side of the barn with enough force that the wood split and a bottle of horse medicine fell off a shelf and shattered.

Arming himself with the broken bottle, Rick rushed toward the men. As Sam kicked the bottle out of Rick's hand, Dr. Ableman leapt up with a jumping spin-hook kick to the side of Rick's face. The blow flipped Rick off his feet. He wallowed in the dirt and groaned.

"Have you had enough?" Sam asked.

Wiping a trail of blood from his mouth, Rick swore harshly. "Think you're better than me? You're nothing! Nothing!"

Rick jumped to his feet and tossed dirt at Sam's eyes. As Sam raised his arm to protect his face, Dr. Ableman jumped up in a flying round-house kick that broke Rick's nose. Sam followed up with a punch to Rick's stomach. Rick flopped against the wall and coughed blood.

As Rick dove toward the door, Dr. Ableman caught him by the collar. Putting him in a chokehold, he hissed, "You hurt the women we love. Now we're going to hurt you!"

As Rick clawed desperately at Dr. Ableman's arm, Sam stepped forward. "How many women have you tortured in the dark?" Sam's eyes blazed. "Did you enjoy hurting Sue? Did you?"

With an iron blow, Sam punched Rick's stomach. Rick doubled over. Dr. Ableman grabbed his hair and held him up. As Sam threw several vicious punches, Dr. Ableman snarled in Rick's ear, "Are you afraid? You should be."

Rick groaned and vomited. Dr. Ableman tossed him to the ground. Rick lay for a moment in his own filth and then struggled to his knees. Dr. Ableman slowly circled him.

"I've had enough," Rick moaned. "Let me go."

"You didn't let Gil go. You almost killed her." With tremendous venom, Dr. Ableman kicked Rick in the face. Rick flopped over and lay still. Dr. Ableman started to kick him again, but Sam put a restraining hand on his shoulder and raised Rick's head by the hair.

"He's out?" Dr. Ableman asked.

"Like a light," Sam replied, letting Rick's head fall limply in the dirt.

Dr. Ableman grumbled and nudged Rick's motionless body with his shoe. "I wanted to hit him some more and threaten him some more—maybe make him cry or wet himself."

"Me too," Sam admitted with a rueful chuckle.

Dr. Ableman looked down at Rick and said slowly, as if tasting the words, "I'd like to kill him."

"So would I, but there's a big difference between subduing a man for the authorities and committing murder."

"Subduing him for the authorities? Is that what we were doing?"

Sam's lips twitched. "Well, that and administering a justified beating, both of which are a far cry from murder."

"I suppose so." Dr. Ableman nudged Rick's body again. "Besides, after all she went through, Gil would never forgive me if I killed him."

"Sue wouldn't like me to become a murderer either. And I'm not about to mess things up with her."

Dr. Ableman backed toward the truck and leaned against its hood. As he closed his fists and inspected his bleeding knuckles, Sam commented, "Those were some great martial arts kicks you landed."

"I'm glad you liked them," Dr. Ableman replied. "You taught them to me."

"I wondered about our last names being the same," Sam said, fingering a cut on his jaw. "Are you some relative I haven't met yet?"

"Never mind, it's complicated. I'll explain later."

Sam looked over at Rick's body. "We should tie him up and phone the police."

"Are you sure we can't just hit him over the head and drop him down a convenient well?"

"Quite sure," Sam replied, "but I'll probably fantasize about that scenario for years—if you'll forgive the impropriety of a pastor admitting to murderous thoughts."

A grin tugged at Dr. Ableman's mouth. "I have no right to throw stones." His grin faded, and his voice lowered. "When I think about what he did to Gil and Sue, I want to—"

"I know," Sam said, interrupting quietly, "but we've gone far enough. We need to let the authorities take it from here. There's rope in the truck. We should tie him up while we have the chance." Sam opened the door with a yank. "Besides, it's better this way. Rick's gonna fry and there'll be deep-down justice in Danny knowing he's on death row."

"I suppose so."

"I'm glad you got here when you did," Sam said, picking up the rope. "I thought for sure I was gonna get shot. I don't understand why I didn't see you at first."

"Never mind, I'll explain later." Dr. Ableman pointed at the blood on Sam's face. "Did any of the bullets graze you? If they did, Sue will have our hides."

Sam shook his head. "I got cut by flying glass. It's no big deal."

Suddenly, Sam saw movement out of the corner of his eye. Without wasting a moment, he dove at Dr. Ableman and pushed him to the ground. A shot rang out and a bullet lodged in the side of the truck. Mentally kicking himself for not securing the gun, Sam stared at the doorway where Rick was pointing his weapon at them.

"Think you got the best of me?" Rick growled. Swearing in a heated rage, he aimed his gun and started to squeeze the trigger.

"This is the police," a voice shouted from outside. "Drop your weapon!"

With a wild curse, Rick swung around and opened fire. As a hail of bullets filled the air, Sam grabbed Dr. Ableman's arm and pulled him beneath the truck. "Did you call the police?" he asked.

Dr. Ableman shook his head and ducked as a bullet ricocheted off the bumper.

Feeling a protectiveness he didn't understand, Sam reached over and covered Dr. Ableman's head with his arm.

"I'm okay," Dr. Ableman said. "Protect yourself."

"Be still and stay covered," Sam shouted, trying to be heard over the gunfire.

Rick's head swung toward them. He locked eyes with Sam. A bullet grazed Rick's arm. He swore and shot toward the door. Sam's heart lurched as Rick rushed at him.

"If I'm going down," Rick snarled, "you're going with me!"

Bracing himself, Sam tried to cover more of Dr. Ableman's body with his own. He saw Nathan and Chief Rogers rushing into the barn.

"Drop your weapon!" Nathan shouted. "Do it now!"

Rick shoved his gun in Sam's face. "Time to say goodbye, preacher."

Suddenly, there was an explosion of sound. A bullet ripped through the side of Rick's head, spraying Sam's face with blood. In silent slow motion, Rick's legs buckled beneath him. His eyes still locked with Sam's, Rick fell to the ground. Blood gushed in a torrent over Sam's hand and pooled in a dark puddle.

Sam felt numb. Beside him, Dr. Ableman was moving frantically. It took Sam a moment to realize he was patting him down, looking for wounds.

"I'm all right," Sam said slowly, his voice sounding strange in his ringing ears. "You?"

"I'm good," Dr. Ableman replied, his voice tense. "I can't believe how close that was."

"Sam!" Nathan yelled, sprinting across the floor. "Are you hurt?"

"I'm fine," Sam replied, crawling out from under the truck—the knees of his jeans getting soaked in blood. "How did you know to come?"

"Someone named Twinkles called in a tip," Nathan replied.

Sam nodded, staring down at Rick's shattered head.

As Dr. Ableman slowly rolled to his feet, Chief Rogers pointed at him and asked, "Who's he?"

Sam tore his gaze away from Rick and blinked. "You know, I'm beginning to wonder that myself."

FORTY-EIGHT

COMING OUT OF row XLIX, Marc watched as Crystal swung a heavy box onto her hip. Before he could talk himself out of it, he walked over and put his hand on her shoulder. Crystal gave a surprised squeak and jumped to one side.

"Whoa," Marc said with a crooked grin, "it's just me."

Glaring up at him, Crystal blew a stray curl out of her face. "What do *you* want?"

Marc shifted his weight onto his heels and stared at her. What did he want? He paused and thought. Truthfully, he wasn't sure.

"Well?" she said impatiently. "I haven't got all day."

Marc reached for her box. "Here, let me help you with that."

Jerking away, Crystal said in a scathing voice, "I can do my own work."

"I know. I just wanted to be helpful. That box looks pretty heavy."

"If you want to help, stop bothering me and get back to work. We'll have this job finished by tonight if you do your fair share."

Marc bit his lip and looked at her. There wasn't anything appealing about her attitude and there certainly wasn't anything alluring about her looks, so why couldn't he get her out of his thoughts? She was like an itch that desperately needed to be scratched. He peered at her messy bun and baggy shirt. *What is it about her that—*

"I know you think I'm weird," she grumbled, "but you don't have to stare."

"I'm not staring."

"Stare." Crystal said in robotic voice. "Intransitive verb. *Per definitionem—De Facto.* Old English—*starian.* Old Norse—*stara.* Middle Low German—*staren. To look directly at somebody or something for a long period time without moving the eyes away, usually as a result of curiosity or surprise, or to express rudeness or defiance.*" She glared at him. "According to definition, you've been *staring* at me for the past five minutes. Cut it out."

Marc blinked and began to laugh.

Crystal's face froze and went completely white. As she tried to step around him, he blocked her path. Looking at her pale face, he cracked his knuckles nervously. She was peering over his shoulder with pursed lips and a steady gaze. It felt as if she'd taken her soul and tucked it far away. Although she was standing next to him, she was untouchable. Unreachable. Unattainable. He didn't know why that should bother him, but it did. It bothered him a lot. A whole lot to tell the truth.

"I'm sorry we keep getting off on the wrong foot," he finally said. "I shouldn't have yelled at you the other day, and I know it."

"Fine," she said briefly. "Now get out of my way."

Marc laid a hand on her shoulder. "Honest. I'd like to apologize."

She shook off his hand. "You already have. Now move."

"Cris—"

Crystal dropped the box on the floor—narrowly missing his foot—and put her hands on her hips. "Look, I know exactly what you think of me, and I'm glad I do. We'll get along better if we keep out of each other's way."

"I don't think that's possible. If we're put on staff, we'll be working together."

"Co-workers don't have to be close." She pushed at her glasses. "I'm prepared to do my job well, but I'm not prepared to get chummy with someone like *you*."

"What do you mean by that?"

"Exactly what you think!" Crystal gave an impatient huff. "You really think you're something special, don't you? You think you're God's perfect gift to women. You think every female is obligated to faint if you smile. You big jerk, the only reason you want to talk to me is because I don't want to talk to you. You need to get over yourself. You're not nearly as handsome and fascinating as you seem to believe. It really peeves you that I'm immune to your so-called charm, doesn't it?"

An angry blush flooded Marc's face. "You don't know what you're talking about."

"Really? Then why did you tell me to stay away and then turn right around and try to be friendly? What am I? A dog you think you can bring to heel?"

"Of course not!" He hunched a shoulder. "I just realized I was out of line, okay? I'm not perfect—far from it. I'm just trying to apologize."

"Fine. You've done your duty. Consider yourself absolved. Now move."

As she tried to push past him, he grabbed her arm. "I'm not going anywhere until I know things are square between us."

"What do you want?" she asked, shaking off his hand. "A written declaration of forgiveness?"

"No, just a friendly smile."

Crystal rolled her eyes and bared her teeth in a toothy grin. "Are you satisfied?"

He shook his head. "Why don't we sit down and talk awhile?"

"About what?"

"Anything you like," he replied. "You can lecture me about the history of paper and Egyptian mummification if you want."

"If you have a burning desire to learn about mummification go look it up. The campus library has a whole section on ancient Egypt."

"If you don't want to talk about that, we can discuss something else—pick a topic."

"How about the underlying symptoms of Narcissistic Personality Disorder?" As Marc's mouth fell open in disbelief, Crystal started counting off on her fingers. "Believing you're better than everyone else, expecting constant praise or admiration, failing to recognize other people's feelings, expressing disdain for those you feel are inferior—"

Marc cut her off. "If you want to talk about psychological problems, why don't we talk about inferiority complexes and passive-aggressive behavior?"

With an angry snort, Crystal tried to brush past him, but he wouldn't let her. Falling back a step, she hissed, "Keep your hands to yourself and let me by!"

"Look, I just want to be friends."

"Why?"

He looked at her pale face and gave a tense smile. "I'd like to get to know you, that's why. You'd probably like me if you gave me a shot."

Crystal glared at him. "Get used to disappointment. I'll work with you, but this is as friendly as we're gonna get."

Marc put his hand on her shoulder and felt her shiver as she jerked away. "Cris, I—"

"Unless it's about work, I don't want to hear it. Is it?"

Marc shook his head.

"In that case, I'm taking a break. You can file that box. It weighs a ton."

As Crystal disappeared through the archive door, Marc leaned up against a shelf and tried to catch his breath. He didn't know why her rejection hurt so much, but he felt as if he'd been kicked in the gut. Ryan was right—once Crystal made up her mind, she stuck with it. She wasn't just stubborn, she was an opinionated mule.

Marc's eyes hardened. Trying to be friendly with Crystal was a complete waste of time. He didn't know why he was bothering. It wasn't like he'd be thrilled to be seen in public with the frumpy campus klutz on his arm.

Poppa's estate was swarming with police. As Nathan left for Westfield to pick up Zara and his grandfather, the coroner came and removed Rick's body. Afternoon had turned into early evening by the time the police had left the house.

In the living room, Gil watched as Twinkles bustled around, setting plates of brownies and cookies on the coffee table. As everyone began reaching for the goodies, Twinkles said soothingly, "That's right, dears. Nothing like a spot of sugar to calm fraying nerves."

"I thought sugar made a person hyper." Poppa chuckled.

"Maybe so, but it's also soothing. Shush now and pass the brownies to Gil. She looks like she needs another."

Deciding that the worry she'd undergone had burned up a gazillion calories, Gil plopped down on the sofa and defiantly took her fifth brownie. Seeing Dan's raised eyebrows, she grumbled, "I love you, but don't get between me and my sugar. After the afternoon I've had, I *need* chocolate—and the more the better!"

As Dan laughed and passed her another brownie, Sam said with a puzzled frown, "Doc, now that the police are gone, can you clear something up?"

"Sure," Dan said absently, placing a gooey chocolate chip cookie on each of Gil's knees and kissing a spot of chocolate off her chin.

"In the barn, why couldn't I see you at first?"

"That's simple," Dan replied, unclipping a box from his belt and handing it to Poppa. "I was using one of the Wonderful Wizard's inventions. A Scan Emitter eliminates the need for brain scans and allows a time surfer to appear or disappear at will."

"That would've helped Gil a lot." Danny chortled. "She was always sitting on shelves and breaking them, or almost getting sat on, or eating when she shouldn't, or—"

Leaning forward, Gil gave Danny's shoulder a playfully slap. "Watch it, squirt!" Turning to Poppa, she asked, "Does the Scan Emitter let surfers eat *real* food without freaking people out?" As he nodded, Gil rolled her eyes in exaggerated ecstasy. "No more kitty-litter bars! That suits me fine—sign me up."

"Not quite yet, dear," Twinkles said. "The Scan Emitter won't be ready for four more years in your time, but I do sympathize about the energy bars." She wrinkled her nose. "Horrible things! I've always said they were the blight of a time surfer's life."

"Did the doc have a Scan Emitter when he jumped through the TV?" Danny asked. "Is that why we could see him?"

"I didn't have the Scan Emitter until Twinkles lent it to me this afternoon," Dan replied. "On D-day, all Poppa gave me was information on how to avoid Rick and stabilize Gil."

Danny looked puzzled. "But how could we see you then? When Gil came, my brain was scanned. I felt the beams inside my head."

Dan smiled. "GAP didn't need to scan your brain. You were predisposed to see me because you'd seen me before in your mirror."

"Whatcha mean? You got my mirror wired up like my PlayFest console?"

Dan's smile grew. "I mean, you'd seen me before by looking at *yourself* in the mirror. Where does your mom always kiss you?"

"On my little freckle."

Turning his head, Dan showed the boy his heart-shaped freckle.

"No way!" Danny shouted. "You're me? That means Gil's gonna be my girlfriend!"

Laughing, Dan said to Gil, "See how he focuses on the important things in life?"

Sue put out at hesitant hand and touched Dan's freckle. "You're my son?"

As Dan nodded and hugged his mother tightly, Sam gave a bellow of laughter. "If you're Danny, I *did* teach you martial arts."

"You did indeed," Dan replied. "You were a great dad and a terrific teacher."

Danny's eyes grew wide. "I beat up Rick when I get old? *Cool!*"

As Danny sat back with a satisfied grin, Sam turned to Twinkles. "If you gave Dan the Scan Emitter today, does that mean you knew Rick was coming?"

Twinkles nodded. "I knew to the exact second. You can't hide much from time travelers when they come from our year."

With an angry sputter, Sue jumped to her feet.

"Why, Sue," Twinkles said, shrinking back in her chair. "Whatever's the matter?"

"How can you ask?" Sue spat. "You *knew* Rick was coming, and you sent Sam to the barn anyway. How *could* you?"

Rising quickly, Poppa stood protectively in front of his wife. "Twinkles only did what I told her. If you want to get angry, get angry at me. But really, there's no need. We sent Dan to help Sam and we called the police. Sam wasn't in danger—at least not *much* danger."

"Yes, dear," soothed Twinkles, peeping out from behind her husband's back. "GAP predicted a sixty-two percent chance that Sam and Dan wouldn't suffer significant harm."

Gil sprang to her feet. "Sixty-two percent! Only sixty-two percent? You sent Dan out there with those *wretched* odds and made me sit in the kitchen with a plate of brownies and fudge sauce?"

Poppa laid a restraining hand on her shoulder. "Just the other day, your odds of success were only fifty percent. Our odds today were much better."

"I don't care!" Gil exclaimed. "Those odds stink!" Her face went white. "When I think about what might've happened—"

"But it didn't happen," Poppa interrupted gently. "Although sending the boys to the barn seems reckless, it was the one scenario in which everyone walked away unharmed and Rick was stopped for good. And that monster *needed* to be stopped."

Gil paused, thinking about the lives Rick had destroyed. She looked over at Sue. Together the women sank back down on the sofa.

Putting his arm around Sue, Sam said to Twinkles, "I appreciated the concordance, but I'm afraid you'll have trouble using it again."

"Don't worry, dear, I bought it to protect you."

As Gil watched Poppa putting the Scan Emitter into his pocket, she asked, "Is the Scan Emitter similar to the technology tested on the files Director Matthews gave me?"

"Similar," Poppa replied, "but far more advanced. The invention to which you're referring was just an early prototype." He smiled. "And I wasn't the one who tested it."

"But aren't you the Wonderful Wizard?"

"Of course I am, forty-five years into your future, but I'm not the Wonderful Wizard who tested the prototype on D-day. That was my younger-self."

"Who's your younger-self?" Gil asked with a furrowed brow. "I know it's not Dr. Moosly. He's bald as an egg, and you have a good head of hair."

Twinkles chuckled. "You know the Wizard, dear. This is just another whimsical time surprise."

Leaning toward Gil, Poppa said, "Kiss my little freckle, will you?"

Twinkles gave Poppa's shoulder a swat. "Oh, no, you don't! No other woman can kiss your freckle—even if she is me!"

Gil's eyes widened. "I'm Twinkles?" Looking over her shoulder at Dan, she sputtered, "Why didn't you tell me you were Poppa?"

"Don't worry, dear," Twinkles laughed, "you'll get even with him, and you'll have a marvelous time doing it." She looked archly at Poppa. "If I remember right, Dan gets quite a bit of enjoyment out of the process too."

Sue turned to Twinkles. "*Your* Poppa is *my* Danny? *My Danny* wrote those love poems?"

As Twinkles nodded and looked smug, Poppa looked absolutely horrified. "You showed my love poems to my *mother?*"

"Just a nice one about my eyes. I didn't let her read the very *warm* ones, dear. I wouldn't let a young girl like Sue read those."

As Poppa's ears turned bright red and laughter broke out all around, Gil slapped Dan lightly on the chest. "What's up with you, you lazy slug? Poppa's a poet. When are you gonna start writing me sonnets about my eyes?"

Dan chuckled. "Don't worry, honey, I'll start tonight." Leaning toward her, he stared at her lips and whispered, "I'm feeling *quite* inspired."

As Dan drew Gil close and kissed her, she saw Danny watching them with a satisfied smirk. When the kiss ended, Danny asked through a mouthful of crumbs, "Am I really gonna invent time travel and run TEMCO?"

Kissing the top of Gil's head, Dan looked at his younger-self and nodded. "You sure will, and Slim's going to be your second-in-command."

"No way! Did I see him when we made contact with the lab?"

Dan grinned. "You sure did—he's Director Peter Matthews."

"*Are you serious?* Slim's gonna flip when I tell him!"

"He will indeed." Dan laughed. "He's your best friend, and his knowledge of physics, and Laura Nelson's expertise in quantum mechanics, will be a great help to you down through the years."

As Danny turned to his mother and started talking excitedly, Gil asked Dan, "Why didn't you let anyone know you were the head of TEMCO?"

"Death Row Daniel and the tangled timeline," he replied. "TEMCO needs grants to keep running, and giving money to an inventor who could vanish from time isn't a wise investment. Peter and Laura thought I needed to keep my identity a secret, and I agreed."

"But how could you put up with Dr. Moosly's condescension? He despises you."

"I just found him amusing. On a weekly basis, he submits a letter to the 'head of TEMCO' demanding I be fired. He's a scientific asset in his own ponderous way, but I'll enjoy seeing his face when I tell him he's been campaigning to fire his own boss."

"I wanna be in the room when you do," Gil said, reaching for a cookie. "His pompous comments about you have been driving me wild."

"Feeling protective of me?" Dan asked, nuzzling her head with his chin.

"Very!" she replied. Turning to Poppa, she said, "That reminds me, do you know why I was sent to protect little Danny in the first place? Do you know what triggered the Time Tsunami?"

Poppa nodded. "Years ago, I discovered a random piece of code in GAP's memory core. When analyzed, it revealed that the Time Tsunami was caused by the foolish arrogance of one person— the first original Dr. Daniel Winston."

Dan blinked rapidly and choked on his brownie. "Are you sure about that?"

"Quite sure. The first Daniel invented time travel just like you did, but it took him longer because he didn't have Peter to help him—you and Slim became friends during Gil's time surf. After establishing TEMCO, Daniel wanted a spectacular test case to take in front of the Grant Review Board to justify an expansion of the program, and that's where the trouble began."

"What kind of trouble?" Dan asked.

"The kind of trouble that gets people killed." Poppa leaned forward and put his hands on his knees. "The first Daniel's time surfers took on small cases—nothing too daring. But he was desperate to make a big splash for the review board, so he went to death row and picked out a likely candidate for time counseling. He was convinced that transforming the felon would get him the grant money he desired."

"What's wrong with that?" Gil asked. "We work with death-row felons all the time."

"The problem was the foolish haste with which it was done," Poppa replied. "In actual fact, the first Daniel made five critical errors, each of which could've led to disaster."

Dan blinked. "When you offered your services as Facilitator, you had me memorize *The Five Immutable Laws*. Were those laws written to prevent Daniel's errors from reoccurring?"

"They were indeed," Poppa replied.

"So, what errors did Daniel make?" Gil asked.

"His first mistake was failing to research the felon's past," Poppa replied. "If he'd done research, Daniel would've discovered that rather than murdering only one woman, the felon in question was a serial killer who made his victims' deaths look like suicides."

Sue made a strangled sound in her throat and looked sick. "Are you saying he chose to counsel *Rick?*"

Poppa nodded grimly. "Yes, indeed, and his choice led to utter disaster." Poppa steepled his fingers. "Daniel's second mistake was neglecting to conduct interviews with Rick on death row. Comprehensive interviews would've revealed Rick's true nature."

"Is that why personality tests are given to time-counseling candidates?" Gil asked.

Poppa nodded. "Some people are so evil it's dangerous to counsel them, as the first Daniel learned to his detriment."

Gil bit her lip and took another cookie. "What was his third mistake?"

"He didn't find Rick's tipping point. He simply surfed back to the day before the murder that landed Rick on death row."

"What's a tipping point?" Sue asked.

"It's the exact moment in which a felon's future is first tipped toward evil," Poppa replied. "It usually occurs during childhood. For example, Danny's tipping point occurred when he stabbed Rick with the butcher knife."

Gil shuddered. "I don't think it would've mattered how young Rick was when he was counseled. He told me he did things to cats when he was a little boy." As Dan tightened his arm around her, she asked, "What was Daniel's fourth mistake?"

"Disclosure. When he confronted Rick in the past, he told him where he used to live."

Sue face turned pale. "You mean...?"

Poppa nodded grimly. "The fourth law forbids time counselors from revealing their last names and personal histories. This law was created because the first Daniel ignorantly informed a brutal murderer that his last name was Winston, his mother's name was Sue, and his hometown was Charlesberg, Colorado."

"I can't believe this," Sue said quietly and numbly. She shivered. "What was his fifth mistake?"

"Arrogance. After he counseled Rick, Daniel was fooled by Rick's fake show of repentance, and rather than checking probability results, he simply surfed back home."

"*A time counselor must never be blinded by conceit or supposition,*" Dan quoted from the fifth law.

"Exactly," Poppa replied. "In reality, rather than being grateful, Rick was furious that Daniel had the audacity to tell him what to do. Determined to get even, he made his way to Charlesberg and found Daniel as a little boy."

As Sue shuddered, Sam put his arm around her and squeezed Danny's hand.

Poppa took a sip of milk and cleared his throat. "Rick killed Sue and Danny. He murdered them both. Their deaths split the timewave firmly down the middle. Two massive waves began crashing toward the temporal shore in a colossal Time Tsunami— one wave in which the first Daniel grew up and created time travel, and one wave in which Daniel was murdered and time travel never existed."

"A Cataclysmic Failure," Dan whispered.

"Cataclysmic indeed," said Poppa. "It was devastating. It threatened to rip apart the fabric of time. When Daniel went home, TEMCO was in shambles. Immediate action was required, and GAP indicated that Gil Montgomery needed to surf back to stop the murder of Sue and her son."

Poppa paused and took a deep breath. "At that time, Gil was a professional time surfer, but her efforts were only partially successful. Sue was murdered. Little Danny was saved, but he killed Rick with the butcher knife and ended up dying on death row. TEMCO was still in danger of collapsing. GAP indicated that Gil needed to try again, but unfortunately, she'd lost her life in the first attempt. Desperate, Daniel traveled a few years back into the past and convinced his younger counterpart to make Gil surf again—this time as a grad student taking a field exam. Her second surf was a success. Sue and Danny were saved and a timeline was produced in which Danny grew up alongside Slim and invented time travel."

"If it was such a success, why was a third surf needed?" Sue asked.

"Because there were still two unique waves crashing toward the shore. A wave in which Danny invented GAP and ran the

404

TEMCO program, and a wave in which he died on death row. The Cataclysmic Failure had shifted, but it wasn't stopped."

"This makes my head hurt," Sue moaned.

Dan smiled. "Don't worry, Mom. The main thing you need to know is that the Time Tsunami was dissipated by Gil's third surf. Everything's fine."

"If you say so."

Gil leaned forward. "Poppa, Dan says consecutive surfs muddy the water, so you can't tell what happened before. That's what happened to Rick, isn't it?"

"Exactly," Poppa replied. "By the time your third surf took place—since it was a triple repeat into a split timeline—the waters, so to speak, were *very* muddy. It's possible that by your third surf, Rick no longer knew about the first Daniel or about time travel. It's possible he just felt inevitably drawn to Charlesberg and Sue."

Gil shivered. "I think he knew something though—even if subconsciously. He wasn't surprised by my invisibility. He took it in stride."

"A regressive memory," Twinkles said with a nod. "Rick may not have realized it, but he was repeating a pattern he'd repeated many times before."

As silence fell, Sue asked hesitantly, "Poppa, were you the first Daniel?"

The old man shook his head. "No, my dear, when Gil's third surf succeeded, the very first Daniel, Death Row Daniel, and the Dan who sent Gil back the second time were all erased from existence. Since the split timewave has been healed, only one timeline now exists. Little Danny is sitting next to you on the couch, Dr. Ableman is Danny twenty-four years into the future, and I'm Danny nearly seventy years into the future."

Leaning back in Dan's arms, Gil asked Poppa, "Do you know if the first Daniel and I were together as a couple?"

He shook his head. "The computer code wasn't that detailed. It only revealed the circumstances surrounding the Time Tsunami."

Gil pressed a kiss to Dan's freckle. "Even if the threat of a Time Tsunami was needed to get me and Dan together, I'm glad we're together. I'm glad things worked out the way they did."

"Me too," chirped Danny. "Especially now that I know I get you as my girlfriend!"

As Gil laughed and tossed her napkin at the boy, Poppa grinned and stood to his feet. "I hate to bring things to a close, but it's time to send Gil and Dan back home."

Danny looked around the room. "How are they gonna time travel without a PlayFest console?"

Poppa tousled the hair on his younger-self's head. "They have Twinkles and me."

"Poppa's inventions, you know," Twinkles said, gathering up the dishes and putting them on a tray. "We stopped leaping through TV portals *ages* ago."

FORTY-NINE

CRYSTAL STARED AT the last two boxes sitting by the archive door. As she reached for one of them, Marc walked out from behind the shelves. Seeing his jaw tighten, Crystal took a deep breath and stuttered, "W-we're almost done."

"I can see that, Einstein."

His frozen voice made her flinch. Squaring her shoulders, she said curtly, "I know we don't get along, but we should pretend to for a while."

"Oh? Why's that?"

"Director Matthews wanted to be informed when we completed our assignment, so he could lock down the archives for the summer."

"It doesn't take two people to deliver a message."

"I know that," she snapped. "But if we want the director to think we can work together, we should try to be civil."

"I'll take my chances."

"Go ahead then, you stupid oaf, act like a jerk and see what happens!" She thrust her angry face toward his. "I'm pretty good at calculating odds, and trust me, if we *both* want a job at TEMCO we'd better walk into the lab side by side."

Marc paused. "What are you trying to say? Do you know something I don't?"

She hunched a shoulder. "I'm just saying that you'd better get the chip off your shoulder and play nice."

"Why do you care? You'd be glad to see me washed out of the program."

"I would not! I may not like you, but I can recognize your talent."

Marc blinked. His voice softened. "Do you mean that?"

"I'm not in the habit of lying."

"You know, Cris, I wouldn't mind calling a truce. I could always use another friend."

Crystal glared through her glasses. "I'm not interested in being friends. I just want a job when I graduate."

Marc's eyes hardened. "You are without a doubt the rudest woman I've ever met!"

"I'm not rude—I'm honest." Shaking her hair out of her face, she mumbled, "Just treat me with civility when the director's watching, okay? Do you think you can manage that?"

"What about you? Every time I try to bury the hatchet, you end up whacking me over the head with it! If anyone needs an attitude adjustment, it's you."

"Don't worry about me," Crystal said, swinging the box on her hip. "I'm smart enough to have a healthy sense of self-preservation. I'll be friendly whenever Director Matthews is around, but the rest of the time I'm staying as far away from you as I can get."

Gil watched as the men carried her luggage into the living room. When she tried to thank them, they began complaining loudly about sprained backs and broken arms. In unison, Gil and Twinkles rolled their eyes.

"Men!" Twinkles said in a disgusted tone. "They can pack light because they never think ahead. Where would they go for a Band-Aid if we weren't around? Feckless creatures! They should be thanking us, not heckling us."

With a naughty twinkle, Gil replied, "I couldn't agree with *myself* more." As the room erupted in laughter, she looked at her new friends and moaned. "I don't know how I'm gonna say goodbye!"

"It's not goodbye." Dan chuckled. "I'm going with you, and you're having dinner with Mom and Dad when we get home—they're flying to D.C. to see you."

"But you aren't little Danny anymore, and twenty-four years is a lot of distance to cover between friends. When I see her again, Sue and I won't be the same age. She'll be older than me and my prospective *mother-in-law*. I'll be intimidated by her."

"No, you won't," Sue said, giving Gil a hug. "I couldn't be intimidating if I tried."

"Don't move! Hold that pose!" Twinkles commanded, rushing forward with an object in her hands. "I want a picture."

As Gil gave Twinkles a puzzled glance, the old woman flourished the device and said, "A holographic camera was a byproduct of the Scan Emitter. Poppa called it his lucky mistake. But mistake or not, it's certainly been a lucrative invention."

Sue blinked. "Danny invents a new type of camera as well as time travel?"

"Your brilliant son is *always* inventing things," Twinkles replied. "I've lost track of all his bright ideas. Now, hug Gil again, will you? I want some pictures for my scrapbook."

After taking the picture of Gil and Sue, Twinkles began taking pictures of everyone else. Eventually, Poppa plucked the camera from his wife's fingers and said, "That's enough, dear."

"I know." Twinkles sighed. "I guess I'm just trying to spin things out as long as possible. I still hate goodbyes."

Smiling at the old woman, Gil asked, "Before I go, any tips for my future?"

Twinkles tapped her finger lightly against her lips. "Let's see...be sure to nudge Laura toward Peter. They're a perfect match. The poor dears are completely blind to it of course, but they'll come around."

Gil grinned. "Anything else?"

"Relish each day with Dan. Your days together are gonna be worth relishing." Suddenly, Twinkles jolted. "Oh! There's one more thing. Don't let your daughter put her hamster in the bathtub when she's cleaning its cage."

As Gil's eyebrows rose, Twinkles groaned. "Don't ask. Just know it involves *lots* of tears and a *very* expensive service call from a plumber late on a Saturday night."

Gil laughed. "I'll remember." Her face took on a puzzled frown. "Can you clear something up? Why did Poppa give me a cookbook when he gave me my scholarship?"

As Poppa began to blush, Twinkles chuckled. "That's easy enough to explain. Poppa loves good food. He was just making sure he got it in the future, the old rascal!"

Dan gave a shout of laughter. "I guess that's one way to ensure your wife can cook." He tweaked one of Gil's curls. "Be grateful, honey, if you didn't know how to cook, you couldn't have resorted to edible bribery to pass the orals."

Gil gave Dan a playful swat. "Be prepared to pay for my cooking with poems, mister!"

Poppa grinned and took a translucent pyramid out of his pocket. After pressing some buttons, he placed it on the floor in the living room doorway.

"What's that?" Danny asked curiously as the sides of the pyramid split apart and transformed into something resembling a lotus flower.

"It's a Wave Trapper," Twinkles said. "It captures timewaves like a spider web and harnesses them for use."

A slender column of silver light streamed up from the middle of the flower. With a burst of iridescent color, the light spread into a sparkling grid that filled the doorway. In rapid succession, the grid sections began filling with blue light.

"Wow!" Danny exclaimed, looking over at Dan. "I—we—made that?"

Dan got a rueful look on his face. "We will eventually. I haven't managed it yet, but I'm getting closer. If Poppa would let me do some reverse engineering, I'd make faster progress."

"You know that's something I can't permit," the old man said. "Besides, I know you'd hate taking a shortcut, no matter how tempting it might be."

"I suppose so. I guess my team and I will just have to figure things out on our own."

"Speaking of your team," Twinkles said, "get ready to say hello."

With another burst of color, the TEMCO lab came into view. Through the glittering wave, Gil could see the shimmering outlines of Director Peter Matthews and Dr. Laura Nelson. They were sitting in the empty lab with their backs toward the emerging portal.

As the silver grid faded and the blue light slowly congealed into an established time portal, Danny said enthusiastically, "I think the Wave Trapper's even cooler than *Extreme Exam*."

Poppa tousled the hair on his younger-self's head. "I aim to please."

Twinkles turned to Gil. "The Trapper's a marvelous invention, but I don't think it has to be so flashy. All those fancy bursts of light are my hubby's way of adding flare."

"Now, honey," Poppa said in a patient voice. "You know the light bursts are unavoidable. The simultaneous cascade of shifting wave patterns captured by the—"

Twinkles gave a snort. "For heaven's sake, don't go all professorish on me! You'll make my head hurt with all your technical mumbo jumbo." Glancing at Gil, she whispered, "I *still* say he's showing off. The light bursts may be unavoidable, but he could tone them down a bit."

As Poppa laughed, Gil saw the enthusiasm draining from Danny's face. He was biting his lip and she could tell he was starting to struggle with tears.

"Hey," she whispered, going to his side. "Are you okay?"

The boy shook his head. "You're really going home, aren't you?"

Gil nodded, feeling the familiar tug on her heart.

A tear trailed down Danny's cheek. "Oh, Gil, I'm gonna miss you so much it hurts."

"I know," she said gently, wiping away his tears. "But we'll meet again. I promise."

Danny pitched himself into her arms. "I'll love you forever."

Gil swallowed a lump in her throat. "I'll love you forever too."

Beside her, Dan clasped Danny's shoulder. "Work hard, little man. Grow up fine, straight, and strong. Don't develop any bad habits that I'll have to break. Save yourself for Gil, and remember that she's absolutely worth the wait."

As Dan and Danny hugged, Sam said to Gil, "I want to thank you for getting me involved. You gave me my family."

Giving Dan a loving glance, Gil nodded and replied, "Getting involved gave me my family too." She looked at Sue through misty eyes. "Thanks for raising Dan to be such a wonderful man."

Sue hugged her close. "Thanks for making sure I had a chance to raise him."

In front of the Wave Trapper, Poppa cleared his throat. "The portal is established. I'm afraid it's time for Dan and Gil to go."

Gil looked through the wave at the lab. As she clasped Dan's hand, sound began traveling through the time portal. She could hear the director talking to Dr. Nelson.

Squeezing her hand, Dan called out loudly, "Hello, the lab!"

Gil watched as the director jolted and looked over his shoulder. When he spotted the portal, he stood up so quickly that he overturned his chair.

"Dr. Ableman," the director said in an unsteady voice, "are you and Miss Montgomery all right? The lack of contact has been alarming."

"We're fine," Dan replied, putting his arm around Gil. "And you can cut the formality, Pete, Gil knows who I am."

Peter raised an eyebrow and laughed. "You're a quick worker, aren't you? But I guess you would be after a twenty-four year wait."

As Dan chuckled, Peter said to Danny through the wave, "Is that you, Danny-boy? Talk about flashbacks! Do you know who I am?"

"Slim the Goon," Danny replied with a teasing smile, brushing the remnants of tears from his face.

Peter groaned. "Am I *ever* gonna live that down?" Tossing a baseball through the portal, he said, "Here you go, wisecracker. Have your dad practice with you—and with me too. Your lethal pitching arm and my home runs are going to win us the state championship senior year."

"Cool!" Danny said, pocketing the ball.

Peter picked up a book called *Hinglly's Formulas Explained* and tossed it through the wave. "Give this to Slim, will you? Tell him when all else fails, look to Hinglly. And tell him not to date Fay Hennly. Got it?"

"Sure." Danny grinned. "I know Fay. I can't believe you dated her."

"Me either," Peter replied.

"Who's Fay Hennly?" Laura asked with raised eyebrows.

"Someone I'd like to forget. When I took her to a drive-in, I had a hard time keeping her hands off me."

As Laura chuckled, Peter smiled and called out, "Mr. and Mrs. Ableman, is that you?"

Sam grinned. "We're not quite Mr. and Mrs. yet, but we're working on it."

"It's great to see you! When I was a kid, the way you opened your home to me was a tremendous blessing. I wouldn't have succeeded without you."

"Don't mention it, Peter," Sam said, putting his arm around Sue. "We'll look forward to meeting your younger-self."

Gil watched with a heavy heart as Dan began tossing suitcases through the portal. Knowing her time in Charlesberg was at an end, she hugged everyone one last time. With tears prickling her eyes, she took one last, lingering look at Danny. He gave her a wobbly grin followed by a thumbs-up sign. Smiling, she squared her shoulders, took Dan's hand, and stepped through the portal.

An icy surge of wind rushed over Gil's skin as she surfed through the timewave. When she entered the lab with Dan, Laura rushed forward. "It's wonderful to have you both home! I was frantic when we didn't hear from you, but Peter maintained that if TEMCO hadn't collapsed, nothing major could've gone wrong."

Peter turned to Dan. "Laura's been more nervous than when we went up for government review the first time. It took all my powers of persuasion to keep her calm."

"I'd object," Laura said, pushing her red hair away from her face, "but it happens to be true. Peter's been a rock through this uncertainty. I never realized how sweet he could be."

Peter's eyes twinkled. "I'm not sure if that's a compliment or not."

"A little uncertainty's good for a man," Laura replied. As Peter laughed, she turned to Gil. "How are you—*really?* We hated to send you back knowing what you were going to face, but we had no choice. I hope you understand."

"Don't worry, I do." Blushing a little, Gil shot Dan a tender glance. "And really, I wouldn't have it any other way."

Peter smiled. "Dan, your mom and dad called. Their plane landed an hour ago. Sue said to tell Gil they couldn't wait to see her again."

"I'm glad they're here," Gil said happily. "That makes everything perfect."

"They want to meet you at Dos Maracas for dinner," Laura said. "But before you go, Dan needs to deal with Dr. Moosly. He's been on the warpath."

"He wants me fired?" Dan asked. "That's normal."

Laura shook her head. "He wants us *all* fired!"

"Even you? What did you do?"

"I refused to ask the board for Peter's resignation. When I told Dr. Moosly that if Peter went, I went, he seemed to think that was a good idea."

Gil saw Dan's jaw tighten. "Get him down here," he said.

Stepping briskly to the phone, Laura made a quick call. "Dr. Moosly, Dr. Ableman and Miss Montgomery have arrived. Would you care to join us?"

A few seconds later, Dr. Moosly came bustling into the lab with a ream of papers. "Dr. Ableman," he sputtered, "an unauthorized trip through GAP is strictly prohibited. Your foolhardy action shows a complete disregard for protocol."

As Gil made an impatient movement, Dr. Moosly turned on her. "I believe your actions should also be called into question. You don't seem to realize that counseling a child is difficult work with dangerous repercussions. You're obviously not cut out for this profession."

When Dan shook his head and started to speak, Dr. Moosly continued furiously, "Don't try to defend her. I've tolerated your opinions long enough! I've listed your infractions, and I'm going to demand your immediate dismissal." He shook the papers in Dan's face. "This report is headed straight to the top."

Reaching out his hand, Dan said, "If that's what you want, I'll take it."

"It's not for you. It's for the person in charge!"

"Yes, I know," Dan replied.

As Dr. Moosly's face turned an alarming shade of purple, Peter said dryly, "Allow me to introduce you to the head of TEMCO. Dr. Ableman happens to be your boss."

Dr. Moosly blinked rapidly. Staring at Dan, he stammered, "You're...? You're...?"

"I'm in charge," Dan replied. "Dr. Nelson and Director Matthews answer only to me."

"But you're...you're..."

"Unconventional. I know. But I'm also the one who does the hiring and firing."

Dr. Moosly shifted uneasily. "All I've ever wanted is what's best for TEMCO."

"I decide what's best," Dan said in a clipped voice. "I've given you leeway in the past, but I'll expect your support from now on."

As Dr. Moosly nodded and ran a nervous finger beneath his collar, Gil saw Peter narrowing his eyes. She never would've pegged the director as having an ornery streak, but she quickly reassessed her opinion when he glanced at Dr. Moosly and said, "Hey, Dan, what are you waiting for? Why don't you kiss your girlfriend?"

Dr. Moosly's eyes bulged. "Here? In the lab? That would be unquestionably ill-advised. Public displays of affection are..." his voice trailed away. After a moment, he said awkwardly, "On second thought, special occasions periodically call for demonstrative actions."

Peter's lips twitched. "Yes, they do."

Gil looked over at Dan and cocked an eyebrow. He shook his head. "This isn't the time or the place."

As Peter gave her a wink, Gil sashayed over to Dan and murmured, "I suppose not. After all, stodgy, old professors like *you* probably don't know the first thing about PDA, do they?"

Gil watched as Dan stood in stunned silence. After a moment, he laughingly pulled her into his arms and leaned her back with dramatic flair.

"Don't you *dare* drop me, you big ham." She giggled.

Dan's eyes smiled down into hers. "You don't need to worry about that. Having finally won you, I'm never letting you go."

Gil's world slowed down as Dan lowered his lips to hers. He kissed her with such a mixture of tender love and burning passion that it took her breath away and made Dr. Moosly sputter, "Mercy me! *Mercy me, indeed!*"

FIFTY

IN COLORADO, SUE watched as Poppa turned off the Wave Trapper. As the glow from the temporal portal faded, he crooked his finger at Twinkles. "Dear delight," he murmured as Twinkles laughed and slid into his arms. "Dan and Gil are going to have a *wonderful* life together."

Twinkles cuddled close and whispered, "I know, Poppa. I remember."

Turning to Danny, Poppa said, "Twinkles and I have something special to give you."

"What is it?" the boy asked.

"It's this," Poppa replied, gently drawing Twinkles's wedding ring from her finger. He placed the ring on a silver chain and clasped the chain around Danny's neck. "I gave this ring to Twinkles the night I proposed, and now we're giving it to you as a special reminder."

Twinkles kissed Danny's cheek. "Wear it always, and keep it safe for me. I'm gonna want it back in twenty-four years."

As Danny nodded and tucked the ring inside his shirt, Poppa showed Twinkles a velvet box. "Poppa!" she squealed. "What have you gone and done?"

"It's tradition, my love," Poppa said, opening the box and revealing a sparkling ring. "Sapphires are the gift of choice for forty-fifth wedding anniversaries."

"You old dear," Twinkles gushed, "this has nothing to do with tradition. I was gonna miss my ring and you knew it. You're the most thoughtful man alive."

Sue gasped. "Poppa, are you the man I spoke to in the jewelry store? I had no clue it was you."

"Of course you didn't." He chuckled. "It's a time surfer's prerogative to keep some secrets."

"So when's your anniversary?" Sam asked.

"Today," Poppa replied cheerfully. "October twenty-sixth." He turned to Twinkles with a wicked grin. "I had your new ring inscribed."

Twinkles read the inscription and blushed. "*Poppa*, someone might see this!"

"Not if you don't take it off your finger." He laughed. "You can't show that inscription to anyone, mind you. It's just for you and me."

Twinkles looked at him innocently. "I can't show it to anyone? Not even your momma?"

"*Especially* not my momma."

Twinkles giggled and said to Sue, "It's so easy to get a rise out of poor Poppa. I know I shouldn't tease him, but teasing him is half the fun of our marriage."

Poppa smiled. "And you indulge in it every chance you get." He looked at the clock and sighed. "I hate to say it, but we must be getting home."

Danny groaned. "Don't tell me we have to move Twinkles's suitcase. I'll bet it's even heavier than Gil's."

Twinkles gave Danny's shoulder a swat. "You little rascal, all I have is my purse."

As Danny raised his eyebrows, Poppa said, "In light of my old football injury, I had to figure out a way around suitcases."

Twinkles gave a loud snort. "Old football injury, my eye!" Turning to Sue, she said with poignant drama, "Promise me you'll *never* let Danny go out for football. He tweaked a muscle once, and now he uses it as an excuse to avoid taking out the trash!"

Sue gurgled with laughter. "I promise. No football." As Poppa and Danny protested, her lips twitched. "No complaining. Listen to your mother, the both of you."

"So how do you avoid lifting suitcases?" Sam asked.

"Cold cash," Poppa grunted. "On extended time surfs, we rent a furnished house and buy whatever clothes we need."

As Sam blinked, Twinkles said with a smile, "Our shopping expeditions are *glorious* fun. When we're done with an assignment, we donate everything to charity. We've hired a moving crew to pick up our clothes and take your wedding gifts to your house tomorrow." She sighed. "Poppa doesn't mind our shopping trips, but if he has his way, they'll be coming to an end soon. He's been tinkering with a gadget that reorganizes atoms or some such nonsense. He wanted to test the prototype on this surf, but I wouldn't let him."

"Why not?"

"He wanted the silly thing to make our clothes, that's why! When I heard what he was up to, I drew the line—*simply drew the line*. I don't care if my toothbrush can poof and disappear, but there's no way I'll agree to go around in clothes that could go poof."

Her voice became scandalized. "Why, what would happen if I was strolling down the street and the dumb thing broke?"

"Now, Twinkles," objected Poppa. "I've *assured* you that nothing goes poof until I decide it should. The quantifiable linear calibration of the—"

"I don't care," she interrupted. "I've heard it all, and I don't understand any of it. I believe you're the most splendid inventor alive, but there are some things a woman just *will not* risk, and ending up in my all-together in the middle of the street is mine."

Sue giggled. "So are you ever going to give his latest invention a whirl?"

Twinkles firmly shook her head. "*Not* on a time surf and *not* in public."

Poppa smiled and kissed her cheek. "I'll have Dave and Cavan test it with me when we get home, okay?"

"Not if you want to use it on clothes. If something goes wrong, I don't want you walking around in your all-together either, and I know the boys' wives wouldn't be happy if their husbands got arrested for indecent exposure. If you want to test the silly thing, you can try it out on something safe like a book or a broom."

"You've got a deal. I'll line up some tests next Monday." He looked at the clock. "I know you don't like goodbyes, but we really must go. The children are waiting."

"Whose children?" Sam asked.

"Ours," Twinkles replied. "Our kids are throwing us an anniversary party tonight."

The smile on Sam's face grew. "Sue and I are going to be grandparents? Is there anything else we should know before you go?"

"I've tendered Sue's resignation for her jobs."

"What?" Sue gasped in dismay. "I need my jobs! I have to have them!"

"Not anymore," Poppa replied, pressing an envelope into her hand. "Here's enough money to pay Dad's old medical bills and keep you comfortable for quite a while."

Sue shook her head. "You've given us so much already. I can't accept any more."

"Of course you can," Poppa said firmly. "When I was a boy, I used to dream about ways to make your life easier. Now that I'm able to do it, don't deny me the pleasure."

Sue looked at the envelope. After a pause, she kissed Poppa's freckle and gave him a strangling hug. "Thank you."

Poppa cleared his throat. "I know you hated Stubby's, but if you ever want to work at the hospital again, your boss said he'd welcome you back."

"But not for a while, dear," Twinkles said, giving Sue's hand a pat. "You're going to be *way* too busy. The painters arrive at Sam's house tomorrow."

"Painters?" Sue asked in a dazed voice as Sam gave a smothered laugh.

"Why, yes, of course," Twinkles burbled. "How could all that nice new furniture go into a house that isn't freshly painted? Poppa remembers the colors of the old rooms, so don't worry, everything will be just right." Suddenly, Twinkles froze. "Now, Sue, *promise me* you won't break your engagement when you see what Sam has in his basement."

Sue looked over at her fiancé. His ears were beginning to blush.

"Just remember," Twinkles said quietly, "every man has his faults, and Sam—exceptional man that he is—has them too."

"What *are* you talking about?"

"Sam's bowling ball collection. It takes up a whole basement wall. Can you imagine? I can see collecting stamps or coins—*but bowling balls?* I tell you, Sue, every wife has her cross to bear and those bowling balls are gonna be yours."

Gurgling with laughter, Sue said, "I think I can handle it."

"You haven't seen it yet," Twinkles replied glumly, "but I'll take your word for it. Anyway, I suppose you'll be too busy to mind anything for a while. You have the house to get ready, and then the wedding, and then little Angelina arrives."

Sue blinked. "Pardon me?"

"Angelina Evelyn. She comes about a year after you and Sam marry."

"Sue and I are having a baby?" Sam said in a startled voice. "I thought Sue couldn't—"

"Of course, you're having babies," Twinkles said. "Two of them—Angelina and Alex."

"Well, at least now we know what to name them," Sam said with a laugh.

Giving him a fond grin, Twinkles said to Sue, "Whenever you picture bowling balls, just think of your babies. Even if a husband collects outlandish things, he's worth hanging onto if he changes poopy diapers." She squeezed Sue's hand. "Be sure to give Angelina music lessons. She's a professional violinist, and she's just as lovely as her name. You named her after your mother."

Giving his wife a wicked grin, Poppa said to Sam, "I tried to convince Twinkles to name our daughter after *her* mother, but she refused."

"Of course I did," Twinkles blustered. "Your man-gene was running rampant that day. I still can't believe you were willing to name our defenseless baby *Moonbeam Frankincense Alabaster!* I loved my family, but their name choices were simply ghastly."

Danny grinned. "Yah, I know how you *adore* the name Gillyflower Meadowlark."

"Actually, I don't mind my name so much anymore—not after Poppa wrote me a lovely poem about it. I have it memorized. Shall I quote it for you?" Giving Poppa an impish grin, she loudly intoned:

"Sweet Gillyflower! Captivating enchantress!
Love blossoms in my heart, and the meadowlark sings in my soul
When the soft morning light gently caresses your sleeping form
Dawn's blushing fingers tremble to touch your—"

Suddenly, Poppa clamped a hand over Twinkles's mouth. As her eyes sparkled naughtily at him, he said with a strangled laugh, "Hush, you *wretch*, or I'll tell your mother-in-law what you sing when—"

Gasping with laughter, Twinkles pulled Poppa's hand away. "Truce! I won't breathe another word." She turned to Sue. "Which is a crying shame because it's *such* a lovely poem."

Sue's lips twitched. "Maybe so, but for the good of your marriage you'd better not recite any more of it."

As Twinkles laughed, Sam said, "You've told us that Angelina needs violin lessons, is there anything we should know about Alex?"

At his words, Twinkles looked uncomfortable. Seeing her distress, Sue asked anxiously, "What's wrong?"

"I'm afraid we have bad news about your youngest." Twinkles sighed.

Clutching Sam's hand, Sue asked in a tight voice, "What's wrong with him?"

"He paints."

Sam's jaw dropped. "But what's wrong with that?"

"It's not bad *that* he paints. It's just awful how *terrible* he does it."

Sue laughed in relief. "I think we can handle it."

"You don't understand," Poppa replied. "Alex's composition is truly awful. It wouldn't be a problem, but he insists on giving us paintings every Christmas. He gets hurt if we don't display them."

Twinkles nodded. "The painting he gave us last year was of a straw hat. Or maybe it was of a donkey. Poppa, which was it?"

"I thought it was a pineapple."

Sam chuckled. "We'll try to curb it a bit."

"Not all the way, mind you," said Twinkles. "Alex does enjoy it so. But a little curbing in the way of gift giving would be appreciated."

Sam pinched Twinkles's cheek. "You might regret that. Picasso wasn't understood at first. Maybe Alex's paintings will be worth a mint of money someday."

"Maybe. But honestly, I'm running out of places to hang them."

Poppa smiled and took Twinkles's arm. "Our children are waiting. We really must go."

"Do we have to?"

"Do you want to explain to Deleena why we're so late? You know she's been planning our party for ages. Besides, the little ones will be getting hungry."

After giving his parents a hug, Poppa turned on the Wave Trapper. Immediately, the doorway was enveloped in a silver grid. Behind the cloudy blue light, Sue could see a group of people chatting beside a three-tiered cake covered with frosting roses. As the swirling light cleared, the crowd cheered. Smiling, Poppa and Twinkles passed through the time portal and into the ecstatic embraces of their children and grandchildren.

Hugging one of his grandsons, Poppa said to Sue and Sam, "Always remember your future holds great joy." With a final smile, he turned off the Wave Trapper. The blue light swirled and faded away.

Sue sighed and stared at the empty doorway. "What do we do now?"

Sam laughed. "I don't know about you, but I'm going home and planning our wedding."

FIFTY-ONE

MARC TYPED THE exit code into the archival keypad as Crystal stood by his side. The echoing noise of the large door shutting behind them had a distinct air of finality.

"A job well done," Marc said gruffly. When Crystal didn't reply, he shoved his hands in his pockets and said waspishly, "Aren't you even gonna talk to me?"

"What's there to say?"

Shrugging his shoulders, he looked away. A thick silence fell between them as they descended the staircase. When they approached the TEMCO lab and reached for the doorknob at the same time, Crystal pulled her hand into a tight fist and backed away. Stumbling sideways, she knocked a framed portrait of Stephen Hawking off the wall and onto Marc's foot. Marc gave an exasperated mutter and rubbed his ankle as Crystal rehung the portrait.

"Wait a sec," Crystal said hurriedly as he reached for the doorknob. "When we go inside, you should do the talking."

"Why?"

She shrugged and looked uncomfortable.

"If you know something I don't, I wish you'd tell me. Is my neck on the line?"

She shrugged again.

"Fine," he grumbled, giving her a glare. "Have it your way."

"For Pete's sake," she said in an exasperated voice. "If you go in the lab looking like that, you'll blow everything!"

"Oh? Just how do I look?" he said stiffly.

"Like an egotistical, arrogant, affronted nudnik who just swallowed a lemon!"

Marc blinked rapidly and gave a spurt of laughter.

"Like the description?" she asked dryly. "On Saturday nights after I read Oedipus Rex in the original Greek, I memorize the thesaurus."

His smile faded. "I'm sorry I teased you about your social life. I—"

She cut him off. "Give it a rest. All I care about is getting through the next five minutes without either of us getting cut from the program."

Marc watched as she gave him a critical glance. After a moment, she said sharply, "Tuck in your shirt and straighten your collar. You're such a neat freak that the director will know we've been arguing if you go in there looking like that."

As Marc obediently tucked in his shirt, he suddenly felt an irresistible desire to tease her. Deliberately messing up his collar even further, he gave her a helpless look and fumbled with the material. He swallowed down a desire to laugh as she glared up at him like an angry wet hen.

"You've *got* to be kidding," she grumbled, batting his hands away and straightening his collar. "Are you completely helpless?"

Standing absolutely still, Marc forced himself not to smile.

"Smooth down your hair," she ordered tersely. "And stop frowning."

His lips collapsed into a grin. Scrabbling his fingers through his hair, he asked, "What about you? Your hair's flying everywhere."

"I don't matter," she snapped. "Everyone's used to seeing me like this." Giving an impatient huff, she demanded, "What the dickens are you doing? You're just making things worse!" Grumbling wildly beneath her breath, Crystal reached up and smoothed down his hair. Marc's smile grew.

"Look," she said, trying to tame his cowlick. "All we've got to do is play nice for a few minutes and then we can go our separate ways and enjoy summer vacation. Do you think you can handle that?"

"I know I can," he replied. "But I'm not sure about you. You're acting like an ice queen."

Crystal gave his hair a defiant pat that was a bit harder than necessary. Backing away, she pinned a cherubic smile on her face. "Don't worry about me. Just keep it together, okay?"

As Marc nodded and opened the door, he gasped in stunned surprise. In the middle of the lab, Gil and Dr. Ableman were locked in a passionate embrace.

Giving a surprised squeak, Crystal clutched Marc's forearm and exclaimed, "Will you look at that!"

Marc didn't bother looking at Dr. Ableman and Gil, he was too busy looking at Crystal. Her eyes were sparkling behind her glasses, and golden wispy curls were dancing on her cheeks. As she held his arm and smiled at him, a shockwave rolled through his body. He suddenly realized what Ryan had meant. Crystal *did* have a lovely face. In fact, it was more than just lovely — it was remarkably pretty. Most women were pretty or ugly all the time, so a man knew where he stood, but all the normal rules flew out the window when it came to Cris. Her beauty was even more potent because it was so shocking. It was like seeing the desert bloom or turning a corner and seeing an unexpected sunrise. He didn't understand how a woman who was normally such a complete dud could suddenly take every bit of breath right out of his body.

Putting his hand gently over hers, Marc murmured, "I *am* looking, and I like what I see."

Marc watched as Crystal froze and stared at him with shocked eyes. Shaking off his hand, she backed away, tripping over a chair in the process. As he tried to help her regain her balance, she gave him an icy stare. Marc began to grin. Maybe getting to know Crystal wasn't going to be easy, but the best things in life never were. Surely she couldn't ignore him forever.

As if overhearing his thoughts, Crystal glared. Lightly catching her arm, he said beneath his breath, "Keep it together, Cris. The director's watching."

Immediately, Crystal pinned a smile on her lips.

"That's better," Marc murmured encouragingly. "You're doing fine."

"Don't be such a condescending twit," she whispered through a frozen smile. As she stepped away from him, she tripped over another chair, accidentally knocking it into the wall.

Hearing a crash behind her, Gil pulled back from Dan's kiss and glanced over her shoulder. When she spotted Crystal and Marc, she began to blush. She hadn't minded kissing in front of Dan's friends, but kissing in front of her own made her feel shy. Dan's arms tightened around her, and she heard him starting to chuckle. Suddenly, he became very occupied with nibbling her earlobe. Giggling, she whispered, "Cut it out, you cheeseball!"

Gil felt a deep rumble of laughter quivering in Dan's chest. Placing a kiss on the tip of her nose, he teased, "Now who's squeamish about PDA? Are you turning *stodgy* on me?"

Gil chuckled. "You're all grown-up, but you're still a wisecracker, aren't you?"

Giving her a wink, Dan said in a jubilant voice, "Well, Marc, how about if your first official act as my new TA is taking over my classes while I go on my honeymoon?"

"I'd be glad to, Doc," Marc replied, shaking Dan's hand.

Gil's smile wobbled as Dan flashed her a laughing glance that was reminiscent of Danny's impudent grin. Taking his hand in hers, she stroked his wrist, shuddering at the memory of the cannulas sticking into Death Row Daniel's arm.

As if sensing her shift in mood, Dan whispered, "Doing okay?"

Nodding, she murmured, "I'm just so glad that we won out."

Stroking her cheek, Dan gave her a smile that warmed her heart. "Me too."

Surging forward, Crystal gave Gil a strangling hug. "When's the wedding?"

"Not for a while," she replied, blinking back the moisture in her eyes. "I'm gonna make this guy court me proper first. But when I finally agree to marry him, I'm partial to October twenty-sixth." She flashed Dan a flirty grin. "After all, I already have that date marked with a giant red heart and a big, fat, sparkling star."

Laughing, Dan pulled her close. "Are you talking about October twenty-sixth of this year or next?"

Gil's eyes twinkled. "That depends entirely on how good you are with your wooing."

432

Acknowledgements

There are many people I want to thank for helping me realize my dream. I never could have done this alone.

Thank you, Dad, for always seeing the best in me and for being so supportive. Your kind words and Godly example have meant the world to me. When you told me how much you liked my book, it was the proudest moment of my life.

Thank you, Mom, for the hours you spent tirelessly editing my manuscript. Thank you for patiently listening as I bounced ideas off you. Your wisdom, love, and support have meant so much to me. The fact that this book is finished is a testament to you.

Thank you, Darla Caudle, Donita Kurtz, Kim Rotharmel, and Tim Caudle for reading my manuscript and making such wonderful suggestions. You helped polish my book, and any praise it receives belongs to you as well. Thank you, Rob Caudle, Kent Kurtz, John Rotharmel, Amy Huang, Bruce Moore, and Paula Mowery for your encouragement.

Thank you, Gloria Penwell, Dave Lambert, Catherine Lawton, Terri Kalfas, Bruce Nygren, Nick Harrison, Sally Apokedak, and John Sloan for your suggestions concerning my manuscript. Thank you for taking an interest in me and making me feel valuable.

Thank you to all of Prism Book Group's wonderful authors. When I joined Prism, you surrounded me with love and support. You showed me the ropes, included me in your group, and offered me your friendship. I am so blessed to have each of you in my life!

Thank you, Larry Carpenter, for your help with understanding the business side of publishing. You made this journey easy, and I appreciate it.

Thank you, Joan Alley, for being so supportive and for publishing my book. I feel very blessed to be part of an organization that tries its best to honor the Lord.

Thank you, Susan Baganz, for "discovering" me. You paved the way for my dreams to come true. You are a beautiful person, a talented writer, and a wonderful friend.

Thank you, Jacqueline Hopper, for being such a wonderful editor. Your support has gone beyond just fixing words on a page—you've taken an interest in me as a person. You've prayed with me. Helped me. Befriended me. You've had such an impact on my life. I'm a better person for having known you.

Thank you to my family and friends for your prayers and support. Thank you for standing by me as I regained my health and embarked on this journey toward publication. I appreciate your encouragement and the way you have promoted my book. I love you all!

And finally, I want to thank the Lord for His love and guidance. Each step of the way, He has shown me the truth of Romans 8:28.

About The Author

Danele J. Rotharmel grew up with a love of the literary word, and by age five, she knew she wanted to be a writer. However, her life took an unexpected turn when a mysterious illness brought her close to death. Eventually, she learned that a low-level carbon monoxide leak from a faulty furnace in her home was slowly poisoning her. This poisoning triggered severe Multiple Chemical Sensitivity and partial amnesia.

During this time, the hardest thing she faced was a crisis of faith. She had to quit her job and stop going to church. She couldn't write, couldn't drive, and could barely remember who she was. To say she was upset with the Lord was an understatement. She began reexamining her faith in light of her illness, and eventually, she came to the firm conclusion that God is real, God is good, God is interested and involved, and God is trustworthy regardless of tragedy.

When her illness became even more severe, she was put into quarantine and could only talk to friends and extended family through the glass of a window. This quarantine lasted for seven years. During this time, she wrote the first six books in *The Time Counselor Chronicles*.

Danele currently lives in Colorado where she continues to write. Although her journey back to health was long and difficult, it provided her with the opportunity to grow closer to God and to write her books. For that, she is forever thankful.

You can learn more about Danele by visiting her blog at https://dragonflydanele.wordpress.com.

Coming soon from Danele J. Rotharmel...

Time Trap

A killer is lurking in the shadows of time itself...

When problems arise during a field exam, Director Peter Matthews and Dr. Laura Nelson are sent through a time portal to investigate. While they search for their missing cadets, they encounter an enemy who is calculating and brutal—a mysterious nemesis who is holding a grudge against the TEMCO program. As Peter and Laura race to unravel clues directing them to their kidnapped cadets, their own survival comes into question. A deadly trap has been set, and they are forced to pit their wits against a serial killer who is intent on playing a deadly chess game through time itself. There is nowhere to hide. No way to escape. Confrontation is their only option...

Please enjoy an excerpt from *Time Trap*...

ONE

May 21ˢᵗ, 11:58 p.m.
Hawking Hall, Washington D.C.
Four years after Gil Ableman's field exam

Wade Kingston stumbled against the wall. Breathing heavily, he raised a hand to his temple and felt blood. Behind him, he could hear footsteps. Forcing his body to move, he lurched down the hall.

His fingers fumbled frantically as he dialed his phone. He'd left a message on William Ableman's machine, but he didn't know when William would receive it—he needed to contact Peter.

"This is W-wade," he said in a slurred voice as the call connected. "We've got trouble at TEMCO. I was working late, and I saw—"

"*You have reached the voicemail box of Director Peter Matthews. I'm unable to take your call right now, but if you leave—*"

With an impatient motion, Wade disconnected the call and dialed Laura Nelson's number. As it rang, he staggered toward the marble staircase leading to the lobby. Suddenly, footsteps rushed toward him. Swinging around, Wade raised his arm to protect his head. A baseball bat slammed across his chest. Wade's phone flew from his hand and fell to the landing below.

Seeing the bat being raised again, Wade stepped back. His feet found nothing but air. In a blind panic, he reached for the banister but missed. White light flashed behind his eyes as he plummeted down the stairs and landed in a heap at the bottom. Looking up, he saw his attacker approaching with the baseball bat in hand.

"You just had to stick your nose where it didn't belong, didn't you?" a voice hissed.

Wade tried to get up but couldn't move his legs. Rolling onto his belly, he dragged himself across the floor. The exit sign blurred in front of his vision. Pain was making him nauseous. Choking on blood, he continued to drag his useless lower limbs toward the door.

Footsteps approached. "Do you honestly think you're going anywhere?"

Wade tried to drag himself a few more inches, but steel toed boots stepped on his fingers. Looking up, he saw the baseball bat smashing toward his head.

May 22nd, 4:00 p.m.
TEMCO Lab, Hawking Hall

"Wade's still not answering," Director Peter Matthews said, hanging up the phone.

"Where do you think he is?" Dr. Laura Nelson asked, glancing at the two cadets sitting by the wall. "Drake and Phoebe have been waiting for over two hours. What do we do?"

Peter made an impatient sound. "We proceed with their field exam. This is getting ridiculous. This surf has already been postponed twice due to scheduling problems. I'm not delaying it again because the cadets' advisor hasn't shown up. TEMCO should already be shut down for the summer. We can fill Wade in when he—"

Across the lab, Zeke Masters interrupted, "Director Matthews, I'm receiving an unscheduled transmission!"

Hurrying over to the GAP computer, Peter leaned over the lab tech's shoulder and looked at the monitor. "Who is it from?"

Zeke's fingers flew across his keyboard. "Doc and Mrs. Ableman."

"It's about time!" Peter exclaimed. "Put it through." He motioned for Laura and nodded at her mute inquiry. "William and Gil are finally making contact."

Laura smiled as the Staging Platform shimmered with a faint blue glow. "I can't wait to hear what they've been up to."

"Me too," Peter said, rubbing the back of his neck. "But I'm also feeling somewhat sympathetic toward Thomas's views about the importance of protocol. A fifty-two hour contact delay is stretching things a bit."

The blue glow deepened as a temporal portal was firmly established. Behind the translucent wave, the form of Dr. Ableman came into focus.

Peter blinked rapidly. William was hunched in front of the portal with a desperate look in his eyes. His hair was sticking up in wild tufts, and there was a bruise across his cheek. Seeing blood on William's shirt, he asked in alarm, "What's wrong? Where's Gil?"

Thank you for your Prism Book Group purchase! Visit our website to enjoy free reads, great deals, and entertaining, wholesome fiction!

http://www.prismbookgroup.com

Made in the USA
Middletown, DE
03 April 2016